Everyone had one, whether they were aware of it or not.

Doctor Burke's desk was a graveyard of broken spectacles. Cracked frames had been discarded under folders or loitered next to empty cups. The doctor's weathered hands fumbled blindly for a pair and shoved them onto his face, only for one of the lenses to fall into his lap. With a sigh, he squinted through the remaining lens at the results of Alice's blood test.

After a moment, he opened his mouth as though to speak, but instead licked his thumb and turned the page. He was a small but hardy-looking old man, shrivelled at the edges like something left out in the sun, with tufts of white hair protruding from every orifice.

Alice glanced at her mother and raised her eyebrows at the unusual display on the surgery wall. A squirrel played a violin directly behind her mother's head. Next to it, a pair of foxes sporting dungarees sat on a miniature tandem. Nothing, however, could top the stuffed owl in a mortarboard, posed in front of a tiny blackboard. Its enormous glassy eyes stared at Alice in vexation, as though she was about to be handed the dunce's cap. Ugly taxidermy littered every shelf. *Not the most encouraging thing to find in a doctor's office.*

It was a good job Doctor Burke didn't know there was a living animal, of sorts, right under his nose. A very small brown bird, its wings tucked against its body, was perched on the doctor's shoulder. He couldn't see it because it was a nightjar, and these particular nightjars were visible only to aviarists like Alice.

The image of a stuffed nightjar flashed briefly through Alice's mind, and her lip curled in distaste. Doctor Burke's soul-bird was tiny, with a streak of faded coppery brown running along its back. Its muddy-coloured feathers were plain but it had a slightly battered look. Two shining black eyes regarded Alice with a solemn air.

By Deborah Hewitt

The Nightjar
The Rookery

THE ROOKERY

DEBORAH HEWITT

TOR

A TOM DOHERTY ASSOCIATES BOOK

NEW YORK

THE ROOKERY

A Tor Book
Published by Tom Doherty Associates
120 Broadway
New York, NY 10271

www.tor-forge.com

Tor® is a registered trademark of Macmillan Publishing Group, LLC.

The Library of Congress Cataloging-in-Publication Data
is available upon request.

ISBN 978-1-250-23979-2 (trade paperback)
ISBN 978-1-250-23980-8 (ebook)

Our books may be purchased in bulk for promotional, educational, or business use. Please contact your local bookseller or the Macmillan Corporate and Premium Sales Department at 1-800-221-7945, extension 5442, or by email at MacmillanSpecialMarkets@macmillan.com.

First published in Great Britain by Pan Books,
an imprint of Pan Macmillan

First U.S. Edition: August 2021

Seb and Archie – to infinity and beyond

THE ROOKERY

PROLOGUE

Doctor Burke's desk was a graveyard of broken spectacles. Cracked frames had been discarded under folders or loitered next to empty cups. The doctor's weathered hands fumbled blindly for a pair and shoved them onto his face, only for one of the lenses to fall into his lap. With a sigh, he squinted through the remaining lens at the results of Alice's blood test.

After a moment, he opened his mouth as though to speak, but instead licked his thumb and turned the page. He was a small but hardy-looking old man, shrivelled at the edges like something left out in the sun, with tufts of white hair protruding from every orifice.

Alice glanced at her mother and raised her eyebrows at the unusual display on the surgery wall. A squirrel played a violin directly behind her mother's head. Next to it, a pair of foxes sporting dungarees sat on a miniature tandem. Nothing, however, could top the stuffed owl in a mortar board, posed in front of a tiny blackboard. Its enormous glassy eyes stared at Alice in vexation, as though she was about to be handed the dunce's cap. Ugly taxidermy littered every shelf. *Not the most encouraging thing to find in a doctor's office.*

It was a good job Doctor Burke didn't know there was a living animal, of sorts, right under his nose. A very small brown bird, its wings tucked against its body, was perched on the doctor's shoulder. He couldn't see it because it was a nightjar, and these particular nightjars were visible only to aviarists like Alice. She was one of perhaps only a dozen aviarists worldwide.

Turning in her seat to avoid the macabre display, Alice studied the doctor's bird. In Finnish mythology it was known as a sielulintu: a mythical bird that guards the soul. Everyone had one, whether they were aware of it or not. Her mother, the human dynamo known as Patricia Wyndham, was completely oblivious to her own nightjar crouched on her knee.

The image of a stuffed nightjar flashed briefly through Alice's mind, and her lip curled in distaste. Doctor Burke's soul-bird was tiny, with a streak of faded coppery brown running along its back. Its muddy-coloured feathers were plain but it had a slightly battered look. Two shining black eyes regarded Alice with a solemn air.

'Well,' said Doctor Burke finally. 'A little out of the ordinary.'

'Oh God,' her mum murmured. 'Is it bad news? I knew we should have made an appointment sooner.'

He put the results down and looked over at Patricia Wyndham, whose face had stiffened. After a moment's pause, the doctor waved her fears away. 'Nothing to worry about,' he said, and Patricia sank into her chair.

'That's a relief,' she said. She turned to Alice. 'Isn't it?'

Alice ignored the doctor's reassuring smile, staring instead at the quivering feathers of his nightjar. Its claws rhythmically tightened and relaxed while its wings made short, jerky movements: all signs of its discomposure. Alice's alertness sharpened.

'When you say a little out of the ordinary,' she said, sitting forward, 'what does that actually mean?'

Doctor Burke's eyes drifted down to the results again. 'Well,' he said, flustered, 'you've low oxygen saturation levels and a touch of anaemia.'

'I've been saying for weeks you were too pale,' said her mum.

'And the test the nurse did last time,' said Alice, 'the low blood pressure – is that connected?'

Doctor Burke hesitated and pushed his broken glasses further up the bridge of his nose. 'If you'd prefer me to make a referral, a friend of mine works at the big hospital in Castlebar—'

'No,' she said firmly. 'Thank you, but no. It's only a bit of dizziness; I'll cope.'

She hated hospitals. Every time she set foot in one, the smell of disinfectant triggered memories of the night her best friend was hit by a car. That night had changed everything. For months afterwards, Alice had believed that Jen was lying comatose on a ward and that it was her fault. Visions of Jen wasting away in a hospital bed had haunted her. But it had all been a lie. Trickery.

Lungs rattling, Doctor Burke coughed into a handkerchief and jolted Alice from her thoughts. She was glad of the distraction.

'Iron tablets,' he said, prodding the handkerchief into his suit pocket and reaching for a pen. 'It's nothing that a course of iron tablets won't fix.'

He beamed at her and she glanced at his nightjar. To the well-practised aviarist, soul-birds mirrored what was hidden in their owners' souls, revealing their thoughts and feelings, insights and lies. Alice wasn't yet as accomplished at reading the birds' behaviour as she hoped to be, but she was a fast learner. Lies made nightjars restless and ill at ease.

'Iron tablets and good country air,' he said, 'and you'll have nothing at all to worry about.' The wings of his nightjar shivered as he spoke and its head rocked back and forth in agitation.

3

Alice frowned. Occasionally, she wished she wasn't an aviarist. Some lies brought comfort.

The car boot slammed shut with such violence the Nissan Micra swayed on its wheels.

'Careful,' said Alice. 'You could've lost a finger.'

Her mum grinned. 'It'd be worth it,' she said, hugging a tea towel-wrapped plate to her chest. 'Just wait till you try this. Breda Murphy's treacle bread,' she said, gesturing at the prize in her arms. 'It's a top-secret Irish recipe, apparently. Breda says she won't tell me what it is until I've been here at least a decade.'

They started up the driveway towards their whitewashed cottage, pausing only to inspect the freshly mown lawn.

'I don't believe it,' Patricia murmured, looking out over the garden. 'He'll think he's got one over on me, mowing the grass before I've had the chance to nag him over it.'

Alice laughed at the accurate assessment.

'Go on then,' said Patricia, shaking her head. 'You do the knocking; you're more musical than me.'

The front door was deadbolted and fitted with more locks than Fort Knox. There was no key hidden under a mat, and no open front door in this quaint little cottage. It was probably the only house in County Mayo with an alarm system that cost more than the car on the driveway and CCTV buried under the ivy on the walls.

Security considerations had been Alice's first priority when they'd moved here. Alongside the locks and alarms, she'd insisted on a secret code to let them know it was safe to open the door to each other. It had been a bit of overkill and was now something of a running joke, but no one had suggested dropping it. Which was why she found herself knocking the beat to *Greensleeves* on the front door for nearly two minutes before it swung open.

'I was waiting till you reached the chorus,' said her dad, beaming down at her. 'But you missed the second verse and the whole thing went to hell.'

Michael Wyndham was a balding man-mountain with kind eyes and a perpetual smile. 'Well?' he said. 'What did the doc say?'

Alice held up her bag of iron tablets in answer. 'Anaemia. He said I'll be fine.' It wouldn't do her parents any good to know the doctor's nightjar had contradicted him. She'd already filed that away to think about later.

'I see you've been busy,' said Patricia, closing the front door behind them. Michael gave her a smug look, and Alice watched them sizing each other up. Patricia was the smallest, most formidable woman Alice knew. Five feet tall at a pinch, faded bobbed hair and oval glasses perched on the end of her nose.

'Cup of tea?' asked her dad, cracking first.

'Oh, lovely. And when we're done, you could run the mower over the bit you missed by the wall.'

Alice snorted in amusement, but was distracted by an explosion of noise in the hallway. Scuttling paws hurtled across the floor towards her, scratching and sliding on the wood. Two shaggy white blurs of excitement, turning in frantic circles, their tails going like windmills: her Westies, Bo and Ruby. She dropped to her knees and they launched themselves at her, wriggling in her arms like eels, arching round to jump at her face and lick her hands while she laughed.

'We've a new postman, by the way,' said Patricia. 'Did I tell you?'

Alice's laughter died in her throat. She got to her feet, her skin prickling, and shook her head.

'What does he look like?' she asked carefully.

'Oh, he's about ninety,' said Patricia. 'Harmless. I checked. We've followed all of your instructions to the letter.'

'No slip-ups,' said Alice.

'No slip-ups,' repeated Patricia, marching off to the kitchen, where Michael was clanking the cups around with increasing haphazardness. She shooed him aside and filled the kettle.

Alice watched them from the hallway with a pained expression on her face. She just wanted to keep them safe. They'd left all their friends behind to move to Ireland – including Jen's parents, the Parkers, who had been their next-door neighbours for twenty years. They'd lived in Dublin briefly before settling in Glenhest, where there was less chance of discovery. And yet, it wasn't just her parents who were in danger – she was too.

Having the ability to read souls and separate truths from lies was a wondrous thing, but the downsides could be fatal. There were those who would give anything to control her gifts, and others who would give anything to destroy them. Alice had already had several run-ins with one such group, spearheaded by a government operative called Sir John Boleyn. His foot soldier, Vin Kelligan, had gone after her parents once, and she wasn't taking any chances now – but the truth was, they'd be safer when she left.

And she *was* leaving. Soon. She'd been offered a research assistant post in the Department of Natural Sciences at Goring University – in London's magical sister-city, the Rookery. Her departure had only been delayed until the blood test results had come through. Patricia Wyndham had made it clear that no daughter of hers would leave home without a clean bill of health.

The circles under her eyes and her shortness of breath on her daily walks had troubled them.

'Will you have treacle bread?' her mum shouted out to her.

Alice watched her parents' nightjars fluttering around the kitchen together, never less than inches apart. They were perfectly synchronized – the result of thirty years of marriage to your soul mate.

'Maybe later,' she replied, with a faint pang in her chest. Watching their nightjars together always brought home the fact that, despite her gifts, she hadn't seen Crowley's nightjar until it was too late. Their nightjars had never been in sync because Crowley had never been honest about who he really was.

Alice shook her head and turned away, but the sharp movement made her light-headed and she swayed onto her toes. She threw out a hand against the wall and scrunched her eyes shut until the moment passed. The gaps between her dizzy spells had been growing shorter lately. Breathing deeply, she pushed herself away, still gripping the bag of iron tablets. Bo and Ruby scurried along next to her like a personal escort; somehow, they always seemed to know when she wasn't feeling her best.

There was a package on her bed. Alice froze in the doorway before approaching it as she would an unexploded bomb. Her name and address were scrawled on the front, but other than her new employer there was only one person who knew where she lived: Crowley.

Alice's eyes roamed over the familiar handwriting; it was every bit as spiky as its owner. A sudden rush of nerves caught her breath. He wanted her to return to the Rookery so he could make things right with her – he'd even sent her the university job advert, knowing she wouldn't be able to resist – but it was too late. She'd told him not to contact her again, so why the package?

Crowley had taken advantage of her distress when she'd believed that Jen was in a coma and her nightjar missing. He'd offered her a chance to save her friend and retrieve the lost soul-bird. But Jen was never in a coma – it was another woman who was lying in a hospital bed: Estelle Boleyn, Crowley's sister. He'd tricked her into saving *Estelle's* nightjar – and in the end, they had both failed. Estelle was still comatose and Jen was now dead.

He had tried to explain, insisting that he had genuinely believed Jen was suffering the same miserable fate as his sister, and that Alice, as an aviarist, could find both nightjars and save both women. But in his desperation, he'd kept up the charade even when he'd discovered Jen was already safe and well. It had been a lie of omission, not maliciousness, he'd insisted. He'd been driven to great lengths out of love for his sister, and she'd have done the same for Jen. But for Alice, his lies were just too big. Even his name was a lie. He had been born Louis Boleyn, and was the son of Sir John Boleyn, leader of the Beaks: the man hell-bent on destroying both the Rookery and Alice herself; the man who had ordered Jen's kidnapping so that Alice would work for him; the man who was the reason they knocked *Greensleeves* every time they came home. Still . . . given her own peculiar situation, she could hardly blame Crowley for wanting to hide the identity of his father.

Alice tore the package open and frowned at her unexpected bounty: half a dozen copies of *The Rookery Herald* and what appeared to be an application form. She knew immediately why Crowley had sent the newspapers. Scooping them into her arms, she carried them to the back garden and dumped them under the rowan tree in the corner. Alice frequently sketched under its branches, sheltered from the sun.

She sat cross-legged on the grass and pulled the nearest *Rookery*

Herald to her. It looked like an old broadsheet, crammed with articles and headlines that screamed from every page: *House Ilmarinen member denies arson! Claims sambuca accident to blame!, Chancellor Litmanen considers naming national holiday after himself* and *Attempt to create waterfall feature in Thames ends in disaster!* Adverts for Oxo Chocolate and Lauriston's Long-Life Candles sprang from between the articles. She studied every page with care before dragging the next one nearer and repeating her inspection. She paused on a piece about a necromancer who'd been jailed for turning up at funerals only to pass on embittered messages from beyond the grave. It felt so strange to sit flicking through stories from another world – a world of magic – while her parents bickered over lawnmowers.

There was a flicker of movement at the corner of her eye. A tiny razor beak, pin-sharp claws and elegant feathers glided past. *Alice's* nightjar. It tucked its wings back and swooped into a barrel-dive, pulling up at the last minute with a dramatic toss of its head. Alice sighed. 'Don't you have anything better to do?'

Nightjars had one important function: to guard the soul. It was the nightjar that brought the soul to the body at birth and protected it throughout life. At the moment of death, the birds departed with the soul for the Sulka Moors, the Land of Death. But Alice's nightjar functioned differently. Her bird didn't protect her soul; it protected others *from* her soul, a fact she'd discovered the night she'd almost destroyed the city. Her nightjar wasn't a guard – it was a jailer.

Something juddered, and the kitchen window swung open with force, jolting Alice from her thoughts.

'You forgot your tea,' her mum shouted through the gap at the bottom. 'Shall I bring it out?'

Alice smiled and shook her head. 'I'll come in for it in a minute. I can always put it in the microwave.'

Her mum looked appalled. 'I didn't raise you as a heathen,' she said, closing the window again.

Alice stared at the window fondly. The Wyndhams had raised her and loved her. They were her parents in the truest sense of the word – but she shared no biology with them. What they did share was so much more important, and yet, over the past few months she had acquired a constant reminder of her difference: her distinctive nightjar.

Aviarists were usually blind to their own soul-birds until the moment of their death. Since Alice had become so intimately acquainted with death, she'd been gifted with the unusual ability to see hers all the time – and what she saw was exceptional.

Nightjars were usually varying shades of brown, but Alice's was pure white. It was a stark reminder that she was *special* in the worst possible way.

Only two others in all of existence had had white nightjars – and both of them were Lords of Death, the Lintuvahti. Alice had met the reigning Lord of Death twice, a young man with ice-white hair. His predecessor, who had abandoned his post as ruler of the Sulka Moors, was her natural father, Tuoni. Alice had been told, once, that she was made of death. And she was – in the most literal way.

Bleached feathers glistening in the sunlight and wings sweeping powerfully at the air, Alice's nightjar circled her head flamboyantly. *Attention seeker.* She ignored it, as she had done for much of the past few weeks.

Moving slightly so that the bird stayed out of her eyeline, Alice pored over the Rookery newspapers. She was searching for something very specific and hoping she didn't find it. After several minutes of scanning the cramped text, she alighted on a phrase that caused her pulse to race: *Marble Arch*.

Fingers beginning to tremble, Alice gripped the pages tightly and began at the top.

> Gas Leak Chaos at Marble Arch! Following reports of a dangerous mains leak last night, the Bow Street Runners responded by evacuating the area around Marble Arch, causing trouble for local residents and late-night business owners. It was declared safe early this morning. A spokesperson for Radiance Utilities has accused the Runners of overreacting to what has now been labelled a false alarm: 'The Runners' heavy-handed approach has cast a shadow over our good reputation. It's a disgrace that they acted against our calls for calm investigation. We can assure the public that the safety of our services remains uncompromised and as efficient as ever.'
>
> When asked for a comment, Commander Risdon said only, 'The Runners take all threats seriously and will continue to uphold the highest standards of security on behalf of this city.' Meanwhile, sources tell us that the death of an unidentified mainlander, found in London on the other side of Marble Arch, was unrelated to the alleged gas leak and is now a matter for the London Metropolitan Police. We ask our readers, were you among those inconvenienced by the Runners' error? Or have you fallen victim to other mistakes by the force that claims to protect us? Contact our hotline today to tell your story!

Alice swallowed heavily. That was the night the world had ended. The night Jen had been taken by Sir John Boleyn's men and Alice had set out to retrieve her from Marble Arch with the Runners' help; the gas leak had been a ruse to clear the area.

With a shudder, Alice reread the article. There was no mention of the real nightmare that had unfolded. Jen had only been a pawn. It was Alice that Sir John Boleyn had wanted, because he'd learned her real identity and knew the truth about her deathly soul – that if it was released, it could wipe out all life in the Rookery.

Alice glanced up at her pale nightjar. A pulsing, incandescent cord was tied to the bird's leg and looped down to circle Alice's wrist. The cord connected them – connected her – and yet, that awful night, Boleyn had sliced through it. Her nightjar had flown free and, without its guard, her soul had escaped and almost purged the entire Rookery. Reuben Risdon, the commander of the Runners, had cut Jen's throat to save the city; he'd sacrificed her best friend on the altar of Marble Arch, using Jen's blood to repel Alice's soul from entering the Rookery – like the lamb's blood on the doors in Egypt during the tenth plague.

With a shaky breath, Alice traced the words near the bottom of the article, *death of an unidentified mainlander*. Jen had died to save their city and they didn't even know her name. There was no mention of Alice Wyndham either, so it seemed she too had retained her anonymity. Maybe Crowley had made a bargain with Risdon to keep her out of it, or maybe it was Risdon's small attempt at penance for his part in Jen's death.

Alice pushed away the newspaper and leaned back against the tree with her eyes closed. Crowley had sent the papers to prove it was safe for her to return and that no one outside their small circle of trusted friends knew who or what she was. But *Alice* still knew.

'Here you go,' said a gruff voice.

Alice's eyes snapped open. Her dad was bearing down on her with a plate of treacle bread and a cup of tea. 'If you don't try it soon, she'll be beside herself. And even if you hate it, you're to tell her it's the best thing you've ever tasted.'

She smiled up at him and accepted the offerings. 'Message understood. Thanks.'

'The wind will have this one halfway down the lane if you're not careful,' he said, bending to grab a loose paper starting to drift over the lawn. He handed it to her before retreating indoors.

Alice watched him go, jumping when her nightjar shot over her head, as aerodynamic as a bullet. She gave it a withering look. It had been pestering her for weeks. Alice knew what it wanted: a *name*. But the bird wasn't a pet, and naming it would give it an identity of its own, making it too difficult to ignore.

'Your showy displays are verging on the egotistical,' she told it. 'And to be honest, as the manifestation of my soul's guardian, I think they're a bit beneath you.'

The bird gave her a guilty look and vanished.

With a satisfied nod, Alice peered down at the other paper from the parcel, the application form. A tree symbol on the letterhead represented House Mielikki: a society for those with specific magical gifts. Almost without thinking, Alice pressed her fingertips into the grass until they touched the soil. A tingle of warmth spread up into her palm and it vibrated gently, as if something was trapped beneath her skin – the magic an itch that needed to be scratched. Alice exhaled slowly, and the grass rustled as she *pushed*. Half a dozen daisies slid out of the soil between her fingers, their heads unfurling rapidly and tiny petals flickering in the breeze.

House Mielikki's members could wield power over plants, trees and wildlife. Alice glanced again at the application form.

She had intended to apply anyway, without Crowley's prompting. When she'd first moved to the Rookery, Crowley had urged her to stay focused on mastering her aviarist gifts rather than becoming distracted by other potential abilities. He'd told her she could pursue them later, if she'd wanted to – and in Ireland she had. Was this another olive branch?

Alice sighed. Exploring her other gifts wasn't the only reason she planned to apply. Joining the House might also help her deny her most terrifying qualities. The magic of House Mielikki was the magic of life itself. Everything that it stood for was in contrast to the identity reflected by her nightjar: death.

She'd developed a strange, grudging bond with her soul-bird, and yet there were still times Alice couldn't bear to look at its pale feathers: a white nightjar for the Daughter of Death. She knew she was capable of being more than that, and she planned to prove it.

The back door banged open and Alice flinched in surprise, her fingers tightening in the grass. Two white blurs burst from the kitchen door, barking happily, and Alice relaxed. It paid to be alert, but always anticipating danger was exhausting.

As Bo and Ruby dived straight over the stack of newspapers, scattering them across the lawn, Alice glanced down. Between her fingers, the newly grown daisies were withering. Their petals blackened and drifted away, and the dull yellow heads began to crumble. In seconds, all were rotted beneath the rowan tree.

Alice stared at them with a dispirited frown, nausea growing in her stomach. Overhead, her nightjar re-emerged in a flurry of feathers, pale wings striking against the air. Alice refused to look away from the corpses of the daisies in the grass.

I can be more than this.

1

Someone was following her. Alice was sure of it. She fixed her eyes on the pavement, watching for movement in her peripheral vision. Tension coiled beneath her skin, magnifying every shadow that crossed her path. The breeze sent a discarded wrapper skittering across the stone and her pulse jumped when her boot crunched down on it. *Litter. Just litter.* A drizzle of sweat slid between her shoulder blades, sticking her shirt to her back. Alice tugged it from her waistband and shook it out with a trembling hand, wafting cool air against her torso. She'd been carrying a fever for weeks; it made her light-headed and sluggish and she could afford neither. Not tonight.

Something rustled behind her and Alice's hearing sharpened. She glanced over her shoulder, but her eyes failed to pick out anything unusual. It was a short, narrow street lined by a row of Georgian terraced houses. A handful of vintage saloon cars sat outside them, their paintwork glinting below the gas street lamp.

This part of the city was quieter; there were fewer pubs and bars here to invite interest after midnight. It made it easier to block out the distant sounds of urban life and listen for the noises that didn't belong: a whisper of muffled panting; the turn of a coat; the heavy tread of footsteps striking the pavement in an alternating rhythm to her own. If she slowed, the footsteps slowed. If she stopped – silence. She peered into the gloom, searching . . . but there was no one there. The street was empty.

A strange sense of claustrophobia tightened her chest and the sound of her breathing was loud in her ears. The dark night pressed in around her, reminding her that she was alone. Fenced in by buildings and high walls. *Trapped.* A bead of sweat gathered at her hairline and she swiped it away with a grim smile. No. That was the fever talking. Just fever-driven paranoia; she'd had months of it. It had started in Ireland, and got worse, not better. Alice loosened another button on her shirt and gave herself a mental shake. She should have been in bed, resting and trying to build her strength; instead, circumstances had forced her to travel across the Rookery in the middle of the night, and she only hoped it was worth the effort. Her pace quickened as she crossed the road and fought to maintain her focus.

She couldn't be far from the entrance to The Necropolis. The private members' club had an invitation-only policy and she'd been warned it would go into lockdown at the first sign of trouble. Trouble in the form of the Bow Street Runners. The city's police force was desperate to get inside the club and shut it down. Luckily, without an invitation they would never discover the hidden entrance.

Behind her, the sound of footsteps grew louder, and Alice's nerves pulled tight. *Not* fevered delusions, real footsteps that smacked and echoed from the stone – and they were growing closer, rounding the corner towards her. What if she had been followed by a Runner? Her foot touched down on a grimy kerb at the junction of an alleyway and she made a sudden decision. Darting into the passage, she pressed her back flat against the wall, the rough brick snagging at her greatcoat. She exhaled quietly. The alley was deserted and steeped in shadows: ideal for lying in wait, unseen.

Removing her clammy hands from her pockets, she curled them into fists, eyes pinned to the entrance. The footsteps stopped abruptly and Alice stiffened. She hadn't been imagining it; someone *had* been following her – and whoever it was had seen her take the detour; they knew exactly where she was. Why, then, were they stalling? The muffled panting had slowed and Alice could almost taste their hesitation. If her pursuer crossed the pavement at the end of the alley, she might see their face in the glow from the street lamp. *Come on*, she urged. *Move into the light.* She shifted her weight to see more clearly, her skin prickling with adrenaline.

Wings. A streak of bone-white feathers at the corner of Alice's eye drew her attention to a stack of abandoned pallets on the cobbles. There, claws gripping the wood precariously, preening itself, was her nightjar. In the right light, it might have been mistaken for a white dove. Doves, however, were tall, with elegant necks and beaks and perfectly proportioned round heads. This bird was squat, with a puffed-up chest, no visible neck and large eyes. Its beak was short and thin, with bristles either side, and its long wings were pointed and kestrel-like.

The nightjar darted its head towards her, peering from its makeshift perch. It churred, low in its throat – a repetitive trilling sound – and Alice knew, suddenly, what to do about her follower. Glancing up the length of the alley and back, Alice crooked her finger at the pale bird and it swooped towards her. She flinched when the nightjar landed on her shoulder.

'Give me a bird's-eye view,' she hissed.

The bird's claws pinched her arm, just briefly, and it stretched upwards, its magnificent wings unfolding as it rose into the air. Despite their strained relationship, Alice had spent months experimenting with her nightjar connection; it had been a revelation to discover that, when focused, she could see the world through her soul-bird's eyes. The eyes were the windows to the soul – so why not vice versa?

Alice steadied herself against the brick wall, took a sharp breath and grasped the cord binding her wrist to the bird's leg. A burst of euphoria rushed through her body, and she blinked rapidly to maintain her concentration. The cord pulsed gently and her palm tingled with shivers of pleasure. Light bled through the gaps in her fingers as she tightened her grip and stared into the dazzling brightness. A flash of white . . . and then Alice's consciousness snapped along the cord like electricity, hurling her mind into the waiting nightjar.

Alice's vision juddered. She could see the top of her own head and shoulders: a sensation that always tripped her nausea. Maintaining the hold on her nightjar's sight meant discarding the solid floor she knew was beneath her and the heavy gravity that weighed down her flesh-and-bone body. She forced her mind to open itself to the steady stream of images pouring in through the glowing cord. She hovered several feet higher, resisting the urge to swoop away. Caught between two bodies, she scanned the alley from above: the top of the pallets, the dustbins, the battered cardboard boxes . . . all laid out beneath her.

With another waft of her wings, Alice propelled herself through the air, gliding along the alley and turning sharply at the end. Around the corner, there was a figure resting against a set of iron railings – oblivious to the nightjar's invisible presence. A roll-up cigarette dangled from his lips, and in his cupped hands he struck a match. It dwindled immediately and he tossed it into the road before trying again. This time, the flame caught and he lit his cigarette, tipping his head back with a satisfied grin. His straw-like hair shone in the street lamp's glow.

'Alice?' he murmured. 'Is it you hiding down there?'

Alice's consciousness shot back to her human body and she jerked upright, thoroughly disoriented.

'August?' she snapped, scrabbling against the wall for balance as she rose. 'Why the hell are you stalking me?'

He stepped out into the road, casting a long shadow into the dark alley. Alice exhaled in a bid to ease some of the tension trapped in her muscles. *Bloody August.* Still, it was good to see him. They'd briefly shared a house owned by Crowley: Coram House, the jewel of the Rookery's version of Bloomsbury and home to waifs and strays. August was one of the trusted few, along with their other housemates – Sasha, Jude and, of course, Crowley – who knew the full and unvarnished truth about who she was. They'd all been at Marble Arch that night, and yet none had retracted their offers of friendship afterwards.

She looked him up and down. He'd lost a little of his trademark scarecrow look in the many months since she'd seen him last. The shock of hair had been tamed, and though his faded black corduroys and jumper were as shabby as ever, they were at least clean. He'd filled out a bit too – the sharp edges had softened and now he was tall rather than scrawny.

'I was early,' he said, 'so I thought I'd come and meet you. I wasn't sure it was you and I didn't want to draw attention to myself by shouting.' He glanced cautiously along the street. 'We can walk together. Are you coming?'

She nodded. August was the one with the invitation to The Necropolis – not her. He was the one who belonged to the private members' club – not her. Alice didn't really belong anywhere.

A curl of smoke wound through the clubhouse. It weaved between the busy tables and darkened booths, snaking over shoulders and wreathing heads that were bent in furtive conversation. Sandalwood and pine incense courtesy of the reeds burning on the bar's countertop. It was, according to August, a security measure: the warm, musky blend was known for its calming effects – just as the drinking den was known for its unrest, heavy on incense, light on trust.

Alice watched the sinuous wisps dance closer. The fragrance wasn't quite a sedative – no one would be reckless enough to come to a place like this and risk having their senses dulled completely – but it paid to remain on your guard. Doubly so when you were battling the lethargic side effects of a fever.

'There's something wrong with you,' said August, squinting at her across the round table, 'and it's not hay fever or flu or whatever else you're going to fob me off with.' He rapped the surface with his fingertips, scattering ash across the polished wood. 'Are you going to tell me what?'

She swigged a mouthful of gin and sat back, shaking her head. 'No. Are you going to tell me what your secret new job is?'

August shrugged. 'It's not important.'

Alice raised an eyebrow. 'It's kept you from coming with Sasha and Jude every time we've met up for the past few months. Sounds important to me.'

He gave her a shifty look. 'If I tell anyone, I'm done. Fired. My esteemed employers have already made that pretty clear.'

Alice's eyes narrowed. 'You're not working for the Fellowship again?' she asked sharply.

He choked on his drink. 'What, you think my IQ is in single digits?'

She relaxed in her chair. The Fellowship were a death cult, led by a sadistic hemomancer named Marianne Northam. Alice despised her, and the feeling was mutual.

'Anyway, stop changing the subject,' said August. 'You don't look right. Tell me what's wrong.'

Alice sighed. 'No.'

'Because?'

'Because you have all the subtlety of a town crier.'

He grinned and leaned back, scraping a hand through his hair. 'Ouch.' Then he added, 'You're worried I'll tell Crowley?'

'No.' Alice sighed and absently drew her finger through a dribble of gin on the table. 'Maybe.' She'd done her best to avoid Crowley since her return to the city. She wasn't ready to see him – maybe she never would be – and he was trying to respect her wishes. 'I don't want this to be the reason we—'

'You don't want a pity party,' said August. 'I get it.'

'No. And no one can know we've come here. Not yet.'

He grinned. 'Clandestine meetings at night . . . secret drinks in strange bars . . . People will talk.'

She raised the glass and pressed it to her forehead, closing her eyes at the cool relief it provided. 'If they do,' she said, 'just tell them . . . tell them you've defied expectations and finally managed to come in useful.'

Something brushed her hand and Alice's eyes flew open.

'Here,' said August, prising the glass from her. He pressed his palms around the sides of the drink and exhaled abruptly. There was a sharp crack and a sudden film of condensation coated the glass. He passed the drink back. A layer of thick ice now sat at the bottom, poking up through the surface of her gin.

'Thanks,' she said, and then paused. 'I thought your magic gave you power over water, not gin. I'm impressed.'

He grinned. 'It's because they water it down. Never trust a bar run by necromancers.'

'You're a necromancer,' she pointed out, pressing the icy glass to her forehead.

'Exactly.'

Across the room, a glass smashed and a lazy collective jeer went up around the clubhouse. A woman pushed back her chair to brush the fragments from her skirt with a sigh. On the table before her, a polished Ouija board was laid out. The woman drew another empty glass closer, tipped it upside down and began sliding it from letter to letter, her lips moving silently.

Alice's gaze trailed around the clubhouse, taking in the oxblood leather sofas, the green velvet armchairs and the dozens of gas lamps and mismatched picture frames on the walls. Somehow, the trappings of a drinking den didn't seem incongruous with the bar's more unusual decor: the metre-wide clock, rusted metal signs and ticket booth. Stone arches, tiled walls and columns divided the space into neat sections. The Necropolis had once been a train station, which was why the rear of the building led to a crumbling platform and a defunct steam train, sitting on tracks that led nowhere.

At the end of the nineteenth century, when an overcrowded London had run out of space to bury its dead, the authorities had come up with a macabre solution: transport coffins and mourners to a cemetery far outside the city's walls, on specially modified trains. The London Necropolis Railway was short-lived, however, thanks to a well-placed bomb during the Blitz.

But in the Rookery, London's darkly magical twin, the station at 121 Westminster Bridge Road and one remaining train had been repurposed in the most fitting way: there was no better location, surely, for a members' club exclusively for necromancers. Considered too unnatural, their magic was banned across the city, but here they were among friends.

Three tables over, there was a sudden frenzy of murmuring and Alice turned towards the noise. A group of bearded men were taking it in turns to examine a handful of small objects they'd tossed onto the wooden floor. Alice assumed they were dice.

'They're allowed to gamble in here?' she said.

'No,' said August with a wry smile. 'They're throwing oracle bones and trying to unpick the future. Funny, though, that none of them predicted the lovely Ouija woman over there was going to smash that glass.'

Even in a city like the Rookery, divination was treated with scepticism. Alice didn't believe in fortune-telling. Then again, a year ago she hadn't believed in magic either – and now, here she was, sitting in a bar accessed by an enchanted door that only opened once a week, and only to those who knew how to find it.

Alice sighed and pressed her fingers into her temples, where a small but persistent pain was beginning to throb. She reached for her glass and took another cooling mouthful. Maybe the gin would take the edge off her headache. Or, if not, maybe it would anaesthetize her to the problem that had brought her to the clubhouse. She rolled her shoulders and tried to sink more loosely into her chair. The incense wasn't helping. It squeezed out the air in the room, filling it with sickly heat that exacerbated her discomfort. A knot of smoke drifted past. She squinted up, watching it thin out as it gained height, dissipating by the beaded lamps that dripped from the ceiling.

A throat cleared nearby – an exaggerated, phlegmatic sound – and Alice flinched, clutching her head, as an extra chair was slammed down opposite her. A woman dropped into it, tossed a battered fedora on the table and gave Alice an appraising stare. Eris Mawkin was the Rookery's only legitimate necromancer – the only one legally allowed to practise her dark art, because she practised it on her employer's behalf: the Bow Street Runners. They were happy to bend the law when it suited them. The Runners' hypocrisy was only part of the reason Alice hated them.

'You're not how I'd pictured you,' drawled Mawkin as she planted her whisky glass down next to the hat. She shook out her bobbed brown hair and leaned back, legs outstretched and dusty boots crossed at the ankle.

'You're . . . exactly how I'd pictured you,' Alice murmured.

Mawkin's eyes glinted with amusement. She turned to greet August and snorted when she saw him hunched over an absurd strawberry vodka. It was decorated with a paper umbrella, a spray of tinsel and a glacé cherry on a cocktail stick.

'Don't ever ask me why I won't mentor you again,' she said when he slid the cherry off the cocktail stick and grinned at her.

'I know, I know,' he said, popping the cherry into his mouth and shoving the paper umbrella into his hair at a jaunty angle. 'With my wholesome good looks and sunny disposition, I don't uphold the dark glamour of necromancy.'

'Necromancy is a serious business, by serious people,' said Mawkin, 'and that is not a serious drink.' She reached for her whisky, swirling the glass between two fingers. 'But the blue umbrella does bring out your eyes.'

She turned to Alice.

'Spit it out then,' said Mawkin, getting straight to the point of their meeting. 'You wanted some information from me, but you already have a necromancer friend. So what do you think I know that he doesn't?' She gestured at August.

Alice paused, considering her answer. 'August . . . has a more *localized* knowledge of necromancy. He knows what he's personally experienced, but anything outside that . . .' She trailed away.

Mawkin raised a sardonic eyebrow and looked to the blond necromancer for his reaction.

August shrugged. 'In my defence, I'm a man of action. Practical. Good with my hands.' He winked, and Mawkin snorted. 'I don't do books and theory; I do whispering to the right people and pricking up my ears at doors.'

He was right. August always managed to find information by devious means; he preferred second-hand information to putting in the hours required to find it first-hand, with research and books and study. It was why Mawkin – twenty years older and the epitome of battle-scarred wisdom – had so far refused to mentor him. And yet, August could do things Mawkin couldn't. He hadn't, however, known the answer to Alice's question. Maybe Mawkin wouldn't either, but Alice had to try.

Alice leaned in closer, anticipation making her hands shake. This was it. This was the moment that could release her from her burden and fix *everything*. 'I want to know . . . how to shut it off.'

Mawkin blinked. 'You've lost me,' she said at last. 'Shut what off?'

'I want to know how a necromancer can cut off their legacy,' said Alice, a desperate edge to her voice. 'Make it . . . make it dormant. Repel whatever death-related gifts they have.'

August threw her a sympathetic look. This was why he'd brought her here: he knew she wanted rid of her father's biology. He'd seen her distress the night Jen died.

'You want to know if a necromancer can neuter themselves?' clarified Mawkin.

'Yes,' said Alice, relieved. 'Exactly that.'

Mawkin's gaze slid from Alice to August and back again. 'And this is, what? Theory? You're not a necromancer, Wyndham, so who are you asking for?'

There was a long pause. So few people knew the truth, and Mawkin couldn't be added to the short list. As the daughter of the Grim Reaper himself, Alice wasn't, technically, a necromancer, but it was close enough. She swallowed the lump in her throat.

'I think she's a late bloomer,' said August. 'You can sense there's something there, can't you? Some touch of the morbid about her?'

Alice flinched at his description but Mawkin didn't respond.

'She's a necromancer with a repressed gift,' August lied smoothly. 'That's why I brought her to you.'

'And, let me get this straight, you don't want me to mentor her to allow these gifts to blossom – you want me to tell her how to shut it off?' said Mawkin, turning from him to Alice. 'That's what you want me to believe?'

Alice held Mawkin's challenging gaze.

'Supposing you are a necromancer,' said Mawkin after a moment, 'and until now you've repressed your gift, either by design or chance, then why not . . . explore it? Under the Runners' radar?'

Alice shook her head impatiently. Mawkin was wasting time with the lie they'd sold her.

'I don't want it,' Alice whispered, the look in her eye growing more haunted as she spoke. 'I don't want a death legacy. I can feel it, crawling under my skin, and I want it out.'

She stared at Mawkin, a silent plea in her eyes. She needed

Mawkin to believe her. She needed to quash her father's deadly legacy, to remove its influence.

'There's nothing wrong with being a necromancer,' said Mawkin, and Alice held her breath. Did that mean that Mawkin had bought it? She didn't dare look at August.

Mawkin gestured around the clubhouse. 'Look. These people are happy enough. They know who they are; they've accepted what they're capable of. There's no shame in necromancy.'

'But no one else has accepted it,' said Alice with conviction. 'They're hiding in here, hoping the Runners don't charge through the door and throw them into Newgate Prison. The Council hasn't accepted it; their laws make necromancy illegal. And I don't have to accept this either. I don't want it.'

'Necromancy is illegal,' said Mawkin, taking a swig of her whisky. 'Necromancers are not.'

Alice exhaled, trying to project an air of calm, and reached for her drink. She was shaking, and she couldn't tell any more if it was the fever or her nerves. 'Semantics.'

'Not semantics,' said Mawkin. 'It's the difference between freedom and persecution. We don't pick the gifts we're born with. It's only exercising them that's restricted.'

'Not for you,' said Alice. Mawkin, after all, was permitted to use them in her work for the Runners. It was a wonder she was welcome in The Necropolis at all; she worked for the people who harassed the other clientele. Mawkin played the game well, however, using the Runners to benefit her fellow necromancers when she could.

'Point accepted,' said Mawkin. She gave Alice a shrewd look. 'You're not a necromancer, Wyndham.' Alice opened her mouth to protest, but Mawkin went on. 'You're not. You don't smell like one of us. But there *is* something . . .' Her eyes narrowed.

'So you can't help her?' asked August, interrupting Mawkin's train of thought with a quick glance at Alice.

She flashed him a grateful smile. She didn't want Mawkin to study her too closely – an experienced necromancer who might somehow sense the impossible truth about her identity.

Mawkin dipped her finger into her drink and drew a whisky circle over the tabletop.

'No,' she said. 'Sorry to disappoint.'

Alice tensed. August had thought there might be a chance, and she'd latched on to the possibility, but if Mawkin was telling the truth . . . Alice's eyes dropped to Mawkin's wrists, searching desperately, willing her aviarist sight to kick in . . . *There.* The glowing cord linking the necromancer to her nightjar suddenly flared across Alice's vision. Her gaze swept up from the pulsing cord wrapped around Mawkin's wrist – which no one but Alice could see – to the small nightjar nestled against Mawkin's neck.

The bird's mahogany feathers were a mixture of plain and tightly patterned, but they appeared frayed at the edges. Its beak was wickedly sharp and its shining black eyes were unblinking. It studied Alice carefully, like an army general watching the enemy from a distance. Alice scrutinized it in return with growing anguish. Mawkin was telling the truth.

'Necromancers can choose not to use their legacy,' said Mawkin, oblivious to Alice's distress, 'but despite what the Runners might want, we can't amputate it.'

Alice inhaled sharply and looked away, frustration biting deep into her stomach. As the daughter of the Lord of Death, she didn't have death magic; she *was* death. Simply not using the legacy wasn't enough. It was a part of her she had to cut loose. There had to be a way.

'I thought Crowley was keeping you leashed in the attic,' Mawkin told August.

August threw her a lazy grin. 'Day release for good behaviour.'

Alice had tensed at the mention of Crowley's name. It wasn't that she'd forgotten Mawkin was one of his only friends – or maybe *friend* was the wrong word. Confidante. Ally. Their paths occasionally crossed at Bow Street Station; Crowley was a thief-taker, skilled in finding stolen goods and employed by the Runners when they were desperate.

'Haven't seen much of him around lately,' said Mawkin. 'He okay?'

'Same old, same old,' said August with a shrug.

Mawkin nodded contemplatively and turned to Alice. After a moment, Mawkin's eyes seemed to darken and her mouth thinned.

'Make yourself useful, Rhone,' she said to August. 'Go get us another round of drinks.'

'You haven't finished your—' he started.

'The grown-ups want to talk,' said Mawkin. She downed the whisky in one and shoved the glass at his chest. 'Give us two minutes.'

August hesitated, but Alice nodded her agreement and he left.

'I knew you smelled wrong,' said Mawkin. 'Does he know?' She gestured at August, who was talking to the bartender. 'Does anyone? Crowley?'

Alice shook her head. 'No. And I don't want it becoming common knowledge . . . please.'

Mawkin sighed and ran a hand through her hair. 'Shit.'

They lapsed into a thick silence before Alice broke it. 'You're sure there's no way to cut out—'

'You can't outrun death,' said Mawkin.

Alice swallowed. 'But maybe if—'

'You can't outrun death,' she repeated. 'I'm sorry. But I can't help you. It's not a necromancer you need, it's a doctor.' She paused, her face softening. 'Are you afraid? There's no need. I have a better idea than most about what comes next. If you want to talk about—'

'I don't,' Alice said quickly.

Mawkin frowned. 'Some people find it therapeutic to spend some time putting their affairs in order so that—'

Alice shoved herself to her feet. 'I don't *have* time,' she said bitterly.

Mawkin graced her with a slow, thoughtful nod. 'Then I'm sorry. Look, if my advice is worth anything to you . . .' She sighed. 'Tell them the truth. Let them take care of you.'

Alice's mouth tightened and she shook her head. She didn't want to hear any more. Platitudes and sympathy were no use to her at all. Mawkin couldn't help her. Her options were now limited to just one.

'Thank you,' said Alice, snatching up her coat, 'for your time.'

Her head was throbbing, making the room pulse around her. She threw Mawkin a meaningful nod and strode away, past a startled August.

You can't outrun death.

What had begun in Ireland had crept up on her with increasing speed. A new tremor in her hands. A now-relentless shortness of breath. Her hold on gravity slipping as rooms spun around her like ballroom dancers, leaving her to slump suddenly into a chair, clutching her head until the world was right side up again.

Sporadic episodes, spaced weeks apart to begin with but growing more frequent, spiralling into fevers and headaches and the nagging certainty that some part of her biology was faulty.

Her lifestyle was too busy, Doctor Burke had said on the second and third appointments. She needed to take yet more iron tablets and slow down. But she *was* slowing down – even her heartbeat had grown irregular, like an offbeat drummer who couldn't keep pace with the lead singer. The worst of it was the days when everything seemed to require so much effort. When the tiredness was so bone-deep she wanted to give up, to let it take her. She'd kept her parents in the dark about the extent of her symptoms, but they had been so concerned in the end that they'd pushed her to return to the Rookery, seeking a cure. And instead she'd found a definitive diagnosis.

This thing inside her – her biological father's legacy, her DNA, or whatever it was – was corrupting her. Overwhelming her. He had loaded so much death on her shoulders it was killing her. And Mawkin had dashed her penultimate throw of the dice. She couldn't sever his deathly legacy; she was sinking under the weight of it. Alice was *dying*.

You can't outrun death?

Alice sighed as she stepped out into the night.

Just watch me.

2

'Slow down!'

The city blurred past as Alice rushed along the pavement. To prevent the Runners from gaining a foothold on its true location, the entrance to The Necropolis was not fixed in place. In the Rookery, a door could lead not to another room but to thousands of possible rooms, depending on where you wished to go. Some of the publicly operated doorways opened to entirely different places dependent on the time or the day of the week – and travel was sometimes like waiting for the right bus.

So it was that Alice found herself in a different neighbourhood to the one she'd travelled through to reach the secretive club-house. Here, there were fewer houses and more shuttered shops. One of the Rookery's more well-known pubs occupied the corner of a tight road, and she paused at the junction. The raucous laughter spilling out from The Rook's Nest was in stark contrast to the secrecy of The Necropolis; no one in this drinking den was concerned about being discovered by the Runners.

A woman smoking outside the pub, glass of wine in hand, was peering irritably at a lantern on the pub's wall. The light inside was sputtering uselessly. With a roll of her eyes, she downed her drink and put her hand over the empty wine glass. The air above rippled with heat, and in the next moment, flames began to lick at her palms. She removed her hand and placed the glass of fire on the windowsill, where it cast a warm glow over the white paintwork. She noticed Alice staring, and nodded with drunken satisfaction at her makeshift new lantern.

Alice put her head down and hurried across the road, turning into a narrow side street of more upmarket shops. She passed the darkened windows of E. M. Saphier: Shoemaker, The Belladonna Bookshop and Dashwood's Fireplaces, splashed with a sign saying, *Coal too messy? Firewood too smoky? Electricity too expensive? Heat your home with our no-fuel fireplaces! Finest House Ilmarinen Craftsmanship – prices starting at only fifty sovereigns!* The last on the row was Barrett's Musical Instruments, trying to entice customers with a sandwich board chained up outside, offering *Self-playing instruments for the busy musician. Something to suit every magical legacy – clarinets, guitars, ocarinas and rainmakers – just ask!*

'Alice, wait!' shouted August from behind. 'For God's sake, I'm a smoker. I don't have the lung capacity for a city-wide chase.'

She turned another corner and found herself standing in front of Mowbray's Perfumery, the moonlight glancing off rows of glass bottles in the window. A sign stretched above them announced a discount on Mowbray's famous poppy and lavender water for members of House Mielikki. Typical. Even the shops showed favouritism here.

Alice sighed and rested her back against the window, her coat clutched in her arms. She'd grown to love this strange city, despite its foibles and its nepotism. The Rookery had been built as a sanctuary for the Väki, a magical race of people who had been fleeing the persecution they'd suffered in their native Finnish homeland during the Crusades. Their descendants had claimed this space for themselves and founded a city on it. For hundreds of years, as the city had grown, they had modelled its architecture on London, right up until the 1930s. Buildings demolished in London lived on in the Rookery. Newgate Prison, Christchurch Greyfriars, Baynard's Castle . . . The Rookery housed the brick-and-mortar ghosts of London's past.

Alice arched her neck to peer again at the perfumery's sign – *10% reduction for House Mielikki!* – and shook her head. The original four Finnish master builders who had created the Rookery were called Ilmarinen, Pellervoinen, Ahti and, of course, Mielikki. Each had an affinity for certain forms of magic and had formed their own Houses for those who shared their legacies. Those skilled with water were typically members of House Ahti. Pellervoinen welcomed the architects, the wielders of stone and brick and the talented travellers of the doorways. Ilmarinen was for the metalworkers and fire-wielders, and House Mielikki took those skilled with flora and fauna.

The reason Mowbray's poppy and lavender water was so famous was because they'd used the magic of their House to enhance it. The scent was said to be so blissfully relaxing the Runners had tested it to ensure it wasn't illegal opium. Far from dampening Mowbray's sales, they'd subsequently rocketed.

'What did Mawkin say?' puffed August, finally catching her up.

'Nothing,' she said, pushing off from the shop window. Her balance swayed for a moment and her fingers tightened on the coat for support. 'Mawkin can't help,' she continued, starting off down the road. 'Tonight was a waste of time.'

He raced ahead of her and spun round, blocking her path.

'Alice, this stuff about your dad – look, your DNA is the least important part of you,' he said, putting his hands on her shoulders. 'Whatever demons you're wrestling, you—'

'I *am* the demon,' she said with a dark laugh. She shrugged him off and stumbled away, feeling off-kilter. It was no use August counselling her; he didn't know that her father's genes were actually poisoning her – no one did. She couldn't bring herself to tell him, because telling him meant telling Crowley. Crowley had sacrificed his sister for Alice – and for what? Alice was dying anyway.

'If you keep racing away, eventually I'm going to stop chasing you,' August called after her.

She ignored him and turned the corner into a residential street. Sandwiched between two houses was a tiny tobacconist's with a green door, which she intended on opening.

There was a muffled curse and then pounding footsteps from behind. August caught up with her, wheezing like a busted accordion. She stopped by the metal railings of a house and leaned against them. A flash of pain shot through her arm and she stumbled away, rubbing the sting from her elbow with an angry hiss.

August nodded at the railings. 'Sadistic bastards, aren't they? House Ilmarinen's newest home security invention – electric shocks running right through the iron. They only work against non-members.'

Alice nodded, barely listening. Her breath was too shallow and her tongue buzzed with pins and needles. Not a good sign. It usually meant a dizzy spell was incoming. She turned her face from August and closed her eyes, trying to push away the light-headedness. *Breathe.*

'What aren't you telling me?' he asked.

Her eyes flicked open to find him frowning down at her.

'August,' she said wearily, 'there are a million things I'm not telling you. Because I don't have to. I'm not your landlord and you aren't renting the space in my head.'

He nodded, and reached for his tobacco box. 'Speaking of landlords, Crowley—'

'No,' she said. 'No Crowley. You promised, and I'm holding you to it.'

He sighed. 'All right. Let me walk you back to the university.'

Alice raised a sardonic eyebrow. She'd been living in staff accommodation at Goring University for months; she certainly didn't need August's help to get back there. If she had to pause on the way, to slide down a wall and sit with her head on her knees, catching her breath and trying to push the stars from her eyes, then she didn't want an audience. She'd managed to keep her bouts of illness hidden from her other friends, Sasha and Jude, during their monthly catch-ups, and she didn't plan on slipping up now. There was no point burdening anyone else with this – no one could help her.

'What?' said August. 'Let me walk you. It's late, it's dark, and this city's no safer than London.'

Her mouth quirked involuntarily. He was worried about her safety? Hers?

'I don't know how to tell you this, August, but a year ago, I almost destroyed this city and everyone in it,' she said, a hint of exasperation in her tone. 'If my death awaits me down a Rookery alleyway, I won't be greeting it with a scream – I'll be greeting it with twenty-odd years of missing Father's Day cards.'

She was aiming for flippancy. Sometimes, if she pretended at breeziness, it was enough to stop her from dwelling on the skin-crawling guilt about Marble Arch and her part in Jen's death.

August lit his cigarette and waved away the smoke with a breezy hand. 'Fine,' he said. 'Then you walk *me* back to the university.'

He grinned at her and reached for the green door of the

tobacconist's. As he pulled it open, a gust of chilled air poured over them, pinching her cheeks. The open door didn't lead to the tiny shop's interior; it led to the void, a dark, barren space between worlds, a corridor like a wind tunnel between the twin cities of London and the Rookery. Alice sighed into the cool air, enjoying the momentary relief. But then it was too much – too cold for her fever to cope with. She shivered, hugged the coat against her chest and stepped through the doorway.

Wind drove into her limbs, chipping away at her skin. She shook out the coat and rammed her arms into the sleeves as August stepped in behind her. He swung the door shut, plunging them into blackness, and when her fingers reached out to check, the door they'd used for entry had vanished. Unable to see, August rested a hand on her elbow, and with the other she sensed him groping at the air for a new door handle. Billowing gusts ruffled her hair and she bowed her head into the pressure. There was a click, and the newly formed door flew open, framing August as he stepped out of the void and onto a worn grass track. Alice took a moment to steady herself before joining him.

'Wasted a cigarette,' August grunted, flicking ash off his jumper. 'Bugger it. Come on then.'

Regimented fir trees surrounded them; clutches of vibrant purple geraniums and bluebells grew thickly at their bases. The lawned university gardens rolled outwards, a colourful riot of scented wildflowers and manicured trees.

The door they had exited – a glossy black door with an iron ring – belonged to an old janitor's storeroom several miles away from the tobacconist's. Alice found it strange that she didn't consider travelling to be noteworthy any more. The ability to move across the city in minutes, reducing miles to inches . . . It was odd how quickly her mind had expanded to make it part of her normal reality.

'What do you mean, "come on"?' said Alice with a tired grin. 'This is where your night ends. You can't come back to my room.'

He frowned. 'Why? I'm not planning to steal your virtue.'

'Rules of using staff accommodation,' she said. 'No overnight visitors on campus and no sub-letting.'

He rolled his eyes. 'Well I've never been a stickler for rules and I've no plans to start now.'

She shook her head. 'Goodnight, August.'

'Will you be okay?' he asked, brow furrowed.

She hesitated, her mouth curving into a brittle smile. 'Of course I will. But thanks. For tonight – for trying.'

'You said it yourself: it was a waste of time,' he said, scratching at his straw-like hair. He found the blue paper umbrella still nestled behind his ear and plucked it out.

'Yes,' said Alice. 'But I needed to hear it. I needed to know what my options are.'

Only one option now.

August glanced up at the towering university building. 'You could come back with me, you know. To Coram House. You could just . . . come home.'

Alice exhaled shakily. Home? How quaint. She'd lost every home she'd ever had: her old flat in London with Jen, the family home she'd grown up in in Henley, her parents' newest cottage in Mayo.

Alice turned away. She had no home.

'Night, August,' she said, moving off through the grass. 'And thanks – I mean it.'

Goring University's sprawling campus was made up of imposing stone buildings and cobbled patios next to rolling lawns and wild mulberry gardens. Alice worked in the Magellan Institute, on the ground floor of the Cavendish Building, one of the four edifices that formed a quadrangle around a large cobbled square. The other university buildings were Sydenham, Whiston and Arlington.

Arlington – home of the humanities faculty – was the first place she'd ever seen in the Rookery, a limestone structure with a domed roof and two jutting wings. One wing housed a two-storey library, while the other held the dining hall on the ground floor and the staff accommodation on the second. She'd been lucky enough to be offered housing when she'd accepted the job; vacancies were like gold dust, but a previous tenant had recently died and they'd wasted no time in finding a replacement.

An unpleasant thought came to her before she had time to extinguish it . . . How quickly would they find *her* replacement if she died? Her shoulders slumped and she trudged onwards, desperate to rest her aching limbs and put the whole night to bed.

Alice gripped the edge of the sink so tightly her fingers blanched. The wave of nausea grew, a soft ache in her abdomen sharpening into a stabbing cramp. She squeezed her eyes shut and gritted her teeth. *I should be used to this by now.* Her shoulders bunched in anticipation as the spasms knifed her stomach, the pain clawing itself higher. Muscles clenching and unclenching, she leaned into the agony, pressing into the edge of the basin. *Here it comes.* The pain twisted and burrowed deeper, needling into her senses. She gasped and her eyes flew open. The toilet cubicle see-sawed around her. Her chest heaved. A jet of hot bile shot up her throat and splattered the porcelain. Her stomach cramped again and she shuddered. Blisters of sweat beaded on her forehead and she snatched a quick breath. *And again.*

She retched, brown hair swaying over the sink with every tremor, but her stomach was empty. Then she spun the taps with trembling fingers and washed away the foul residue. She straightened up and leaned against the bathroom mirror, her back cooling on the reflective glass.

A harsh buzz from the doorbell announced an early visitor, and Alice wiped her mouth on a towel. She staggered into her bedroom, stripping off her pyjamas and squinting up at her clock. It was barely 8 a.m.

'Give me a minute,' she managed. Pulling on a pair of work trousers and a shirt, she lumbered over to the door and swung it open.

A young woman – athletic, with platinum-blonde hair pulled back into a ponytail – was standing in the doorway with a bored expression. Her sailor pants and fitted floral blouse reminded Alice of something a pre-war model might wear on her day off; they were pristine next to Alice's rumpled outfit.

'I'm here for my book,' she said.

Alice frowned, momentarily confused.

'Holly?' she murmured. 'What are you . . .?'

The visitor took advantage of her disorientation to move past her, into the room. She peered around Alice's quarters with interest.

Like the other four staff lodgings on this part of the floor, it was small, with a kitchen-diner open to the bedroom, and the very definition of utilitarian. The magnolia walls were bare and the wooden furniture was solid and unfussy. Old kitchen appliances were stacked by the window; their yellowed plastic suggested they'd been purchased in the 1970s, which made them positively youthful compared to the age of everything else in the Rookery.

When she'd moved in, there hadn't been anything for Alice to eat on, so she'd persuaded the janitor, Eugene Reilly, to let her have the broken flip-top desk and chairs he'd been storing in his outhouse. The room's only extravagances were the huge window that overlooked the gardens near the Whiston Building, a small shelf for her sketchbooks and the avocado-coloured carpet, which was so thick she lost her toes in the pile. She was also lucky enough to have her own toilet – though she did have to use the communal bathroom for showering. Alice didn't care about the cramped size or the terrible furniture; she loved the lodging because it was hers. What she didn't love was having it invaded by the second-most-abrasive person in the Rookery – the first, of course, being Crowley.

Alice's lips thinned as Holly moved towards the chest of drawers, which was cluttered with personal belongings: Alice's hairbrush; a small ring box her mum had given her when she'd left Ireland; her main sketchbook, filled with dozens of annotated nightjars; and a cricket bat. The bat had been mouldering in the humanities faculty's lost property box; she'd claimed it because owning something capable of smashing skulls had seemed common sense for a woman who lived alone.

Holly's green eyes swept over the mess and Alice eased past her, tipped the ring box into the top drawer, tossed the hairbrush onto the bed and stacked the rest more neatly. She threw Holly a challenging look, waiting for the anticipated remark about her untidiness.

'Are you pregnant?' asked Holly, studying her with a raised eyebrow.

Alice's mouth dropped open. '*What?*'

Holly shrugged. 'The walls are thin. I heard you throwing up and it's early. Do you have morning sickness?'

Alice was too shocked to reply.

'If you're pregnant, you'll have to rescind your application. You can't sit the test; it's dangerous for the baby.'

'There is no baby,' said Alice. 'I'm not pregnant, Holly. I'm ill, for God's sake, that's all.'

Holly's eyes drifted over her, coolly assessing. Finally, she gave a sharp nod. 'Fine then. I'm here for my book.'

Alice turned away, careening a little as the room tilted with her – a movement that did not go unnoticed by her visitor. Holly Mowbray was her next-door neighbour. A standoffish twenty-something, just a few years younger than Alice, who worked in the Faculty of Medical Sciences. It was an appropriate place for her to work: Alice had never met anyone so clinical. In ordinary circumstances, their paths might never have crossed. However, alongside the fact that they shared a corridor and a party wall, they had both applied for membership of House Mielikki.

There was no chance at all that Holly would fail in her bid. She was the youngest of the Mowbray family, who were not just a dynasty of talented perfumers and herbalists but also one of House Mielikki's most prominent families.

The success of Alice's bid was much less guaranteed. Her skills as an aviarist were utterly distinct from the House system. Aviarists didn't inherit their magical gift, and they had no specific House. Like necromancers, they were a genetic accident. Though some anomalies, like August, had found a conventional home; his water legacy had recently won him a place in House Ahti. And Alice knew she had the same potential. There was no doubt she had Mielikki's legacy – but whether it was strong enough to win her a place in the House was another matter.

A vision floated across her memory of the ivy she'd conjured to swaddle her parents' house in Mayo: at her touch, its waxy star-shaped leaves had unfurled from strong vines, wrapping around the stone to whimsical effect. Alice had been so proud; the place had been rundown when they'd moved in but they'd revived it together. Growing ivy over the old walls had been the finishing touch. And then the vision was swept away, replaced by the memory of daisies rotting between her fingers and, soon after, the ivy withering on the brickwork, its stems turning brittle and thin. As Alice had sickened, so had the plants she'd grown.

'Did you make this?' asked Holly, moving to examine the ornate window frame.

Alice frowned, distracted. 'What?'

'Did you make this?' Holly repeated slowly.

'Oh. Yes,' she said. 'A fortnight ago.'

The frame's design had been as plain as the rest of the room when she'd first arrived, but Alice had spent months practising on it like a canvas as she researched her potential.

She'd worked hard – coaxing life from its surface until whip-thin branches had sprung from the knots of wood, teasing and curling them into entwined swirls and laying them flat around the window with their leaves artfully fashioned either side. It hadn't been her intention, but from a certain angle, it looked like a piece of living baroque architecture, all theatrical leaf scrolls and winding branches.

The labour had become part of her training. Her application to join House Mielikki would involve an entrance test and Alice had to sharpen both her reflexes and her understanding of their legacy. She allowed her eyes to trace the window frame, still miraculously bursting with life weeks after she'd grown it: proof

43

she was capable of creating as well as destroying; proof that she was more than an architect of death.

'It's good,' Holly offered grudgingly. 'Except here,' she said, turning a vine over and directing Alice's gaze towards it. 'The leaves are starting to crisp and curl at the edges. It's drying out. Or dying out. One or the other,' she said casually as Alice's stomach clenched. 'You should redo it before it spreads.'

There was a heavy pause. Holly stared curiously at Alice, taking in the dark circles ringing her brown eyes, her dull hair and too-thin face. Alice's vanity had become laughably unimportant to her lately. She wondered what Crowley would make of her now.

'You look like there should be a plague cross on your door,' said Holly finally.

'Thanks.'

'Whatever you've got – is it contagious?' she asked, a note of concern creeping into her voice. Not concern for Alice, of course. Holly had all the warmth of an iceberg – specifically, the iceberg that had downed the *Titanic*.

'No.' Alice pulled a tight smile. 'You're safe enough, don't worry.'

Holly raised a sceptical eyebrow. 'So what's wrong with you then?'

'Nothing,' Alice murmured, wiping moisture from her top lip. 'Look,' she said, 'the book you've come for . . . Which one was it?'

Holly moved away from the window, turning on the spot, her eyes searching. '*Dugdale's Exercises in Advanced Blooming*,' she said. 'I need it by this afternoon. Lester wants to quiz me on it.' She tutted. 'As if I can't already recite the whole book backwards and forwards in my sleep.'

Lester was Holly's mentor. Every candidate applying for membership of a House was assigned one. The idea had been introduced about two decades before in an apparent bid to make the membership process more democratic, to ensure that no candidate was disadvantaged by their lack of House experience. Holly had little need of a mentor; she'd been primed for membership since birth.

'I returned it to the library on Tuesday,' said Alice. 'I don't think anyone else had reserved it so it might still be available.'

Holly gave a peeved sigh and turned to go, then paused and retraced her steps to the window. As her fingers caressed the branches and leaves, there was a rustle and clusters of yellow-green flowers burst open beneath her palm, their growth spreading rapidly through the dense ivy.

A dark bud surged up through the tangled vines and bloomed into a red rose before Alice's eyes – then another appeared, and another, on thorny stems.

'There,' said Holly, stepping back with a satisfied expression. 'A little pre-test gift for you. Forget Dugdale, I should be writing my own guide to blooming.' She gave a tinkling laugh that faded into a sigh. 'I'll be glad when this is all over,' she said, strolling towards the door. 'Won't you?'

Alice stared at the new window frame. If she had wanted roses, she'd have installed them herself. She pinched the bridge of her nose and closed her eyes. A familiar fluttering sound whispered by her ear, and Alice opened her eyes to find her nightjar clacking its beak in Holly's direction. She frowned. It was the first time the bird had seemed to share her thoughts. It was unsettling. Narrowing her eyes, Alice willed it to leave, and it vanished with a quiver of feathers.

'I'll see you later,' said Holly with a wicked grin, 'if I can't find the book you've cost me.' She laughed again and waved her comment away before closing the door smartly behind her.

Alice crossed to the kitchen, poured a glass of water and sat at the battered wooden table. Most days, Holly was perfectly tolerable, but Alice did sometimes have to grit her teeth. The muscle under her right eye twitched and she took a mouthful of water. She would indeed be glad when this was all over – assuming she passed House Mielikki's tests, which was increasingly doubtful.

Joining House Mielikki had become vital to Alice after her disappointment at The Necropolis.

Though Eris Mawkin knew of no way to shut off her connection with death, Alice refused to allow it to kill her. Her father might be Tuoni, the former Lord of Death, but she also possessed the Mielikki gifts, presumably through her mother's bloodline.

As much as Alice would have liked to believe she was the product of a grand love affair between her parents, the likelier explanation was that she had been born of some sinister bargain or ritual. House Mielikki was the very antithesis of such a union and would likely react badly to Alice's heritage should they discover it. Their House produced even fewer necromancers than the others – their legacy was life, not death.

And they were the masters of it. When the Rookery had been created, Mielikki's greatest contribution had been the Arbor Suvi – the Summer Tree – a tree so powerfully magical that its roots had provided the city's foundation and given it life. Even its sap possessed healing qualities – thanks to Crowley and Sasha, it had once saved her life.

This Tree of Life, House Mielikki and the hope they represented had quickly become an obsession for Alice. If she could pass their test, the House could help her to balance the two halves of her biology: death constrained by life. She was sure of it. Joining House Mielikki could save her.

She glanced at the window frame, searching for the decaying leaves, but Holly had buried them beneath abundant fresh growth. Alice shook her head and turned away. She had no hope of success while Tuoni's legacy prevented her from showcasing her true Mielikki potential. Eris Mawkin had been her last hope of solving the paradox. Alice bit her lip and stared through the glass. If only oracle bones really could reveal the future.

3

A storm was brewing. An academic storm, Alice called it. Her boss, Professor Reid, was in one of her moods. Alice sat by the lab window, pretending to leaf through an old dissertation while her eyes flicked sideways to follow Reid's rigid motions.

The older woman's temperament fluctuated with the successes and failures of her research. A month ago, Reid had discovered a Finnish-to-Latin translation error that would set her research back six months and, in a rage, she had smashed a window with a mug of tea. *Alice's* tea. Three weeks before that, Alice had found a sought-after reference to René Descartes in a book on metaphysics, and a tearful Reid had almost embraced her. Almost. Alice was faster than she looked.

The professor's footsteps cracked sharply on the wooden floor as she paced in front of the research lab's vast arched window. It was a big, airy room, but it seemed to shrink whenever Reid was in one of her frenzies, as though the woman's mood acted on the space like a vacuum.

'Ethereal transcendence?' mumbled Reid, her horsey teeth chewing her bottom lip. 'Animism?'

Reid scraped a hand through her hair, fingers snagging in the grey streak running through dark chestnut. Her hair was always a reflection of her frame of mind. Neatly pinned back was a good sign, but if her curls escaped their nest throughout the day, it was an omen of her temper unravelling.

'Pardon?' Alice asked cautiously, one eye on Reid's mussed-up hair. She wondered if it was too late to cloak herself from sight and sneak out. Two little words, *look away*, and she could make Reid's nightjar – and therefore its owner – simply stop seeing her, an invisibility trick that lasted a few minutes. Just long enough.

'Doesn't it all come back to dualism and trauma?'

Alice sighed. 'Is this rhetorical or—'

Lips tight, Reid waved a dismissive hand and Alice bristled. Reid ripped a Post-it from her desk and shoved it at Alice, before turning away, muttering to herself. *Clement weather with clear skies and low-pressure winds*, Alice noted. *Storm abating.* She glanced down at the Post-it: another library book request.

Alice was employed by the university as a research assistant, a job title that she and Reid had interpreted in very different ways. To Alice's mind, her role was to assist with research. Reid, however, understood the job to be *researcher's* assistant, which was quite similar and also wholly different.

'It'll take me a while to find this,' said Alice, holding up the Post-it note and wondering how long she could drag out the library search. An hour? Two? Perhaps until Reid retired? Unfortunately the professor was in her early fifties, so there would be a long wait.

Reid shrugged, then paused and took a step towards Alice, her unfocused eyes suddenly sharpening. She frowned.

'Are you ill again?'

Alice tensed. After her morning encounter with the sick bowl and Holly, she'd taken a hot shower and washed her weariness and nausea away. Her headaches and fever tended to come and go, but as long as she didn't overdo it physically, right now, she felt . . . adequate. Alice's whole future was riding on the next two days, so adequate was the best she could hope for under the circumstances.

'You look terrible,' said Reid. 'You realize your contract says nothing about sick pay?'

Alice gave the woman a saccharine smile. Reid's heartfelt concern for her welfare made Alice feel like such a valued employee. 'I'm fine; it's just my hay fever playing up.'

Reid stared at her, her long, humourless face scanning Alice's tired eyes and pallid complexion. Then she turned away.

Professor Vivian Reid's research was funded entirely by the Magellan Institute, a small offshoot of the university subsidized by a bursary from the Magellan Estate. When Alice had first arrived and realized exactly where she'd be working within the Department of Natural Sciences, she'd assumed it was Crowley's idea of a joke. Then she'd wondered if it was another olive branch. Or perhaps a whole olive tree. Magellan had been a renowned aviarist and had written the *Nightjar Compendium*, the guide Alice had used to help hone her skills. It was Crowley who had managed to source her a copy of the rare text. Magellan had also written about the nature of the soul, an uncomfortable subject, given Alice's history. He was the one who had theorized, in his seminal work, *Sielun*, that Tuoni's nightjar had a different function to others – that it didn't protect his soul but imprisoned it.

The Magellan Institute could only afford to fund one research project at a time, and Reid and Alice made a team of two. Alice had quickly discovered that the professor was a woman whose grudges ran so deep she could have used them to tunnel to Australia. Her work had once been mocked during a brief post at the Sorbonne in Paris, and she was now fixated on producing a paper so groundbreaking it would wipe her critics off the map. Privately, Alice thought this was a stretch. She'd read the professor's research and, despite an initial fascination with the topic, she'd soon realized that Reid's focus was not exactly titillating stuff.

The project, as might have been expected from an institute linked to the most famous aviarist of all time, was related to the concept of the soul. Alice very much doubted that Reid's work would ever receive the acclaim she was hoping for. It wasn't going to cure disease or end famine; it only sought to prove a centuries-old philosophical argument that had bothered bearded old men and no one else.

Even so, before signing the employment contract, Alice had scoured the woman's nightjar for any sign of ulterior motive in offering her the post. She had to be careful. After Sir John Boleyn's actions at Marble Arch, she'd even considered that he might be funding the Magellan Estate. But Reid's nightjar had shown nothing more dangerous than a foul temper and a propensity to throw mugs. Alice was satisfied that the woman's ambition had no significance to her own troublesome soul. She kept her mouth shut and got on with the job.

Reid trusted Alice to carry out mundane errands like photocopying, but nothing more. For a while, it had given Alice some spiteful pleasure to know that Reid had overlooked the one person who could have given her project some real insight. But her aviarist skills were better off hidden; nothing good had ever come from people knowing she could reveal their secrets and read their lies.

Reid's dismissal of her talents had worked to Alice's benefit in the end. As long as she was available for humdrum tasks, she was free to do pretty much as she liked. She had a living wage, some-where to sleep, and she didn't have to spend her time and energy on someone else's business, which was just as well, since her time was running out and her brain felt like it was barely functioning some days.

'Bring me back a coffee,' Reid called over her shoulder. The professor was obsessed with two things: her project and caffeine. 'Use those beans I like – the arabica. And make it black. I'm work-ing late.'

Alice reluctantly bit her tongue at Reid's tone and slipped out. She had no plans to hurry back; library errands were the best part of her job description. Not only did they keep her out of Reid's way, they were also a legitimate reason to while away hours with a book. Never the ones Reid asked her to find, of course, but usually books related to Mielikki's legacy. Today, however, would be different. Today she would set aside the texts on botany, trel-lising and blooming, and use the time to sharpen her reflexes and prepare. At sunset, she would be taking part in the first member-ship test for House Mielikki.

The wind had picked up. When Alice opened the door to the university's central courtyard, a gust nearly snatched it from her fingers. She took a moment to savour the cool draughts across her clammy skin. The mulberry tree in the centre rattled its branches at her, its wine-coloured berries swaying precariously. It was her favourite tree; she often had her lunch beneath it – a strategic feat because Professor Reid usually insisted on breaking for lunch just after noon, at the same time as the undergraduates. On warm days, when no one wanted to be stuck in the dark dining room in the Arlington Building, it was a race to grab the bench under the tree before the undergrads did.

As she hurried across the cobbles, Alice glanced up at the tree's dangling fruit. Her eyes narrowed in concentration and she squeezed her hand into a fist. Her fingers tingled and throbbed. Then there was a susurration of leaves waving in the breeze . . . and the berries began to lengthen, growing bloated at unnatural speed. A rich, tangy scent hit the air, bursting out from the tree in clusters, like the residue of a dozen tiny explosions. A small robin hiding among the branches hopped out and darted towards a clump of mulberries. Its beak attacked the fruit's flesh, staining its feathers purple as it gorged itself on the juices.

Alice smiled as the robin suddenly paused and darted its head to watch her pass.

'You're welcome,' she told it. The weeks spent poring over *Dugdale's Exercises in Advanced Blooming* had been worthwhile after all.

But as she reached the back door to the Arlington Building and pulled it open, Alice saw the bloated mulberries drop from the branch and splatter across the cobbles, decomposing at a rapid speed. A pain began to tick behind her eyes and she turned away, disappointment pinching her throat.

'Alice!'

She sidestepped small pockets of students ambling through the corridors with satchels and armfuls of books. In keeping with the Rookery's 1930s fashion, the boys all wore shirts with club collars and high-waisted trousers and the girls tended towards long skirts and blouses, though a few were in wide-leg culottes similar to Holly's. Up ahead, a larger group held a heated discussion outside the dining hall – literally: one of them was gesticulating with a sandwich until the others groaned in unison and flicked their hands, laughing uproariously when his bread roll went up in flames. A familiar face appeared over the tops of their heads, playing peacemaker and trying to put out the fire – a bearded face with serious eyes and square glasses: Tom Bannister, one of the technicians in the environmental engineering department.

Tom spent almost as much time in the library as Alice did; it was the best place to hide from his departmental bosses. He liked to hunker down by the pharmacology shelves, where there was no chance he'd be found by anyone who was actually looking for him. She waved at him. He gave her a thumbs-up before he vanished down a corridor, carried along by the arguing students like a piece of driftwood.

When Alice reached the library, Bea was kneeling on the rug, surrounded by piles of water-damaged books.

'Look at this,' said the librarian, holding up *Vancy's Nine Methods of Incision*. 'The entire foreword has faded. That bloody janitor attached the outdoor fountain's pipes to the mains upstairs, and it blew the whole lot. Two hundred fucking gallons of water. The ceiling nearly fell in.'

Alice smiled briefly. Why was it that swearing sounded so brilliantly wrong in a cut-glass accent? Last term, the Dean of Ancient Languages had insisted on Bea using a swear jar in a bid to stop her corrupting the younger students.

Bea staggered upright, her beaded necklace jangling against her brashly patterned dress and large hooped earrings. A London-born aristocrat in her late thirties with a penchant for eccentric clothes, Lady Beatrice Alberta Pelham-Gladstone hadn't been so much born with a silver spoon in her mouth as a forty-eight-piece cutlery set. She could always be found tending her books, a pencil tucked behind one ear.

'Go on then,' said Bea, sorting through her ruined pile. 'What's she sent you in for this time?'

'Philosophy section,' said Alice, glancing down at the title on her Post-it note, and then at the waterlogged hardbacks. 'Do you want some help with those?'

Some of the editions had turned to pulp, others papier mâché bricks where their soggy pages had fused together. If they were allowed to dry out, they could be used to build a very flammable house.

Bea clasped the leather cover of one sodden block between her fingers. Very slowly, its mushy contents let go of their binding, slid from the cover and hit the rug with a dull splodge. Bea stared at it with a mournful expression and shook her head.

'No use,' she said. 'This is a job for a highly skilled librarian.'

Alice smiled. Bea was much more than a custodian and curator of books. She was Alice's mentor and lifeline. For six months, she'd force-fed her student a diet of books and set her a series of hard mental and physical challenges; it was a lot like having a personal trainer, only with less shouting.

'Besides,' Bea continued, 'we both know the books can't bear the sight of you – yet.' She raised an amused eyebrow.

Bea spoke about her library as though it were filled with living things that could express preferences and desires. In a way, she was right. The books Alice searched for always seemed to evade her – pages fell out, front covers fell off, and those she plucked from the shelves at random seemed to attack her deliberately with paper cuts.

'Are you feeling okay?' asked Bea, frowning.

'What? Oh.' Alice nodded. 'Yes. Fine. I'm just getting over a stomach bug.' She licked her lips; they were salty with sweat. 'Has Holly been in? She's trying to hunt down the Dugdale book.'

'Not yet,' said Bea. 'But surely she's not going to spend the day of the first test trying to learn something new?'

Alice shook her head. 'Lester's going to quiz her on it, apparently.'

Bea's expression was withering. 'Pointless,' she said. 'They should be warming up for tonight with some practical exercises.'

Alice sighed. 'Maybe he thinks Holly doesn't need them.'

They lapsed into silence. Holly wielded her legacy without thinking. Alice had seen her drop a glass bottle in the courtyard once, and a claw of twigs from the mulberry tree had shot out to catch it before it hit the ground. Holly wasn't boastful about her gifts, and she wasn't modest; she simply accepted them as her unquestionable birthright and didn't think they warranted much attention. For Holly, the testing process was merely administrative. All she really cared about was passing more successfully than her sisters.

'Are you ready to start now?' asked Bea. 'I was expecting you after lunch, but the more time we have, the better. Tom said he'd try to stop by to give you a pep talk as well.'

Like Bea, Tom also belonged to House Mielikki. Most members had day jobs alongside the functions they performed for their House. Bea had taken up mentoring duties and Tom helped to administer the test results. Alice would have preferred some insider tips on how to pass rather than a pep talk, but she'd take all the help she could get.

Alice gestured at Reid's Post-it. 'Let me just get Reid's book request out of the way first.'

'All right. Show me what she's asked for again,' said the librarian.

Alice held it out and Bea glanced at the scrawled writing. There was a slight tremor in Alice's arm from the effort of keeping it raised. Bea noticed, so she made an effort to steady it.

'Look for *198 DAV*,' she said. Bea was renowned for her encyclopedic knowledge of the Dewey Decimal filing system. She turned back to her sodden book pile and Alice drifted away.

It was very easy to get lost in the library. It was two storeys high with polished wooden columns supporting the mezzanine floor above. There was a wide set of steps at the far end, but there were others – small spiral staircases set at random intervals around the library that led to alcoves and cubby holes midway between the two floors, their entrances concealed by bookshelves, and others that led to dead ends or just stopped in mid-air. The library had been designed by someone who saw logic as a minor complication, and not as a basic architectural aim.

Leaded windows and two immensely sturdy chandeliers gave light to the room, throwing long shadows from the wooden rafters across the parquet flooring. On the ground floor an array of mismatched lamps glowed warmly across equally mismatched tables and comfy chairs. It was very snug, perfect for curling up with a book.

Alice hadn't curled up with a book for months. She tended, instead, to slump over them in exhaustion, or build towering stacks of them as she laboured through page after page of dense academic jargon. Bea was a hard taskmaster and she had a book for every purpose, but Alice could only cram so many words into her brain without feeling she might burst at the seams.

She came to a stop in the philosophy section. Someone had posted a flyer on the end of the rack:

Compete in the annual Cream of the Crops competition!
Face off against your foes in the Legacy Games.
Entry available only to full House members.
No associates allowed. Must be registered to
your House's student society to apply.

Bea would kill the event organizers. She'd already banned them after the last batch of flyers. Alice whipped the poster down and crumpled it up, quickly resuming her search. Here, the books were crammed onto their shelves, the covers pressed so tightly together that the spines were buckled. She ran a finger along the dusty line, searching the alphabetical author names . . .

Alice paused at the sound of movement nearby and spun towards the source of the noise, but there was no one there. She hesitated before returning to her search, a vague sense of being watched leaving her unsettled, and continued to scan the titles until she reached the end of the shelving unit. Nothing.

She gave a frustrated sigh and moved back to the first shelf to start again. She must have missed something. This time she moved even more slowly, but the twisted letters began to swim across her vision. Alice shook her head to clear it, and frowned. It was nothing to do with her sickness; she was used to that. She was sure the books were making her search impossible on purpose, because she was House-less.

Thanks to the university's archaic rules, only members of a House were allowed to remove volumes from the library for personal use. Alice had had to resort to putting all her books on Reid's account. And without a House, the books were not inclined to treat Alice kindly – they sliced her fingers and made themselves impossible to find. She hoped that winning entry to House Mielikki might make her ability to conduct research much easier.

She sighed heavily and shoved her brown hair out of her face. Looking down, she saw not her book but her nightjar, sitting on the rug. With a flutter, it shuffled closer to the bottom shelf, cocked its head and raked its claws along one of the spines. Alice raised an eyebrow. It stared back at her with slit eyes, then tilted its head again and pecked at a book. She moved closer and yanked the volume free from the press.

The Weight of the Unknowable Spirit, by C. P. Davies. A surprised grin spread across Alice's face. 'All right,' she murmured to her nightjar. 'That's worth a thank you, I suppose.' If it was possible to look self-satisfied, her bird managed it.

Rising, Alice marched off to find the librarian, but Bea found her first, appearing at the end of an aisle with a potted sunflower in her arms. 'Ready for a final practice session?' asked her mentor.

Alice pushed aside the sudden flicker of nerves and the spike in temperature that usually preceded a headache. *Not now.*

She forced a smile and nodded. 'Ready as I'll ever be.'

'Excellent,' said Bea, thrusting the sunflower – grown from a seed during their last session – into Alice's hands.

Alice glanced down at it, her smile fading fast. The sunflower's petals were withering. They shrivelled and crisped as she watched. The stem began to droop under the weight of the flower head and then the petals broke free, scattering to the library floor.

'Must be infested with cutworm,' said Bea, whipping the decaying sunflower from Alice's arms with a nervous laugh. 'The buggers are everywhere.'

'Must be,' agreed Alice gratefully. Even the thought of Bea discovering her secret was enough to make Alice's blood run cold. Would the mentor really want to help her win a place in House Mielikki if she knew her heritage? If necromancers were social outcasts, Alice would be practically leprous.

Alice stared at the petals lying like small cadavers at her feet. The two sides of her nature were out of balance and at war – and her father's deathly legacy was winning. She'd run out of time. It was poisoning her Mielikki skills and strangling her chances in the House membership tests.

She was going to fail.

4

The sky was bruised with purples and warm yellows: the dying embers of the sinking sun. Street lights glimmered across the pavement, chasing away frail shadows. It was warm and sluggish, the kind of night that trapped the city odours. There was no breeze to carry away the exhaust fumes or the scent of stale beer and unwashed dray horses.

Alice marched along the pavement, paying no attention to the city's assault on her senses. Her thoughts were focused on the skills she had acquired over the past year. She ran through the circumstances in which, under Bea's tutelage, she'd grown branches from knots of wood, teased life from young buds and turned summer leaves autumnal. She recalled the desire she'd felt before she'd worked the magic, the sense of calm determination and the tingling in her fingertips – all sensations she'd need to recapture to do whatever was asked of her tonight.

'Chamomile?' said Bea, her relaxed pace lagging a few steps behind.

'A mild sedative,' Alice responded automatically. 'Useful for its calming effects and for treating insomnia.'

'Preparation?'

'Pour boiling water over the dried flowers and add alcohol.

Leave it and then strain it to remove the herbs from the tincture.'

'Container?' asked Bea.

'No metal, no plastic. Glass is best; it keeps the mixture free of other chemicals like bisphenol that might taint it.'

Bea smiled. Alice had slowed, deep in thought, and Bea overtook her, the heavy necklace she wore swinging against her dress as she trotted past. A car horn honked, and Alice glanced at a commotion on the road.

The driver of a vintage green Bentley gestured impatiently at a street sweeper to let him pass. The street sweeper – a thin man with a pencil moustache and a battered trilby – glared at the driver, brushed the litter and debris to the roadside and bent over. He laid his palm on the stone kerb and then, very carefully, lifted it, the entire pavement tilting up at a slanted angle.

Alice lost her footing and slid sideways, but Bea merely adjusted her balance and kept walking. The street sweeper brushed the litter underneath as though sweeping it under a rug and then lowered the pavement again, the kerb thumping back into position. Then he spun round and tipped his hat sarcastically to the driver, who sped off with a roar.

Alice shook her head and tried to regain her focus. Catching up with Bea, she worked furiously to remember the herbs she might be given if she was asked to concoct a tincture: chamomile, echinacea, valerian . . . She ran through the flowers she'd managed to bloom by thought alone – marigolds and pansies were the easiest; the perennials always presented her with more difficulty. If they asked for a demonstration, she hoped there was no yarrow or English lavender.

She had been concerned that the tests might involve some sort of combat. Bea had scoffed at this, telling Alice, 'Darling, you're not being conscripted into the army. At House Mielikki, a group of hobbyist basket weavers meet in the clubhouse bar every Wednesday. That's the sort of place you're attempting to join.' Alice had grudgingly accepted there was no need to hone her defensive skills. Besides, in case of emergency, she could cloak herself to hide from an opponent's sight, or call on her own nightjar's help if she needed a better overhead viewpoint. However, she would be expected to use her Mielikki legacy to win a place in their House – and relying on her aviarist tricks might see her fail their test.

'Remember,' said Bea as they walked, 'if you're good enough, you'll join. The first test is just about you. You're not in competition with the other candidates today. Not with Holly or anyone else.'

Alice nodded. 'I'm in competition with myself,' she said.

'Exactly, darling.'

Alice frowned. Bea's words hadn't relaxed her; far from it, they'd highlighted her biggest fear.

The dome of St Paul's Cathedral rose above the distant rooftops, and they hastened along King Edward Street towards it. In London, the ruins of Christchurch Greyfriars sat at the bottom of the street, partially destroyed by German bombers in the Blitz. Two perpendicular walls remained standing and a beautiful wild garden had burst to life in the building's broken shell. Where the stone pillars had once stood, there were now wooden frames crawling with fragrant roses and trails of clematis, overlooking a patchwork quilt of hardy shrubs and plants.

But this wasn't London – and it wasn't Christchurch Greyfriars that occupied the space at the end of King Edward Street. Here in the Rookery, the site of those ruins was home to House Mielikki. Though the Rookery had been untouched by war, the church walls had been torn down to mirror the damage suffered by the original building and then replaced with walls made of flowering vines and climbing plants. The governor of House Mielikki had considered it a fitting tribute to the London dead: a reminder to all that life could bloom in death's shadow.

Alice had come once or twice to draw the building. Sitting on the corner of Angel Street, her back resting against the iron railings and her sketchbook on her knees, she'd marked out the clean lines of the two original stone walls that stood at a corner. But it was the other walls – those created in memoriam – that had really captured her attention. Built not from stone but from a dense thicket of entwined boughs and twigs – willow, cherry blossom and horse chestnut – the walls had been knitted together in overlapping weaves of leaf and wood.

She had sketched hurriedly, trying to keep pace with the transformation unravelling across the building, her eyes fixed on the botanical walls as the bare branches evolved, tender green shoots and buds exploding from the bark. Berries and flowers fountained from the buds, their petals rippling in the breeze; the waxy green leaves thickened and multiplied, before the colours shifted – the greens fading and autumnal browns and oranges catching hold of the leaves, spreading like fire across the walls, then twisting away from the stems and branches and spiralling through the air to scatter across the pavement. Winter, spring, summer, autumn – the walls cycled through the seasons at speed, producing the most beautiful display of nature, and of power, to all who passed by.

House Pellervoinen, a huge edifice made of pale Portland stone, neighboured House Mielikki, and it too demonstrated its unique character. Its architecture frequently morphed into different iconic styles, the walls melting into the clean lines of art deco, or a more decadent gothic style, or the many columns of the neo-classical. But Alice had only ever had eyes – and a sketchbook – for House Mielikki.

She crossed the road towards it, this time without her sketch-book, and breathed it in while Bea waited patiently. The House had a musky fragrance, heavy and earthy one moment, then light and fresh with hints of citrus and spice the next. An arched bough formed the entrance to the building. A warm glow flickered in the gloom beyond, as though the entrance was illuminated with candlelight. The first time she'd seen this building a haunting melody had seeped out into the night: the notes of violins and tambourines carried faintly on the breeze, the penny whistle partly hushed by the rustling of wind through the leaves.

Crowley had been with her then. She'd found herself trapped in the entrance and dashed out in a panic; he'd caught her by the arms and held her steady. Something in her chest tightened and she turned away, staring at the cars rumbling past, their head-lamps like searchlight beams seeking out the dangers ahead. Was she ready for this? For the possibility of—

'Alice Wyndham?'

She jumped, startled, and whirled around. A severe-looking old man with dark skin and greying hair in tight curls stood in the doorway. He was dressed, like most of the Rookery's resi-dents, in an outfit more suited to the previous century: rounded club collar, skinny tie and sharply creased trousers. The tweed waistcoat, complete with dangling pocket watch, told Alice he was dressed for formality. He watched her closely from behind circular wire-framed glasses.

'Yes,' she said. 'I'm—'

'And, of course, the honourable Lady Pelham-Gladstone,' he said, a sparkle in his eye.

Bea wagged an amused finger at his face. 'Stop goading me, Cecil. You know I'm a socialist now, not a socialite.'

He turned to Alice, the smile fading to an expression of polite interest. 'I'm Cecil Pryor, Head of Membership Admissions. Follow me, please.' He turned on his heel and disappeared into House Mielikki. Alice ducked inside without hesitation.

The wicker ceiling was strung with twinkling pinprick lights, leading her down a dimly lit corridor. The walls either side were not made of seagrass, as she'd initially assumed; they were woven from willow, with vines sewn through the gaps for additional strength. There was a doorway at the far end, and the sound of music, muted voices and clinking glasses drifted out from the gap at the bottom of the door. The clubhouse bar, she assumed.

Cecil stopped midway along the corridor and brushed the willow. Alice watched, impressed, as the branches began to unravel and twist, opening up a gap in the wall, which he stepped through.

It led to a room filled with leather chairs, a glossy walnut desk and a boldly patterned rug. On the walls there were ornamental animals, carved in ebony wood or sculpted in terracotta, flashing their teeth and claws. The array of potted plants and flowers lined haphazardly on a shelf behind the desk seemed too quaint in contrast.

'Please sit,' Cecil said brusquely, taking a seat behind the desk and reaching for a handful of papers. He glanced up at Bea, who lowered herself into a leather chair with a grateful sigh. 'Can I interest you in a drink?' he asked Bea, indicating two cups – one empty and one filled with boiled water. 'Green tea, isn't it?'

Bea waved his question aside. 'I've given it up. I'll have a rosehip, if you have it.'

He turned to the plant pots, his hand drifting left and right while he searched with his eyes. His hand paused and then plucked several small red fruits from a rose plant. He crushed them in his palm and dropped them into the cup of hot water. Alice watched in silence as the water turned scarlet, noting that he hadn't asked her if she would also like a cup. With a flourish, Cecil whipped out his handkerchief, laid it over the empty cup and poured his concoction over it to strain out the rosehips.

'Don't worry,' he said. 'It's clean.'

He discarded the handkerchief and passed the tea to Bea, who took it without batting an eyelid. 'Thank you,' she said. 'It really nips at the tongue, doesn't it?'

Cecil turned to Alice and raised both eyebrows, his lined forehead crumpling. 'So . . . you consider yourself worthy of joining us, do you?'

Alice hesitated. It was an odd way to phrase it, as though answering yes indicated her vanity.

'I think I have Mielikki's legacy,' she said carefully.

'Many do,' he said, retrieving a bundle of paperwork from his drawer, 'but not all become members.'

Bea had told her this. Those who failed the tests – or weren't prepared to take the risk of failing – were considered instead for an associate membership, which acknowledged they had a degree of Mielikki's legacy but one of no great significance. The fully fledged members of a House often ridiculed associate membership; it was a status that broadcast your lack of power, or lack of courage. It mollified those with weaker legacies, but they didn't really belong to the House; they didn't enjoy the same benefits or respect as full members, and they weren't even allowed full access to the building in case they stumbled across some secret knowledge reserved for their betters. She thought of the flyer in the library, advertising the Cream of the Crops competition – banned to associates. They weren't even made to feel like real members of their own student societies.

Cecil gestured at the paperwork on his desk. 'You'll have to sign to show that you accept the risks involved in the testing process. Your mentor should have made these clear when she was assigned to you, but would you like me to clarify them for you now?'

Alice shook her head. Bea had been quite alarmingly detailed about the risks. With unnerving relish, she'd recounted stories of the candidates who had not survived the testing process: those who had made fatal errors in brewing tonics; those who had failed to differentiate correctly the edible mushroom from the poisonous; those who had tried too hard and suffocated under the weight of the flowers they'd grown in a room too small to accommodate them; those who hadn't tried hard enough, who had been paralysed by anxiety and failed to secure the roots of a redwood as the trunk crashed down on top of them. Then there were the injuries: the candidates who had lost limbs and fingers carving wood into elaborate shapes; those who'd accidentally ingested plants that stole their eyesight; those whose skin had erupted with blisters following mishaps with giant hogweed.

But for Alice, the benefits outweighed the risks. She was dying anyway. What difference did it make if she died in the testing room? She had nothing to lose and everything to gain.

'Aside from the risks involved in the tests, you are aware of the nature of membership? The binding draught?'

Alice nodded. Of course she was aware; it was the very thing that had cemented her determination to join the House.

'Membership is awarded,' said Alice, reciting one of Bea's books from memory, 'after the consumption of a draught made from the Summer Tree, a tincture of its essence. Anyone who refuses to take the draught is refused membership. It binds the drinker to House Mielikki—'

Bea nodded encouragingly. 'The draught binds you to the tree itself rather than the House,' she corrected.

'Yes,' said Alice, with a brief frown. 'Sorry, that was what I meant.'

She had pored over the guidance she'd been sent in advance. She'd considered the implications of binding herself to Mielikki's tree, the Tree of Life . . . and she'd known instantly that she'd wanted it – *needed* it. A small, illegal dose of the tree's sap had once saved her life, nullifying the toxins of the Arbor Talvi, the winter trees, in the Sulka Moors. Now she needed something even greater to nullify Tuoni's poisonous legacy. The binding draught was it. The Rookery's most controlled and precious substance.

Cecil pushed the paperwork across the table, towards Alice.

'The draught is too powerful and too dangerous to be consumed in one sitting,' said Cecil. 'That's why it's given in moderation. There are three tests for admission; if you pass today's you will be offered your first portion of the draught. Failure to drink it will result in a rejection of your application, regardless of your success in the test.'

Alice forced a smile. 'I know. That's fine.'

He nodded. 'It's a very great honour,' said Cecil, 'to be bound in service to the Summer Tree.'

She didn't respond, but he didn't seem to have expected her to. The tree was a wondrous and magical thing, but the draught ensured honourable servitude at best. The binding tied members to the tree's life force; it was in their interests to tend it well, because they would face personal consequences if the tree came to any harm. The binding would pass on the damage to them. There could be no weak links, no one who would care poorly for the tree and let the House down.

'Could I ask a question?' asked Alice.

Cecil peered at her over his glasses.

'If the draught links us to the Summer Tree, and we feel the effects should it grow weaker, isn't the reverse also true? Could we damage the tree if we became ill? Or died?'

It was the only fear that had held her back. Bea's books had already provided the answer she'd hoped for, but she needed to hear the words confirmed out loud.

Cecil smiled. 'No.'

Alice's shoulders relaxed just a fraction.

'Members of the House can't damage the tree in return,' said Cecil, 'or every time someone linked to the tree died of old age their death would harm it. But they don't. The tree is too powerful to accept such damage. Do you see?'

She nodded, the tension she hadn't realized she'd been carrying now beginning to ease.

'Do you have any questions regarding the binding draught?' he asked.

Alice shook her head.

The binding draught was also a part of the tests. If your legacy wasn't strong enough, the drink itself could kill you. Like a drug, it could act as an overdose. Only those with the strongest constitutions could withstand a tincture harvested from the most ancient and powerful tree ever grown. Bea had been quick to provide Alice with the statistical chances of death as a result of the draught – but she'd tried to smooth over the danger by suggesting it was, at least, a good way to die, a pleasant delirium.

The binding draught held no fears for Alice. It was why she was here. It was the *prize*. Tying herself to a tree renowned for its life-giving properties was exactly what she needed.

Cecil patted his waistcoat pocket and retrieved a gold pen. He placed it on top of the contract.

'We can't be held responsible should the tests result in grievous injury or death,' he said. 'If those terms are agreeable to you, then go ahead and sign.'

She did as instructed. An undercurrent of nerves had just begun to kick in and her signature was unrecognizable.

'I won't be a moment,' he said, stepping out from behind the desk.

'Someone else finishing up?' asked Bea over her teacup.

Cecil checked his pocket watch. 'Yes. The youngest Mowbray girl.'

Holly, realized Alice.

'Where's Lester?' asked Bea, her voice dropping an octave.

'In the bar, I believe,' Cecil answered with a private, knowing look at the librarian. 'Enjoying a celebratory drink in the name of his mentee's success.'

Bea snorted.

'A little presumptive,' added Cecil with a smile. 'Since she hasn't finished her test yet.'

'Oh, she'll pass all right,' said Bea. 'He only takes the dead-certs from the highest-profile families. Snob.'

Cecil chuckled and left the room.

Bea twisted around in her chair to face Alice, who had begun to pick anxiously at the dry skin on the back of her hand.

'That looks suspiciously like a nervous tic,' said Bea, her expression serious.

'It looks suspiciously like dermatitis,' said Alice, dropping her hands to her knees. She flashed a smile.

'How are you feeling?' asked Bea.

Alice's smile faded into a wince. 'Like . . . this chair is too small,' she said, rising from it, 'and I need to keep moving, because if I stop and think about it, I might start picking at my hands again.'

Bea nodded sagely. 'Alice, darling, I have total faith in you.'

'Really?' she said, a crack appearing in the mental wall she'd built for the test. 'And my recent disaster with the sunflower?'

'That was cutworm, darling. My faith in you,' said Bea, sipping from her cup, 'is as unshakeable as my love of tea.'

Alice raised an eyebrow. 'Rosehip or *green?*' she countered.

Bea laughed. 'That's the spirit.'

Alice sighed. It was an act of self-sabotage to think of the dead sunflower and what it meant. She couldn't dwell on it. Not now. She moved off to distract herself with the portraits decorating Cecil's walls. Dignified men and women, painted in oils or photographed in black-and-white daguerreotype and faded colour Kodachrome; they looked out from their frames with pompous or sombre expressions. She examined them closely, scanning the plaques attached. Chancellor McGillen, Rector Sullivan, Governor Whitmore, Governor Harlin, Treasurer Helsby, Chancellor Westergard, Chancellor Franzen.

'House Mielikki's finest alumni,' said Bea. 'Cecil says he keeps their pictures up because it's aspirational, encouraging new recruits to imagine the heady heights they could reach in the Rookery. All nonsense,' she said cheerily. 'He keeps their pictures up because he was the mentor for at least two of them – Helsby and Sullivan – and it's a matter of House pride that we've produced more than our fair share of chancellors.'

Alice's eyes paused on the photo of Governor Whitmore, the current head of House Mielikki. If the newspapers were to be believed, the four governors spent as much time at the Houses of Parliament, arguing with the chancellor who ran the Rookery Council, as they did in their own Houses.

'The whole testing thing . . .' Alice said at last, turning away from the portraits. 'Don't you think there should be more . . . I

don't know . . . pomp and ceremony?' She glanced down at Bea.
'A cup of tea and a bit of paperwork doesn't exactly capture the
excitement of the occasion. And *I* didn't even get offered any tea.'

Bea shook her head, smiling. 'It's exciting for you – not so
much for Cecil, who's been through this process about a thousand times. Besides,' she said, 'they save all the pomp and ceremony for later. I can give you the speech, if you like. Cecil's given
the same spiel to every single candidate I've ever mentored. Let
me remember . . .' She squinted into her cup, thinking hard. 'Oh
wait, I've got the start of it,' she said, clearing her throat. 'We take
only those who have a clear legacy inherited from Mielikki. We
don't take those who show only a modicum of talent. A jack of all
trades has no place here. We are elitist and proud of it.' Bea
paused. 'This is the bit that'll interest you . . . There are no fan-
fares and parades for those who merely apply for membership –
because many will fail and we do not reward or encourage failure.
If suitable, the governor—'

'I don't know whether to be insulted or flattered,' said Cecil,
appearing in the doorway.

Bea's eyes widened and she choked on a fresh mouthful of tea.
'Flattered, Cecil. Without question.'

'Did you manage to finish?' he asked, his mouth lifting into a
muted smile.

'Not quite,' Bea mused. 'Isn't there a bit about the deciding
vote? A nice, summarizing flourish, I've always thought.'

'That's right,' said Cecil, turning to Alice. 'The governor
retains the power to confer membership. Though I'm Head of
Admissions, Gabriel Whitmore will have the deciding vote on
your success, should you reach the final stage. Now,' he said,
'would you like to begin?'

Alice nodded, but Cecil didn't move. He glanced over her shoulder at Bea. 'No parting words of wisdom?'

Bea leaned over and placed her teacup on the table. She rose from her seat and approached Alice with a broad smile. 'It's very simple, darling,' she said. 'All you have to do is . . . not fail.'

Alice pulled a face. 'Thank you. I'm sure that inspirational speech will make all the difference.'

'Well,' said Bea, her bosom heaving, 'it's never failed me yet.' She patted Alice's arm a little too hard, her tone growing more sober. 'You're ready. Now off you go,' she said, waving Alice into the corridor, 'and don't come back until you've passed.'

Alice thought she heard Cecil mutter something under his breath as she followed him back into the corridor. It was the same corridor she'd arrived by, except that this time there were two new doorways opposite. One of them was open.

A towering, broad-shouldered man with a chin you could crack walnuts on was leaning casually against one of the door frames. He wore shirtsleeves rolled to the elbows and braces that seemed to highlight his strapping chest. He heard them approach and turned a smug grin on them.

'I think we can safely record that as a pass,' he said, crossing his burly arms over his chest.

'Thank you, Lester, I'll be the judge of that,' said Cecil.

Lester's eyes – too small for his face – swept the full length of Alice's body before sharpening. Alice couldn't help but stare at the sweat glistening on his upper lip.

'Are you one of the Callaghans?' he asked.

'No,' she said. 'One of the Wyndhams.'

'Never heard of them,' he said, turning away with uninterest.

Holly emerged from the room. Closing the door behind her, she asked, 'Was I faster than Cassandra?'

'Easily,' said Lester. 'Your sister isn't a patch on you.'

Holly gave a small, satisfied smile. 'Good. I've had to wait two years for my chance to wipe her family record.'

She gave a high, bright laugh as she sashayed down the corridor with Lester swaggering ahead like a bodyguard. 'I can't wait to tell her.' She paused by Cecil's office. 'Oh, Alice – good luck,' she called out behind her. 'But not too lucky – don't even think of beating my time!'

Alice attempted to return the smile, but her stomach was knotted with anticipation.

'The theme of your first test is rejuvenation,' said Cecil, who was standing by the other of the two doors. 'House Mielikki is famed for its ability to rejuvenate natural objects.' He pushed open the door. 'We would like you to demonstrate that you can think outside the box and contribute to the House's future endeavours in this area.'

She moved past him, into the room. There were no obvious dangers. The room was bare save for a table in the centre, which held a wooden tray covered with a faded patterned blanket.

'Remove the blanket,' he said.

She did as he told her and examined the contents of the tray. There was a small terracotta pot filled with soil and fine grey dust; poking from the top was a withered seed. Next, there was a rotted, trumpet-shaped flower with burgundy petals in a vase of murky water: a tropical hibiscus – they only ever bloomed for a single day. The only other item was a burned match, one end blackened and as brittle as charcoal.

'You have fifteen minutes.'

He closed the door, but she didn't watch him leave; she couldn't afford to waste the limited time she had.

5

Rejuvenation. This wasn't combat against a challenger; this was combat against herself, against her destructive Tuoni legacy. But if she could just channel the right energies and restrict the others, wasn't this something she could do? The decorative plants on her parents' home had lasted weeks before they'd died, and she only had to make these rejuvenations last fifteen minutes.

Alice reached for the terracotta pot, clutching it tightly in one hand while she pushed the fingers of her other hand into the soil. The seed was half planted, protruding from the topsoil. Taking a deep breath, she studied every millimetre of it: the mottled brown pattern, the flaking crust, each furrow and slope on the shell. She imagined it germinating, a shoot sprouting from the bottom, bursting through the shell, and deep roots plunging into the soil to take hold. With every fibre of her being, she willed it to vibrate with life. The tendons in her neck strained and her fingers tingled. But the seed remained inert. Lifeless.

Lifeless. Again, the fears pushed themselves to the forefront of her mind – *I am made of Death. How can I create life?* – but she swallowed hard and forced them away. No time for doubts. She *had* brought foliage to life before – and she'd already wasted five minutes.

She dumped the potted seed back onto the tray and snatched up the vase of decayed red hibiscus. The stems were weak and the flower heads drooped pitifully over the side of the glass. She scooped up the heads in the flat of her palm, moved closer and breathed warm air over the crisped petals. A shiver of relief ran through her as a rich scarlet bled through the petals, the edges uncurling and the stem straightening. But her resuscitation lasted only moments. The colour swiftly faded and dulled once again, and the soggy stems bent under the weight of the heads. Alice peered into the vase, debating what to do about the murky water; she couldn't clean it – this was a test for entry to House Mielikki, not House Ahti – but could the dirty water be inhibiting her efforts?

Frustration dug into her thoughts, and she hurriedly discarded the damp flowers. She snatched up the match and examined it carefully. One end of the wood was smooth and undamaged; the other was crooked and blackened, the burned phosphorus sulphide crumbling against her skin. She replaced the match on the tray, took one final confirmatory glance at the terracotta pot and stepped backwards.

This wasn't a test – it was a trick. The seed was planted in a terracotta pot, in soil mixed with a dusting of fine grey cement. It was tainted with materials more suited to House Pellervoinen, the House of stone and rock. The rotted flowers had drunk their fill of filthy water – House Ahti, the House of water. And the burned match had been destroyed by fire – House Ilmarinen, the House of metal and flame. Everything in the tray was linked to another House and designed to work *against* her. Well, Alice had already spent months trying to wield Mielikki's gifts while another force attempted to quell her; she was used to that. But how to approach this now? She'd never had to produce her skill in defiance of another *House's* magic before.

She glanced at the clock on the wall. Five minutes left. Five minutes to save her life. Chewing furiously on her bottom lip, she began to pace. The soles of her shoes squeaked on the wooden floor, setting her nerves on edge, while she tried to assemble a plan from her scrambled thoughts. What had Holly done to pass? Had her test been the same as Alice's?

She toured several lengths of the room, the minutes dwindling still further, before she stopped fixating on the items on the tray and widened her focus to the tray itself. *We would like you to demonstrate that you can think outside the box and contribute to the House's future endeavours in this area . . . We would like you to demonstrate that you can think outside the box . . .* The box . . . The *tray* . . . Had Cecil been giving her a clue? She froze. Her eyes roamed the breadth of the bare room, taking in the table and tray, the blanket, the patterned wallpaper, elegant ceiling rose and hardwood oak floor. Her breath hitched. Could she . . .? Was there time?

She dropped to her knees and ran a hand over the floorboards: planks of smooth timber, with dark knots spattering the grain like freckles. Literally outside the box. In some places there were small, haphazardly positioned knot clusters on the planks. Perfect. She crawled closer on all fours, and then sat back to better examine her options. One of the knots was small, and noticeably darker than the rest; she picked it out as her main target.

Rubbing her palms together until the friction warmed them, she slammed her hands down on the cluster of knots. Bent over, with her shoulders almost touching the floor and her head hanging so low that her hair trailed over the wood, she sucked in a deep, slow breath, inhaling the scents of polish and musky resin – and when she exhaled, she held the small dark knot in her mind's eye and pushed her breath, her will, her desire towards it. Her stomach fluttered with exhilaration. The tips of her fingers blanched against the wood grain, tingling and throbbing, the blood carrying the pulsing sensation up her arms, into her chest and her pounding heart. *I can do this. I can. I'm made of life too.*

It began as a nudge. Something prodding at her skin. Her index fingertip first . . . then her thumb . . . her left hand – and her right . . . the palms, the forearms . . . small protrusions pushing their way out of the ground. Not out of the small dark knot. Out of *every* knot. Poking her, jabbing her with hardened tips.

She opened her eyes and forgot to breathe. All around her, growing branches snaked out from the knots of wood. They moved sinuously, up and up, extending over her head until they butted the ceiling and began to bend under the pressure from below. Twigs sprouted rapidly from the arms of the branches. Buds blossomed and leaves unfurled, draping the room with foliage and colour.

Energy poured out of her like a surge of water escaping a reservoir. And Alice could only watch in silent amazement as she grew a forest from a polished wooden floor. What *was* this? Her chest swelled with a dizzying euphoria. This was a *pass*.

She moved to the door to find Cecil, to show him what she'd done. But the branches were in the way, pressing against it. Alice's hands scrabbled with the doorknob, twisting it and trying to yank it free. With a muffled click, the door jerked open a few inches and she peered eagerly through the crack.

Cecil wasn't waiting outside the room, and Alice was just about to close the door again to wait when she caught a blur of movement. A pale man wearing a trilby and a long dark coat swept along the corridor towards the closed door of the clubhouse bar. He stopped and glanced around him as if checking he wasn't being followed, then stroked a hand over the willow wall opposite. The willow unravelled and peeled back to reveal a hidden door. With one final look over his shoulder, he hurried through it, and the wall weaved back into place. Alice exhaled softly. Despite the hat, she recognized him. It was the governor. Gabriel Whitmore. Maybe there would be some pomp and ceremony for her after all.

'Cecil?' she called out into the corridor. 'I think I've . . .'

The beatific smile dropped suddenly from her face and she staggered sideways, grabbing for the branches to steady herself. Her hands slid painfully down their length and she crashed to the floor on her knees. The room spun around her and a bright, fierce pain charged in to hack at her temples. Pins and needles tingled through her body, the buzz of pain expanding, folding back into itself, like a wave gaining strength. The muscles in her limbs clenched and spasmed as agony washed over her. Alice gasped, her fingers rushing desperately to press into the gnawing in her head, to push it away. Her eyes screwed up as a fresh pain clawed at her chest, tearing her in half, stealing her breath away.

What's . . .? I . . .

There was a flash of white at the corner of her eye – pale feathers and flapping wings. Alice's nightjar swooped into view and shot her a reproachful glare. She reached out to it, for comfort, as her last clear thought arrowed into her brain.

I'm dying.

And then darkness engulfed her.

'Over-exerted herself . . .' *Cecil's voice?*

'. . . just a short rest . . .'

'Remember Finn Conroy's test three years ago? The very same thing . . .'

'. . . was one of Lester's, wasn't he?' said Bea.

'. . . Conroy failed, of course . . .'

'That's right,' said Bea. 'I heard Lester broke Finn's nose when he failed, for embarrassing him . . . terrible shame. The family disowned the boy.'

Alice's eyes snapped open. She found herself lying on her side, on the floor of Cecil's office. With a wheeze of pain, she pushed herself upright. Stars danced at the edges of her vision and she slumped back to the floor again. The ceiling, she thought. Concentrate on that. If she could just make the ceiling stay still, she'd be okay.

A hand smoothed Alice's hair out of her face. 'You're burning up,' Bea muttered. Something clinked as though a glass lid had been removed, and then a powerful smell – ammonia and eucalyptus – burned the back of Alice's throat. She gagged, coughing and spluttering into the rug.

'Smelling salts,' explained Bea as Alice struggled to turn her head away. 'No, don't do that,' said Bea, wafting the scents closer. 'You need it. Just lie flat and catch your breath, that's it.'

Alice's eyes stung. She gave a watery blink and released a trembling breath. Bea patted her arm and vanished from sight.

'Generally, people go for the blanket,' said Cecil, his voice floating from the corner of the room, where his desk sat.

Alice frowned, trying to regain her senses. The blanket? What was he talking about?

'It's half a century old. The pomegranate dye is very faded and the cotton worn through with holes.' He paused. 'Fixable, for those who have the presence of mind to remain calm when the items on the tray prove difficult. They're specially commissioned from each of the other Houses,' he said conversationally.

'I don't remember any previous challenges featuring a blanket,' said Bea.

'I suppose it's been a few years since we've used that particular test,' Cecil conceded.

Alice's mind went blank. The *blanket*? Her brain had slid right over it as soon as she'd seen the knots. She tried to open her mouth to speak, but found her energy so lacking she could barely move her lips into the right shapes. What was *wrong* with her? Was this the hangover from working Mielikki's legacy? She recalled the feeling of energy pouring off her in waves. Had she gone too far? Given too much of herself?

There was a heavy sigh from the corner. 'It's been an additional twenty minutes,' Cecil said slowly.

'Just give her another minute,' said Bea. 'She's almost come round fully.'

They were talking about her as though she wasn't in the room. And yet she was – she was right there. But she couldn't seem to move or communicate with them.

'Tell me about – oh Christ, Cecil, I don't know,' said Bea. 'Holly? Who's administering the draught for her? Is it Tom?'

'Yes,' said Cecil. 'She and Lester should be in the grove right now. And I should be there with them, overseeing stage one of her binding.'

'But you're here enjoying my company instead,' Bea responded brightly. 'I'm sure Lester won't mind waiting. He'll probably enjoy dragging it out for all it's worth.'

'Bea—'

'Tell me about your plans for the holidays,' she said.

Alice's eyes flickered with the effort of keeping them open. She was so tired. So very . . . All she wanted to do was sleep . . .

'*Bea*,' said Cecil. 'Your candidate . . . This is only the first test and it has depleted her resources, utterly. The second test might ask so much of her it kills her. I'm sorry, but it's time to bring this to a close.'

'No,' said Bea, her voice steely. 'I've seen what she can do, Cecil. She has the strength to go all the way with this. And if she doesn't . . . I'll take responsibility for it.' She took a deep breath. 'Now – please, tell me about your holidays.'

Cecil grunted, and Alice heard the shuffle of paperwork.

'I was thinking of visiting Edinburgh, if the weather is good,' he said at last, his tone grudging.

'How lovely,' said Bea, and from her prone position on the floor, Alice could almost hear the relief in her voice. 'I can recommend a visit to . . .'

A faint clicking sound, like a cicada, made Alice's jaw vibrate and Bea trailed away. *Was that noise in my head?* Alice wondered. But the noise grew louder, transitioning into a whirring, ratchet-like sound as the noise gathered pace, and then a screeching klaxon. A fire alarm?

'No,' Cecil breathed. 'No, it can't be . . .'

Cecil got to his feet and Alice caught sight of him by the door. His expression one of horrified disbelief, he hurried from the room without another word.

Bea sprang up and made to follow him, but hesitated and hurried back to retrieve her handbag. She ferreted around in it and pulled out a small bottle of liquid. With a quick check to ensure there was no one coming, she sank down beside Alice and lifted her head.

Alice blinked up at her groggily as Bea unscrewed the lid and poured the thick liquid down Alice's throat.

'Do *not* tell anyone I've given this to you,' hissed Bea. 'It's a restorative tonic. Capsaicin for pain relief, plus powdered maca, guarana, ephedra berries and golden root. A powerful stimulant and also absolutely illegal. I only carry it for emergencies.'

Bea quickly stowed the empty bottle in her bag and sat back to stare anxiously at Alice, who was licking her lips and appeared to be relearning how to use the muscles in her jaw.

'Cecil is considering failing you for your own safety,' said Bea, leaning closer to be heard over the sound of the klaxon outside the room. 'What went wrong? You've never fainted before!'

Alice said nothing, but she managed to push herself into a sitting position. Warmth flooded her body, massaging relief into her limbs. The pain had dwindled to a vague, dull vibration beneath her skin. Manageable. She swallowed thickly, marvelling at the lack of discomfort when she inhaled.

'If Cecil knows I've given you a stimulant, he'll fail you regardless. I might as well have fed steroids to an athlete. You can't let him smell it on your breath. Let me see your eyes.' She grabbed Alice's face and tilted it sideways, studying her carefully.

'Damn. Your pupils are huge. Don't let him look at you either.' Alice nodded.

'Speak,' said Bea desperately. 'Show me you understand, Alice. They'll *expel* me from the House if they suspect I've had possession of that tonic.'

Alice's tongue unstuck itself from the roof of her mouth. 'Okay,' she croaked.

'Oh thank fuck,' said Bea. 'Come on, stand up.'

She made to hook Alice's arm and pull her up, but Alice shook her head.

'No, it's . . . it's okay,' said Alice. 'I can do it. I feel . . .' She hesitated, frowning. The tumbling wail of a siren was still echoing through the building: too loud, too invasive. What was it?

'I feel okay,' said Alice. 'I can stand.'

She pushed upwards and found her feet. Her head felt clear, maybe a little buzzed but . . . alert. She rolled her shoulders and stretched her arms out in front of her, cracking her fingers.

'What's the siren for?' she murmured.

'I'm not sure,' said Bea. She frowned. 'I think it's coming from the grove, but . . . It must be a false alarm.'

'The grove?' said Alice. 'Isn't Holly there with Lester and Tom?'

Bea nodded. 'Tom's administering the draught.' She patted her bag down, ensuring the tonic bottle was out of sight. 'Listen,' she said, gesturing at one of the leather chairs, 'you just . . . just sit here and wait.' She scanned Alice's face. 'Hopefully the more obvious effects will have worn off by the time I get back.'

Bea darted to the door, paused and waved again at the chair. 'Sit,' she said. 'Stay. And do not, for the love of God, let anyone see your ridiculous eyes!'

Without another word, Bea vanished. Alice glanced at the chair. There was a long pause while she battled her conscience, but the boosted adrenaline in her blood made the decision for her. With an apologetic grunt, she rushed after Bea, but the corridor and the entirety of House Mielikki had come alive, and it was impossible to spot her. People had spilled from the room of clinking glasses and music, and were milling around outside it with an air of confusion. The clubhouse door had closed behind them, but a fresh door had opened opposite. And it was to this door that the people were drawn like moths. *This* was the door she'd seen Governor Whitmore entering before she'd fainted.

The siren drowned out the crowd's frantic conversations, but Alice caught one or two words as she drifted closer, wary and expecting at any moment to be asked to leave – or to be spotted by Bea or Cecil.

'Arbor Suvi,' someone murmured.

'. . . Summer Tree.'

'. . . does it mean?'

The klaxon grated her eardrums and she winced. The crowd funnelled through the door at the end of the corridor and Alice hung back, watching them go. In minutes, she was alone. Curiosity itched beneath her skin and the emptiness of the House seemed to mock her. *Follow them.* Taking a deep breath, she ploughed forward, pulling open the door.

A gentle breeze brushed her face as darkness settled around her. She'd travelled using the void plenty of times, and yet it felt different here, the wind warmer and less cutting. She remained very still, trying to catch her bearings and work out what to do. To travel, it was important to visualize the door you wished to travel to, but Alice had no idea where the others might have chosen to go. She frowned into the darkness, frustration beginning to chafe. And then there was light – a tiny glowing spark, followed by another, and another: fireflies. They radiated faint light, like a trail of breadcrumbs, showing her the way. They floated around a door frame that the darkness had hidden from her. Alice peered at it in the gloom. *Is it a door or an ancient tree?* It was misshapen, the rough wood crooked and gnarled but thick as an oak trunk. There was no handle. Alice reached out to the wood, and with a soft creak, it swung open.

She had expected to find herself in another corridor; instead she found herself in a wood. The dark sky was pierced with tiny stars. Thick clouds cloaked the moon, stifling the light – yet a diffuse glow shimmered between the trees and Alice caught her breath in wonderment. Hundreds of fireflies drifted lazily through the woods, illuminating the motes of dust floating past her eyes. She stepped forward, crunching through bark and bracken. The others must have come this way too; many feet had trampled the undergrowth.

Ahead, a rope bridge hung over a deep gully filled with creeping ferns. Its entrance, lit like a runway, invited her into the copse beyond. Clusters of glowing lights lined the timber rails, and as she drew closer, Alice realized they were bioluminescent mushrooms. *Omphalotus nidiformis.* She'd seen them in one of Bea's books. Funnel-shaped with overlapping clusters, they reminded her of white lilies and were strangely beautiful.

The rope bridge swayed when she stepped onto it. Alice paused, her adrenaline spiking with the rattling of planks. She doubted the House would take kindly to trespassers in these woods. She squinted into the distance, picking out silhouetted figures moving between the trees. Too many people with too many nightjars – she couldn't cloak herself from them all. Alice moved off with more caution, willing the bridge not to give her away, and reached the other side with relief.

It was quiet here. The klaxon had been silenced, and the crowd trudging ahead spoke in hushed whisperers as though a raised voice would defile the sanctity of the woods. The only sounds were the leaves stirring in the breeze, the groaning branches and the soft footfalls of the crowd stepping through the grove. Alice followed silently behind, careful not to garner attention. The siren had sent them here, and she wanted to know why. Where were Holly and Bea?

She crept behind a thick trunk and peered around the edges of the crusted bark. Dark figures obscured her view, and she moved from tree to tree to see properly. She considered calling for her nightjar, but she wanted to see this with her own eyes – and she wasn't sure Bea's stimulant was strong enough to fight off the disorientation of a bird's-eye view.

Something glittered over the heads of the crowd and she inched closer. They were gathered around a tree no bigger than a small fir in the centre of a clearing. The tree had captured the attention of everyone in the forest. For a moment, she thought there were glistening raindrops falling on its leaves, but in fact it wasn't rain – it was light, particles of sparkling lights, and they weren't falling – they were floating *from* the branches, flittering into the air like sparks of ash from a bonfire. She moved out from behind the tree, mesmerized by the dancing glints streaming upwards through the dark night.

She recognized this tree. But it was too small. The twisted trunk rose from the soil and not from an atrium floor. Crooked boughs held up a vast crown dripping with elegant, tapered leaves that were a dull green on one side and brighter on the other. The branches twined around each other, chasing empty space like a halo around the trunk. Its shape was that of something bursting at the seams, exploding outwards and falling back in on itself. Pinpricks of yellow light danced around the spindly offshoots: fireflies.

This was the Summer Tree in miniature. The Arbor Suvi. The Tree of Life. The original was caged in the atrium of the Abbey Library in Bermondsey. This one could have been a model, but unlike normal trees, its roots were moving. Just barely, but enough to draw the eye from the sparkling branches to the gentle twitch of shifting topsoil.

'It's growing,' murmured a voice nearby.

'It can't,' came the urgent, whispered response. 'If the replica is growing, the original would be too, and that's not possible. Is it?'

'But the roots . . .'

The crowd fell silent as all attention fell on the soil. Alice found a ridge of thick moss and clambered onto it for a better vantage point. Her eyes swept left and right, searching the faces in the crowd without success. A small cluster of huddled figures stood a short distance from the glittering tree, but Alice couldn't quite—

'Get help!' a familiar voice bellowed. *Tom's?*

And then a scream of terrified agony knifed through the grove, a sound so dreadful it sent a shockwave of revulsion through the waiting crowd. Alice's foot lost its grip. She slipped from the ridge and careened into the crush of people, gravity pitching her forward into the throng. Bodies pressed against her on all sides, stealing her oxygen. She threw out her elbows and forced her way through, plunging into the clearing with a gasp.

For one dizzying moment, she couldn't make sense of what she was seeing. A shadow play of figures, backlit by the glowing tree, were attending to someone on her knees.

'Upright. Get her upright,' shouted a slim man now instantly recognizable as Tom.

'Give her to me,' demanded another voice. *Lester?* 'I'll get her back to the House.'

'No,' ordered Cecil. 'Talk to her. It's the best way to help her.'

There was a jangle of beads and Bea appeared, shifting into focus. 'She's going into shock,' she said. 'Come on, sweetie. Dig deep. Focus your mind.'

Alice frowned. *What—?*

Cecil moved towards the assembled crowd, his hands up as though in surrender. 'Please,' he said. 'Go back to the House. A false alarm triggered the siren.'

'But the tree!' someone yelled, and the grove erupted into murmurs of assent.

'A false alarm,' repeated Cecil. 'Please . . . please just go. Allow the young woman some privacy.'

At this, silence fell like a guillotine, and then, slowly, people turned and began to drift away. Alice watched them leave, indistinct figures moving through the trees, their frantic whispers carrying eerily through the grove.

'What's happened?' asked Alice, moving closer. 'Is that . . .? Holly?'

Bea's eyes widened at her presence but she turned away quickly.

'You shouldn't be here,' said Cecil, his mouth drawn into a frown.

'Holly?' said Alice, sidestepping him. 'Are you . . .? Is she okay? Tom?'

The blonde was now standing, held steady between an anxious Tom and Lester, whose face was beetroot red.

'Stand up,' Lester hissed at Holly. 'Don't you dare do this. You remember what I told you. Failure's a state of mind. Weakness is a choice.' He spoke at furious speed, punctuating his words with a blast of spittle.

Holly's eyes were glazed but she was staring straight ahead, the cords of her neck bulging as she swallowed convulsively.

Alice cast around to discover what had happened, and her eyes alighted on a tree stump, polished and inlaid with the crude tree symbol that represented House Mielikki. Was it a table of sorts? On top, there was a round wooden tray served with a half-empty decanter and a roughly carved wooden chalice on its side. A golden-hued liquid oozed from the lip of the chalice, dribbling onto the tray.

A tight, high-pitched moan issued from Holly's mouth, drawing Cecil's attention, and Alice grabbed Bea's arm.

'Is that the binding draught?' asked Alice, gesturing at the chalice. 'Did she take it?'

'Yes,' hissed Bea.

'Have you given her any valerian?' barked Cecil.

'Yes,' said Tom helplessly. 'It . . . it didn't work. She can't just . . .'

'Get another dose of valerian to ease her pain,' snapped Cecil, his patience gone.

Tom stared at Holly in shock, as though he'd heard nothing. 'It was supposed to be routine. Lester said she'd be—'

'Don't you dare blame this on me,' roared Lester, shoving Holly at Tom, who stumbled but managed to keep her upright. 'If she can't handle it, it's not my—'

'Tom!' yelled Bea, barging past Lester with a vicious glare. She grabbed Holly and began to loosen her buttons to help her breathe. 'Get the valerian!'

The technician's eyes widened and he nodded vigorously. 'I'll . . . I'll just . . .' he mumbled, and hurried off.

Holly began to keen softly, a sound so pitiful the hair rose on the back of Alice's neck. A panicked flutter disturbed the air above Holly's head: her nightjar. Alice glanced at it, but its motions were too fast to see it clearly; in desperation, it jerked and bucked as it circled. Below, Holly's fingers curled and flexed in spasms. Bea put both hands on the side of Holly's face and pressed their foreheads together. She murmured to her, frenzied and without pausing for breath, while Alice watched helplessly and Lester stormed off to lean against a tree, his fists clenched.

With a strangled gasp, Holly snapped upright, her spine giving a series of cracks like falling dominoes, and Bea stumbled, caught off balance. Holly stood rigidly in the grove, her elbows slightly bent.

Alice searched the younger woman's face, frozen in a rictus of horror, but her eyes . . . her eyes seemed to send out a silent plea, and Alice – not quite sure what was happening to Holly – found herself stepping closer to offer her comfort. Alice reached for Holly's hands, which were still contracting rhythmically. The fingers clenched painfully around Alice's and she flinched.

'Holly,' she whispered. 'It's okay. The draught . . . It's just caught you off guard a bit with the side effects, but this will pass. You just . . .' She glanced behind her at Cecil, who was staring at Holly, his face lined with regret. 'Can she hear me?' she asked. 'What's happening?'

'Taking the draught is as much a test as the test itself,' said Cecil, his voice faint. 'You must have the strength to use your legacy, but also to control it. And the binding draught . . . If you can't exert your power over it, then it will overpower *you*.'

Alice spun back to Holly. 'But she *is* strong,' said Alice. 'She breezed her test! I've seen her do some incredible things with her legacy. Bea? Haven't we? She's . . .'

Bea nodded, her lips pinched. Alice frowned and turned to Lester, who was watching in silence, his face a study in rage and shame. The hairs on the back of Alice's neck stood up at their reaction – at their lack of reaction. Why weren't they helping her?

'Holly?' Alice croaked urgently. 'Holly, listen—'

But the blonde shuddered and relaxed her hold on Alice's hands. Her arms suddenly whipped out as though clawing the air for balance. Jaw clenched, Holly's eyes widened, giving her a haunted expression. Breath whistled through the gaps in her teeth, and she began to pant, the sound reaching a crescendo in the quiet clearing, filling Alice's senses so that all she could hear was Holly's panic.

Alice peered at her, confused, examining her face, her arms, her *fingers*. Alice's head darted up to Holly's in horror. Their eyes locked, Holly boring the message of her terror into Alice's brain.

'*No*,' Alice whispered.

Holly whimpered and her arm jerked. The gorge rose in Alice's throat and she couldn't seem to look away as something small and hard pierced the flesh at Holly's wrist and pushed through. Long and dextrous, it slithered out from beneath her skin. A bloodied twig, tapered at the end. Alice blinked at it, unable to accept what she had seen. Like an escaped vein, a twig . . . a spindly twig had poured out from Holly's right arm.

And the other . . . There was something moving under the skin of Holly's left arm. Something that snaked from side to side, stretching the flesh, a hidden pressure below the surface. The blue veins in her wrist stood out boldly against her pale skin.

Another jerk and Holly moaned quietly as an eruption of needle-like branches burst from her fingertips. She stared at Alice, her face a fixed mask of pain, and Alice's stomach lurched violently as another branch shot through Holly's left arm. The bone snapped as the wood smashed through her torn limb. Blood coursed from the punctured wounds, pooling on the long grasses.

Alice's eyes filled with panicked tears, her heart pounding at the nightmarish sight, her whole body trembling with shock. *Holly . . .*

'H . . . help . . .' Holly rasped through her agony.

Frantic, Alice's mind fractured into a dozen hopeless responses. What could she do?

'Save her,' Alice begged, turning desperately to Cecil, and to Bea, and to Lester, to anyone who could step forward and fix this.

'Alice . . .' murmured Bea.

And, of course, she understood. No one could fix this. This dreadful consequence of failing the test of the binding draught. Of being too weak to quash the power of the Summer Tree as you imbibed it and made it part of you: a part of you that shattered bone and mangled flesh. The Summer Tree was life itself, unleashed – the explosive vitality of unhindered growth.

And then there was a flutter, and a pale nightjar appeared on Alice's shoulder. It churred in her ear and she inhaled sharply as dread slid down her throat and settled heavily in her stomach. Alice's eyes desperately searched out the air by Holly's head . . . There. Her nightjar, less frantic now and more purposeful: a sleek, pale brown bird with a curved beak. The cord attaching it to Holly's wrist was growing thinner, its luminous glow dimming as her nightjar pecked at it, urging it to break.

The cord would snap, and Holly's nightjar would leave, taking her soul with it. But it was too slow. Holly's physical body would be torn apart before the cord broke, and she would be forced to feel every moment of it. Every fibre of broken muscle, every shattered bone, every puncture of her flesh . . . She would feel it all before she died.

'Pl . . . ease . . .'

Holly's voice was no more than a breath on the wind.

And Alice, without stopping to consider what she was doing, or how, knowing only that she had to end Holly's pain, turned to her own nightjar and whispered a single pleading word to it.

'Go.'

The white nightjar shot into the air. It arced around the grove like a bullet, pulling at the cord that bound it to Alice, picking up speed and gaining height . . . and then dived. It swooped towards Holly's nightjar, its beak wide . . . and sliced straight through her cord. There was a simultaneous gasp from Holly and Alice. A pain tore through Alice's chest and she clutched her heart as the trees tilted and swam around her.

Her trembling legs sagged and she sank to her knees, her head bowed against her chest and her eyes screwed tight. With every blink she slid further away from the grove – the bloodied grass, the shouts calling her name, the concerned faces of Bea and Cecil, a shocked Tom, downing the valerian to calm his nerves, Lester's red-rimmed eyes watching her, awash with bitterness.

A ruffle of feathers vibrated against Alice's cheek and she heaved in a great, calming breath as the pain under her ribs eased. The cord linking her to her bird draped across her face, so bright it pressed uncomfortably against her eyelids. Opening them to a dazzling pulse of light, she rolled onto her back as her nightjar pecked at her hair.

I killed Holly.

Panic seized her, leaving her shivering and cold.

No. I saved Holly.

Pushing herself up onto her knees, her hands clenching the grass, Alice retched and retched.

6

'I can't allow her to proceed.'

Alice blinked. She felt as though she were very far away, sitting at the end of a long room while distant voices argued her fate. She felt indifferent, though she knew that she shouldn't. Nothing mattered more than joining House Mielikki.

Mentally, she felt completely displaced. She had seen death before. She'd watched her best friend bleed out on a road; she'd seen her work colleagues violently stabbed to death on the London Eye. But watching Holly being torn apart from within . . .

There was a smear of blood on the back of Alice's hand: Holly's blood. Or was it Jen's? Alice was always failing to save people. She hadn't saved Holly either; she had only ended the girl's pain, quickened her fate. The test was as brutal as the toss of a coin. But – Alice thought numbly – she hadn't changed the way the coin landed, only hastened its fall. You either survived the binding, or you didn't. No one could interfere with destiny. But how had she, even in the heat of the moment, embraced the part of her she'd despised and denied for so long? Where did that leave her?

The voices had stopped murmuring, and there were anxious faces staring at her.

'Alice,' Cecil said kindly, as though he weren't about to ruin what remained of her life, 'I've been forced to reach a decision about your test. Given how drained you were after the practical assessment, I can't, in all conscience, allow you to . . .'

He trailed away as a figure appeared in the doorway, and some of the tension went out of his face.

'Governor Whitmore?' he said in tones of relief.

Alice stared blankly at the new arrival. The governor was a pale man with alabaster skin and blue eyes as dark as the bottom of the ocean. Despite his solid, sturdy build, his movements were graceful as he strode into the room and greeted Cecil with a nod.

'I thought you were tied up in the chancellor's meetings all evening,' said Cecil. 'We weren't expecting you.'

'I wasn't expecting to be here,' said the governor, tossing his trilby onto an empty chair. 'And I certainly wasn't expecting to find the House in such a furore on my arrival.'

'You've just arrived?' asked Cecil.

Whitmore nodded, picking up the decanter of left-over binding draught on Cecil's desk and studying it closely. 'This very moment.'

'Then you haven't heard about the Mowbray girl—' began Cecil.

'But I saw you . . .' Alice interjected, staring at Whitmore.

The governor replaced the decanter on the table and regarded her with curiosity. 'Yes?'

She frowned and fell silent.

'Do I know you?' asked the governor, his eyes narrowing as he drew closer.

Alice didn't respond, taking the opportunity to observe him. His nightjar wasn't visible. Had he – like Crowley – learned to hide it? But she didn't need to see the governor's nightjar to know he was a liar. She'd *seen* Whitmore entering the door to the grove, glancing around as though to check for witnesses. He hadn't arrived in time to find the House in a furore – he'd been in the House *before* the siren rang out. Either he'd left the grove before the siren sounded or he'd been in the grove the whole time Holly had been dying. Why was he lying about his arrival?

'This is one of our membership candidates,' said Cecil. 'Alice Wyndham. I don't believe you've met.'

Whitmore's eyes travelled over her face. 'I see. And did you pass our little test, Alice?'

Little test?

She lifted her chin a nudge higher. 'Yes,' she said. 'But I'm being denied the chance to cement my pass with the binding draught.'

Whitmore raised an eyebrow and looked at Cecil. 'Surely not?' he said, his voice silky.

'The youngest Mowbray girl has just . . .' Cecil cleared his throat and continued more evenly. 'We've just lost a candidate who performed more strongly in her test. I don't think it's appropriate to risk—'

'But the young lady wishes to take the risk,' said Whitmore, waving blithely at Alice. 'It's not our job to tinker with the judgement of the Summer Tree,' he said. 'If she still wishes to take it . . . let her.' He gave her a humourless smile. 'The young fear boredom far more than death, isn't that so?'

A muscle under Alice's eye twitched at his comment. Bea, who had sat watching this exchange in silence, leaned closer to her.

'Alice, maybe you need a clearer head before you—' she began.

'I'll take it,' said Alice.

'Bravo,' said Whitmore, reaching for the decanter with long pale fingers. In the absence of a chalice, he snatched up a teacup from Cecil's desk, tipped the contents into one of the flowerpots behind the desk and thrust it into Alice's hand. He uncapped the decanter and poured the draught into the cup. Then he clinked the glass decanter against the porcelain.

'Cheers,' he said softly.

Alice's eyes slid from his face to the liquid in her hand: it was the colour of oatmeal, with an oily golden sheen. She ground her teeth and glanced up at the governor. Was he trying to help her by forcing Cecil's hand? Somehow, it didn't feel that way as he towered over her – too close.

This draught was the first step in binding her to the Summer Tree and, by extension, House Mielikki. If she was dying anyway, wasn't it worth the risk to bond with the most powerful life force in the world? Wouldn't this life-giving tincture energize her in a way nothing else could? A life-giving tincture that had just torn apart a woman before her eyes.

Alice's hesitation lengthened. Whitmore had been inside the grove – maybe at the time Holly had taken the draught – and he was now encouraging her to make the same choice.

'The tree,' she said suddenly, remembering. 'In the grove – is it a miniature of the Summer Tree?' There had been no mention of the replica in the books Bea had given her to read.

'It's . . .' Bea glanced from the governor to Alice. 'It was grown from a cutting centuries ago. House Mielikki cares for it. The miniature helps us to monitor the original; they mirror each other perfectly.'

'But they said it was growing,' said Alice.

'An illusion,' said the governor. 'The Summer Tree can't grow.'

Alice nodded. She pulled the drink closer, but paused. The action caused Whitmore to sigh.

'Don't worry about the grove,' said Whitmore, his expression suggesting he'd grown bored of her. 'If you have no intention of continuing your membership application, which – it seems – you do not, then it doesn't concern you.' He glanced at the untouched draught in her hand. 'Pity,' he said, turning away from her. 'I'm heading to my office,' he told Cecil. 'Two minutes to finish up here and then we'll debrief?'

Cecil nodded and the governor swept out, leaving them in silence. Bea sat tight-lipped, apparently unwilling or unsure of whether to intervene and take the cup from Alice.

'I think we shall leave it there,' said Cecil. 'Miss Wyndham, if you could—'

Alice brought the cup to her lips and swiftly downed the liquid. It burned her throat, setting it alight. She winced at the heat on her tongue and her eyes welled up. Bea shoved half a cup of cold rosehip tea at her.

'Drink,' she urged.

Alice swallowed, dribbling scarlet tea over her chin as she choked it down.

There was a tense silence as they waited for something to happen. But there were no side effects. No repeat of Holly's fate. Nor was there a sudden burst of energy. No euphoria, no pleasant delirium. In fact, she felt no different at all.

'Thank God. Let's go home,' said Bea.

Alice stared at the bathroom sink. She'd had precious little sleep, crawling into bed sometime around midnight and then staring at the ceiling for hours. Bea had given her a mild dose of valerian – perfect for insomnia – but she hadn't taken it until around two in the morning, when the images of Holly's terrified face grew too disturbing.

She'd neglected to turn off her weekday alarm in the madness of the previous day, so she was now awake far too early for a Saturday. But even so, something felt unusual about the morning. She had the feeling she'd forgotten to do something.

Frowning, Alice dismissed the sensation and went about her morning ablutions. It was only when she spat out the toothpaste that it occurred to her. The bathroom sink was pristine. Usually, she emptied the contents of her stomach into it the moment she rolled out of bed – that or the toilet bowl, depending on how fast she moved. And yet, this morning . . .

Her eyes drifted to the mirror. Crumpled, stripy pyjamas and hair hopelessly dishevelled: so far, so normal. Alice shuffled closer to examine her face. Turning her head this way and that, it soon became clear that the dark circles under her eyes had begun to fade. The once sickly pallor of her skin was now . . . glowing? She looked better than she had done for months.

Sasha, one of her first and most eagle-eyed friends in the Rookery, would definitely notice the change; she visited her on campus every few weeks, occasionally with Jude, always commenting on the fact that Alice looked haggard and exhausted. Alice had explained it away as a consequence of being overworked. Sasha was visiting tonight to see how she'd fared in the first test, and Alice wondered what she might say when she saw the improvements.

She backed away from the mirror and trudged into her room. Instead of taking the pyjamas off, she wrapped herself in a dressing gown, made a hot drink and settled down at the table. Her hands were no longer chapped, she realized as she nursed the cup. The dermatitis she'd been scratching at the day before had cleared up. And – she placed a hand on her forehead – no temperature. She barely remembered what life was like without fevers and headaches, stomach pains and breathlessness.

A sudden balloon of excitement rose in her chest. She quashed it mercilessly. It would do her no good to get her hopes up. She'd only taken one portion of the draught, and there were two others left to take, assuming she didn't squander the opportunity. This didn't mean anything. Besides – it felt wrong to be happy about her own good fortune with the binding draught when it had gone so horribly wrong for Holly.

She took a sip of tea and allowed her gaze to wander out of the window. The wind was up and the branches of the mulberry tree were dancing in the breeze. It could have been her imagination, but it seemed as though there were dozens of ripe new berries hanging from it.

7

'Tom's struggling,' said Bea over the breakfast table.

The Arlington dining hall was wonderfully cosy in the winter: arched ceiling, chequered tiles, rich wooden panels halfway up the stone walls, oil paintings in ornate frames and plain circular chandeliers hanging low over the wooden tables – each of which had a lamp in the centre and leather seats lining each side. In summer, however, it felt too dark, despite the tall windows and many lamps. Alice couldn't help but feel that the season wasn't supposed to be cosy; it was supposed to be bright and airy, and fresh with promise. It was why she preferred taking her lunches in the quad.

She reached for a slice of toast and a pot of marmalade. Her eyes were focused over Bea's shoulder on a long-haired student who was showing off to a girl. He was telling her he'd entered the Cream of the Crops, and doing something to the table – warping the mineral streaks in the wood into different patterns and shapes for her, as though it was a canvas.

'Is that a portrait? It doesn't look anything like me.' The girl laughed. 'Write my name in it again.'

Alice was so busy watching them she knocked the marmalade into the butter. 'Did he go home last night?' she asked, slathering her toast.

'I think he spent the night drinking,' said Bea, taking a sip of her tea. 'I found him sitting on the kerb after the test with his head in his hands, just devastated. He didn't want to talk.'

'It's not his fault,' said Alice. She shoved her plate away, suddenly losing her appetite. It felt wrong to sit here attempting normality. Holly had once sat in this hall.

'Of course it's not his fault,' agreed Bea. 'He's administered dozens of binding draughts without a problem. It was no one's fault – not unless you want to blame a tree.' She swallowed a mouthful of tea and peered closely at Alice. 'How are you feeling about . . . what you saw?'

Alice paled. 'It was . . .' She shook her head and stared at the table.

Bea reached over and patted her hand with sympathy. 'Best to keep your mind busy,' she said. 'You become hardened to it eventually, but even then . . .' She sighed and then fumbled for something on the bench next to her. 'Here,' she said, plonking a book on the table. 'Not as useful as some of the other books I've given you, but I was obliged to pass it on.'

'*House Mielikki: Models of Success*?' said Alice, reading the title aloud.

'A gift from Cecil,' said Bea. 'He said he hopes it'll prove aspirational for you after your difficulties in the first test.'

Alice raised an eyebrow, unsure whether to be insulted or grateful.

'Just humour him,' said Bea. 'Look at the author.'

Alice's eyes tracked to a few words eclipsed by the cover image of a stately woman in an oval frame, plaited brown hair pinned into a business-like yet elegant style.

'Cecil Pryor,' said Alice. 'He wrote this himself?'

She nodded. 'I think he sold ten copies. Eight of which I ordered for the library out of kindness. I'm sure he has a few hundred stashed in his office, ready for handing out to every new candidate.'

Alice flicked through it. It appeared to be a list of the accomplishments of other House Mielikki members, going back a few hundred years.

'Tell him . . . thanks.'

Bea nodded and reached for a breakfast pastry. 'About Tom,' she said. 'He feels responsible because he prepared the draught, but—'

'My draught was from the same batch,' said Alice. 'And it didn't harm me the way it did with . . . I feel fine.'

'I know,' said Bea. 'That's the risk everyone takes. Tom's just . . . I don't think anything we say will make him feel better. What happened was so awful. I've seen some dreadful things in my time, and I've heard stories about others, but to see *that* . . .' She shuddered and replaced her pastry, apparently losing her appetite. 'But Holly knew what she was signing up for,' said Bea matter-of-factly. 'As a Mowbray, she'll have heard the same stories and known the risks. It's hideous, terrible and tragic, but . . . everyone has to make the choice for themselves about whether to take that draught. I did, Tom did . . . you did.'

There was a flicker of movement and Alice shifted in her seat. Tom had appeared in the corridor outside the dining hall, visible through the open doorway. Even from a distance she could see that all was not well. He was usually smart, buttoned up in a preppy shirt and tweed trousers, his sandy beard neatly trimmed.

But now he looked like he'd slept in his clothes and had lost control of the beard. His glasses were slightly askew and his blue eyes were weary. It appeared as though he'd aged ten years overnight, and yet he was a year younger than Bea and still a few years off forty.

'Speak of the devil,' said Bea. 'Tom!' she boomed across the dining hall.

Several heads turned to look, but in the corridor Tom flinched. Spotting them, he shook his head as though warning them to stay away. Alice frowned as the light caught the other side of his face. Tom's cheek was bruised and his lip was bloodied. Before he hurried off, Alice glimpsed his nightjar, hovering anxiously near his head. There was only one emotion rolling off it in waves: guilt.

'Something's wrong,' said Alice, getting to her feet. It wasn't his guilty nightjar that concerned her; it was his split lip. Tom hadn't given it to himself.

Incoherent shouting exploded outside the dining hall, and Alice's hackles rose. She recognized the timbre of one of those voices. As the noise worsened, others in the dining hall cast awkward looks at each other. Alice ignored them and hurried into the corridor with Bea following close behind.

Most of the students and staff had taken advantage of the warm weather and were eating on the lawns, leaving the corridors unusually empty. In the humdrum atmosphere, Alice quickly found the source of the commotion.

Lester stood midway up the stairs to the staff accommodation, his hand clutching the banister. Hair greased with sweat and a five o'clock shadow on his lantern jaw, he looked terrible. His hulking arms and barrel chest seemed at odds with the growing paunch poking from his T-shirt.

'Leave him alone, Lester,' Alice snapped.

Beneath his fingers, the banister spindles had been transformed, the solid wood now as flexible as vines. At Lester's urging they grew longer, creeping and slithering towards Tom, who was trapped against the wall lower down the staircase. Tendrils already held him in place, lashed around his wrists, while others climbed up his body and curled around his throat.

'Let him go,' demanded Bea, her voice steely, 'or I'll have Whitmore expel you from the House for assault.'

Lester laughed and turned towards her, his small, piggy eyes bloodshot.

'What makes you think Whitmore won't give me a medal for cleaning up the membership?' he sneered.

His hand twitched and the slithering wood around Tom's throat tightened. Tom's face paled and his eyes widened.

'This bastard was the one who made the draught, and then tried to blame me.' Lester spoke through gritted teeth, his face suddenly flushed with effort as the wood around Tom lifted him off the floor. Dangling in the air, Tom gasped desperately, his face puce and his feet twitching.

'He can't breathe,' shouted Alice, while Bea ran to help yank the vines from Tom. 'Let him go or—'

'Or what, you stupid bitch?' snarled Lester. 'You were there last night as well. Touching her. Pretending you wanted to help. Maybe you sabotaged her. Why did you collapse after she did?'

'I . . . I didn't—'

'I saw you,' he said. 'I watched you.'

Alice glanced at Tom and Bea. The librarian had dropped to her knees and was raising each wooden stair so that Tom could stand on solid ground.

'Whitmore—' Alice started.

'Go ahead,' said Lester, with a twisted smile. 'Tell the governor whatever you want.'

Tom's eyes flickered and he made a low gurgling sound. Heart slamming against her ribs, Alice looked from him to Lester and grabbed the banister. She could feel the dull tingle of his magic in the wood as she strengthened her grip on the rail. Alice's fingertips whitened.

'Someone's to blame for Mowbray kicking it in the grove,' said Lester, his voice harsh, 'but it isn't me.'

Anger and guilt snuffed out Alice's sensibilities. She squeezed the banister, her palm smarting with the buzz of magic. Beneath her hand, the wood began to rot. It blackened and flaked, and splintered against her skin. A crack grew, snaking up the length of the banister, spreading decay through the brittle wood. Too fragile for Lester's weighty grip.

The banister crumbled to dust. Lester's nightjar, a plain-feathered light brown bird, shrieked a warning he couldn't hear. A brief expression of shock crossed Lester's face as he fell over the edge of the staircase. He smashed to the floor, and Alice flinched at the echoing thud. The moment he landed, the vine-like spindles holding Tom turned to ash and the technician also fell to the ground.

Lester was silent, and Alice stared at the strange angle of his neck with dread. His small nightjar fluttered anxiously, pecking at his hair and then his cord. Alice's pulse raced and her ears buzzed with fear and adrenaline. *I had no choice.* She looked down at her hands. *Did I have no choice?* Alice shuddered. She'd either just killed a man or made an enemy.

There was a muffled groan from the heap on the floor and Alice exhaled sharply. Lester was alive. Further down the corridor, office doors had begun to open. Finally drawn by the noise, half a dozen onlookers appeared, curiosity and concern on their faces. 'I knew that stairwell was dangerous,' muttered one. 'I told the janitor it needed looking at.'

'Is he all right?' asked another.

Lester answered for him. With a rumbling grunt, he staggered to his feet, patting himself down in confusion. He looked furiously over his shoulder, his eyes locking on Alice, before barging through the crowd and stomping from the building with a limp.

'It's not Lester's fault,' said Tom, hunched over the table, nursing a cup of coffee.

Bea had dragged Tom and Alice back to the Arlington dining hall for a stiff drink, but in the absence of alcohol they'd had to make do with caffeine.

Alice's tea had gone cold. She stared into her cup, thinking about the look on Lester's face as he'd fallen – and the expression of rage as he'd stormed out.

'Are you suffering from Stockholm Syndrome, darling?' asked Bea. 'Of course it was Lester's fault. I'll be reporting him first thing tomorrow.'

'Don't,' said Tom, his forehead furrowed. 'Please. Just leave it.'

Alice glanced at him. He looked utterly defeated. 'You can't make yourself Lester's punch bag,' she mumbled. 'You didn't kill Holly.' Her stomach clenched and she took a mouthful of cold tea to disguise the tremor in her hands.

'He didn't even come here for me,' said Tom quietly. 'It was just unlucky I bumped into him.'

'What was he here for then?' asked Alice.

'His books,' said Tom, glancing up. There was a shadow behind his eyes she hadn't seen before. 'He loaned Holly a stack of books when he was mentoring her.' Tom shook his head, his voice dull. 'He was trying to get up the stairs to her apartment to find them, but . . .' Tom shrugged. 'He shouldn't be allowed to root around in there. It's not right. I asked him to leave but he followed me, and . . .' Tom trailed away. 'I hope Lester's okay,' he said after a moment.

'Tom, he nearly killed you,' said Bea, aghast.

'I know, but still . . . It wasn't his fault.'

They lapsed into silence and Alice watched the couple on the other table for several minutes. They hadn't left despite all the commotion. The long-haired student had taken a wooden coaster from under his coffee cup and turned it into a carved wooden rose. The girl he was trying to impress was refusing to accept it, telling him with a laugh that she preferred orchids to roses.

Roses, Alice thought with a pang. *Holly.*

'Are you busy tonight?' said Alice. 'I have an idea.'

Sasha was supposed to be coming to the campus for a drink that evening, but there would be time for an important job beforehand.

They were trying very hard to be normal for Tom's sake, but the atmosphere had become a distorted pantomime.

'Shhh,' Bea whispered dramatically as they crept across the gardens. 'If Eugene sees us, he'll cave the library ceiling in again as punishment.'

'I don't think he actually has a vendetta against you. He's always very cheerful when I see him,' said Alice with forced jollity.

'Rank favouritism,' said Bea. 'I once asked him to help me move a shelf and he refused. He took offence because it contained the complete works of Capability Brown, landscape gardener extraordinaire, who is apparently his personal nemesis despite being dead for over two hundred years. Meanwhile, he brings you a full set of dining furniture to your quarters, up how many flights of stairs?'

'Technically it's Victorian classroom furniture,' said Alice, her feet sinking into the thick grass as she trudged across the lawn.

'Where are you taking me?' asked Tom.

They both looked up at him sandwiched between them. Each had linked an arm through his – not easy with someone as tall as a lamp post – and were steering him to a secluded part of the vast campus.

'On a secret adventure,' said Bea shiftily as they trekked beyond Cavendish and the Whiston Building, in which he worked.

He sighed and allowed them to guide him onwards. The part of the gardens they were heading towards had manicured lawns that eased into wilder, longer grasses, and a small hedge maze populated with oddly shaped bushes at every dead end. The janitor, Eugene, had wrested total control of its design from the university gardener some years previously. Eugene had a passion for topiary, despite being a member of House Pellervoinen and hopelessly mismatched for such a hobby. His enthusiasm was that of the grimly determined, and no matter how many times he'd tried to shape the hedges into grand sphinxes and magnificent lions, they always resembled deformed ducks. A professor of animal anatomy in the Sydenham Building had once tried to burn them to the ground, and had the next day returned to his office to find someone had bricked up the door. No one had ever complained again.

They urged Tom into the maze. He was tall enough to see over the top of the hedges. A few swift turns and they were soon at the centre, stretched out on the grass while Bea rummaged in her bag. It was a quiet evening, and the sun was setting behind the Whiston Building, painting warm streaks across the sky.

'Red sky at night,' said Alice.

'Shepherd's delight,' Tom finished in a monotone voice.

Bea thrust a bottle at each of them and sighed with satisfaction as she uncapped her own and put it to her lips. It was cloudberry wine sweetened with honey. The amber liquid in the glass caught the last rays of the sun and reminded Alice of the binding draught. She glanced at Bea, who appeared to have had the same thought, and they cleared their throats to urge Tom to drink.

'To Holly,' said Alice, raising her bottle.

Tom stared morosely at his feet, so Alice grabbed his sleeve and pulled his arm up into the toast.

'To Holly,' she repeated, her voice cracking, 'who was strong and brave and always did *exactly what she wanted.*'

'And to the hundreds of other souls who've taken that test over the years and met the same fate,' added Bea, 'because sometimes life is cruel and there's nothing at all we can do about it.'

Alice took a sip of her wine, her mouth twisting at the rush of sweet and bitter flavours on her tongue. She'd never been much of a wine drinker.

They drank in silence for several minutes, before Alice got to her feet and approached the circular mound at the centre of the maze. She crouched down and slid her fingers into the grass, digging into the soil. Then she pressed a single red berry into the earth and took a deep breath.

When she was done, Alice glanced up to find Bea and Tom looming over her. Bea's arm was around Tom's shoulders and she was squeezing him hard. Tom offered Alice his hand and pulled her upright. Together, they stood for several minutes, peering down at the memorial Alice had wrought in the grass: a perfect, neat little holly bush, blooming with vivid red berries and spiky leaves.

'To Holly,' said Tom, his voice hoarse, raising his bottle.

'To Holly,' they agreed, clinking their wine and drinking deeply. Alice's eyes darted to meet Bea's, who smiled in honour of a job well done. Alice looked away, taking another swig of wine to disguise her own pensiveness.

Drowsy with drink and barefoot, they lay on their backs and watched the sky darken.

'Ursa Major,' said Alice, pointing at the clouds. 'It'll be somewhere over there later.'

'When the clouds aren't in the way,' said Bea, squinting upwards.

'What's Ursa Major mean?' mumbled Tom. 'Sounds like a piano key.'

She craned her neck to see him. He was stretched out on the grass, his eyes heavy-lidded. He'd finished off his own wine and then hers and Bea's. At least one of them was feeling better.

'It means . . . "the great bear",' she said. 'My dad used to draw the constellations for me when I was little.' Her dad. Her real dad. The one who'd given her a love of sketching and Swindon Town Football Club. *Tuoni* was nothing more than a bogeyman she intended on shoving in a closet.

Bea snorted. 'And there's . . . the great mallard,' said the librarian, pointing at one of Eugene's mangled topiary ducks.

Alice rolled onto her front and pushed up to her knees. 'We should head back,' she said, fumbling in the grass for her empty wine bottle. Sasha was due soon – they were meeting in the quad – and Alice planned to introduce her to Bea and Tom. She glanced at Tom, whose eyes were closed and face was plastered with a languid, drunken smile. Okay, maybe not Tom, just Bea.

Between them, they hauled Tom to his feet, reeling backwards when he tipped too far forward on his toes.

'Everything's spinning,' he muttered.

Alice swung his arm over her shoulder and they began to totter back towards the quad. They'd made it out of the maze when Bea said, 'Hang on, I'll meet you in the courtyard in five minutes.' With a wink, she slipped away and cantered back towards the maze.

Alice was forced to plough on alone, because every time she stopped, Tom stumbled about like a deer on ice. She glanced up at him. His nightjar was relaxed on his shoulder, its head bobbing with every footstep.

'Alice,' Tom whispered at about a thousand decibels, 'I think Holly's in a better place now.'

'Yes,' she said tightly. 'Me too.'

'The maze,' he said, the arm around her shoulder squeezing in thanks. 'It was a good idea . . . and the wine.' He raised a pointing finger and gesticulated, only able to focus one eye. 'A *very* good—'

Tom's foot knocked his own ankle and he lurched sideways. She tumbled with him and they hit the grass in a shabby heap, gasping in surprise.

'We fell over,' he whispered with a loopy grin.

Exasperated, she peered over at him, splayed out on the grass next to her, one leg slung over hers. 'Well spotted.'

She sat up, picked grass and flowers out of her messy hair and tossed them at him. They landed on his face, and he spat a daisy out of his mouth with a mumbled protest.

'Hello, Alice.'

She shot round, and everything – Tom, Bea, the gardens, the buildings around the quad – faded away. Her stomach clenched, and when she rose she found that her heartbeat thrummed against her ribs like a trapped butterfly, and every thought in her head vanished.

Crowley.

He was standing in the shadow of the Arlington Building, his dark hair overlong, reaching past his ears and falling into his eyes. He drank her in, his gaze searing her skin as it travelled over her mussed-up hair, her rumpled shirt and bare feet.

Despite the warm night, he wore the long, sweeping coat he always wore – so dark green it was almost black – a white buttoned-up shirt underneath it, black trousers and scuffed boots. There was a hint of stubble on his jaw and her fingers tingled at the thought of running her hand over it.

'What are you doing here?' she found herself saying. Sasha was supposed to have come, not Crowley.

'I wanted to congratulate you,' he murmured. 'I heard about your recent success, and I wanted . . .'

He trailed away, and they stared at each other in silence. A whole year lay between them. A year in which they hadn't spoken, in which she'd nursed her wounds and tried – and failed – to forgive his lies. A year in which she'd reconnected with everyone in Coram House except him.

'I wanted to see your face,' he admitted in a low voice, his glittering eyes roaming over her as though he might only have this one chance to imprint her in his memory.

He straightened, his hands withdrawing from his pockets and his gaze dropping to Tom, collapsed on the grass. Crowley grew very still before offering her the briefest of smiles. 'I'm . . . glad for you,' he said with a slow nod of understanding. His lips curved into a more forced expression. 'I won't intrude' – he took a step backwards – 'but I just wanted you to know that . . . I truly wish . . . only the best things for you.' His mouth tightened again, and he gave her a nod before turning away, the coat flying out behind him.

Alice was slow to react, still dazed to find him in front of her after all this time. It took a moment before the meaning of his words sank in. He thought she was with *Tom*.

'Crowley, wait!' she shouted. She raced forward but skidded to a stop, watching him stride off around the side of Arlington. She couldn't seem to make her feet move any further, couldn't seem to bring herself to dash after him to explain that he'd misunderstood. Her throat was clogged with emotion – but her feet just wouldn't move.

She watched his coat rippling out in the breeze and stood speechless as he disappeared between the fir trees.

'Eugene's going to be furious,' shrieked Bea as she hurtled into the quad and almost fell on top of Tom.

Alice turned towards her, barely comprehending.

'I've vanished all of his hedge ducks and grown a fox that looks like it's eaten them,' she panted with a beaming grin. 'I'll grow them back again tomorrow night,' she said, waving a hand while she caught her breath, 'but that'll serve him right for waterlogging all my books.'

Alice said nothing. A small voice in her head was screaming at her to run after Crowley. But a louder one had pinned her to the spot.

'What?' she said.

Bea frowned. 'You look like you've seen a ghost.' She glanced down at Tom. 'Help me get this drunkard to his feet before he falls asleep on the lawn.'

Alice nodded and took a step towards them. She felt like her ears were full of water. Crowley had been here. Crowley had come to see her, to congratulate her, and she was letting him go. She swallowed and tried to shake it off. She *had* let him go. That was the point.

'One arm each,' said Bea, her handbag clinking with empty wine bottles. Alice trudged closer and reached down to help.

'On the count of three,' said Bea. 'One . . . two . . .'

The lawn juddered beneath them. The soil and grass vibrated between Alice's bare toes – gently at first, and then rising with force into a shuddering rumble from deep below the ground. Every flower began to quiver and the berries on the mulberry tree were shaken off, the fruit bouncing across the quad. Alice staggered backwards, fighting to keep her balance as something rose under her heels. It was the grass. Fresh grass was growing, sprouting rapidly from the soil until it was waist high. And then, just as quickly as it started, everything stopped – the tremors, the growth, everything – and the lawn was still again.

'What was that?' Alice breathed.

'I think that was . . . a small earthquake,' said Bea.

'And . . . are they common in the Rookery?' asked Alice, staring in confusion at the reverse crop circles enclosing them.

Bea shook her head, staring at the wild grass with a frown. 'No,' she said. 'They're not.'

8

On Monday morning Reid's hair was a disaster of epic proportions. She slammed open the lab door, her heels whip-cracking on the wooden floor as she stormed over to her desk and thumped her paperwork and a mug of coffee down on it. *Mayday. Mayday. Category-five hurricane incoming.* Alice resisted the urge to laugh – even the sound of her exhalations had been known to send Reid into a fury. It wasn't Alice's fault her nose occasionally whistled with sinusitis.

Ignoring the anger that was radiating from her boss, Alice made another note on her page. Now that she'd passed the first stage of the testing process, Bea had set her some research on one of House Mielikki's main responsibilities: the upkeep and monitoring of the Summer Tree – something Bea was particularly keen to do, in light of the grass's growth spurt and the mini quake. Alice was only allowed to observe Bea's work, but still felt like some invisible barrier had been crossed, like she had one foot in the door of House Mielikki. Throwing herself into the opportunity had become a useful distraction from poring over her short encounter with Crowley – and the letter folded in her pocket.

Her fingers twitched with the impulse to pull it out and read it for the fifth time, but she resisted. It had been delivered earlier that morning, with a Mayo postmark. When she'd left Ireland, they'd agreed that Alice wouldn't write home. Rookery mail was transported to London and sent around the mainland from there, and Alice couldn't risk Sir John Boleyn's Beaks somehow intercepting it and tracing her parents' newest address. It had been a difficult decision, but a necessary one. She could only contact them if she travelled into London to use a telephone. The only silver lining had been that they could still write to her using a mainland post box specifically for Rookery mail.

Her pen poked a hole through her page and she blinked in surprise. Too distracted. And she really couldn't afford distractions. Maybe if she just scratched the itch again . . . With a sigh, she tugged the letter from her pocket and smoothed it open. Her mum's looping handwriting sprang out at her.

> . . . *turned up out of nowhere, just like last time . . . with his long hair and that coat of his . . . Your dad nearly punched him in the face! . . . insisted on showing us how it works . . . the downstairs toilet door and if we step through it, it takes us right to your dad's favourite pub in Westport . . . exit plan, just to be on the safe side . . . have warned your dad he's not allowed to use it just because he wants a pint of Guinness . . . He offered to hide the house, if you can believe it . . . don't know what kind of magic . . . but the postman would never find us if the house was invisible! . . . Told us not to tell you he'd been, but . . .*

Crowley had visited her parents on Sunday – the day after she'd seen him – to fit them with new safety measures. He was exceptionally talented with the doorways, but how he'd managed to provide an escape hatch without them having to use the void between the two locations, she didn't know. Alice glanced down at the last lines, about hiding the house, and frowned. She'd never heard that was possible; her mum must be exaggerating. Flutters shivered in her stomach, and she squashed them down. He'd assumed she was with Tom, and yet he'd still taken it upon himself to make sure her parents were safe. She exhaled slowly.

'Would you stop that infernal whistling?' snapped Reid. 'This isn't the fucking seven dwarves' workshop.'

Alice's eyes narrowed. 'It's my *sinusitis*,' she said testily, folding the letter and shoving it back in her pocket.

'Well you're fired,' Reid shot back, downing her coffee and storming to the window to throw it open.

Alice stared at the professor in bemused shock. Reid's hurricanes usually involved broken glass and smashed pottery, not provocative statements. But she would not allow the woman's temper to deflate her. For the third morning running, Alice had woken up feeling well: no sickness, no fever. It was the binding draught – she was sure of it – healing her of Tuoni's influence.

'You can't fire me for *breathing*,' said Alice. 'That's not even legal.'

Reid had pulled out a short cigarette holder. She wafted it around while she prepared to light the match. 'Sweetie, no one cares about legalities,' she said in a patronizing tone. 'They're threatening to fire me too.'

Alice frowned. Maybe Reid was serious.

'Who's *they*?' she asked.

Reid shrugged. She leaned out of the window, one elbow resting on the sill, the cigarette holder held loosely between two fingers. She took a drag of her cigarette and blew the smoke over her shoulder, back into the room.

'The Magellan Estate,' said Reid, still staring out of the open window. Alice squinted at her, trying to work out if she was bluffing. 'They're not happy with the direction of my work. Too narrow, apparently, and not enough visible progress.' She paused, then added bitterly, 'What the hell would they know? If it's to stand up to peer review, it has to be narrow to be properly rigorous! Those fools at the Sorbonne will have a field day if my funding's pulled *again*.'

Reid spun round and Alice was struck by how vulnerable she looked. She seemed to have shrunk over the weekend. She'd lost all control of her hair, and the over-large shoulder pads in her suit jacket made her look tiny.

The professor shrugged and stubbed out her cigarette on the stone. 'Just my life's work ripped from my fingertips, that's all.' She slammed the window shut and sighed, then made a grab for her mug but instead poked it off the table. It smashed onto the floor, the cracked porcelain landing with a clink. With another irritated sigh, she scooped her hand through the air and the pieces came back together, perfectly re-forming the mug. It was lucky for Reid, given her frequent outbursts, that she was a member of House Pellervoinen – otherwise the amount of money wasted on shattered plates, mugs and windows would have bankrupted her.

'Get me a black coffee,' said Reid, thumping the healed mug onto Alice's desk. 'Use the arabica beans again.'

'I don't work for you any more,' said Alice with a sigh. 'You just fired me.'

'Fine. You're un-fired. No sugar.'

Alice closed her notebook, fighting the temptation to spite Reid and walk out. She didn't owe the professor any kindnesses, but she supposed she'd grown used to her wild moods. Alice couldn't help but feel a sliver of sympathy for her; it must be exhausting being Reid all the time. 'Tell me how I can help you with the research,' Alice offered with only a slightly grudging tone. 'If we can salvage your project then maybe neither of us will lose our jobs.'

Reid narrowed her eyes. She hesitated on the verge of speech, before shaking her head.

'I've spent months photocopying and filing,' Alice pressed. 'I'm perfectly capable of taking on part of your research and making notes on what I find – if you'd just let me help you.'

'You've proofread my drafts,' said Reid defensively. 'I've kept you involved.'

'You've kept me at arm's length,' Alice corrected. 'But fine.' She shrugged and turned away. 'Your choice.'

'I've . . .' Reid started, and quickly trailed away.

Alice waited, doubt beginning to creep in. Maybe she shouldn't have offered; she was quite happy with their current arrangement and the freedom it gave her to pursue her own interests.

'I've pored over Magellan's published and unpublished manuscripts,' Reid said at last, her voice tight. She gestured at the tinted-glass and marble cabinet beneath her desk. 'His letters, his notes – all passed on by his estate. But there's something missing.' Reid swiped a curl out of her face irritably. 'You've read my latest work? You're up to date?' she asked with faint scepticism.

'Yes.' Alice nodded, feeling vaguely patronized. 'It was very interesting,' she lied. It wasn't the subject that had been dull, really – it was Reid's writing style.

Reid had been studying Magellan's belief that the soul was composed of three parts. In most modern-day religions, the soul was believed to be a single complete entity, but Magellan had travelled the world meeting people of different faiths. By the time he'd returned to the Rookery and sat down to write *Sielun*, he was convinced by soul dualism – that people could have multiple souls, each with different functions. Initially, he'd been very taken with Chinese Taoism and the belief that each person had two souls – the spiritual hun, which left after death, and the corporeal po, which remained with the body. But he'd gone back to his roots in the end, with the early Finnish belief in the three-part soul – made up of henki, luonto and itse – forming his own belief model. Reid's entire project was founded on one goal: to prove that soul dualism, and therefore Magellan, was correct.

'And you've read *Sielun*?' Reid said sharply.

Alice stared at her. Reid's fraught snappiness did not make her inclined to be too helpful. 'I have,' she said coolly. 'Where's your stumbling block? What is it you think is missing?'

Reid frowned as though it was obvious. 'Everything. The fact I *haven't* been able to prove that the soul has three parts in the first place, never mind their functions. I'm trying to prove something I'm fundamentally blind to. I can't dissect a soul the way a surgeon can dissect a heart, because it can't be seen or touched.'

Alice's cheeks burned. She may not have been able to see souls themselves, but she was entirely familiar with nightjars, which mirrored the souls they guarded.

'I've studied Duncan MacDougall's old twenty-one grams experiment in detail,' Reid went on. 'He weighed the body before and after death and found it grew lighter, suggesting that the soul leaving the body caused the drop-off in mass. He claimed he'd proven the soul weighed twenty-one grams. Does that mean that each of Magellan's three parts – henki, itse and luonto – are seven grams, then? Or was MacDougall's work flawed? He claimed no difference in weight before and after death when he trialled his experiment with dogs, and I utterly refute the idea a dog has no soul.'

Alice thought of her two elderly Westies, Bo and Ruby, living with her parents in Ireland, and had to agree.

'At the very least, animals and plants must have the henki soul, which is—'

'*Plants* have souls?' said Alice. She'd agreed about dogs, but the idea of a nettle having a soul felt like a stretch too far.

'All living things have souls,' Reid answered impatiently. 'The soul is what animates the physical form; it brings life to what would otherwise just be a body, a sack of skin and bone. According to Magellan, the soul that gives the body *life* is known as the henki. Without it, we die.'

Alice's brow furrowed in thought. She was rustier on the difference between the three soul parts than she'd thought. Maybe she ought to study Magellan's *Sielun* more closely once her membership bid had been dealt with. If she survived the tests.

'But it *is* possible to live without the other two soul parts, the itse and the luonto,' Reid went on, 'because *they* don't give us life; they only give us personality. They shape who we are as individuals.'

Reid stopped for breath and stared into the distance. Alice shifted uncomfortably.

'I thought I was getting closer,' Reid murmured. 'But it's all conjecture, in the end.' She paused, eyes glazed. 'And Magellan's estate doesn't really care about my research. It's plaudits and awards they want in his name. They care nothing about the nuts and bolts of the work, or the fact it'll shame *my* name if it's torn apart because I've holes in my evidence.' She shook her head bitterly. 'Magellan had the advantage of being an aviarist. If I manage to prove his theory without assets like his, I'll have outdone him. I'll have outdone *all* of them.'

Her gaze drifted over Alice, whose face had flushed at her final comment. Reid frowned as though surprised to find Alice there, still listening. Her spine snapped upright and she cleared her throat. 'You want to keep your job? Make yourself useful then. I need you to copy some of Magellan's notes on the Ditto machine for me. His estate has sent over the last bundle from his files and I hate taking the originals out of the lab. I'm going to be working into the evening, and red wine and irreplaceable items don't mix well.'

Alice stared at her, a peevish glint in her eye. After a moment, she mentally shrugged. Fine. Let Reid battle on alone. Alice had more important things to do. Preparing for her second test and catching up with Bea's Summer Tree reading list meant that she already had more than enough on her plate. Which, incidentally, was why she couldn't afford to think about Crowley too. No distractions. She had to throw everything at her House membership bid. There would be time to think more clearly about Magellan, the security of her job and Reid's complete lack of teamwork skills later.

Alice reached gladly for Reid's notes. Trips to the Ditto machine were always good for giving her some additional thinking time. The Ditto machine was an ancient mimeograph, a pre-Xerox photocopier, kept in the reprographics room in the Arlington Building. Like the architecture and clothing, the Rookery's scientific and technological development had stalled somewhere around the 1930s. Alice had briefly harboured fantasies about revolutionizing the city with London tech, importing Steve Jobs' inventions and becoming a billionaire. Unfortunately, the electrical systems were also from the dark ages and barely powerful enough to run a pocket calculator.

'Get me some coffee on your way back,' said Reid, shoving a folder at her chest. 'Use the—'

'Arabica beans,' said Alice, snatching up her own notes. 'Yes, I know.'

She'd decided she might as well go the long way round and pop in to see Bea on her way back. They were heading out to see the Summer Tree after work the next day, and Alice wanted to check she had everything she needed.

9

The sounds of movement on the other side of the wall caused Alice to pause later that night: drawers scraping as they opened and closed, wardrobe doors creaking, the muffled whisper of dull voices. They were clearing out Holly's room. Not Eugene, the university janitor – her family. Alice hesitated, torn between knocking on to pass on her condolences and not wanting to intrude on their grief.

When something smashed – a mirror? A vase? – and the fragments of a furious argument seeped through the walls, she decided it wasn't the right time to pay them a visit.

'Negligence,' a woman's voice snapped. 'Lester . . . fault . . . whatever he claims . . .'

'. . . can't simply . . .' A deep masculine voice, striving for patience. '. . . Runners won't . . . civil suit . . .'

'. . . not enough!'

Alice pressed her fingers to her eyes and exhaled calmly. Holly's poor family. The holly bush they'd planted in memoriam suddenly seemed so irrelevant in the face of their anguish. Alice undressed and slid into bed, thinking of her parents – happily pottering around their new cottage, learning to bake treacle bread, fixing up an old car. She didn't ever want them to be in the position Holly's parents were in, falling apart at the news of her death. She screwed her eyes shut and burrowed under the covers. God, she missed her parents right now. A sudden desperate need forced her from the bed. She whipped back her covers and yanked out the top drawer of her chest. Nestled among the socks and underwear – and now her mum's letter about Crowley – was the small ring box she'd tidied away on Holly's last visit.

Alice cracked it open and gently lifted out the ring inside, sliding it onto her finger. Just a touch too big, it was an oval signet with a worn pattern, partially hidden by the scuffs and bumps that had left four scratches over the dull gold surface. Her mum's ring; she'd given it to her when she'd left Ireland. Alice had never seen her mum wear it – she'd always said it was an heirloom and so its sentimental value was too great. It was a battered-looking thing, but as she folded herself back under the covers, it brought comfort to keep a visible souvenir of her parents close by.

Red hair fluttered at the corner of Alice's eye. She reached out, fingers stretched in anticipation. It brushed against her wrist, soft and silky. She smiled in relief, her lips forming a word. *Jen*. But her voice leached colour from the hair. It faded into a brittle blonde and broke off in her hand. There was a clump of it in her palm. She stared at it in horror. Jen's hair? Holly's hair? There was a peal of high-pitched laughter, and then a rasping voice, too close.

'Alice . . . don't beat my time!'

She bolted upright, her fists clenching the damp sheets and her eyes wild. The room was dark and haunted by shadows. Grappling with the bedside lamp, she banished them with light and sank back into her pillows, her heart thudding against her ribs. A waft of air kissed her forehead and she squinted gratefully at the white bird perched on her headboard, flapping its wings to cool her.

'Thanks,' she murmured begrudgingly, her throat dry.

The bird tucked its wings in and shifted closer. It was so pale that its feathers seemed luminescent. She knew, suddenly, what to call it, but she bit her tongue. To name it would be to recognize it, to honour it and all it stood for. Her nightjar gave a regal toss of its head and cooed softly as though offering comfort, and Alice was struck by a fleeting sense of guilt. Was she being fair, always keeping it at a distance?

'Your name . . . is *Kuu*,' she murmured, raising a shaky hand to stroke it. 'Because you *coo* over me. And because kuu means "moon". Pale, glowing, hovering in the air . . . with a dark side no one else sees.' She studied it closely. 'Yes. Your name is definitely Kuu.'

It churred in response and nuzzled her hand with something like affection. Sighing heavily, Alice switched off the light and lay rigid in the dark, staring at the patterns on the ceiling. The moonlight was obscured by long shadows from the trees in the gardens. The breeze tousled their leaves and the shadows undulated so that her ceiling seemed to pulsate with life.

She hadn't dreamed of Jen for months. Back in Ireland, her dreams had been filled with fleeting visions of red hair turning grey and lifeless in her hands. Every time she woke sweating and with a heavy sense of dread – but something had seemed to settle when she'd returned to the Rookery. She'd taken it as a positive sign that the nightmares had finished with her. But now Holly was haunting her dreams.

She sighed and closed her eyes, concentrating on the sounds of wind and leaves, and the white noise of her nightjar's song. If she concentrated she could hear the occasional rumble of a night bus on the distant roads and the clop of dray horses' hooves. Underneath the quiet city noise there was another sound: the cracking and splitting of wood under pressure, of fibres snapping . . . She frowned in the darkness. It wasn't coming from the soft whisper of the mulberry crowns bending in the wind. It was something else. Something closer.

Her nightjar shrieked in sudden warning and Alice leapt from the bed on instinct. She landed off balance, her heels striking a ridge in the wooden floor. Biting back a flurry of swearing, she lurched sideways and flattened herself against the wall. She tensed and peered into the shadows for the source of the noise, shaking with adrenaline. There was something *in her room*.

She crooked her finger and her nightjar appeared on her shoulder with a flutter of pale wings.

'Bird's-eye view,' she whispered into its ear.

It lifted upwards, wings unfolding as Alice focused on her breathing and reached for the glowing cord around her wrist. It pulsed warmly in her hands and she pushed her mind into the connection. Her vision travelled through it, throwing her consciousness into her nightjar.

Through Kuu's eyes, Alice hovered above the bed, scanning the room for the source of the noise. From the higher vantage point, her sense of the room sharpened: the spaces within it, the layout of the furniture cast in darkness, the stillness . . . Except, the room was not entirely still. She barely saw the movement at first – a flicker against the window . . . and then the slow progress of a shadow slithering along the ground, creeping closer.

Something long and narrow brushed against her leg, prodding her skin like questing fingers. It crawled over her bare foot and coiled around the ankle . . . Her vision snapped back to her physical body and she staggered. She felt heavy and lumbering, all lightness gone. Helpless in the face of her cumbersome frame, she inhaled sharply as a nimble rope of vine unravelled swiftly across the floor and curled around her other ankle. She jerked backwards, but another twig circled her leg and tightened, strangling the blood supply and firing her pain sensors until she cried out. The floor . . . the floor was *alive*. A mass of branches, twigs and leafy vines writhed across it, pouring out from the window frame. It was her decorative window, the one she'd proudly teased into shape, practising her Mielikki skills and injecting some personality into her room.

A branch snaked up and wrapped around her torso. Another around her wrists. Forcing her fingers between skin and tree branch, she tried to prise them away, but they only increased their stranglehold. A vine travelled up her spine and curled around her shoulder – this one thorny and blossoming with roses. Holly's roses. Alice's eyes widened in horror.

'*What* the f—'

It slid around her throat and squeezed, choking her protests.

Her free hand flew to her neck, pulling at the vines, but they entwined, pinching the soft skin beneath.

Alice's nightjar swooped to her aid, its claws outstretched, tearing at the flexible wood, pecking and slashing at the bark with its beak. But it was no use. The branches tightened. She was trussed up like a fly in a web. The squeeze on her windpipe sent the room spinning like a carousel. Her eyes bulged and stars popped across her vision. *Shit*. She couldn't . . . couldn't breathe . . . Her woodwork – of all the fucking things, her *woodwork* had turned against her.

Her thoughts beginning to darken, she focused her gaze on the window, imagined the branches and vines that spilled from the wood pulling back to their source, shrivelling under the power of her stare. But the pressure on her windpipe increased and her concentration lapsed. Her hands were numb, her head tingling – and her Mielikki skills utterly ineffectual. She sagged at the knee, all her energy bent towards staying upright. Not falling. Not collapsing to the floor, where the writhing vines would surely envelop her.

Her fingers scrabbled again at the vine circling her neck, and she suddenly remembered another attack – a stranglehold of vines just like these, the look of fury in Lester's eyes as he'd stormed from the university. The banister. She'd rotted the banister beneath her hands. If her Mielikki legacy was failing her, then why not use Tuoni's? She clawed uselessly at the vine, willing it to decay. *Why won't this fucking stuff die?* It squeezed harder instead, and she swayed drunkenly.

Her nightjar tugged at the cord lashed to her wrist, pulling away from her, urging her to action. She stared at it, confused, double vision making it swell in size, a hazy blur dancing at the edges of her consciousness. The bird opened its beak and shrieked at her, pulling at her arm, her hair, her shoulder – and whether by instinct or design, she raised her free arm and forced it away, batting it off.

'*Stop*,' she croaked. '*Go.*'

And it did.

The cord thinned, its glow dim yet unbroken, as Alice's nightjar flew – far beyond her sight. A pain tore open her chest and she slumped over, her grip on herself loosening as the vines tightened. A jolt of pure electricity hit her in the spine and she snapped backwards and exhaled what felt like her last breath.

Except it wasn't a breath at all; it was something else: power and spirit, and darkness and hunger. Pure energy, expelled from the prison of her body . . . a *soul* in flight. And she rose into the air – *like* a bird, but *not* a bird. Without wings, she stretched herself wide, learning the shape of herself, a billion glittering particles suspended in the air above the catatonic body she'd discarded. Slumped on the floor, she observed the top of her head and shoulders, but the familiar nausea escaped her this time. Instead, she felt lighter than air, free, exhilarated . . . and hungry. So hungry. And cold. She moved towards the window, desperately seeking heat. The branches and twigs throbbed with life. Warmth. She reached out for them . . . but they dissolved into ash and dust. The air rained with it, floating past her like specks of grey snow. A fluttering of white wings drew her attention. Pale wings and pulsing light danced around her . . . Her nightjar cried out and Alice shrank back in alarm. Shrank back. Shrank. *Back.*

Her eyes flew open. With a gasp, she crashed to the floor and a cloud of dust blossomed up around her. Ash. Dust. It covered the wooden floor. She traced a finger through it in confusion. The vines and branches were gone. The window frame: plain and ordinary, utilitarian in its lack of decorative elegance. Only a single red rose petal remained.

Her nightjar swooped down and landed on the floor next to her, churring in the most soothing way. It sidestepped closer and nuzzled her hand. The stranglehold of the vines had left marks in her skin.

Alice swallowed thickly. She had sent her nightjar away. Not far enough to break the cord – but further than she should have. And in the distance between them something had slipped out, something strong and deadly that had consumed the life pulsing through the branches – something that had saved her life. Something she did not want to name.

What's wrong with me?

The sawdust on the floor began to shift as if blown by an

unseen wind to reveal letters freshly gouged onto the wood. A message, carved into the grain: *MURDERER*. Alice's breath hitched.

Then the floorboards creaked outside her living quarters. Light footsteps pattered in the corridor outside. But with Holly dead and her family long gone, no one else but Alice lived at this end of the corridor. She ran for the door – snatching the cricket bat as she passed – and flung it open, her chest heaving.

The corridor was empty.

Alice slumped back against the wall, her head pounding but her mind suddenly tack sharp.

Lester.

Her jaw clenched and she slammed the door shut.

10

'Are you listening?' asked Bea, elbowing Alice as they crossed the university gardens.

Alice started guiltily – she hadn't been listening at all. Her hand drifted up to her neck where the thorny vines had pressed their spikes into her skin. She'd spent hours thinking about the carved message. *Murderer.* And hours studying the window frame which had once blossomed with Holly's uninvited roses. She shuddered involuntarily. The message was wrong. She'd helped Holly; there was no doubt in her mind about that. What worried her was how instinctively it had happened. That, and whether someone knew what she'd done in the grove that night. Yet it hardly seemed possible. Alice had barely known what she was doing, and no one could have seen her nightjar slice Holly's cord – not even Lester.

In the stairwell, he'd thrown out accusations to shift his guilt, even suggesting she'd sabotaged Holly out of jealousy. *I saw you . . . I watched you.* Was it possible he *had* seen something to paint her with suspicion – not her nightjar, but *something*? Or was he only calling her a murderer because she could have broken his neck letting him fall down the stairs?

The possibility that Lester might make another attempt was at the back of her mind, but wasn't her primary concern. Greater was the awful worry that, for an instant, her *soul* had been freed – or, if Reid and Magellan were to be believed, a part of it at least. Her nightjar had failed to restrain it; her Tuoni legacy was too strong. She had to get it under control, or she would become a danger to everyone around her.

'The Juhannus?' Bea prompted, herding Alice towards the janitor's shed door.

Alice glanced at her. She hadn't been able to tell Bea about the attack. If Lester did know something – even if he was only bluffing – she couldn't take the risk of losing her mentor and friend. If Bea really knew what she was . . .

'*Alice*,' said Bea. 'Are you all right?'

'What? Oh, sorry. I was just thinking. Did you report Lester to Whitmore in the end?' Maybe he'd been reprimanded and that had been his catalyst last night.

Bea shook her head. 'No. I think it would knock Tom even more if he felt responsible for the big idiot's membership being revoked. I want to wring his neck, darling, but . . .' She sighed. 'Tom has suggested *mediation*.'

Alice pulled a horrified face. Lester could've killed him. Her hand drifted to her neck again.

'Yes,' said Bea, nodding in agreement and shooing her through the door to the void. 'Precisely. Anyway, forget that great pillock. About the Juhannus—'

The door shut, and darkness folded around them, but not before Alice saw Bea raise an eyebrow at her blank face.

'The *Midsummer Festival*,' said Bea. 'We won't go to the big festival at Hyde Park. Everyone goes there and it's always full of students. We're doing the one at Crane Park Island – the Ukon Juhla. It's smaller and more intimate. The focus is more on the traditional, pre-Christian celebration – in honour of Ukko the thunder god rather than John "Juhannus" the Baptist. Plus the food is to die for. There'll be bonfires – kokko – by the river Crane, hot food, drink, music, pagan rituals . . . You'll love it. You have to come.'

Alice hesitated. 'Maybe.'

She shivered and huddled closer to her mentor. They couldn't see each other's faces clearly in the void, but Alice felt Bea's chest inflate with indignation at her lack of commitment. It wasn't that she didn't want to go, but now didn't seem the right time for a frivolous excursion. She still had two tests to concentrate on, and the small matter of her deathly soul and Lester, her new sworn enemy, to worry about.

'Midsummer is our biggest festival,' said Bea with feeling, 'and we only have weeks to prepare.' She shook her head. 'I'm sorry, but if you don't embrace this tradition, our friendship is over and you're going to have to leave the Rookery forever.'

Alice forced a smile and tried to rouse her spirits. 'Tad over-dramatic,' she said. 'But fine. I'll come.'

'Excellent,' said Bea, clapping her hands with delight. 'You've got less than a week to get things ready.' She thrust open a well-hidden door and light poured into the barren space.

'What "things"?' Alice said suspiciously as they stepped out into a busy street.

Bea gave her a coquettish smile. 'We're single. That means we're midsummer maidens, darling. If we pick seven flowers from seven different meadows and leave them under our pillow at midsummer, tradition says we'll see our true love's face in a dream.' She paused and gave an offhand shrug. 'And if you want one blessed with a *pretty* face, the growing wisdom is you have to pick the flowers naked.'

'Oh God,' said Alice.

'Or if you go to a river – naked – you'll see the face of your true love reflected in the water.'

Alice's cheeks warmed and she looked away. Romance was about as far from her mind these days as . . . well, as Crowley. Which was to say, not far enough.

'I didn't think you cared about meeting anyone,' said Alice.

'I don't,' said Bea. 'But we owe it to our ancestors to uphold the traditions. Especially the one where the midsummer maiden rolls around in a wheat field—'

'Naked?' Alice asked.

'Of course. Then it means she's destined to meet her future husband before the next Juhannus.'

'Do the men ever get naked in these traditions?'

'If I'm rolling around in a wheat field with my knickers off, darling, I certainly hope so.'

She laughed throatily and marched across the road, towards their destination. Alice watched her go, struggling to maintain the happy mood in Bea's absence. Her footsteps slowed at the memory of Crowley's face, attempting to smile at the imagined relationship between her and Tom. She'd tried so hard never to think of him; in the year apart, she'd put herself first, focusing on what she needed to do to survive Tuoni's cursed genes. She hadn't wanted pity or help; she'd just wanted to move on and fix things herself.

Alice could accept he'd made amends as best he could. Forced to choose, he'd sacrificed the thing that had mattered most to him in the world to save her: his sister's nightjar and her one chance to recover from a coma. Yet, there was still a mental block, a wall she'd built to protect herself – not from him, but from the emotions he might stir in her. Nothing could be allowed to distract her from her purpose. Not the uncertainties Crowley engendered in her, not anything. She sighed heavily and hurried across the road after Bea.

The Abbey Library in Bermondsey was so imposing it could be seen from several streets away. Rising from a cobbled square, it stamped its authority on the busy landscape and cast deep shadows over those who stood in its presence. Originally, the site had belonged to an eighth-century monastery and then to a Benedictine order. In London, the building had been destroyed during the dissolution of the monasteries. In the Rookery, however, it had remained standing, used not as a place of worship in the traditional sense but to house the Summer Tree.

'Oh look,' said Bea, gesturing at a hodgepodge of stalls crowding one end of the square. 'The Travelling Market's here. I wonder if they'll have anything I can wear to the festival.'

'I've never understood why it's inside,' Alice murmured.

'It's a street market,' said Bea, staring at her as though she was mad. 'It's *out*side.'

'I mean the Summer Tree,' said Alice. 'The replica is allowed its freedom, planted in some Rookery forest somewhere—'

'No, it's not,' said Bea, diverting them towards the market. 'It's in Oxleas Wood in South East London.'

Alice stared at her, surprised, and then darted after the librarian as she plunged through the thin crowd of people milling around the makeshift stalls.

'It's . . .?' She snagged Bea's sleeve. 'You mean to say the grove that Holly—that the binding draught is taken in *London*?'

'Yes. You're wondering why the place isn't full of humans

who've stumbled across it by accident,' said Bea with a knowing grin. 'Darling, those people only see what they want to see.'

'But—'

'And of course the House has made sure to hide it from view completely. It's in a small, hidden grove we cultivated ourselves. They couldn't find it if they tried; the only point of access is that door in the House.'

Alice stared at Bea. Crowley had offered to hide her parents' house in Ireland. So such a thing *was* possible?

'If entire houses and groves can be hidden with magic,' she asked, 'why are we not all living in London? If the Beaks can't see those places, then—'

'Oh God, no,' said Bea. 'Would you really want to? And besides, do you have any idea how much magical skill is required to *hide* a place? I doubt even the House governors have legacies powerful enough for that any more.'

Alice frowned. Maybe Crowley had just been showing off.

Bea's eyes drifted over a table of beaded necklaces. 'What do you think?' she asked, holding a garish gold and fire opal necklace to her throat.

'I think the Mayor of London probably wants his chain of office back,' said Alice.

Bea sighed and replaced the necklace, waving away the trader, who tried to pass a dozen others into her hands. 'Seen anything you like?' she asked.

Alice glanced around the small market. The stalls seemed to consist mainly of haberdasheries and curios. There were table-tops laden with painted masks, corked bottles of drinking water from the river Walbrook, gift boxes of asbestos-suede fireproof gloves and stacks of yellowed letters handwritten in faded ink. She wondered why anyone would buy second-hand letters, and then her eyes fell on a stall selling *Petrified-wood tables, House Pellervoinen certified!* The tables glistened with a polished sheen, and Alice moved closer to study them. Marble patterns rippled across their surface, yet there were wood-like knots and a grain. She rapped one with her knuckle, and it rang with a deep bass as though stone rather than wood.

'Can I interest you in this beauty?' tempted the trader – a long-haired old man in a waistcoat. 'Originally from fossilized oak, this one's made of quartz and silica minerals. Look at the way it catches the light. Or this one – opalized rowan?'

Alice shook her head, bemused.

'This ornamental piece, then?' suggested the trader, snatching up a piece of dull grey stone that appeared to have been cut to look like a piece of tree trunk. 'Top-quality stone trees, with the grain intact just like nature intended. They fetch a high price but I'm willing to let you have it for—'

'*Stone* trees? Like nature intended?' said Alice sceptically.

'Pellervoinen-certified,' he threw in eagerly. 'These ones were petrified by their finest craftsmen.'

She shook her head. Stone trees? 'I'll leave it. Thanks.' She spotted Bea near the tail end of the stall's stock, next to a display of *Finest House Mielikki living furniture*. There were intricately carved cherry and beech wood chairs sprouting flowers and foliage. The tapered shape of the leaves reminded her of those belonging to another tree . . .

'The Summer Tree,' said Alice.

Bea raised an amused eyebrow. 'I'm afraid it's not for sale, darling.'

'What?' said Alice, with a confused laugh. 'No, I mean the fact it's inside; it just doesn't seem right.'

Alice moved through the throng with Bea following behind. The smell of fried onions and hot roasted chestnuts wafted closer and her stomach rumbled involuntarily. Towards the edges of the market, the miscellaneous clutter gave way to food stalls. Smouldering metal drums had been lined up on the kerb and were spilling charcoal smoke into the air. Round metal plates punctured with holes rested on top of the drums, slowly cooking heaps of dark chestnuts, their skins cracked open and revealing the tender, nutty flesh inside.

Alice quashed her sudden craving and peered up at the abbey's bell tower. It was wrapped in ivy and its spire pierced the clouds. 'The miniature is outside, enjoying the wild freedoms of nature, and the most important tree ever grown is trapped in a building in the middle of a city. It just seems wrong.'

'It's Pellervoinen's fault,' said Bea. 'Apparently. The story goes that it was a power play. Mielikki had created her greatest work – a tree with life-giving properties, securing the Rookery's foundations so that it didn't crumble – and then Pellervoinen slapped an enormous abbey around it, ultimately trapping her tree in a stone prison.'

'Ah, so a real gentleman,' said Alice as they trekked away from the entreating cries of the market sellers and towards the imposing abbey.

'Exactly,' said Bea, pulling aside the heavy entrance door. 'A man trying to compensate for his insecurities with an act of aggression,' she added in her cut-glass voice as they stepped into the abbey. 'Who'd have thought it?'

The abbey's bell tower was an empty shell, and the long nave inside – which should have held aisles, wooden benches and an altar – was simply an enormous dusty room. Its only feature was the hole in the floor which announced a winding subterranean staircase. The wonders of the Abbey Library were far below ground.

Alice followed Bea through the hole and down the worn stairwell. The oil lamps illuminated roughly hewn walls that became smoother the lower she went. Corridors sloped off from the stairs, receding into darkness, but Alice stayed the course until they emerged together onto the upper floor of a vast atrium.

The library was the most magnificent open space she had seen. The earth below the abbey's shell had been hollowed out. Far above them, in the cobbled square behind the bell tower, was a cordoned-off glass surface that acted as a vast skylight for the underground library. In the centre of the atrium stood a two-hundred-foot-tall tree: the Summer Tree. Its leafy crown reached far over Alice's head to press against the glass ceiling, which was bracketed with elegant steel girders arching up from the upper stonework.

Leaves spilled from the tree's branches, beautifully tapered: matt green on one side and a glossy, richer green on the other. The tree's twisted trunk was buried in the atrium floor five storeys below, and flagstones lay over its swollen roots.

She paused for a moment to appreciate the tree's immensity. It seemed to throb with life and reminded her of a caged animal, fighting to free itself. Stooped boughs were crushed against the walls; branches and twigs curled around corners and ran along corridors, their spindly shoots coiling around pillars and arches. A granite staircase wrapped around the tree and landings ran off it, leading to other floors filled with narrow passageways, shelves and alcoves, all spilling over with books.

The early evening sky outside was dull, but the atrium was alight with the glow of tens of thousands of fireflies. Signs everywhere warned visitors not to touch them – the Lampyridae. They had been known to bite.

Alice followed Bea down the staircase to the courtyard on the ground floor. Around them, and moving purposefully along corridors, were librarians wearing black aprons with front pockets full of books. Other members drifted around, leafing through journals and stacks of reading materials.

'Something's wrong,' Bea murmured. 'This doesn't . . . feel right.'

Alice glanced at her, but Bea was staring up at the leaves with a frown.

A handful of people wearing small wooden badges on their collars were also ignoring the library's stock, and were, like Bea, focused only on the Summer Tree. They moved with quiet industry, murmuring among themselves, hurrying to inspect the roots with an extended clinometer and standing back to peer up at the branches. Alice watched as a man with red hair in a severe parting approached the trunk, a tape measure in hand and a pair of polished mahogany-and-leather binoculars hanging from his neck.

'What's he doing?' asked Alice, distracting Bea from whatever had caused her to frown.

There was a long pause as they stared at the man, fascinated. His face was as red as his hair as he repeatedly approached and retreated from the tree in a crab-like motion. It was like watching a matador dance with an invisible bull.

'I think . . . he's trying to measure the tree's girth without the fireflies turning on him,' said Bea. 'He hasn't got a chance. They're rebuffing him quite politely so far, but if he persists he'll be lucky not to lose an arm.'

The fireflies – stationed at the tree to protect it from potential attackers – were carnivorous.

'Which reminds me,' said Bea, turning to Alice. 'Keep your distance. The only reason they haven't yet gone for his throat is that they can sense he's bound to the tree they're protecting, and so less likely to do it any harm. You, however, with your one portion of the draught, don't have that same security.'

Alice nodded, turning from the redhead and his increasingly daring lunges. She had seen the fireflies at work the previous year; they'd savaged August's arm like a pack of wild dogs. She knew the risks – but they hadn't attacked her then, though they'd had the opportunity.

Bea strode off to collar one of the workers holding a clipboard while Alice peered up through the tree's branches. She couldn't help but feel a strange sense of affection for it. She'd had a single dose of the binding draught, and all of her aches and pains had vanished – she'd felt well again, after months of illness. She owed this tree a debt of gratitude.

Her eyes drifted down the trunk and followed the course of the tangled roots. The courtyard stones were laid over them unevenly. Had they been so irregular on her last visit a year ago? She bent down to trace a hand along one of the exposed roots, her fingers tingling at the throb of power emitted by the tree. Magellan must be right: if any plant was likely to have a soul, this one surely would. A single humming firefly drifted closer, and Alice hurriedly removed her hand from the bark – but it landed on the back of her palm, glowing gently. She stared at it in fascination.

'Governor?' said the redhead behind her in surprise. The firefly darted off at the noise.

Gabriel Whitmore was standing by the wall at the edge of the courtyard, his arms folded across his broad chest and his brow furrowed. He was so still that Alice wondered how long he'd been watching, unseen.

'If I'd known you were coming, sir . . .'

Whitmore's mouth pinched.

'Pass me your measuring tape,' said the governor dismissively. He approached the group of librarians, his usual elegance replaced with abruptness.

The group of badge-wearers hovered uncertainly around the perspiring redhead, apparently unsure how to behave in the presence of the head of their House.

'You don't have a yardstick?' Whitmore asked him, striding purposefully around the trunk.

'No, sir,' he replied. 'If I'd known you were coming, sir, I'd have—'

'Well perhaps in future,' said Whitmore, his voice laced with sarcasm, 'I'll ensure you're fully briefed on my daily diary. That way, you'll always have precisely what I need, when I need it.' Staring up at the tree from the other side of the courtyard, he shook his head and tossed the tape measure aside. 'The clinometer,' he said, clicking his fingers for attention.

The redhead snatched it from someone else's hands and hurried to hand it over. Then they watched in silence as Whitmore squinted up at the crown and made some measurements from a distance. Finally, he returned and handed back the equipment.

'Everything is as expected,' he said with a tight smile.

A middle-aged woman with hair in old-fashioned rolls frowned at her clipboard. 'But Governor, our measurements suggest—'

'Do they suggest,' he interrupted smoothly, 'that the tree is being tended as it should?' The light in his eyes was cold despite the thin-lipped smile. 'Is that . . . what the numbers on your clipboard suggest?'

Silence.

'Good,' he said brightly. 'That's as I thought.'

He turned sharply and his gaze fell across Bea and Alice. A flicker of interest crossed his face. 'Beatrice,' he said with a nod of acknowledgement. 'And our successful candidate. You took the binding draught in the end, I see.'

'Yes,' said Alice.

'Congratulations,' he said, his smile widening. 'I do like the brave ones.' Then he turned and swept up the winding staircase.

Bea watched him go with a shrewd look, before murmuring so that only Alice could hear. 'It looks like someone's trying to avoid a scandal,' she said. 'The Council and Houses must be putting real pressure on us to order an investigation like this.'

'Has the tree actually grown?' Alice asked quietly.

'Who knows, darling?' said Bea, glancing up at it and ushering Alice further away from the others. 'It's been stable for hundreds of years, but you felt that rumbling in the grass the other night.'

'Surely it's a good thing,' said Alice. 'The tree is growing stronger.'

'If it gets out that the tree is growing,' said Bea, glancing around and urging Alice to keep walking, 'the other Houses might consider it a challenge to their authority. There's been a rivalry between the four Houses since they were founded. It doesn't help that we currently have a Pellervoinen chancellor in charge of the Rookery, and frankly, darling, they hate us.'

Alice's forehead grew lined. 'Why would that be a challenge? Because it'll look like – what? Posturing, if Mielikki's tree grows?'

'Because it will look like a power grab,' said Bea, clutching her jangling necklace in one hand. 'There's always been speculation about our connection to the tree. Rumours – started by us, of course – that if the tree grows, the strength of Mielikki's legacy could grow with it.'

Alice's blood began to race at the prospect. The grass had grown so quickly outside the maze.

'And is it true?' she asked quietly.

Bea sighed. 'I want to say no,' she murmured. 'But really, who knows?'

Alice swallowed and peered up at the canopy. Her pains and fevers had stopped after a normal dose of the binding draught. If the tree's growth signalled a power surge for the members of the House, then she could only imagine how invigorated she would be by a second, more powerful draught. And if her Mielikki legacy were strengthened, might it enable her to control the flight of her deadly soul and ensure it was never released again?

Excitement and relief fluttered together in her chest, and she smiled as she peered into the depths of the tree's branches. She needed that second binding draught to increase her link with it. Fast.

11

'Watch this,' said Tom, peering over his glasses.

Alice had plonked herself in one of the squashy university library chairs, hunched over as she tried to organize copies of Magellan's notes for Reid. Tom was lounging in the modern languages aisle, a book open on the floor next to him. He twitched his fingers over the paper and the pages began to turn of their own accord.

'That's the laziest use of our legacy I've ever seen,' said Bea, appearing from an aisle to shove an armful of books onto a metal trolley shelf.

'I've never been able to do it before,' said Tom.

'Oh give over,' Bea scoffed. 'I've seen you move wooden tables with a flick of your wrist.'

'Brute force,' said Tom. 'This is different. The fine motor skills are harder. It's . . .' He slowed the movements of his fingers and the pages followed the pace. His jaw was tight with concentration. 'Very delicate work.'

He pinched his fingers and the book snapped shut. 'Have either of you noticed things getting easier?' he asked, a curious look in his eye.

'If you're finding the mastery of books so easy,' said Bea with a heaving sigh, 'feel free to help me sort out the shelf that's been infested with booklice.'

'Booklice?' said Alice, twisting her mum's signet ring around her finger. Slightly too big – she wondered if she ought to have it altered so it wouldn't fall off. She glanced down at it. With its scuffs and the four scratches over its face, she doubted anyone else would care about losing it.

'Our waterlogged books have somehow, despite hours of care, grown mould – and booklice can't get enough of the stuff,' Bea said bitterly. 'If I lose the whole collection because of that bloody janitor, I'll go after his topiary ducks again. I mean it.'

She marched off with an irritable huff and Alice turned back to Tom, wondering about his sharpened skills. A sign the Mielikki legacy *was* growing, surely?

'I've started reading Cecil's book,' she said after a moment. 'It's actually quite good.'

'Swot,' said Tom with a grin.

She swiped up a book and was about to throw it at him, when a disapproving look from Bea, at the end of an aisle, forced her to lower it.

'Tell us what it says,' he said. 'No one's ever got further than the front cover before.'

'Well, it has a foreword from Chancellor Litmanen—' she started.

'Abort, abort,' Tom hissed urgently.

'And he . . .' She trailed away at Bea's expression of white-faced rage.

'Is the worst chancellor the Rookery has ever had,' spat Bea, drawing closer. 'A big Pellervoinen lummox who thinks far too much of himself!'

Alice's eyes widened at the strength of Bea's reaction. 'He's . . .

quite complimentary about the last Mielikki chancellor,' she said. 'Speaks . . . very highly of the House in general.'

'Well, he would,' said Bea with a moue of distaste. 'It's a book of House Mielikki's biggest stars and he's good at playing to a crowd and telling them what they want to hear. Insufferable man,' she muttered. 'He's not fit to speak the name of Leda Westergard. She was the best leader this city's ever seen, and everyone knows it.'

She stormed off with a stack of books under her arm, and Alice looked to Tom for an explanation.

'Lady Pelham-Gladstone has moved in the same circles as the Rookery's finest,' he whispered. 'She and our current chancellor had . . . a bit of a falling out.' He smiled, shoved his glasses further up his nose and went back to his book.

Alice cleared her throat and smoothed a hand over Magellan's notes. Reid had split them into sections and had insisted Alice allocate each its own folder. A tedious job, because the professor had not seen fit to label each section properly, making it impossible to find where one ended and another began. With a sigh, Alice flipped through them, and then suddenly she stopped.

There was a piece of paper that didn't belong. It was a different texture to the rest of the stack – thin, with a light sheen. She slid it out and frowned at it, a flare of anger rearing up from nowhere.

It was a leaflet, emblazoned with the words *He is Coming* above the picture of a white feather. It belonged to the Fellowship of the Pale Feather – August's one-time employer, and the hopelessly twee name of a Rookery death cult who worshipped Tuoni. She glanced at the feathers of her own pale nightjar, sitting on the back of her chair, and back at the picture.

She felt disconcerted. Why did Reid have this in her stack of notes? It could be accidental; Alice had seen other leaflets and fly posters around the university, trying to spread the word of Marianne Northam and increase her followers. Or maybe . . . Reid was one of those followers herself? Marianne had infiltrated the Runners with her people, so why not the university too?

Alice pinched the thin paper carefully between two fingers as though it might contaminate her. By rights, a death cult who worshipped her biological father should have extended its worship to Alice – their very own messiah. Except that Marianne had seen Alice as a rival and they'd hated each other at first sight. So what might it mean for her if Reid was in the Fellowship?

'Oh,' said Tom. 'You've got one of those as well? They're everywhere.' He held up his book with a smile. 'I've started using one as a bookmark.'

Alice stared at it. Maybe she was being too suspicious. She scrunched it into a ball and let it fall into her lap. However, in light of recent events, she didn't feel like taking any chances, and decided to examine Reid's nightjar again at her earliest opportunity.

With a puff, Bea slapped a handful of books down on the nearest table, causing the students nearby to jump. 'If we're doing this properly, we should do it at a table,' she said.

Alice watched, confused, as Tom staggered to his feet.

'Doing what properly?' Alice asked.

Tom licked his lips nervously. 'Lester's meeting us here. To talk.'

Alice's eyes widened in alarm and she rose from the chair. 'Now?'

Bea nodded. 'I thought a public place was best, and this is a more neutral ground than the House.' She opened a book at random and sighed. The pages looked like Swiss cheese. 'You can sit in, if you like. The big wazzock's due any minute—'

'I've had better welcomes,' grunted a voice over Alice's shoulder.

She gritted her teeth but didn't turn to face him. Lester limped to her side, stopped and bent down. She could see the back of his head and his thickset neck, glistening with sweat. An old scar stretched up into his hairline. When he stood again, the scrunched Fellowship leaflet was in his hands. He opened it, glanced at the text and shoved it at her.

'Thinking of joining?' he asked with a sly smile. His tiny rosebud mouth was too small for his broad face. 'What makes you think Marianne would have you?'

First-name terms? Alice thought, her eyes narrowing. She glanced at his offering, her stomach tensing at the sight of his stocky arms, where other scars crossed his skin. Marianne was a powerful hemomancer who controlled her little cult using their blood. She cut them with a lancet to do it . . . and she enjoyed leaving a scar. Were Lester's scars ordinary, or something more menacing? She stared at him, at the calculating glint in his eye, then snatched the leaflet from him and stuffed it into Reid's folder.

With a snap of wings, Kuu rose higher, fluttering about in a supportive temper and clacking her beak at him. Alice felt a rush of affection for the bothersome bird and raised a single eyebrow at Lester, emboldened.

Lester's gaze flickered down and Alice hugged the folder to her chest, hiding the Magellan Institute name stamped on the front. The less he knew about her, the better. If he was one of Marianne's, he might already know *everything*. She swallowed hard, the message carved in wood flashing across her memory. *Murderer.*

'I'll leave you to your mediation,' she said, her face carefully blank.

He snorted a laugh. 'I'm not here for mediation. I'm here for an apology.' He cast an accusing eye over Tom, who was sitting at the table, his legs twitching underneath, and Bea, who looked back at him critically.

'One of you has been bad-mouthing me to the Mowbrays,' he said, his gaze pausing on Tom. 'They're sending solicitors after me for something *you* fucked up.'

'None of us have spoken with the Mowbrays,' said Bea coldly. 'But unless you want us to speak with the *Runners* about your assault on Tom, and on university property, I suggest you *sit down* so that we can iron this out.'

Lester didn't move a muscle.

'You'll get one chance to do this Tom's way,' said Bea, her voice bright but edged with steel, 'or we can do it my way, which ends with you thrown out of the House on your arse, darling. Which is it?'

He yanked a chair aside and thumped down into it. 'Talk, then,' he muttered.

Alice hovered for just a moment and gathered up the rest of her things. 'I'll catch you later,' she told Bea and Tom – who was white-faced.

Lester turned his whole body around to watch her, his right hand rubbing his knee unconsciously. The limp, she realized. She'd given it to him.

Alice walked away, certain she could feel his eyes on her back. But when she reached the corridor and glanced over her shoulder to check, he was staring at Tom across the table. She paused, taking advantage of the space between them to concentrate. Her eyes narrowed. *There.* His nightjar stood on his forearm, which rested on the tabletop. A small bird with plain, light brown feathers, its wings were stretched as wide as possible and its head was bowed, its beak tucked down into its feathery chest. It exuded menace. But if it showed signs he was a member of the Fellowship, she couldn't see them. She would have to look into its memories to confirm that, which required her to get right up close and personal with him.

Lip curling at the prospect, Alice breathed deeply and slipped away.

'More copies,' Reid had demanded. She wanted a second copy of her notes run through the Ditto machine – one to keep in the lab and another to keep at home, presumably in case she was struck by inspiration while she was brushing her teeth for bed.

The Ditto machine was close to the library. After her brief run-in with Lester, Alice had been tempted to put off Reid's request until another day, to avoid bumping into him on his way out. But she'd had a swift change of heart when she'd realized that a one-on-one meeting with the hulking brute was exactly what she needed.

If she could just get him alone, without Bea or Tom or anyone else seeing her, she could try sliding into his nightjar's memories. It was unlikely his soul-bird would agree to this, so it would require either guile or force. Since Lester was twice her size and a fully fledged member of House Mielikki – a mentor, no less – it would have to be guile. Maybe she was leaping to conclusions about the Fellowship, but she needed to know for sure. If Lester was a member of the death cult, it added a disturbing new dimension to his attack. It might be a sign Marianne was moving against her . . . a sign the new life Alice was building could still fall apart.

Alice breathed shakily. She wished one of her friends from Coram House were here. People who knew her secrets, who had been there when she'd dealt with Marianne before. It was exhausting keeping parts of her identity hidden all the time. For the first time in months, her need to see Crowley felt overwhelming. But of course, Crowley knew exactly what it was like to live with secrets, and to lie to those closest to you. She swallowed thickly and shook it off for another time. Right now, Lester was still in the building. She needed to find him.

Alice grabbed Reid's folders and set off with a determined stride. The Arlington Building was quiet. Alice could sense the scholarly industry behind the doors in the corridors: the hum and murmur of lectures and seminars on law, English, philosophy, art, languages and history. She passed the offices of the various deans, and the reprographics room loudly churning out papers in purple ink. She paused outside, just briefly, before continuing past, the folders clutched under one arm.

The library was nearby, and her shoulders tensed as she rounded the corner towards it. No sign of Lester. No sign of anyone. She breathed in the perfumed polish on the wainscoting which reflected the light from the tall windows along the hallway. Huge paintings sat on the walls between the rooms, adorned with elaborate gilded frames and depicting the sort of pseudo-religious scenes that she felt sure Marianne Northam would admire. A shiver of disgust rippled down her spine at the thought of the woman, and she hastened along the corridor, eyes scoping left and right.

She heard footsteps behind her and sidestepped to the left, turning towards the noise just a fraction too late. A glancing blow struck her from behind and Alice's skull vibrated as she was pitched forward. The folder tumbled from her hands and slid along the corridor as the momentum sent her crashing into the wainscoting. Her back slammed against the polished wood, knocking the breath from her lungs. Struggling for air and punch drunk, she pushed herself onto her hands and knees with a groan. She swayed back and forth, her arms trembling and eyes searching for her attacker.

But the corridor was empty.

'What the hell—'

A deafening crack resounded overhead and she flinched. *Crack. Crack. Crack.* A series of sharp blows snapped through the corridor like falling dominoes. *The walls!* The wainscoting was fracturing. The wooden panels split in half, one after the other. Splintered fragments burst from the seams as snaking cracks opened in the grain.

Dazed, Alice made to crawl sideways, but jagged shards of wood sprang loose from the panelling and thudded onto the floor, barring her path. *Too close.* She hitched a breath and spun on her knees in a bid to clear the danger, but stilled as she turned into a serrated chunk of oak. It pressed against her chest, the pointed tip digging under her ribs. She didn't dare breathe again as she slowly inched backwards. But a sliver of pointed wood jabbed the back of her neck and she froze. *Trapped.*

Spiked shards of broken wood surrounded her, all of them pointing inwards. The wood panelling . . . had ruptured and reassembled itself around her body, hemming her in. Keen-edged spears of oak angled inches from her skin. Her adrenaline surged, telling her to get away, but she ruthlessly stamped it down. One wrong move and she would be skewered.

Against every instinct, she became utterly motionless. There was no more sign of movement.

'Okay,' she said, trying to keep her voice steady. She was trapped so neatly she couldn't move her arm to check the wound on her head. It wasn't painful – shock had numbed it – but she could feel warm blood seeping down the back of her neck.

'How about we call it a draw?' she said into the empty corridor, trying to lure him out. 'My head for your knee?'

Laughter, short and abrupt, echoed like gunfire. Her pulse jumped.

'Kuu?' she whispered.

Her nightjar blinked into view with an agitated flutter. Alice steadied her breathing and held its gaze.

'Bird's-eye view.'

Stretching its pale wings, the nightjar rose into the air, its tail feathers extended and its legs tucked under its breast. Alice opened her mind to the sensation of flashing images, and then reached for the composure to separate her cumbersome human body from her nightjar's vision. The scene laid out below her was one of destruction. Plaster dust and debris were strewn across mangled wooden planks – choppy piles of spiked timber surrounded Alice on every side. From above, she appeared trapped between the teeth of a vicious predator.

The nightjar swooped lower before gliding to the window. It was then that Alice saw the shadow fall across her back. There was someone watching – hiding in a nearby doorway or approaching from the corner.

With a screech, the nightjar looped around, picking up speed, determined to identify Lester's exact position . . .

Alice gasped.

The link with her nightjar's vision broke.

The wood . . . She blinked fiercely, tears of panic and pain forming in her eyes. The shard of jagged oak pressed under her ribs was *moving*. Embedded in a cluttered mound of shattered timber, it drove towards her. Its tip pierced her cotton jumper. She scrabbled to push it away, wrapping both hands around it and thrusting, but it was no use. The wooden spike met flesh.

'Bea!' she shrieked, fear chilling her blood. '*Bea! Tom!*'

The spike punctured her skin . . . Her nightjar soared through the air and landed on her shoulder. It churred comfortingly, rubbing its head against her wet cheeks. Alice pushed the bird away and tightened her grip on the wood. With an explosive exhale she urged the surface to disintegrate. Her palm tingled with pent-up power and the wooden spike turned to ash under her fingers.

Her relief was short-lived. Another spear shunted closer to take its place. Hands still smarting, she grabbed it and willed it to wither and rot. It too crumbled. But another took its place, and another. *Too many, too close.* Alice stared at her nightjar in disbelief, her hands trembling as a shard slid under her ribs. All thoughts vanished as the wood began to push into her chest. A drop of her blood splattered on the tiles . . .

She couldn't stop the wood. But she could stop a *person*. A person whose lifeblood would attract her deadly soul like a magnet . . . *No.* Oh God, what was she thinking? She could never—

Another bead of blood splashed the floor. The pain sharpened and she gave in. 'Kuu,' she moaned. 'Go.'

Her nightjar cawed and butted her shoulder in understanding. Then it unfolded its wings, bent its legs and lifted off, just as a clatter of footsteps turned the corner and came to a skidding halt.

'What in the name of Ukko's hammer is going on?' shouted Bea, aghast.

The cord linking Alice to her nightjar grew thinner as it increased its distance. The glow dimmed, and Alice stared at it in horror. 'Bea,' she breathed. 'No. Go away.'

A bolt of electricity hit Alice in the spine. She snapped backwards, her muscles cramping, and relaxed as she exhaled sharply.

She fought to maintain her consciousness, to hold her human shape. A dark hunger pricked at the edges of her consciousness. A throb of warmth nearby stirred some part of her buried deep inside. No. No. Not Bea. Her deadly soul began to peel away from her body, particle by particle. She mentally fought to hold it down, to trap it inside. But it was drawn to the life pulsating in the corridor – vivid and dynamic. To Bea.

'Kuu,' she begged. '*Kuu. Come back.*'

12

Alice's chest was tight. She prodded it with a finger and found it wadded with cotton dressings and surgical tape. Cranking open one eye, she squinted at her surroundings. She was in her room, bundled up under a blanket on the bed. A whisper of rain pelted the windows and slid down the glass, distorting her view of the gardens beyond the Whiston Building. She frowned into the gloom.

'It's not supposed to rain in June,' she murmured.

'Actually, for the past few years, June has been the fourth-wettest month of the year.' Her gaze drifted sideways and found Tom sitting on a Victorian school chair, peering over at her. 'Fifty millimetres of rainfall, on average.' He smiled, blue eyes gleaming.

She made to sit up, and hissed at the sudden sting under her ribs.

'Careful,' he said. 'The nurse had to use butterfly stitches.'

'Tom, I . . .'

She trailed off, her eyes sliding away from his, searching out the room. There was a distinct absence of aristocratic dynamism. An absence that slowed her heart and stuck in her throat.

'Where's Bea?' she croaked. 'Is she – oh God, Tom—'

'She's downstairs,' he soothed. 'She had to put the corridor back together.'

Her mouth opened and closed. 'She's – she's not—'

The door swung open and Bea burst into the room, necklace jangling and long patterned dress flowing around her like something alive. Alice sank into her pillows, weak with relief. Bea's hair was pinned back into a bun, shot through with what at first appeared to be two long pins but which, on closer inspection, turned out to be shards of wood.

'You've got wainscoting in your hair,' Alice said, brows furrowing.

Bea patted the bun. 'I had some pieces left over and I couldn't for the life of me figure out where they went. Jigsaws were never my forte.'

Tom cleared his throat, and it was so unusually assertive that they both turned to him in surprise. 'Alice,' he said with a penetrating look. 'What happened?'

They listened in silence while she recounted what she knew of the scene in the corridor. She found herself spilling the news that she'd had a previous attack, though she left out the message that had called her a murderer. While she talked, Bea moved closer to examine the window frame, her expression serious.

'And you think you heard someone outside your door?' said Bea. 'The night of the first attack?'

'Yes.'

'Well, who's got access to the staff accommodation, other than us?' she asked, gesturing at herself and Tom.

Alice shook her head. On this part of the floor there were only four apartments: hers and Holly's empty unit at this end, and at the other end one belonged to a nervy old woman who worked in the Department of Legacy Disciplines and the other to a reclusive researcher in the Sydenham Building. She'd checked out their nightjars when she'd first moved in, and they were dull as ditchwater and totally harmless.

'Holly's parents,' she said, 'and *Lester*. He knew which entrance led up here; he was trying to access it the day he . . .' She swallowed. 'And the way Holly used to talk, I think he'd visited her up here. If he knew which apartment was hers, he'd have known which was mine.'

'Oh God,' said Bea. 'You don't think they were—'

'No,' said Alice with a shudder. 'I hope not.'

'You think . . . Lester did this?' asked Tom, his face falling.

'I think he blamed me for his fall from the banister,' she said.

'Then it's my fault,' Tom said quietly. 'That would never have happened if he hadn't felt justified in attacking me. It's only because of me that you were even there.'

'No,' said Bea, her face pale. 'It's my fault. I could have reported him to Whitmore for what he did to Tom, but I didn't.'

'But only because *I* asked you not to,' said Tom, staring down at his lap, his face unreadable.

Alice glanced up at Tom's and Bea's nightjars, competing for guilt as they swooped overhead with twitches and agitated jerks.

'I'm going to resign my post at the House,' said Tom, rising, his face strained. 'I can't administer the draught again. I should have done it sooner.'

'No, Tom, don't be silly, darling,' said Bea, grabbing his sleeve and pulling him back into his chair.

'You can't let him have that much power over you,' said Alice.

They lapsed into a tense silence, only broken when Bea spoke again, her nose wrinkled in thought.

'Two revenge attacks because of the incident in the stairwell?' she said. 'Even for that awful cretin, it's a bit extreme.'

Alice hesitated. 'Maybe that wasn't the only reason,' she said carefully. A memory flashed into her mind that left her cold. *Murderer.* 'Maybe it was because I was the only candidate who survived the binding draught, on the night his own protégée died?'

Tom flinched.

After a moment, Bea nodded and Alice relaxed. 'He's always been bitter about others' success,' said Bea.

'We'll have to be on our guard from now on,' said Alice.

'Never mind being on our guard,' said Bea. 'We've got to report him to the Runners.'

'No,' Alice said quickly. 'I don't want them involved. I'd rather . . .' She couldn't explain to them why she despised the Runners so much. Infiltrated by Marianne's Fellowship bent on their own plans, Alice had lost faith in them long ago – even before their commanding officer, Reuben Risdon, had killed her best friend.

'No Runners,' she said firmly. 'Not yet. We don't have any solid evidence.'

'No,' said Bea in a clipped voice. 'Darling, I'm sorry, but look at you. He could have killed you.'

'Please, Bea. Just . . .'

Bea sat back in her chair, crossing her arms with a deep frown.

'I should be the one to contact them,' said Alice, changing tack. 'Let me be the one to do it. Okay?'

Bea's eyes narrowed, but she gave a grudging nod.

Alice's wound had healed rapidly. The university nurse had said it might be a fortnight before the butterfly stitches came off, but in only two days, the cut on her chest had scabbed over and she was bursting with energy. She needed to burn it off after forty-eight hours in bed – most of which had been spent sketching and trying to communicate with Kuu about how, if they were to trust one another, the bird must never allow Alice's soul to be released again. It wasn't some accidental mishap or unknown flaw that had forced Kuu to 'go'; Alice had done it herself. She'd *told* the bird to leave – but the nightjar must never follow that order again. And as soon as Alice shored up her Mielikki legacy with the second portion of binding draught, those reckless instincts might fade away too.

Sketching had always calmed her mind, and now her sketchbooks were filled with nightjars and buildings, trees and people. She had drawn Bea from memory last night, but she was out of practice and the likeness had been disappointing. She'd drawn the Summer Tree, over and over. For some reason, it had proven so much easier to remember the curves and texture of the tree than it had the planes of Bea's face – and yet she'd only seen the Summer Tree once in a year, while she saw Bea's face almost every day.

Finally, the cut healed, and Alice returned to work to find the university's entire student body buzzing with anticipation for the annual Cream of the Crops competition, being held on the lawns that evening.

Easing herself into a chair, she glanced over at the professor, wondering if the woman had even realized she'd been missing for two days. One quick glance told her all she needed to know about Reid's current state of mind. The professor's nightjar looked frazzled. Its dark feathers were rumpled and its wings refused to lie flush with its body. With its complex pattern of chocolate browns striped with beige and its distinctive speckled breast, it resembled a song thrush, save for the wider, flattened head. Alice watched it carefully. *Magellan's Nightjar Compendium* had had a lot to say about feather patterns. The speckles clearly marked Reid as having Pellervoinen's legacy.

Alice chewed thoughtfully on the end of her pencil. Kuu's feathers were plain white. There was nothing to indicate she had the patterns associated with Mielikki. Was that a sign that her Mielikki skills were genetically subordinate to her Tuoni legacy?

Reid's sharp footsteps recaptured Alice's attention. There was nothing particularly sinister about the professor's nightjar. It seemed tired, like Reid, but not in a state of active aggression. Alice wondered if it was worth probing the subject of the Fellowship and watching for lies or unusual responses. Because of the attack she still hadn't dealt with the matter of the leaflet she'd found in the folder.

The professor stood back from the blackboard erected along the length of the room. It was not a blackboard in the traditional sense, since it was in fact a block of polished hematite mounted to the wall. Dark greyish-black and formed from crystals of glimmering iron oxide, it seemed to sparkle in the right light.

Reid examined a calculation she'd chalked up. One hand stretched up to trace it from the start, along the messy algebraic equation to the solution at the end. Which, judging by her reaction, was wrong.

'It's *not* a simple change of direction if it creates a domino effect that changes everything else!' she hissed under her breath.

She hurled the white chalk across the room, where it pinged off a coffee cup and rattled under a desk. Both hands went to her hair and she scraped it back, clutching the curls, pulling them so tight her wrinkles smoothed out.

'I'm done,' she announced. 'I'm done for today. For *every* day!'

With a petulant grunt, she yanked her hands free of her hair, and Alice's eyebrow lifted at the sight of the white dust covering the curls. She looked like a Georgian noblewoman in a powdered wig.

Reid flicked her hand at the blackboard and the chalk equation vanished. With one vicious finger, she stabbed at the hematite and scrawled something across it. She stood back, and Alice squinted at the glittering black rock, where the professor had used her legacy to carve the word *Done!* into the hard surface as though it was butter. Then Reid snatched up the folders piled on her own desk and stormed over to Alice's.

'Did you copy those files I asked you to sort *days* ago?'

Alice winced. She'd forgotten. Bea had kept them safe for her after Lester's attack, but they were now sitting, un-copied, in Alice's in-tray again.

'I'll do it now,' she said with forced breeziness. She'd just reached out for the topmost stack of papers when Reid emitted a strangled sound. The folders Reid was carrying thumped to the floor, several pages skittering under the desk. The professor's bony fingers yanked at Alice's sleeve and shucked it up, exposing her wrists.

Reid bore down on her, squeezing Alice's arm, her eyes wide with apoplexy.

'What is it?' said Alice, peering up at her in alarm. 'What's wrong?'

Reid's face was nearly bloodless. Her stare was wild – manic – as her eyes darted over Alice, studying her with an intensity that was intrusive.

'But you . . . Where did you . . .?' Reid hissed incoherently, her gaze flickering over Alice's clothing, the ring on her finger, her cluttered desk. 'How could you *possibly* . . .?'

Reid's fingers clenched harder around Alice's cotton shirt, her nails digging deeper. The skin pinched, and there was a small flare of pain. Alice tried to pull away, confusion and irritation swiftly transforming into anger.

'Stop it,' Alice snapped. 'What the hell do you think you're—?'

Reid's hand flew open with such force that Alice's arm was flung back to the desk. Her elbow caught the folder of papers in her in-tray and sent them cascading over the floor.

Reid stared at them, her face twisted and her hands shaking.

Alice's eyes darted straight to Reid's nightjar. The little bird was trembling with shock and panic – and overlaying her emotions, Alice was able to pick out another strong sense washing over the professor. Vivian Reid had a shameful secret – and her nightjar had never even hinted at such until this very moment.

Alice opened her mouth to question her, but without a single word of explanation, Reid grabbed her folders, spun around and staggered from the room like a drunkard.

Alice sat in confused silence for several minutes, unable to process exactly what had happened. Reid had once thrown a mug through a window. She'd shouted and spoken harshly, her words barbed. But she'd never stooped to manhandling Alice in one of her temper tantrums before.

Alice rubbed her arm, frowning. That deranged woman would never touch her again, that was for sure. But what the hell had set her off? And what was she hiding? Something to do with that Fellowship leaflet? Alice examined the red marks on her skin, left by the professor's nails, and shook her head, disgruntled.

Well, she could forget the photocopying, Alice decided bitterly. She moved to snatch up the folder of papers that had slipped to the floor. Gathering them together, she shoved them into

Reid's marble cabinet, under her desk. But the professor didn't return.

There was a rap at the door several hours later and Alice stared at it suspiciously. If that was Reid, back for round two . . . She slipped off her stool and swung the door wide.

'Yes?' she demanded.

There was a figure waiting for her in the corridor, leaning against the wall with hands in her pockets. It wasn't an apologetic Reid.

'Sasha?'

Alice's shoulders sank with relief at the sight of her.

Thank God.

Right now, a familiar face outside the myopic university campus was exactly what she wanted to see. Someone she could unload on without holding back. Someone who knew exactly what she was going through – Sasha had once feared her own legacy. Skilled with water, she'd blamed herself for her sister's drowning and suppressed her gift until it exploded out of her. The frequent cause of flooding when they'd lived together at Coram House, Sasha had taken tentative steps towards accepting her legacy. They might not see each other every day – or even every fortnight now – but there was always something comforting about being with Sasha, even if she was the least sentimental person Alice had ever met.

She moved forward to greet her friend, and Sasha held up a hand. 'Oh no. We're not huggers. Put those arms away.'

Alice couldn't help but laugh. It punctured the tension building in her chest, and she felt a new lightness steal over her.

'You have no idea how pleased I am to see you,' said Alice.

Sasha had caught the sun, and her already-dark skin was a deeply rich shade of brown. She was wearing a pair of wide trousers with braces over a maroon blouse, her halo of springy black curls tied back with a matching bandana. Her unique sense of style always made Alice feel depressingly unfashionable.

On her shoulder sat her nightjar. The bird, simply patterned, with downy, mussed-up feathers in an earthy palette, was calmly watching Alice.

'Fancy a drink?' said Sasha. 'And then you can explain why you're looking at me with heart eyes, and why you've been sneaking around with Worzel Gummidge.'

'Who?'

Sasha pushed away from the wall, leaving Alice to quickly grab her bag from the lab and hurry after her.

'The human scarecrow . . . August,' Sasha tutted. 'I can't deal with your lack of eighties pop culture references. *Modern history.* Aren't you supposed to be a history graduate?'

'Funnily enough,' said Alice, 'eighties pop culture didn't come up much in my dissertation about Bismarck's unification of Germany.'

They looked at each other. A grin crept onto Alice's face, and an answering smirk slid across Sasha's before she rolled her eyes and pushed through the door that led out to the quadrangle.

'He's been cagey about it,' said Sasha. 'But I have spies everywhere. One of them saw you together. Not *together* together – Crowley would kill him – just *together*.'

'Someone saw us at The Necropolis?' asked Alice.

'You went to The Necropolis?' asked Sasha, suddenly animated. 'Why?'

'What? But *you* said—Then who saw us?' said Alice, confused.

'Pippa Stridley was drinking at The Rook's Nest and said she saw August with a woman. As soon as she described her – terrible hair, boring clothes, total lack of eighties pop culture knowledge – I knew straightaway it was you.'

Sasha stopped, and Alice shunted into the back of her.

'My curiosity,' said Sasha, 'stems from the fact that each time me and Jude arranged to meet up with you, August declined – he was always too busy with his top-secret new job to join us. But now it looks like he wasn't that busy after all.'

Alice winced. 'He was doing me a favour, that's all, but I didn't want to worry anyone.'

A new batch of wine-coloured berry clusters had erupted from the branches of the mulberry tree, drawing blackbirds and finches from the skies to feast on them. 'So go on then,' said Sasha, detouring across the cobbles towards the bench beneath the branches.

A pair of students approached from the other side of the quad with the same destination in mind, but Sasha beat them by seconds. She dropped down onto the bench and shot them a raised eyebrow.

One of them elbowed the other as they slunk away, the bronze telescopes poking from their satchels rattling and clinking. Astronomy students. One of them picked a berry from the tree as he passed and held it out on his palm. It swelled to the size of an apple, then a grapefruit. His friend murmured, 'How the hell are you doing that?'

'I don't know!' he answered, laughing. 'But it won't stop!'

'You should've entered the competition,' said his friend.

'I tried! Failed the preliminaries months ago!'

Two blackbirds, circling overhead, swooped towards the melon-sized berry with aggressive flutters and squawks. Hooting with laughter, the students tossed it away and pelted across the lawn towards the crowd packed in to watch the competition.

Alice watched them with a keen eye, thinking of her conversation with Bea at the abbey and Tom's new page-turning skills.

Sasha grabbed Alice's sleeve and pulled her down onto the bench.

'Go on then,' said Sasha. 'It's been a month. Fill me in.'

'You know I saw Crowley?' said Alice.

'Of course I do. He stole my visiting night, then came home and barely spoke for days.'

A solid thirty minutes or so later, in which Alice had opened the floodgates and allowed everything to spill out – the trip to The Necropolis, her death sentence, Holly, the House Mielikki test, the binding draught, the attacks, Reid – a frowning Sasha said, 'But you're okay now? Whatever you think had gone wrong, the draught has healed it?' Sasha leaned back, running a contemplative eye over Alice. 'You look better than last time I saw you.'

'I'm not sick any more,' Alice confirmed.

Sasha blew out a breath and shook her head in disbelief. 'Shit, Alice. Why would you keep that to yourself? Why didn't you tell me?'

Alice's mouth ran dry. 'I just . . . I didn't want to worry you with something you couldn't fix. But it's okay. As long as I get my hands on the other two doses of binding draught, I won't get sick again.'

Sasha looked at her, her expression serious, and Alice waited for the verdict. Then Sasha shook her head and made an apparent effort to normalize the tense atmosphere.

'So,' she said. 'You've been back in the Rookery about – what, six months? – and you've already found yourself with a mystery enemy. Classic Alice.'

Alice managed a wry smile. 'Not that mysterious.'

She tipped her head back and allowed her gaze to wander over the sky; dusk was beginning to draw in and there was no heat left in the air.

'So you don't know if this Lester guy is making lucky guesses or whether he's one of the Fellowship?' asked Sasha, pulling out two flasks and handing one to Alice.

Alice shook her head, uncapping the flask and taking a swig: gin and elderflower. 'Nope,' she said. 'And now I don't even know whether my boss, Vivian Reid, is caught up with Marianne too.'

'Sounds like you've been winning over lots of new friends here,' said Sasha as she loosened one of her braces. 'Where's your evidence your boss is involved with Northam?'

Alice struggled to raise a smile. 'I found a Fellowship leaflet in her paperwork.'

'Incriminating,' said Sasha, following Alice's eyeline to the sinking sun. 'Mind you, they toss those leaflets out like sweets. You'd probably find one in half the houses in the city. I once caught Jude using a folded one to clean the spokes of his wheel-chair, and he knows they're banned from the house.'

'Well . . . yeah, maybe. I just don't know any more. And I don't know how things stand anyway now. I mean, I know Marianne hates me, but technically . . . *technically*—'

'They should be worshipping you,' finished Sasha with a grin. 'A testament to how screwed up their thinking really is.'

'I think Marianne's a fraud,' replied Alice. 'I don't think she worships Tuoni as much as she worships power. If I hadn't been the fly in the ointment – if she'd actually managed to birth her own . . . *messiah* . . . with Tuoni . . .' Alice frowned and took a sip of her drink. 'Imagine if she'd been successful. She'd have used a baby to bring about total destruction – but only, I think, because *she'd* have enjoyed the power.'

'You've got to hand it to these tiger moms.'

Alice glanced sideways at Sasha and laughed shortly.

'If it was possible for that woman to have a child, it'd be the spawn of the devil, not the spawn of Death,' said Sasha, her hair bouncing as she leaned back. Then she added, 'You come out with the upper hand in that comparison, in case that wasn't clear.'

Alice smiled, and then lapsed into a sigh. She was suddenly very, very tired. A roar went up from the crowd on the lawns, and Sasha narrowed her eyes.

'Cream of the Crops competition,' explained Alice.

'Show me what kind of rubbish goes on in this place then,' said Sasha, getting to her feet and scooping up her flask of gin. She strode towards the source of excitement and Alice trekked after her.

Groups of students stood around with glasses of weak lager in their hands, laughing and cheering at something on the grass. Others sat cross-legged, watching with one eye as they chatted to friends. Every now and again, a whoop of delight would ripple outwards. The atmosphere was not so much that of an organized competition as a Sunday kick-about at the park. Drinking appeared to be the real priority.

On the grass, however, there were four competing groups – all wearing T-shirts bearing their House's symbol. The furthest two teams, half a dozen students representing Ahti and Ilmarinen, sat opposite each other with an old log between them. The bark was hissing with both steam and smoke while the students flicked and gestured at it, faces sweaty with determination.

'What are they doing?' asked Sasha.

'I think,' said Alice, 'the Ilmarinens are trying to set it on fire and the Ahtis are trying to keep it wet enough to stop them. It's a war of attrition.'

Sasha snorted derisively, and they both turned to peer at the groups representing Mielikki and Pellervoinen. A log lay between them too, except that this one was partially submerged in what appeared to be a huge glass basin of mud and steaming water. The outer layer of bark was ridged but appeared almost polished – and it was changing colour. Ripples of translucent orange, deep red and dark grey moved through it before returning to an earthy brown.

'What's going on there?' said Sasha.

'Pellervoinen are trying to petrify the wood into stone,' answered the person in front of them. It was the berry-growing astronomy student. He shot Sasha a nervous smile and then an admiring glance. 'It's how you fossilize wood. They're trying to replace the organic matter in the wood's cell walls with minerals and sediment. Stone versus plant. House Mielikki are trying to resist.'

Alice squinted to try to watch them more clearly, remembering the slices of ornamental stone tree and petrified tables made of quartz she'd seen at the market. She smiled to herself. She'd thought the trader was trying to scam her. *Stone* trees?

The astronomy student cleared his throat and then threw in casually, 'Hey, next year I'm going to enter this myself, if you wanted to come and . . .'

Sasha stared at him until he trailed away, red-faced. She stepped back from the crowd, shaking her head in bemusement. 'Weird,' she said, necking back a mouthful of gin. 'All of them.'

They headed back towards the quad and Alice glanced over at her.

'You know Crowley assumed I was with someone?' said Alice as the crowd erupted in another roar.

'I do know.'

'A guy called Tom. He works as a technician, but there's nothing – literally nothing – between us. Not like that.'

Sasha nodded and sat heavily on the empty bench. 'And . . . this is something you want me to slip casually into conversation?'

'I don't know,' said Alice, looking up at the cloudless sky. 'I don't know how to get past what he did.' Then, '*You* got past it,' she added. After all, Crowley had lied to all of them.

'We sat down and talked it through with him. Fully. Everything out on the table,' said Sasha. 'Have you tried that?'

Alice pulled a face. Sasha knew she hadn't.

'I'm still worried that if I talk to him I'll forgive him.' She shrugged. It sounded ridiculous when she said it out loud. Alice was just glad Sasha had come today. The way she'd been feeling about her situation and the possibility of Marianne rearing her ugly head again, she might easily have caved and sought him out, just to be with someone – anyone – that she didn't have to pretend with. But Sasha had scratched that itch for her instead.

Sasha nodded and took a slug of gin from her flask. 'Forgiving Crowley isn't a weakness,' she said at last. 'It isn't giving in, it's . . . moving on. And sometimes that takes more courage. It's harder to climb out of a trench and run across no-man's land than it is to hunker down and wait out the war.'

Alice's mouth curved into a faint smile. 'Nice analogy.'

'Thought you'd appreciate the history theme,' said Sasha.

They sat in silence for a few minutes, resting on the bench and drinking together. Alice was grateful for the edge Sasha's visit had taken off her nerves. Reid's manic behaviour had left her jumpy.

'I need to get back,' said Sasha, getting to her feet. 'I've got work in the morning.'

'See you in a couple of weeks?' said Alice, standing too.

'Maybe instead of me coming here, you could come to Coram

House for a change?' said Sasha, one eyebrow rising sharply in question.

'Maybe,' said Alice. 'I'll think about it.'

'Don't think too long. Someone might just come along and snap Crowley up while you're dithering. I know a lot of women who go wild for men that look like stoic undertakers.'

Alice snorted and looked away. Crowley had once been stoic to the point of indifference. There was an emotional echo left by Sasha's words, and it took Alice a moment to figure out what it was. Then it struck her: Jen had once described Crowley as an undertaker too.

'I'll let you know,' she said, forcing a smile.

Sasha nodded and made to leave, taking a shortcut across the lawn.

'Oh,' Sasha added, turning back. 'This Lester guy . . . I'll make some enquiries – see what I can find out about him. But he doesn't stand a chance against you. If he tries it again, you show him what you're really made of.'

Alice's cheeks flushed and something caught in her throat. 'Hey, keep your voice down,' she managed with a grin. 'Anyone would think you care.'

'Well, I care about August and Crowley too,' said Sasha, 'so the bar is set pretty low.'

Alice laughed, and Sasha paused for a moment. They shared a quick smile, and Sasha turned again to go.

'Wait!' called Alice. 'Come to the Midsummer Festival with me! I'll introduce you to the mentor House Mielikki assigned me. You'll like her. And Tom too.'

'Which festival?' asked Sasha, stopping by the fir trees.

'The Ukon Juhla at Crane Park Island.'

Sasha shook her head. 'I've already made plans to do the one at Hyde Park.'

'Please, Sasha,' said Alice. 'It'll be fun.'

'I can't. Jude's taking me to meet some of his friends from the Royal Mint.'

Alice's eyebrows shot up. 'Oh. At *midsummer*? Wait, are you two . . .?'

It was Crowley who'd once revealed that Sasha had feelings for Jude – but as far as Alice was aware, things had never got off the ground between them, and they'd moved past it months ago.

'No,' said Sasha emphatically. 'We've drawn a line under that. Jude's my best friend, and some friendships are too important to risk on romance. And maybe it's just what happens when you wait too long – the chance passes you by.' She shrugged. 'There's a life lesson there,' she said, cocking an eyebrow at Alice.

'You've been reading the philosophy books again, haven't you?' said Alice with a groan.

Sasha laughed. 'Actually, I have. Philosophy of rationalism versus empiricism, trying to make sense of my life during my lunch breaks at work.'

'I should introduce you to my boss,' said Alice, shaking her head. 'So what do the books say?'

'They say . . . don't wait for the spark to die before you tell someone how you feel. Not unless you want to try sparking a wet match.' She heaved a sigh. 'Or maybe that's me, not the books. Anyway – midsummer? We'll see. We might swing by Crane Park after the first bonfires are lit at Hyde Park. It's all downhill from there, so . . .' Sasha turned and started walking backwards, towards the fir trees and the door. 'I'll see you soon,' she said, with a quick wave.

Alice smiled at her retreating back. 'Yes,' she shouted, 'at the Midsummer Festival.'

'Maybe,' said Sasha, shaking her head from afar.

'Definitely!' Alice called after her.

A sudden cheer reverberated around the campus, and a distant voice yelled, 'House Mielikki takes the trophy!'

13

Bea wasn't in the library the next morning. She'd left a note explaining that she'd be gone for a few hours. All members of House Mielikki's governing committee had been summoned to an urgent morning meeting. Bea wasn't a committee member, but she took the minutes during the monthly governance meetings.

Alice examined the two books Bea had left for her alongside the note: *The Craft of Carving* by Bridie Walsh and Mary Lynch, and *Eradicating the Uninvited: Weeding Out Pests Permanently* by C. Carrasco. Bea had highlighted the pages she wanted Alice to read before Monday. There were a lot. She tucked the books under her arm and headed off to the lab, wondering what it meant that there had been an urgent meeting at House Mielikki.

Alice's boots crunched over broken glass and she paused in the doorway. It was a scene of total devastation. Face slack with shock, she peered around the room and stepped further inside, allowing the door to fall closed behind her. The brittle crunch of glass echoed in the empty lab.

She trudged to her desk and laid Bea's books on it. Then she turned back to examine the room, her breathing shallow. Reid's desk had been upended and was lying in pieces. Her polished hematite blackboard was cracked in two. The shelves had been pulled down, their skeletal frames smashed, and the books scattered around the room, their pages missing and covers torn. Plaster from the walls crumbled over everything, a fine mist of grey dust and thick, broken chunks. Reid's chair had been flung on its side, the legs snapped off. Everywhere was shattered glass, shards of wood and fragments of masonry. Torn papers blanketed pockets of the chaos.

What had happened here?

The door was shoved open, scraping the glass across the floor, and Alice turned slowly, expecting a horrified Vivian Reid. It was the janitor, Eugene Reilly – he always reminded her of an old sea captain, with his white beard and the navy cap pulled down over his fluffy hair.

'I've phoned the Runners,' he said. 'They're going to send someone. You'd best come away.'

'Who did it?' she asked blankly.

He shrugged. 'Vandals, probably. Too extreme for a student prank. I'll clear it up once the Runners have gone.'

'Does she know? Has she seen it yet? The woman who works in here with me?'

'Professor Reid? No. I think we'd have heard the shouting a mile away if she'd walked in on this,' he said with a knowing look.

'Probably,' she agreed, looking around at the carnage.

It looked like someone had been searching for something, smashing the office in a rage when they hadn't succeeded. Then another thought came to her. The look in Lester's eye when he saw the name of the institute on the folder she'd carried in the library. He knew where she worked. But if this was aimed at her, what was the point of it? She looked around. Was it just an attempt to spook her?

Alice frowned, lips pursed. If Reid suspected the lab's destruction was linked to Alice she'd fire her; there was no doubt. Fucking Lester. The man must be deranged. Her jaw clenched.

'It's not safe in here,' said the janitor. 'Come to the staffroom and we'll have a hot drink while we wait for the Runners.'

Alice flinched. She didn't want any contact with the Runners. She hadn't even reported her own attacks to them. 'I'll . . . just get my stuff,' she said, forcing a smile. He nodded and trudged out, leaving her alone.

Alice hesitated. What if something had happened to Reid? It was so unlike her to be late for work. Out of the corner of her eye, Reid's glass and marble cabinet caught Alice's attention. It had once sat beneath her desk but now lay exposed. A crack ran down its centre and the drawers were out of alignment. Reid kept her research notes in it. Someone – Lester? – had been interested enough to search the drawers. But why? Reid had always kept it unlocked.

She stepped carefully through the mess to reach the cabinet and bent to examine it. The damage had wedged the drawers shut so it was impossible to know if Reid's papers were still inside. She yanked at the handles, but the drawers wouldn't give. Casting around for something useful to jimmy open the narrow gap, her eyes alighted on one of the wooden shards on the floor. She shoved it into the space and forced it down, but the wood snapped off in her hands.

A quick glance at the door, to check for the Runners or Eugene, and she hurriedly studied the ruptured wood. She broke off a splinter from the end and rolled it between her palms. Warm tingles seeped from her hands, up her arms, as she held the image of the tiny wooden shard in her mind. She held out her palm, and the wood seemed to vibrate like a grain of boiling rice. Eyes narrowed in determination, Alice tipped the splinter through the gap, into the cabinet's middle drawer, and quickly moved aside.

She counted out the seconds, her palms still tingling. With one sharp exhale, the middle drawer exploded open as the splinter inside it grew larger. Like an exploded bomb, its growth burst inside the drawer and jolted it open with such force the cabinet expelled every drawer. Heart pounding at the possibility that Reid's research – which Alice had failed to copy for her – had been taken, she bent and peered inside.

It was empty.

Alice felt sick. If she'd just copied the research when she'd been asked . . . She swallowed, searching desperately for something she could salvage. A few scraps of paper littered the bottom of the last drawer and something was wedged into the corner. She picked at it, trying to gain some purchase, and managed to pull it out. It was an envelope. She turned it over. A very old envelope, the writing on the front faded and illegible. Alice slid a finger inside and pulled out two photographs. One was familiar. It was an exact copy of the photo on the front of Cecil's book. An elegant woman in an oval frame, the very model of cool composure. Why would Reid keep a photo of Leda Westergard stuffed in a drawer?

Alice frowned and studied the second photo. A group of women and girls sat on a picnic blanket in a garden, their smiling faces tilted towards the sun. Alice paused on one of the figures in the image. She was little more than a child, but with the shark-like eyes there was no question who it was: Marianne Northam. She looked again, lingering over the slightly older teenager with curls next to Marianne, her arm around a wet Labrador. Was that . . . *Reid?* Turning it over with trembling hands, she could just make out a faded message written in pencil:

Left to right: Helena, Leda, Emmi, Catherine, Marianne, Hanna, Florens and Tilda.

23rd August – Annual Jarvis Fundraiser. Look at Tilda's wet dress! She told me she's banning either dogs or pond-dipping next year! I almost told her I'd rather she banned herself but I bit my tongue to keep Mother happy!

Alice frowned, a tightness in her chest easing just slightly. Not Reid then – there was no Vivian listed. But she'd been right about Marianne. As for the others . . . She turned to peer at the faces, squinting to sharpen the camera's slightly unfocused blur. Second from the left, according to the list, was Leda. She glanced at the official portrait of Leda Westergard. Marianne had known the Mielikki chancellor. How deep did her scheming run? Marianne had her claws into the Runners – had she once held more sway with the Council too? Alice looked around the room, taking in the destruction, and was acutely reminded that Marianne also wanted to get her hooks into the university.

Footsteps and mumbling voices outside the window caused Alice to flinch. She snuck out from behind the cabinet and moved to peer outside. Eugene was leading two Runners along the gravel path by the side of the Cavendish Building. He stopped to point at the lab window, and Alice ducked.

Reuben Risdon. Reuben fucking Risdon had come. Wasn't vandalism a bit beneath his pay grade?

He hadn't changed. Even his burgundy waistcoat, overlaid with a worn blue greatcoat, was the same as she remembered. Tall and lean, in his early fifties, his tangle of grey hair glinted in the sunlight. Slate-grey eyes examined the outside door – no doubt checking for signs of forced entry to the building itself. His eyebrows slanted fiercely as he studied the frame.

She hated him.

Every cell in her body burned with her hatred. She had never, really and truly, hated anyone before. It was strange to think she was capable of it. She'd thought, after Jen's death, that it might lessen with time, or that she might become more understanding of his reasons. But she had surprised herself by nursing her contempt until it grew roots in her heart. He had murdered her best friend in the world. She didn't care that he had done it to save the city. She didn't care that he had done it to save her *own* soul from the burden of massacring the Rookery. It wasn't rational, she knew that. But hating Risdon was the only thing that had made it possible to live with herself after Jen's death. Hating him meant she didn't have to hate herself.

His eyes tracked in her direction and she drew back sharply.

Time to go.

She grabbed her two books and the envelope of photographs and scrambled to the door. Without a backward glance, she darted into the corridor and hurried away. She needed some fresh air and time to think.

There was a bouquet of flowers on the floor outside her apartment. She froze at the flash of colour wrapped in hessian and tied with ribbons. Sympathy flowers for Holly left in the wrong place? She glanced down the corridor, to Holly's empty apartment. No doubt they'd have a new tenant in there any day now.

She scooped up the bouquet, wondering whether it might be coincidence that flowers had appeared the day after Sasha's visit.

Either sent to cheer her up, or . . . perhaps they were from someone who'd just been told there was no relationship between Alice and Tom. Crowley wasn't the type for flowers, but . . .

A small rectangle of white card nestled among the blooms, and her stomach tightened at the possibility of seeing Crowley's familiar angular scrawl.

'Miss Wyndham?'

Alice started, and almost dropped the bouquet. It was Reuben Risdon, followed by a uniformed younger man in a blue tunic.

She tensed as Risdon strode the length of the corridor, his regal bearing at odds with the shabbiness of his greatcoat.

'Could I have a moment of your time? I'd like to discuss what you know of the vandalism in your workroom.'

Her mouth thinned and she looked away. She'd have preferred an ambush from Lester.

'No, sorry, I need to get these in water,' she said, waving her flowers in explanation.

The card tucked inside floated to the ground. There was no sign of Crowley's handwriting on it. The message printed on the card was simple and direct: *Murderer*. She gritted her teeth.

With a swift glance at Risdon, who was fast approaching, she retrieved it and shoved it into her pocket. Examining the flowers, she frowned into the bouquet as realization struck. Purple foxgloves, calla lilies, hydrangeas, oleander and hemlock. Poisonous flowers, all wrapped in hessian like a gift. But it was too late: she must have accidentally touched them when she'd reached for the card. She turned over her left hand. Her palm had turned an angry red; it swelled at an unnatural speed. The creases in her skin tightened, smooth and shiny, and itchy.

'Damn.'

She flexed her hand and the skin cracked, exposing the tender flesh underneath. Her palm burned with hot agony and she couldn't stifle a soft moan. Water. She needed water.

'That looks nasty,' said Risdon, his expression serious. 'Let me take you to the medical bay.'

The university nurse slathered a dollop of cream that smelled heavily of eucalyptus across Alice's hands and smiled down at her.

'You've been very lucky to have avoided serious side effects . . . and *death*,' she said, shaking her head and bustling over to the sink to wash her hands. 'Come and see me again tomorrow.'

Reuben Risdon was watching from the door, his arms folded and a concerned expression on his face. 'Could you give her something for the pain?' he asked.

Alice stared at him. She didn't need him to speak for her, and she certainly didn't want him offering his false kindnesses.

The nurse spun round, apologetic. 'Would you like something?'

'No thanks,' said Alice. Her hand was tender and swollen, but at least the signet ring wasn't so loose any more, she thought grimly.

She flexed her fingers, examining the redness, and smiled. The sting was already fading. Maybe the so-called 'rise of House Mielikki' had given her some additional protection.

'Might I have a moment with the patient, if you're done?' asked Risdon, and Alice became very still.

'Oh,' said the nurse, and paused. When Risdon raised an impatient eyebrow, she said, 'Of course, Commander,' and left her office looking taken aback.

Risdon closed the door carefully behind the nurse and the young Runner who'd accompanied him.

'I spoke with Beatrice Pelham-Gladstone earlier,' he said. 'Would you like to report the other attacks you've suffered?'

Alice stilled. Bloody Bea. 'No.'

The room fell silent, but she was very aware of his studious gaze. He knew who and what she was – both that she was an aviarist and that her soul was infused with death.

'Given this afternoon's events,' he said, 'I'm willing to extend an offer of protection to you. An officer, stationed here at the university to—'

'I don't need your spies,' she said, looking up at him for the first time.

There was a steely glint in his eye and his jaw tensed. 'You are a citizen of my city,' he said, 'and I have a duty to ensure your safety equal to any other.'

She tried to calm the tremble of anger in her voice. 'Or maybe,' she said, 'you want to protect the other citizens from me?'

Their eyes locked and his expression softened. 'Would you like to discuss the events of Marble Arch?'

'No thank you,' she said in a clipped tone. 'When the commander of the Runners can murder an innocent and walk away without a blemish on his character, that says more to me than words ever will.'

His forehead creased, the fierce eyebrows slanting. 'Defence of the city is not a crime,' he said. 'Many lives were saved that night.'

A blush rose on her cheeks and she glanced away, gnawing guilt chipping away at her. She wanted to hold on to her anger.

'Nothing was put on record that night,' he said. 'I have kept your confidences, and respect your right to privacy.' He paused. 'But a watchful eye over you—'

'How about opening that watchful eye to the corruption under your nose,' she said offhandedly. 'I told you that the Runners were infested with Marianne's Fellowship. Her followers are wearing your uniforms. Maybe you should be dealing with that first.'

'I am,' he said quietly.

Her mouth snapped shut and she graced him with a suspicious look.

'I've engaged one of her ex-members to help root them out,' he said. 'Someone who knows the signs.'

Alice frowned, and then understood. '*August?*' she asked in surprise. August's top-secret job was ratting out the Fellowship?

Risdon nodded, a conciliatory look in his eye that threw her. 'I took your information seriously. I won't accept corruption in my ranks.'

Alice stared at him, suddenly torn.

'And I will take the allegation given by Miss Pelham-Gladstone seriously too,' he went on. 'I can assign a Runner to you, one with an unblemished record, so that—'

Her expression hardened and she shook her head. 'No. You can send your spies to watch me, claiming it's for my own protection all you like, but don't expect me to be grateful to you.'

The card shoved in her pocket poked her thigh and she hesitated. *Murderer.* Well, Risdon was the murderer in this room.

'I think I would like something for the pain after all,' she said, rising from her chair. 'Nurse?' she called, opening the door. 'Do you have something for an irritating headache?'

The next morning Bea was in a foul mood, and Alice's was no better.

'I can't believe that corrupt, venal bastard is using us for a photo opportunity!' seethed Bea, sprinkling black pepper on her poached eggs.

They were sitting at a long table in the Arlington dining hall, newspapers spread out among the plates of hash browns, toast, jam pots and teacups. The corner of *The Rookery Herald* was sitting in the milk jug and the print was slowly bleeding from the front page. It was just as well: the article announcing that Chancellor Litmanen was cutting the ribbon at the Midsummer Festival had not gone down well with the librarian.

'Geraint Litmanen. What an absolute shit.' Bea slammed the pepper pot down and knocked the marmalade into her green tea. 'He came here two years ago,' she said, reaching for her teacup. 'They gave him an honorary doctorate in political science. Can you imagine? And in his speech, he claimed he was related to the Welsh Picton family and wore a sash with their coat of arms on. My mother plays bridge with the Dagsworth-Pictons once a year, so I double-checked the genealogy books after he'd gone and they don't even have a coat of arms!' She sipped her tea and pulled a face. 'Don't drink the green tea. It tastes of oranges.'

'Not a fan then?' asked Alice, eyes travelling over the soggy front page and the chancellor's face. In his early forties, with sparkling green eyes, slick dark hair on the verge of receding and a dazzling smile thanks to porcelain veneers, he was wearing a waistcoat pulled tightly over the early stages of a paunch.

'Some men,' said Bea, stabbing her poached eggs with a fork, 'are the type you'd take home to your mother. And others are the type who'd sleep with her.'

Alice contemplated her over her slice of buttered toast, watching the obliterated yolk ooze across Bea's plate.

'I want to go to House Mielikki,' said Alice. Bea paused at the sudden change of subject. 'If Lester's been going there, then I want to find him and—'

Bea shook her head. 'He isn't. I reported him to Cecil – Whitmore wasn't there. Cecil's suspended his membership. I spoke to Cassie Mowbray, too – Holly's sister – and they think he's gone to ground because they've put a solicitor on his case.'

Alice sighed irritably and added another sugar to her tea.

'Whenever he re-emerges, the Runners will find him,' said Bea. 'Don't worry.'

'I'm not worried,' said Alice, 'I'm pissed off.' She shook her head. 'And you *knew* I didn't want the Runners involved.'

Bea reached for her cup. 'I have a duty of care for your safety,' she said. 'If you die before the second test, who's to say it wouldn't be *your* family setting solicitors on me?'

Alice sighed, but the frown lines remained etched on her forehead. 'Do I have a date yet?' she asked. 'For the second test? I'm ready for it. I want to get it done.' She didn't just want it, she *needed* it – what if Lester attacked again and her soul was put at risk? She was determined never to give Kuu the order to 'go' again, but she needed that link to the tree strengthened.

'There's been a slight delay because . . .' Bea glanced around and leaned closer. 'Concerns over the Summer Tree's growth have taken precedence.' She sat back up straight. 'But it'll be soon. We should hear about the date early next week. And Cecil has thrown me a little pre-warning about the next test.'

'Oh?' asked Alice with interest.

'They're setting you against other candidates. Four of you for two spots in the House.'

Alice grimaced. She didn't like the sound of that. Not when she'd already watched Holly die the last time round.

'Look at this,' said Alice, putting the test to one side for now. She pulled out Cecil's book and found space for it next to a rack of toast.

'I don't think he's going to test you on that, darling,' said Bea. 'Most people smile politely and put it on a bookshelf unread.'

Alice shook her head and tapped the photograph on the cover. It was the same portrait she'd found locked away in Reid's drawer.

'Look at what she's wearing on her finger,' said Alice, pointing to the woman in the oval frame.

She'd studied the photo all evening, holding it up to the light at different angles to see if there was something written on it, some hidden message she hadn't yet spotted that might explain its significance to Reid. But then she'd noticed something curious.

Bea hunched over, examining the spot in the photo that Alice was pointing at. On the woman's little finger was an engraved oval signet ring. Alice held up her own gold signet ring. It had the same criss-crossed pattern around the setting. 'Don't you think they look the same?' she asked. 'Isn't that weird?'

Bea squinted at Alice's ring, then back at the photo. 'Maybe,' she said in an indulgent tone. 'But every man and his dog has a signet ring with a coat of arms on it – except the Dagsworth-Pictons. My mother wears one with a bear on it that belonged to her father. Unless you can inspect it with a magnifying glass, they all look the same to me.'

'But look at the scratches on my ring,' Alice persisted, drawing Bea's attention back to the photo. 'Couldn't they be the same as these lines on here?'

Bea laughed. 'Darling, I can't even see any scratches on your ring, never mind a photo. My eyes just aren't good enough.'

Bea reached for the salt again, and Alice sighed. It had been a bit of a leap, she supposed, but it was the only thing that stood out about the photograph. She couldn't fathom why it might be special to Reid. Of course, there was also a huge question mark over the other photograph, but . . . Alice shook her head. The woman hadn't returned to work since she'd manhandled Alice, not even after her workspace had been destroyed. Either she'd finally lost it or something was wrong. Still, that was for Risdon to follow up on in his investigation into the vandalism.

Alice stared absentmindedly at her arm, remembering the manic glint in Reid's eye as she'd grabbed her. What had tipped her over the edge? That Alice had forgotten to copy her notes?

'These old genealogy books of yours,' said Alice. 'Do they have *all* the old crests in them?'

'I suppose so,' said Bea. 'All the ones from the big old families, anyway. You want to see if you can find the pattern on your ring?'

Alice sighed. 'I don't know. My mum gave me this ring and she's never set foot in the Rookery, but . . . it's just odd. It looks so similar to that one.'

Bea gestured for Alice's hand. 'It *could* be a coat of arms,' she conceded. 'But the engraving's so smooth, darling, it's almost worn away to nothing. You'd have a real job trying to match it up with anything.' She paused. 'I take your point, though. As far as I can tell, the pattern on the side of the ring is quite similar to the chancellor's portrait. But I imagine thousands were.'

'If I can make the engraving clearer . . .' Alice began.

'How?'

Alice smiled. 'I have a very clever friend who works at the Royal Mint. He makes weaponry in his spare time and coins in his day-to-day job. If anyone could do it, he could.'

Jude was a member of House Ilmarinen, the House of fire and metal. Next time Alice saw him, she was going to ask for his help. In fact, if she wore the ring to midsummer and Sasha and Jude could be persuaded to meet her there, she could kill two birds with one stone.

14

The moon hung low in the sky. It was the first thing Alice saw when she fumbled her arrival, staggering sideways and bumping her shoulder into the brick archway. Bea was so distracted she barely noticed. Despite weeks of planning, Bea had changed her mind about her outfit at the last minute, ditching the green floaty dress for a deep maroon silky number, which she'd paired with a slash of bright red lipstick. The dress switch had made them late for the Midsummer Festival. The bonfires were due to be lit a little before sunset, at around 9 p.m., and they'd hoped to be among the first to arrive and circulate. That plan, so far, had failed.

'Was that smoke?' asked Bea, her voice fraught.

'I don't think so,' said Alice, emerging from the doorway.

'Definitely steam,' said Tom, nudging them forward.

They'd travelled through the Crane Park shot tower, a two-hundred-year-old circular brick erection at least eighty feet tall. Right next door, accessed via a short bridge, was Crane Park Island itself. The island had been created to contain water for the Hounslow Gunpowder Works near the site. Now, it was a nature reserve back in London, and here in the Rookery, a largely uncorrupted woodland allowed to grow wild.

Bea hurried on ahead, her eyes fixed on the steam dissipating over the treeline. Tom's long legs caught her up with ease, but Alice held back. She wanted to take her time, to appreciate her first Midsummer Festival. And if she was hoping a face would spot her moving slowly through the crowd, she didn't allow herself to think on it too much.

There was a path trodden through the woods, worn grasses giving way to dry soil. She followed its curve, leading her between a grove of trees and out into a glade. She stood absolutely still, savouring the scents and sounds permeating the air. Very slowly, a smile spread across her face and her eyes gleamed. If ever she was to believe there was magic in the air, then this midsummer eve was certainly it. And tonight, she wanted to believe in magic.

Drifts of people in high spirits meandered through the glade and off into the woods. Others stood around in groups, drinking and laughing. A small huddle watched a woman in a headscarf cooking at a huge metal plate. Pan-fried minnows sizzled in butter, sending flashes of steam billowing into the sky. She turned the fish with a spatula and tossed a handful of flour and seasoning into the pan, watching it crisp and crackle. A few feet away, smoked bream cooked on a metal rack next to an open fire, while garlic-stuffed trout was laid flat across a grill, the scales shimmering in the flickering light.

There were tables and tables of food laid out under the trees: tureens of soup and warm bread; plates of buttered potatoes; salad bowls filled with dewy tomatoes, ripened peppers, watermelon and feta cheese, dressed with wine vinegar and sour cream; and plates of homemade munkki doughnuts alongside pulla pastries with whipped cream. The air was fragrant with sweet smells and sharp, salty tangs, mingling with the scents of fresh grasses, birch wood and flowers.

Glasses clinked, and bearded, smiling men beckoned Alice closer, urging her to taste their sahti beer and liquorice-flavoured salmiakki. She grinned at them and shook her head, ambling away from the glade and deeper into the trees.

Bright flashes of orange fire exploded through the sky, and Alice paused to watch as a bare-chested man in face paint tossed balls of flame with his bare hands. The crowd cheered him on when he introduced a fifth, juggling the fire higher and higher, the tapered flames like shooting stars against the dark night.

Overhead, midsummer poles – midsommarstång – had been raised: timber logs fashioned into crosses with circular wreaths on each arm. Birch leaves and flowers wrapped the timber, hiding the wood beneath. They stood thirty feet tall, marking out a trail through the scattered festival celebrations.

Alice glanced over her shoulder every few metres or so. She'd been torn over the dangers of the festival – on the one hand, a busy area full of people would be a foolish place to attack her; on the other hand, she was surrounded by nature: in other words, a ready supply of weaponry for anyone with Mielikki's legacy to launch an attack. But as long as she kept her wits about her, she intended to enjoy herself.

She passed old ladies with stalls selling woven blankets and crocheting. They stood by the piles of fabrics, fingers at work with drop spindles, the yarn spinning uniformly around the wood. As she passed, they grabbed her and gestured for her to try. Beaming, she took one end and rotated the spindle, but the wool clogged and tangled; they laughed as she smiled her apologies and pressed the wool back into their soft hands.

'Wildflower crown?' asked a young woman at the next stall. 'Hand-woven using the freshest flowers to symbolize rebirth and growth . . . the best way to capture the magic of midsummer for the best price.'

She held out a handful of seeds in her cupped palm. 'Primrose, daisies, red campion and white clover,' she said – and in her hand, the seeds cracked open and sprouted. In moments, budding flowers unfurled their petals and the woman fastened them together with a thin vine.

She took advantage of Alice's surprised silence to settle the floral garland firmly on her head. 'Five shillings if you don't want to haggle,' she said, 'and six shillings if you do.'

Alice laughed at her audacity. 'They're beautiful,' she admitted, admiring the many midsummer crowns laid out on the table. 'I'll take it.'

'Now you're ready,' the trader said, exchanging money.

'For what?'

'To dance,' she said with a wink.

A soft, mellifluous sound swelled through the trees. By turns haunting and lively, the clear, bright notes of a piccolo drifted through the darkening night. It was joined by a mournful harmony knitting the melody from other voices: the rich staccato plucks of the kantele, the wheeze and whine of an accordion and the tremulous tones of a violin swaying through the trees.

Alice followed the tumbling rhythm beneath the leafy canopies, weaving between the birch, willow and oak trees and skirting closer to the trickling sounds of running water. Were the plants always so verdant here, she wondered, or was it another sign of House Mielikki's increased power?

A steady stream of dark figures left the woods to follow the riverbank, the edges of their silhouettes flickering with orange light. Alice trekked after them, emerging from a dense copse, her boots finding firmer ground. The river Crane flowed smoothly downstream towards Isleworth, sloshing against the reeds and spraying a fine mist over the reed warblers hiding there. Iridescent dragonflies hovered and darted low to the water, their reflections rippling across the surface.

Dotting the riverbank were heaped piles of dry branches and bracken tapering to points. Bonfires. Most had now begun to flame. They'd missed it – the ceremony of lighting the brushwood – but the reflection of dancing flames on the water was so beautiful it didn't much matter. Slashes of golden fire painted the sky and rained sparks like meteorites. Smoke billowed up from the smouldering bonfires, musty and fragrant.

And then she saw movement in the river: arms scything through the water or stretched out and floating. Men and women discarded their clothes on the riverbank and slipped into the shallows, their shrieks and giggles muffled by the folk melody seeping from the woods.

'Alice?'

She turned quickly, peering into the thicket. The bushes rustled and Bea stumbled out, tailed by Tom.

'Told you it was her,' said Tom. 'You owe me a glass of sahti.'

'Yes, well,' said Bea, 'panoramic views *are* one of the many benefits of being sixteen feet tall.' She straightened her dress and assembled a knowing smile on her face. 'So? What do you think of the Midsummer Festival?'

'I . . .' Alice sighed. 'Love it.'

Bea grinned. 'I knew you would. Nice crown, by the way.'

Alice brushed a hand over the circlet of flowers.

'Come on,' said Bea. 'You have two options now, and you have to show willing and participate in at least one.'

Alice's brow furrowed with suspicion. 'What options?'

'Well, you've already missed your opportunity with the seven flowers under your pillow—'

'I am *not* rolling around naked in a wheat field,' Alice said firmly.

'Quiet, darling – you so clearly don't know what's good for you,' she said with a smile.

'And with that,' said Tom with a laugh, 'I'm off to find a comfortable wheat field. I'll catch up with you both . . . tomorrow, hopefully.'

He smiled and moved off through the woods, into the promise of the night.

Bea rounded on Alice, eyes sparkling. 'Midsummer is time to worship nature with our most sacred traditions – we ward off evil with fire, we give thanks to the old gods . . . and if we're lucky, they grant us healthy, fertile crops and wombs. Midsummer is a night of magic and promise. A night of – oh, everything, multiplied a thousand-fold. Fertility, rebirth, love—'

'I don't want to multiply my fertility,' said Alice, alarmed. 'Especially not for one night only.'

Bea laughed. 'You have to be open to anything – all of our Rookery traditions. This is midsummer. Who knows? Tonight, you might see your true love reflected in the river. Or on the other side of the bonfire when you jump over it.'

'When I jump over a *bonfire*?' Alice spluttered. Some of the bonfires along the river's edge had to be at least seven feet high. 'And burning to death like Guy Fawkes . . . this is "what's good for me", is it?'

Bea smiled and patted her arm. 'Absolutely,' she said, towing Alice back through the woods.

Alice found herself dragged into a crowded clearing, which turned out to be the source of the music. The tune had picked up a faster tempo now, and the musicians had switched from haunting melody to playful quickstep. Couples danced around the glade's distant edges, spinning in circles far from the glow of a blazing fire. This one was considerably smaller than those lining the riverbank.

A ring of people stood drinking around the small bonfire, laughing and shouting encouragement at a short man who was preparing to leap over the searing flames. Judging by the way he was swaying, the true love he was likely to see on the other side of the bonfire was another glass of beer. Alice winced as he set off at a tilted canter. Predictably, he mistimed his jump and his trailing foot kicked the smouldering branches as he landed. The bottom of his trouser leg caught fire and the crowd jeered as he rolled in the grass. The flames finally doused, he got to his feet sheepishly, and a taller man shoved a beer at him and clapped him on the back.

'See,' said Bea. 'Easy.'

A woman trotted over and hurled dried birch wood onto the heap. The fire sparked and the smoke thickened, warping the night air and shrouding the furthest trees from sight. In the distant gloom, there was a flicker of movement as a tall figure at the edge of the glade leaned back against a trunk, his head tipping back, arms folded, and the stern, disapproving stance was so familiar that Alice's pulse raced, just for a moment, until another figure appeared, took his hand and slipped deeper into the shadows. Not him. In fact, looking around at the laughing, the clinking glasses and the dancing, she couldn't imagine a less likely place to see Crowley. There was an infinitesimal slump of her shoulders, but she lifted her chin higher and tried to focus on Bea's conversation.

'Go on then, Lady Pelham-Gladstone,' said Alice. 'Since you're so keen, let's see *you* jumping through fire to see your true love.'

'Less of the lady, please,' said Bea. 'Anyway, I don't want to see my true love through a bonfire,' she added with a smutty laugh. 'I'm enjoying my maidenhood, thank you. I wouldn't mind finding myself a horizontal companion, however.'

With that, she turned away, gathered up her skirts and hurdled the bonfire. A man emerged from nowhere to catch her on the other side and there was an audible gasp from the watching crowd as they realized who it was. Alice recognized him from her soggy newspaper. With two dour, hulking men looming nearby – bodyguards, no doubt – and the ceremonial chain around his neck, the dark receding hair and impossibly white teeth, it could only be . . .

A middle-aged woman bumped into Alice from behind. 'I've had too much sahti,' said the stranger, squinting across the clearing. 'I thought I just saw Chancellor Litmanen catch that woman.'

There was a heavy pause.

'You did,' said Alice. 'And now you're seeing her shove him into the bonfire and his bodyguards drag her away.'

Alice hesitated for a moment, wondering if she should hurry to Bea's aid. Then she watched dandelion stalks slither from the ground and wrap around the bodyguards' ankles and decided Bea had this one covered.

She grinned and moved off to find some refreshments.

The moon shimmered across the water, its cool rays blending with the warm firelight in a discordant blaze of colours: fiery reds, oranges and yellows, tinted by the blue-grey of the night sky. Alice sat on the riverbank's edge, her shoes skimming the rippling surface. It was calm here. Peaceful. If she concentrated, she could fade out the distant folk music and hear instead the gentle shushing of the river and rustling of the bushes as water voles and mice scurried through the undergrowth. Moths flitted past and crickets chirped their rhythmic mating call, and she breathed it all in, revelling in the small taste of nature parcelled up inside a busy city centre.

She took another long sip of her drink, rolling the flavours around her mouth. Barley and juniper with an illogical hint of banana. She'd never been especially fond of beer, but somehow the flat, cloudy sahti was growing on her. Or maybe it was the mellow sensation in her limbs and the pleasant warmth in her stomach that she enjoyed. She stared into the depths of the river Crane, thinking no particular thoughts. Somewhere further down the bank, a handful of couples hid in the shadows, hands entwined, savouring the magic of midsummer; she was perfectly alone, and she was . . . okay. More than that. She was very okay. Midnight had long gone, and she'd seen no face reflected in the water – no great love, just herself, smiling and tranquil. And maybe that was as it should be. Why shouldn't she love herself first? Why shouldn't *that* be the magic of midsummer?

She sighed and stared into the water.

'I love myself,' she murmured. She grinned lopsidedly, and laughed at herself. 'And why not?' she added, emboldened by the tingling in her head and the taste of juniper on her tongue.

She lurched to her feet, her shoes slipping on a weaker chunk of soil and scattering mud into the river. She loomed over her smiling reflection, the tumbler of beer raised as though in toast.

'I love myself!' she declared.

'And they say the story of Narcissus is a myth,' drawled a low voice over her shoulder.

She whirled around in shock, sloshing sahti over the grass. Her heart gave one great thud – and everything stopped. The music, flowing water, the songs of crickets and warblers, the flittering moths . . . Everything evaporated. Everything but the tall figure standing on the riverbank, white shirtsleeves rolled to his elbows, his dark hair overlong and choppy, falling almost to his jaw, and green eyes watching her calmly. And that glorious nose, like something carved from rock or minted on Roman coins.

'*Crowley?*' she breathed.

He stepped closer, the familiar scents of burned pinewood and cloves engulfing her, causing a small shiver to run down her spine. She stared up at him in wonder. He was here. Really here.

And then – suddenly – he wasn't.

The weak soil gave way beneath him and he landed with a mighty splash in the river Crane.

15

Eyes wide, Alice watched in stunned silence as Crowley struggled to his feet. His sopping white shirt stuck to his skin, almost transparent, and the sleeves had begun to unravel with the weight of the water. His black trousers were slick as oil, and somewhere in the murk – wedged in silt on the riverbed – were his scuffed boots, utterly waterlogged. Every part of him was drenched, even his hair, hit by the spray that had fanned up on his crash landing.

'*Oh*,' she said at last.

Crowley shot a stern glance at the water, as though to chastise it for its insolence. It was this that tipped Alice over the edge. A helpless splutter burst from her mouth and her shoulders began to quake. She folded at the waist, creased with laughter.

'Oh Crowley . . .' she managed. 'I can't even . . .' She trailed off, unable to speak, her stomach cramping.

He waded to the bank, planted a boot heel on the soil and hauled himself from the river. He stood before her, soaked to the bone, his clothes hanging from his lithe frame while droplets slid down his face, sticking wet tendrils of hair to his cheekbones. The water trickled along his collarbone and under his shirt, and as she followed its path with her eyes, her laughter died as quickly as it had started. Visions of Fitzwilliam Darcy emerging from the lake at Pemberley in his white underclothes superimposed themselves on the riverbank and she swallowed thickly. *Bloody BBC. Bloody Jane Austen.* Crowley raised an eyebrow and she bit the inside of her lip, using the sharp sting to jolt her to her senses. Absence might have made the heart grow fonder, but it didn't heal it – not quite – and standing with him now, the lies he'd once told her, the hurt he'd caused, all came rushing back.

She took a deep breath in a bid to release the tension in her chest.

'Mr Darcy did it better,' she said.

He huffed out an irritable breath and strode past her with all the grace and dignity he could muster, his boots squelching in the grass.

'You'll catch pneumonia!' she called after him.

He flourished a lazy hand in the air . . . and exploded in a blast of flame. Alice gasped involuntarily and staggered backwards. Engulfed in a fireball, the heat blistering, Crowley merely paused and ran a hand through his hair. It lasted only seconds. Alice blinked in shock as the fire spent itself, the last flames dwindling on the collar of his shirt before winking out.

'What . . .' she started.

'Evaporation,' he said in an amused tone.

She watched him, her eyes tracing every inch of his face. The atmosphere thickened, the levity in his tone burning away under her inspection. Crowley. Here. All this time fighting the urge to see him, to forgive him. How had Sasha and the others managed to when she couldn't?

She took a deep breath.

His chest stilled, like a man awaiting the executioner's axe.

'I need another drink,' she murmured, tramping past him and vanishing into the shadowy grove.

The bonfire had been fed since Bea had hurdled over it, trebling in size and casting a warm glow across the musicians and dancers. The music stopped abruptly, and as Alice padded across the grass, her footsteps seemed thunderously loud in the silence. Head still buzzing with sahti, she paid for another and stared into the fire, clutching the glass like a lifeline.

Crowley weaved through the crowd until his eyes found her. Standing side by side, they said nothing. Inches lay between them that might as well have been kilometres, and neither seemed to have any words that could bridge the gap. They watched the musicians, who were stepping away from their instruments and gathering closer together. Crowley's elbow brushed Alice's. She tensed and took a swig of sahti before placing it in the grass; she wanted no more of it clouding her decisions.

The musicians had formed a quartet. One of the women nodded at the others, and they began to sing – a cappella, voices accompanied only by each other. It was a quick, jaunty folk tune. The singers' voices jumped in and out of the song, creating a percussive rhythm. It was both strange and wonderful – or wonderfully strange, perhaps. And soon, her smile broadened as the tempo picked up and the melody grew more complicated.

Crowley turned to her and raised a sardonic eyebrow. Then he bowed and held out his hand, long fingers urging her to take it.

'You can't be serious,' she said.

He gave a wry smirk and twitched his fingers. 'Deadly.'

She stared at his hand for a moment, and shook her head. 'I can't dance.'

He rolled his eyes, then took her hand and spun her into his arms with a gasp.

'Crowley!'

The crowd had begun to join in with the beat, couples in the waltz position dancing in neat steps across the clearing. The demanding pace increased and a few broke apart and began to clap the beat from the edges of the glade instead.

He spun her away from the bonfire and she laughed at the landscape smearing past her vision. She was very aware of his hand on the small of her back, of the feather-light touch as he guided her around the clearing, his movements sharp and practised.

'How did you know I'd be by the river?' she asked.

'I didn't,' he said. 'Sasha told me you'd be here. I've been wandering for an hour, searching for you.'

His chest vibrated with his words, and she felt a small thrill of anticipation at their closeness. But she sensed the danger: it would be so easy to get swept up in the music, the scents, the heady magic of midsummer.

'Crowley . . . I can't forget,' she said after a moment.

'I know,' he murmured. 'But if you'll let me, maybe I can give you new things to remember.'

They changed direction, and she lost her balance. He pulled her closer. 'The song is called the *Ievan Polkka*,' he mouthed into her ear. 'Eino Kettunen composed it in the 1930s.'

Faster and faster, the rhythm increased. Around her, couples danced with light half-steps, a complicated pattern of leg crosses and turns, and Alice had no hope of keeping up. Every misstep brought her feet down on Crowley's toes, but he only caught her with a laugh and spun her away. They danced through the shadows, following none of the synchronized shapes made by the other dancers. Spinning quarter- and half-turns, whirling her with a gentle pressure on her waist, gliding left and right and smoothly forward and back again. Step after step, after step . . . and then the song ended. And he was staring down at her, not smiling, his mouth no more than a line, but his eyes glittering with humour and something that made her stomach twist and her mouth dry.

'Your crown has slipped,' he said in a low voice, and she tilted her head back for him to adjust it. His fingers reached up, brushing her hair gently aside, and settled the garland in place. Then he allowed his gaze to drift lower until their eyes met. The longing in his eyes scorched her. They were so close she could almost feel the heat rising from his body.

'Alice,' he whispered. He lowered his head, and she raised hers, one hand clutching the front of his shirt. Inches away, centimetres, millimetres . . . His warm breath ghosted over her lips as she arched upwards to close the gap . . .

But then the ground rumbled beneath their feet and the screaming began.

Alice's hair whipped back as they sprinted over the thick grass. Crowley's grip on her hand was firm as he pulled her through the woods, stumbling over roots and fallen boughs and slipping on glass bottles abandoned in the grass. She lost her footing completely and crashed onto her knees.

Stampeding feet ploughed past her, the swollen crowds of people rushing to escape the island, to find safety. Without pausing, Crowley hauled her upright and accelerated, his hand squeezing hers for reassurance as thunder shook the clearing. The hard-packed soil, the ditches, the scrub and riverbank – all began to tremble.

'An earthquake?' she shouted.

The grass vibrated and tingling pulses shot up her legs. Her knees throbbed with the sensation and her jaw buzzed. Together, they surged across the woodland as the convulsions tossed stones and broken branches into the air. Then a juddering tremor and a *crack* resonated, like the mantle of the earth had ruptured, and a thin crevice opened up in the grass metres ahead.

Alice skidded to a halt, her free hand grabbing the back of Crowley's shirt to stop him plunging into the sudden rift. Others were not so lucky; a blond-haired man tumbled past them, his eyes raw with panic, his hands grasping fruitlessly for a ledge as he plummeted into the dark sinkhole.

Another hurtled past, plunging towards the chasm – the wild-flower crown seller. The woman flicked out a hand as she fell, her lips working quickly as she called on her legacy to save her. Tufts of ragweed buried in the crust shifted at her urging. The roots shot out of the soil to wrap around her waist and stop her fall. But the magic was too powerful and Alice watched in horror as she lost control of it. The roots tightened and pulled the crown seller back into the soil, her mouth filling with thick mud as she suffocated.

'Crowley!' Alice gasped, shoving him away from the edge to free up her hands. 'We have to help—'

'They've gone!' Crowley shouted.

An echoing boom knocked them off their feet. Tossed backwards, Alice smashed into a fallen food table and landed face down, her nose smarting and her chest winded. Her fingers sank into the grass as she pushed herself up to her feet. Alice lurched towards Crowley, panting, and thrust a hand at him. He scrambled to his feet. Crane Park Island was fracturing in half. Branching fissures severed the ground all around them, slicing more chasms into the grass.

'The shot tower!' he shouted.

A scream tore through the clearing, lifting the hairs on Alice's arms. She darted a horrified look at Crowley but he shook his head, his expression grim.

'The shot tower,' he repeated urgently. 'Let me take you to safety.'

She stared at him, her bruised face streaked with mud.

And took a step back.

'Kuu?' she shouted, turning on her heel and stumbling away. 'Find me the ones with unbroken cords. Find me the ones still alive.'

Her nightjar, trilling in agitation, led her back through the grass. All around her, a terrible symphony of panic and fear and terror echoed between the creaking trees: full-throated sobs and shrieks, a mumbled chorus of prayers and moans in the undergrowth.

The sinkhole. There might still be some I can help. But then the woods began to moan and she froze. There came a deep, yawning rumble, a whining rasp, and then a shuddering, splintering explosion of noise. The trees rocked. The grass surged higher as something slid beneath it, bunching the soil. Something thick and curved – the body of a python turned to wood. *A tree root*, Alice realized as it looped through the rifts in the ground. She stared at the devastation, the churned-up soil, the obliterated grass and tilted trees, the ruptures and cracks.

Then it began to slow. A curtain of stunned silence fell across the island, a collective intake of breath as the vibrations diminished, the chasms stopped expanding and the trees stilled. It was over. Something brushed her arm. *Crowley.*

She stared at the devastation, her throat tight and her pulse racing.

'Whitmore's been trying to keep it secret,' she said in a strangled voice. 'But the Summer Tree is growing.'

16

They waited. An hour? Two? They waited until Alice was sure that Bea was safe – with the chancellor – and Tom, who had left with a woman hours earlier. They waited until they could no longer bear the quiet sobs and soft, pleading moans. Caked in dirt, they had moved brushwood aside with a snap of fire, and fallen trees with the sweep of a hand. They had searched for the lost until their voices were hoarse and their feet were numb.

When the Runners had arrived in their navy tunics, shining gold buttons and polished shoes, *then* they had left. Reuben Risdon had been there – commanding his men to help those who were conscious before attending to the silent ones. His shocked eyes had found hers across the clearing, and she had been too stunned by the night's sour end to take her measure of him. A tangle of silver hair and sharp eyebrows, his face was pale as he examined the scene. His fingers had crept to his pocket to retrieve a tin of snuff tobacco, and he had clutched it like a security blanket, barking orders left and right.

'Coram House,' she murmured to Crowley, her bones aching and her mind numbed. She didn't want to be alone. She needed to be with her friends. 'I want to go home.'

Crowley's eyes glittered, and he reached for her hand.

The showerhead blasted her with needles of hot liquid, sloughing the mud off her damp skin. She tilted her face into the spray, eyes closed, allowing bubbles to gather at the corners of her mouth. *Wash it all away*, she urged. Wash the stains on her soul clean and scrub her mind of the night's events. She turned up the heat, the punishing sensation of boiling liquid easing the tension in her muscles. Her skin was pink, her palms and soles wrinkled, when the water finally ran clear. She turned the dial and the water cut off, a few drips splattering the back of her neck. Crowley had given her one of his old shirts to wear. It smelled of him. A pang of discomfort tightened her stomach as she slipped it on.

She didn't want to be with him. But God, she didn't want to be without him either. Maybe Sasha was right. Maybe it was time to let go of her pain and try to move on. In all the chaos and the terror she'd witnessed tonight, Crowley's hand was the one thing that had kept her steady.

'It was just . . . awful,' said Alice, her tone expressionless.

She sat on a kitchen chair, her knees drawn up to her chest and Crowley's shirt pulled down over them. The fire flickered in the grate but she was cold with exhaustion.

'Risdon was still commanding the clean-up operation when we left,' said Jude. He looked drawn. His usually tanned face was wan, his stubble grown out too long, and his blue eyes, usually brightly inquisitive, were now dulled and bleak. He tapped the arm of his wheelchair as though the repetitive action might bring back some order to the world.

Jude and Sasha had burst through the door of Coram House an hour after Alice and Crowley had arrived, and a brief, frantic comparison of the night's experiences had left them lapsing into longer and longer silences as the hour wore on. August hadn't returned at all, and although they knew he hadn't been at Crane Park Island, no one knew which of the other festivals he'd attended. Crane Park Island was the only one with fatalities and serious injuries, so he was safe, at least.

'I need to go to bed,' said Sasha, standing abruptly. 'I can't keep . . .' She shook her head, shot one last look at Jude and trudged from the kitchen.

'We should all probably . . .' Alice started.

Jude nodded, but no one moved. They stared into space for several moments longer, each lost in their own thoughts. The soft moans, the whimpers . . . Shaking herself, mentally and physically, Alice finally slipped off the chair and stood, wrapping her long sleeves around her chest. Crowley's eyes were on her back as she left, concern creasing his brow. She would never sleep tonight.

Red hair rippled in the wind. *Jen.* Alice spun towards her – but she wasn't there. Distant laughter echoed across the moors. Alice turned again. Gone. Red hair always at the corner of her eye, always disappearing when she reached for her. Alice looked down. Her bare feet were nestled in frosted grass. Crystallized tendrils between her toes. The floor began to rumble. The grass shook violently and she stumbled.

'Alice?'

Jen's voice. Not rasping, not taunting. Just Jen.

'Alice, *run*! He wants you!'

She sat up with a gasp, her hands clenching the bedsheets.

The curtains weren't fully closed, and the street lamp outside bobbed around the edges of her vision like a yellow orb. She whipped back her sheets and wriggled her feet. They were white with cold. Numbed and icy to the touch. Trembling, she wrapped the covers around them and squeezed her toes for warmth. Was it just a dream? She glanced over at the dormant fire in the grate. This room had always been cold. But her feet were *frozen* . . .

Alice sighed and stared blankly up at the ceiling. After a few moments, she frowned and squinted into the shadows. They were moving. Wiry oak twigs curled out of the white plaster above her head and she realized what she was seeing: life had blossomed out from the wooden joists supporting the floor above. She tensed, expecting an attack – but they dangled immobile, posing no threat. As she sank into the pillows and tried to empty her mind for sleep, Jen's voice reverberated through her mind.

Alice, run! He wants you!

She had no intention of running – from anyone.

'Why is it so cold in here?' asked Alice as she prepared a bowl of lingonberry porridge for breakfast the next morning. The entire house was chilled.

'The underground mains pipes have burst,' said Sasha, who was sitting on the countertop in stripy blue pyjamas, eating breakfast yoghurt with a tense expression. 'I was out there half an hour ago. Three streets away, there's a sinkhole in the road that's taken out the heating in every house up to half a mile away. Ours included.'

'Aftershocks,' said Jude, 'from last night.'

Alice nodded, her shoulders sinking at the thought of there

being yet more damage caused by the Summer Tree, like ripples in a pond.

'The Council will fix the pipes,' said Jude, flicking a hand at the fire, where an explosion of flames suddenly leapt into the grate. 'And in the meantime, warmth won't be a problem for us.'

She nodded. Jude was dressed in the clothes he usually wore to his forge – turned-up jeans and a grey shirt with *J. Lyons* embroidered on the pocket. He seemed quietly contemplative. Not that that was unusual for Jude, but there was an air of solemnity about him this morning that was strangely detached.

The door swung open and Alice glanced towards it, but it was August, not Crowley.

'He's gone out,' said Sasha, sensing what she'd been hoping to see. 'He left at the crack of dawn, but he said he'd be back before lunch. I think he thought you'd be sleeping in till then. It was a long night.'

Alice nodded and moved to sit with her porridge and a cup of tea. Crowley vanishing was common practice. Alice suspected he'd gone to check on his sister – comatose in a London hospital – to check that the chaos of last night hadn't left echoes in London.

'I've been doing some digging,' said August. 'And your biological mother . . . If she was a member of House Mielikki, then she wasn't a practising necromancer.'

Alice jerked upright, caught off guard by the randomness of his comment. 'What?'

August ruffled his straw-like hair and threw himself into a kitchen chair, long legs stretched out like a spider's. He looked like he hadn't slept all night. Like the rest of them, she supposed.

'Is there any coffee?' August asked through a yawn.

'Just tea,' said Jude, holding up his flask. He always carried a flask of emergency tea. As a compulsive tea drinker, it was one of the things Alice loved most about him.

'No good. I need double the amount of caffeine that tea can give me,' said August.

'Well, genius,' said Sasha, throwing her bowl into the sink, 'you could always have two cups.'

'Point noted,' he replied. He gestured for the flask, and Jude wheeled closer, uncapped it and poured him a cup.

'You look like you could do with a shot of something in this,' said Jude. 'Where were you last night?'

'Running errands,' said August.

'You've been doing some research into my family history?' asked Alice, placing her spoon on the table with great deliberation, as though any sudden movements would distract him. The possible overstepping of boundaries hung in the air for just a moment.

'Call it professional interest,' he said. He looked around the kitchen. 'Oh come on. No one else was curious about how Tuoni, basically the chief necromancer, managed to meet a woman and . . .?'

He trailed away and gestured at Jude as though for support. Sasha shook her head in disgust, while Jude sighed.

Alice sat up straighter, her tiredness falling away. 'Tell me what you've found out,' she said. 'Please.'

August raised a smug eyebrow at Jude, before turning to Alice.

'They keep a record of all the registered necromancers, going back years, at the Council's White Tower offices,' he said. 'And Eris Mawkin owed me a favour.'

'Eris doesn't work for the Council,' said Sasha.

'Maybe not,' he said, 'but she's got a nice shiny badge from the

Runners that says she's allowed any file she asks for. Anyway, I went to see her last night.'

'At midsummer?' said Sasha.

He shrugged. 'We had a drink at Hyde Park.'

'At midsummer?' Sasha repeated, crossing one leg over the other. August gave her a strange look and Sasha frowned. 'I'm just surprised you gave up an opportunity. All those lovesick women dropping their standards for one night only.'

'Sasha, please remember the house rules,' said Jude, forcing a smile and clearly trying to rally his mood. 'You've been banned from cooking for us, cleaning the bathroom and bullying August. We've spoken about this.'

'Deprived of all my favourite hobbies,' she replied, shaking a curl out of her eyes. 'Fine, so you saw Eris Mawkin and . . .?'

'Mawkin is the only registered House Mielikki necromancer for at least three decades.'

Alice's eyebrows shot up. She'd had no idea Mawkin was a member of the House – so few necromancers ever were. 'What about unregistered ones?' she asked. 'The ones who've gone off-grid to avoid the Runners taking too much of an interest in them?'

'No unregistered necromancer belonging to House Mielikki either,' he said.

'But how would she know?' Alice pressed. 'If they're unregistered and underground, no one would know who—'

'Mawkin would know,' August said. 'You know what she's like, always propping up a bar somewhere or other. Twenty-odd years ago she'd have been a wildcat. Same trade, same House; they'd have crossed paths.' He turned to Alice, his expression serious. 'Whoever your mother was, I don't think she met Tuoni through necromancy.'

Alice nodded. She knew so little about her biological parents. Even Tuoni, who had become such an overwhelming presence, was a mystery to her.

'What are your theories on the incident last night?' Jude asked quietly.

Alice started. Her mouth opened, and swiftly closed again. She didn't really want to talk about last night.

'I'll tell you mine,' said August, with morbid relish.

Alice dropped out of the conversation, unable to concentrate. All she could think about was her ceiling and the fact that she had woken feeling tired, but without a single ache or pain. She and Crowley had clawed through mud, had fallen against tables and been flung about by the uneven ground. She should have woken with muscle burn and bruises blooming across her skin. And yet she didn't have a scratch. Every full member of House Mielikki – even those with only one foot in the door – seemed to benefit from the growth of the tree. She was starting to believe that its extraordinary power was already beginning to balance Tuoni's deathly legacy and save her life. A prospect that was desperately welcome and hideous in equal measure, because if correct, she was benefiting from the Summer Tree's growth while others died. The echoes of the screams and shouts of Crane Park Island washed over her and she shuddered.

'Jude?' she said, slipping off her oval signet ring and glancing down at the faded crest. 'Can I ask a favour?'

17

Alice had deliberated long and hard, but in the end she hadn't waited for Crowley to return to Coram House before she left. Jude had taken himself off to his workshop to try to clarify the engraving on her ring, and Alice took the opportunity to check in on Bea again. She wanted news about last night – real news, from the House and not gossipmongers or newspapers – and only Bea could give it to her.

Bea, however, was not at the university when Alice arrived. There was a sombre air over the entire campus. Students and staff, or their loved ones, may well have been caught up in the Crane Park disaster. There were no lectures in the halls, no seminars in the fusty rooms, no sounds of the Ditto machine cranking out paperwork. One or two of the administrative staff passed her in the corridors and nodded solemnly as they went on their way, but there was a blanket of silence draped over the place that was unnerving during term time.

Alice found herself at a loose end, waiting for Bea's return. She had walked the length of the Arlington Building several times, and sat in the library, staring at the same page for half an hour while the words slid off the paper. It was impossible to concentrate on her training books. She needed to do something practical to distract her mind.

Genealogy books. That's what she needed. Jude had the ring with the faded crest on, and she couldn't truthfully remember what it looked like without it in front of her, but she could make a start. Bea would not be pleased at the state of the shelves. The ripples of Crane Park's destruction had stretched further than Alice had expected: one of the shelves had snapped and another had tipped its load onto the floor. She stacked them up neatly and moved on to the genealogy section. The volumes found here were arranged in House order, with titles like *Esteemed Houses of the Eighteenth Century*. She traced a finger along those in the House Mielikki section and settled on *The Roots of House Mielikki*.

She flipped through the pages, searching for crests, but there were very few on offer. In fact, it appeared to be less a genealogical study and more a salacious story of five-hundred-year-old sex scandals and political marriages between the Gardiners and the Florins – apparently two of House Mielikki's oldest families.

Alice paused, book in hand. She was tempted to return it for a more serious tome, but last night had been serious enough. So maybe sex scandals and centuries-old gossip was exactly the sort of levity she needed right now. Besides, if House Mielikki was on the rise, it was useful to know exactly what it had risen from. Trudging back to the comfy chairs, she settled down, slung one leg over her knee and scanned through the book.

She was deep into the tale of how the Gardiners – the longest-surviving dynasty and the original bloodline of Mielikki herself – had married into the Florins and found themselves erased from history. The last Gardiner daughter married a Florin who stole her inheritance, divorced her and then married a Lynn. And the Florilynns, as they became known after scrapping the double-barrel, went on to found *The Rookery Herald* before losing their entire fortune to gambling debts at the end of the nineteenth century, when the bloodline dwindled and vanished for good. There was a whole chapter devoted bitterly to the fact that Maurice Beale, a newly moneyed industrialist, had swept in and bought the newspaper, despite being a member of the opposing House Pellervoinen.

'Where the hell have you been?' asked Bea, sweeping into the library, her voice instantly breaking the mournful silence.

Alice blinked up at her, closing the book with a snap. 'I could ask you the same question.'

Bea shook her head. 'Not here,' she said. 'Out on the lawns. Let's go.'

'Outside?' asked Alice. 'Why?'

'The House has been debating whether to postpone the membership applications until this whole palaver with the Summer Tree is over.'

'They're cancelling my test?' asked Alice, horrified.

'No,' replied Bea. 'They're bringing it forward. To tomorrow night.'

The university gardens near Holly's memorial were empty, but they took the precaution of choosing a secluded clearing behind the laurel hedges. Here, the grass was long and a neat arc of crab apple trees lined the area.

'You're imagining a knife instead of a fist,' said Bea.

Alice was standing over a pine log suspended by laurels. She felt like a black belt martial artist, chopping wood for the approval of a trainer. Every now and again, Kuu churred loudly as though attempting to cheer her on.

'If you're slicing strips off the trunk, you're narrowing your focus,' said Bea. 'Fist, not knife, darling. Fix it up and try again.'

Bea's instructions were incredibly specific. Split the log, but don't carve through it; use force but don't physically touch it; snap it cleanly without splinters. Alice's lips pursed. She pressed her hand to the log, and under her palm the nicks in the bark smoothed out.

'Geraint has fobbed me off.'

'What?' asked Alice. Bea's surprising relationship with Chancellor Litmanen was the least important thing that had happened lately.

'He doesn't think it will play well with the voters if he's seen getting too cosy with a member of House Mielikki. Or, to put it another way, the House is on the public's shit-list and he wants to come out strong against us.'

'*Against* us?' said Alice, flexing her hand for another go. 'But the House hasn't done anything wrong. It's not our fault that the tree is having a growth spurt.'

'Yes, well, not quite true, but nice try. We are, all things considered, in the middle of a shit-astrophe.' Bea relaxed against a small apple tree and buried her head in her hands. 'I'm sorry. I don't even like that word; I'm just having a moment.' She took a deep breath and murmured, 'Shitshitshitshitshit.' Then she lifted her head and wafted cool air onto her face. 'Okay. Okay, I'm good now. The fresh air helps; we should work out here more often.'

'Why isn't it quite true?' asked Alice, ignoring the brief meltdown. 'Are you saying it *is* House Mielikki's fault?'

There was an expectant pause. Alice bent her arm, took a deep breath and shoved from the elbows. Her hand snapped forward – a little too curved – and lopped off a chunk before the log broke in half.

'When the hand's about to land, it needs to be—'

'Straight,' said Alice, 'I know. Channel it evenly through the ball of my palm.'

She picked up both halves, pressed her hands over it and resealed the log. Breaking the wood was easy. But she was used to relying on the tingle in her fingers and the feel of Mielikki's legacy surging up her arms. Bea wanted to sharpen her ability to focus her power through the fleshy part of her palm – it was the most stable part of the hand, and if the legacy poured down her arms rather than up, she could exert much more force into the pressure point.

'*Is* it House Mielikki's fault that the tree is causing problems?' asked Alice, replacing the wood, ready for another try.

'Possibly. Mielikki's tree is our responsibility,' said Bea, closing her eyes and tipping her head back. 'It's always been the responsibility of her House, in one way or another.'

'What happened at Crane Park . . .' Alice began.

'Awful,' said Bea, her eyes flying open and her expression darkening. 'We lost so many to the sinkholes.'

'I saw tree roots in the trenches, in the cracks. I'm sure I did. The Summer Tree's roots?'

'Yes,' said Bea wearily. 'There's no hiding it now, I'm afraid. The other Houses know. The Council knows. Like I said – Geraint's throwing us under the bus for votes.'

Alice nodded, sinking briefly into her own thoughts before resurfacing. She stared at the pine log, focused on its weakest point in the middle and arched her arm over her shoulder. Imagining the desire starting in her chest, the back of her neck prickled and she shivered. The blood raced through her arms. She swung her hand out like a punch and stopped a centimetre clear of the bark. The air warped around her closed fist and smashed through the wooden log. Obliterated it. Annihilated it. Pine dust and splinters exploded across the grass, and Alice's sleeve was covered in it.

'Fuck,' she muttered.

'Yes,' said Bea, spitting out sawdust. 'A little heavy-handed, I agree.'

Alice flicked the powdered debris off her clothes and swiped up a second log. She slammed it into position with a vengeance.

'Tell me about the tree,' urged Alice. 'Tell me the things that aren't in the books you've given me so far.'

'Oh, darling—'

'You're my mentor,' Alice pointed out, fixated on the wood. 'Come on, mentor me. I want to know . . . everything. Like – when it's said that the foundations of the Rookery are built on the tree, is that literally or metaphorically?'

'I'm not sure I know a great deal more than you, any more,' Bea murmured. 'It's not *in* the books. That's the problem. Everything we know has been passed on by word of mouth, and people are fallible – we make mistakes, we misinterpret what we've heard.'

There was a rustle of movement in the grass and Tom appeared, striding out from the trees and into their glade.

'That's not strictly true,' he said with a solemn smile. 'There was one book that put forward a theory about our foundations.'

Bea threw him an exasperated glance. 'A book that burned to a crisp hundreds of years ago.'

Tom slumped down next to Bea in the grass and kicked out his long legs. 'There are rumours that Governor Whitmore has a copy of it.'

'All nonsense, darling,' said Bea with a sigh. 'If Gabriel Whitmore owned one of the Rookery's greatest losses to litera-ture, I think I'd know about it.'

'What was the book?' asked Alice, staring at the pine wood.

Tom gestured at her. 'You know, sometimes it can help to tackle it from a diagonal,' he said. 'Try standing at a forty-five-degree angle.'

Alice nodded and adjusted her stance. He was right. She felt steadier.

'Oh, it had a Latin title,' said Bea. 'Something hopelessly long and fussy. But it was *apparently* a scientific study of the Rookery's geography.'

'There was a national outcry at the time about the secrets of our creation having been lost,' said Tom.

'Apparently,' added Bea.

'And what was its theory?' asked Alice, squinting at the log with one eye, to perfect her aim as though staring down the barrel of a gun.

'It told us how parallel cities like this one were built,' said Tom.

Alice stepped back from the pine to listen, and Bea bristled. 'Can we please focus on the matter at hand?' said the librarian, gesturing for Alice to resume her practice.

'Am I causing a distraction?' asked Tom.

'Yes, darling, you are,' said Bea, patting him on the hand. 'But I'm just glad to see you're safe after last night.'

He rose to his feet and dusted himself off. 'I just wanted to let you know that I've offered to administer the binding draught in your next test,' he told Alice. There was a nervous pause. 'I thought . . . maybe jumping back into the saddle is for the best.'

They very carefully avoided looking towards the holly bush.

'But I won't be offended at all if you'd rather—'

'I want you to do it,' said Alice.

He let out a rush of breath and nodded. 'Good. Well, I'll see you both later.'

They watched him lope off. After a moment, Alice turned back to Bea and said, 'How *was* the Rookery built?'

Bea sighed loudly, but her expression showed she'd given in.

'The world is an onion skin,' she said. 'Cities layered upon cities. And in that gap between the layers is the void. An empty space, like a corridor. The problem is, some layers are stronger than others. Take an *actual* onion skin,' she said. 'In the centre is the bud. If I drop an onion, the chances are the layers on the outside will be bruised and the bud will be quite safe.'

Bea paused, to take in Alice's raised eyebrows.

'*London* is the bud,' said Bea. 'We're the weaker layer on the outside. Once you cut the layers off the onion bud to make your dinner, that's it, they're gone, so for us to survive intact, we have to stay attached to the onion bud. Oh, I don't even like bloody onions,' she said after a moment. 'But do you see what I'm saying? The Rookery is on its own layer. Here, the Summer Tree is what keeps us stable, by connecting us to the' – she rolled her eyes – 'onion bud. We're anchored onto London. And the tree's roots stretch through every part of our city's foundation layer. The Rookery is built over them. Without them the city would crumble – possibly into the void, who knows?'

'How do the *roots* tie us to London?' asked Alice, trying to keep up. 'Do you mean literally? They stretch through the void and into London's foundations too?'

Bea shrugged. 'No idea, darling. The theory was explained in the book, but it's gone. I doubt we'll ever know. The important takeaway is that without the tree, the Rookery would disintegrate.'

'But . . . the tree isn't going anywhere,' said Alice, pausing. 'Setting aside what happened last night, if the tree's growing bigger and stronger, won't it strengthen the ties?'

'Look, big is beautiful – you'll get no argument from me on that score,' said Bea. 'But think about this for a minute, darling. House Mielikki controls the natural world; it doesn't let it run wild. I can grow a rose for you, exactly twelve inches tall, with alternating red, white and yellow petals. I control the rose. It grows to my specifications, not its own. We manage the unmanageable.' She paused. 'Look at parasites, diseases and tumours . . . Uncontrollable cell growth can be damaging. There has to be balance – something to restrict it, to hold it back.'

Alice tensed. Those words were familiar to her in a way that Bea could never imagine.

'Have you ever seen an infestation of knotweed?'

Alice nodded cautiously. When she'd been looking around flats with Jen, one of the first that the estate agent had shown them had had knotweed in what the particulars had claimed was a garden but was in fact a tiny square of concrete. The plant had smashed through the concrete, its invidious roots piercing the flat's mortar and cracking the brickwork. The whole building looked like it was about to collapse, and they'd laughed in the estate agent's face when he'd asked if they wanted to pay the deposit by cash.

'You're saying . . . the Summer Tree might grow like knotweed and destroy the Rookery's foundations in its bid to expand?' she said.

'Yes,' said Bea. 'And I think last night shows that's exactly what it's capable of.'

Alice shook her head in disbelief. How could this possibly be true? She had only discovered this world eighteen months ago – people she cared for were here. Jen had *died* to save this city. And now . . .? It was unthinkable. She couldn't lose the Rookery when she'd only just found it.

'But . . . Look, if House Mielikki has responsibility for the tree, why can't they use their legacy to stop it? The legacies are growing stronger. Do something with them!'

'Because we protect it,' said Bea, 'but we don't control it. Mielikki's family bloodline died out years ago, and with them all our control over the tree.'

'The Gardiners,' said Alice. 'Or the Florilynns, you mean.'

'How do you know?' Bea cocked her head in interest. 'You've been reading up?'

'I've been reading about stolen inheritances and gambled fortunes,' said Alice.

'Ah, *The Roots of House Mielikki*,' she said. 'Apparently, it caused a bit of a stir when it was published about a hundred years ago.' She paused and then shrugged. 'No. It was the Gardiners who were the original bloodline. When Nathaniel Florin threw out his wife, Elizabeth Gardiner, they had no children. He boasted of his connection to the Mielikki line but it was rubbish – as soon as he divorced her, the connection was ended, and Elizabeth died of consumption soon after.' Bea sighed and leaned back on her elbows. 'Mielikki's line ended, and that's where the House has always had a problem. Mielikki grew the Summer Tree, and when she died, her children became its . . . its . . .'

'Gardeners?'

'Exactly,' said Bea, snapping her fingers. 'The *Gardiners*. We're talking thousands of years ago. On-the-nose surname bastardizations were all the rage.' She brushed splinters off her dress. 'First Mielikki, then her children and grandchildren looked after it, for thousands of years.'

'But then years of mixed marriage corrupted the bloodline, and the . . . original line died out?' said Alice, understanding beginning to emerge from the potted history.

'Yes. Of course, to some degree or other, each of us has her blood inside us, since we've inherited her legacy.'

'The House system is so incestuous,' Alice murmured.

Bea snorted. 'I suppose. But only in the way the entire human race is. You could be my great-to-the-power-of-a-billion grandmother for all we know. Anyway, none of us are direct descendants. But we do have her legacy, however diluted it's become. So we took on responsibility for the tree. It was House Mielikki who pushed for the fireflies to be introduced to protect the tree. Decades ago, it wasn't necessary because Mielikki's most direct bloodline could still protect it. But when that family died out, we needed an alternative. Politically,' she went on, 'it's always left us vulnerable. We take credit for the good the Summer Tree does, but it's difficult to avoid the pointing fingers when things go wrong if you've spent years crowing about being responsible for its successes.'

Bea stopped and tucked a loose straggle of hair back into her chignon. 'So,' she said. 'Those crowing about the rise of House Mielikki are going to have a shock heading their way. I hope whatever spike in legacy power they get from the tree's surge is worth it, because we're about to become the most hated House in the Rookery's history. Tomorrow morning's *Rookery Herald* is running with a headline blaming us for the deaths at midsummer. And do you know what, darling? That's probably the best we can hope for right now. Because if things get worse . . .' She shook her head, her face deathly pale.

Alice thrust her hand forward. The log split cleanly and rolled into the grass.

Bea tried to smile, staring at the wood but clearly distracted. 'Well at least that's something.'

Alice nodded with satisfaction.

'By the way – there's something you should know,' said Bea.

'What?' asked Alice, wiping her palms on her jeans.

'Lester's dead. He fell into a sinkhole at Crane Park.'

Alice's eyebrows rose. He'd been there? She wasn't sure what to feel about it. Relieved? She shook her head. Actually, after all she'd seen, more than anything she just felt . . . sad.

There was someone in her apartment. She could hear their nightjar fluttering through the crack under her door. Alice hesitated, a chill prickling down her spine. *Lester's dead. How could there be a stranger in my apartment if Lester is dead?*

Alice froze. Her heart began to pound and adrenaline slid through her veins. *Catch them by surprise*, she decided, quickly formulating a plan. The cricket bat was just by the front door. It was the perfect weapon, in fact, for someone who claimed Mielikki's legacy: she could turn it into anything she needed, an explosion of wooden shards, maybe . . .

Alice glanced over her shoulder and quickly placed her hand against the wooden door. She exhaled steadily, the even rhythm of her breath helping her to focus as she pushed her will into it. Tingling shivers ran down her arm and she pressed harder . . . until the door shattered into thousands of splinters, falling to the floor like hail.

There was a gasp of surprise from inside and Alice charged into her apartment, snatching up the cricket bat as she went.

'Don't swing that at me.'

It was Reid. Pale and drawn, and wearing clothes that looked slept in.

'What the hell are you doing in here?' asked Alice, letting the cricket bat fall to her side.

'I needed to talk to you,' said Reid. 'I wanted to . . .' She trailed away and visibly stiffened, her back straightening and her eyes narrowing. 'Were you followed?'

Alice gave her a baffled look. 'What's all this about?' she asked. 'Have the Runners been in touch? They've been investigating the vandalism in the lab. You didn't show up for work, and—'

'It was me,' said Reid dismissively. 'I smashed up the lab.'

Alice dropped the bat. '*What?* You? Why?'

Reid shrugged the question aside. 'It doesn't matter. The bulk of my research . . . is gone. Destroyed. You didn't make any more copies?'

Alice stared at her. 'No. 'But *why* would you—?'

'Because I was lied to!' said Reid in a shrill voice. 'I thought my research was only theoretical, but the project backer . . . He wanted to *use* it. To make me an accessory out of a twisted vengeance. What happened at Crane Park Island . . . If I'd known, I would never have . . .' She shuddered, running a shaky hand through her nest of hair.

'Crane Park?' Alice said sharply. Had Reid's project had something to do with the Summer Tree's damage?

'I need you to come with me,' said Reid, dropping her voice to a barely audible whisper, 'to my apartment. It's only a matter of time before he discovers my address.' Her tone was urgent. 'I want to show you what remains of my research. You have to help. We need to go before—'

It began as a rattle. Wooden boards tremored against each other, long edges vibrating. Then a clacking sound that made it difficult to hear as the ends tipped and crashed back down again. It was the floor beneath them. It was lurching unevenly.

'This . . .' said Reid, looking about her with an anxious scowl on her face. 'It's not . . .'

The joists in the ceiling shifted out of place with a thunderous crack, and Alice darted a glance overhead. The ceiling was going to fall in. A sprinkle of plaster bloomed from above, raining dust over the floor, and as the creaking boards rocked beneath her feet and the door frame strained against the walls, she was catapulted to Crane Park Island – the earthquake, the sinkholes . . . the screams.

Not again. Not here.

'Reid!' she shouted over the noise. 'Let's go!'

But Reid was bleeding. A red blotch was seeping through the cotton shirt by her collar bone. The wooden lintel on Alice's window frame had cracked, a shard tumbling free and striking her near the shoulder. Reid fell back against the wall, too weak to push herself upright. Diving forward, Alice flung Reid's other arm around her neck and hauled her across the tilting floor-boards. They didn't quite make it to the door. Reid was a dead weight in Alice's arms. The professor's limp foot caught the edge of a lifted board and sent them stumbling towards the bed.

Alice ricocheted off the bedpost and hit the wall with a winded breath. Reid lay collapsed on the mattress, her crumpled blouse riding up over the waistband of her trousers and her curls utterly undone. Shit. Alice's back smarted with the pain of her landing.

But the room had stopped vibrating. The floor was still, the door frame no longer straining against the walls. Alice didn't have time for relief: she had to get Reid out of here, quickly. The vibrations had stopped, but between the precarious joists, the ceiling, the floor and window, the place was a death trap.

Kuu suddenly screeched a warning, and Alice's eyes darted up. Tension tightened every muscle and ligament in her body. Kuu jerked her head at Reid's nightjar, and Alice paled. Reid's nightjar, sitting next to her on the mattress, spread its wings and tottered closer to the radiant umbilical cord that linked bird and human. Squatting down, it pecked at the cord in a frenzy, then wafted its wings and soared into the air. The cord looping from its clawed foot . . . was beginning to dim. The glow was fading as it prepared to leave. Reid was dying before her eyes.

'What? No!'

Alice dived onto the bed, her knees sinking down into the springs. How was she dying? Why?

Blood had pooled out across the mattress, rich and glossy. *Oh God.* The broken lintel hadn't struck the professor – it was *embedded* in her. The angle was a steep diagonal, the wooden fragment stabbed through like a rapier. *How close to the heart?*

She grabbed up handfuls of bedsheets and padded them around the pumping wound, careful not to remove the shard of broken wood.

'Reid?' she shouted, one eye on the professor's deathly pale face, the other on the blood. Her stomach fluttered. It wasn't stopping. The blood wasn't stopping. It soaked into the knees of her jeans, and she shuddered at the warm wetness against her skin.

'Help!' she bellowed. 'Someone get help!' But of course, there was no one else upstairs.

The pillows, she decidedly frantically. She reached for the pillows, pressing them harder, silently pleading. *Come on.* And then, seconds or minutes or hours later, Alice glanced up at Reid's nightjar – the cord now blooming with light. *Thank God. There's still time to get help.*

Reid mumbled something inaudible, and a shiver of relief ran through Alice.

'Vivian?' she shouted. 'Stay awake, okay? Just . . .'

Reid's eyes flickered and she forced them open. She squinted up at Alice. Her mouth worked silently, and Alice strained to listen.

'You should never . . . have come back. You were safe . . .'

Reid closed her eyes and winced in pain.

'With your parents . . .' she hissed. 'You were safe . . . They were chosen . . . because . . . safe . . .'

Alice stared at her in shock.

18

'Vivian, what do you mean?' asked Alice, fighting the confusion that threatened to disorder her thoughts.

Reid's eyes rolled back and she wheezed.

'Science,' she mumbled incoherently. 'Magellan . . .'

'Vivian?' Alice said more forcefully, kneeling down so that they were eye to eye. 'What do you mean about my parents? You chose them? What does that . . .?'

Reid peered at Alice, trying to focus through her pain. She tilted her head, mouth puckering.

'I didn't know who you were,' she said, her skeletal hands reaching out to tighten around Alice's wrist. 'I didn't know . . .' Her grip relaxed and her hand slid down Alice's, pausing at her bare finger. 'Where is it?' she asked, squeezing Alice's hand.

'My signet ring?'

'I left it for you . . . wanted you . . . to have it . . .' Reid rasped.

Creeping fingers of icy dread slid down Alice's spine. She stared at the bare finger, and back at Reid's slack face. No. Alice's mum – Patricia Wyndham – had given her the ring months ago. Alice's ears were buzzing, and the walls seemed to close in around her.

'What are you saying?' Alice whispered. 'What are you . . .?

Reid, wake up!' she demanded as the older woman's eyelids flickered. 'Reid, don't you dare – tell me what you mean!'

Reid opened her mouth, but her words were garbled and nonsensical as she struggled to stay awake. The professor hissed, frustrated at her inability to speak, and her eyelids drooped. Alice's hands darted to the wound. The blood flow had eased off. Reid's cord was aglow, her nightjar intact.

Out in the corridor, a distant door swung open – the one that led from the stairs up to the corridor. Brief footsteps echoed along the hallway.

'Call an ambulance!' Alice shouted. 'Someone's had an accident!'

There was a sharp intake of breath and the footsteps hurried away, the door swinging shut behind them.

Alice looked down at the professor. She was breathing in a steady rhythm, as though in a peaceful rest.

The glimmering cord linking Reid to her nightjar looped down between them, pulsing with muted vitality. Alice's old tutor, Proctor, had once told her that an aviarist couldn't touch someone else's nightjar – but Proctor had been wrong; she had once stroked Sasha's, and it had given her a glimpse of Sasha's most secret memories. But that had been accidental and deeply intrusive. Sasha's memories had been private and none of Alice's business.

But this time . . . now . . .? Reid had been trying to tell her something.

With only a moment's hesitation, Alice reached for Reid's nightjar, avoiding the cord. Her fingers brushed gently against the feathers and circled back to stroke the soft head. The professor's nightjar opened its eyes and blinked at her.

'*Show me,*' Alice breathed.

She caught the bird's gaze. Eyes like the dark, glossy surface of a lake locked on hers. The light from the incandescent cord glowed brighter, haloing the nightjar's head, and Alice was mesmerized. *Dark . . . glossy . . . surface of a lake.* The room flickered around her. She felt herself mentally tip forward, falling towards the bird's gaze . . . and broke through the surface of the lake. She sank into the bird's mind like a lead weight. Memories – Reid's – flashed across her vision like gunfire: snatches of her school days, holidays, her graduation . . . glimpses of laughing faces, some unknown and some faintly recognizable – a younger Marianne Northam? They burst in front of her and died away. Another memory rose to take their place, then another . . . Alice screwed her eyes shut. Reid exhaled softly next to her . . . and a new memory rose up and thickened around Alice, came to life like the outline of a sketch painted in. The living room at Alice's old house; she remembered it from old photographs: familiar carpet, furniture, trinkets . . .

Her eyes flew open. She was *Reid*. Not Alice. And her body was alive with grief and dread, sparking through her limbs like electricity. A terrible fear, smothered by an even more terrible hope, sat in her gullet, waiting to choke her. *Keep her safe. Make it count.*

'And here she is.' That was Tilda. Business-like. Trying to make it quick.

The couple had eyes only for the Moses basket. Their hands were gripping each other so tightly their skin was blanching. They didn't think she could see it – their naked desperation, their swollen hearts – but she saw everything now: how foolish she'd been, how naive . . . everything.

'You'll take good care of her,' said Tilda. Not a request – a command. Tilda bent down to tuck in the blanket without looking inside; she hadn't wanted to look too closely on the journey here. Too painful, she'd said, her lined face crumpling. Her hair was so grey. Was it the grief that had aged her?

'We'll give her everything we have,' said the man. A tall man, with broad shoulders – he'd need those – and the sort of face that was quick to smile. Mike, that was his name. He put a hand on his wife's shoulder, squeezing reassurance into her muscles. The woman – Patricia – barely seemed aware of what he'd said. Her eyes were fastened to the baby.

'The other social worker—' he began.

'Retired,' said Tilda. 'Uncontactable now, I'm afraid. She's moved to the south of France.'

'Oh, how lovely,' said Patricia, smiling fixedly into the Moses basket.

'We . . . did have a small complication,' said Tilda.

Patricia's eyes shot up, her panic palpable. She was worried they would take the basket away again. Maybe they should.

'A mistake with the paperwork.' Tilda gestured at the sleeping baby. 'Her file was misplaced. We moved offices – you understand, these things happen. Still.' She smiled tightly. 'It's not a problem, is it?'

'No,' replied Patricia, the relief clear in her tone. 'Not a problem at all.'

'Her mother – her natural mother, that is – is dead. It's all very sad.' Tilda turned away to busy herself with the sheaf of papers they'd signed. She stuffed them carelessly into her handbag. Was she hiding her face? 'Well,' she said, spinning back with a grim smile. 'We'd better leave you to it. Catherine?'

A shake of the head. No. Not yet. Not like this.

She saw Patricia tense. Saw the worry written over her face.

'We'll take the best care of her. We'll love her to the ends of the earth.' She glanced nervously at her husband. 'Won't we, Mike?'

He nodded vigorously. 'She'll want for nothing – not money, a nice home, love. Nothing.'

'We've been waiting for her all along,' Patricia said quietly. 'I knew the minute I laid eyes on her. I've waited all my life to love her.'

A pain. In her chest. Take the basket from them and run.

'We've . . . we've got some names picked out,' said Mike, casting around for something to say: a convincing sales pitch to make them leave, and leave the basket behind. She knew it.

'Rose. For my grandmother. Or—'

'No.'

He stopped short and looked over at Patricia. His wife glanced at Tilda.

'My colleague here . . . is Catherine Rose,' said Tilda. 'And she's never been especially fond of her own name.' Tilda smiled, trying to ease the strange atmosphere in the room.

'Oh.' A warm, defusing laugh from the husband. She had been right – he was quick to smile.

They all smiled. A roomful of smiles. Smiling was the thing that would carry them through to the end.

'Well,' said Tilda. 'We wish you all the very best. We know you're the right match, and we hope you will all be very happy together.' She paused and gestured as though to encourage speech, or a last goodbye.

But she had already said her goodbyes: to the child and to her mother.

'Good luck,' she said, the words like ashes in her mouth.

Mike and Patricia were bent over the basket, enraptured.

Later, they would find the signet ring, tucked into the folds of the blanket. It had been important to pass it on. Fitting, some-how. No other trace of her mother would be left. Tilda planned to destroy the books, but the ring was special. She would never know who she was. But she might wear the ring one day, and touch hands with her past.

Alice shrank back from Reid's nightjar with a gasp, her fingers tingling and her head pounding. Kuu fluttered onto her shoulder and pecked at her hair. The bedroom blinked into existence, the mattress creaking under her and Reid wheezing softly, only semi-lucid.

Alice blinked rapidly, still trying to focus. 'Vivian?' she managed, disoriented. That had never happened before. The first time she'd done this, with Sasha and without her permission, she'd been a bystander in Sasha's memories. This time, she'd not merely been right in the centre of things, she'd slipped behind Reid's eyes. She'd experienced the memory as though *she* was Reid – feeling her feelings and thinking her thoughts – and the next minute was thrust back into her own mind and her own body, in the very real here and now. It was like time travelling; she'd just been standing in her old living room, twenty-six years in the past: the day her adoption had been finalized. Had she experienced the memory differently this time because she'd featured in it, her infant self perhaps recalling some unconscious connection with it too?

Alice peered closely at Reid. Rifling through her memories hadn't hurt her; Sasha had never even been aware.

'Vivian?' said Alice. Then, more insistently, 'Catherine? Catherine Rose? Is that your real—?'

'No,' moaned Reid, her eyes flickering open. 'Not that . . . If Marianne . . . He did this. He's here . . .'

'Tuoni?' Alice threw out sharply.

Reid's glazed eyes widened and she released a strangled gasp. The cracked ceiling groaned. A thick wooden joist, destabilized by the quake, swung loose, and before Alice had time to react, it crashed down across Reid's abdomen, pinning her to the bed. Her eyes bulged at the pressure and Alice yelped in shock, diving towards the already injured woman.

Alice thrust her hand out, all of the tension focused on the ball of her palm. The air warped and the wooden joist exploded into dust.

'Reid?' she yelled.

Reid's shoulders twitched and she began to convulse, her legs kicking out. Alice leapt the bed and ran for the door.

'Help!' she screamed. 'An ambulance! Now!'

The door of Coram House swung open, and there was a long pause in which Crowley studied her intently. 'What is it? What's wrong?'

She opened her mouth to speak, to explain, but found she didn't know where to begin. So instead, she moved past him, into the house, without a word.

He sat her in a kitchen chair and pressed a hot tea into her hands, then frowned and waved a hand at the fire. Flames burst into the grate, the orange glow dancing across her face. She wasn't cold. It was the shock.

He didn't sit with her. He seemed to understand she didn't want to be examined. She just wanted to sit in peace – and Coram House had always brought her that.

The tea grew cold in her hands. Alice was utterly motionless. Her breathing was so shallow and so calm that she could have been mistaken for dead. She had spent the afternoon thinking unthinkable thoughts.

What if Reid dies in the hospital? She tried out the idea in her mind, imagining how it might feel to be told the news. But she couldn't seem to absorb the possibility. Reid had been a constant fixture, a blunt thorn in her side, for months. She couldn't just die.

The shock of seeing her parents and childhood home in Reid's memories had ebbed away, and now she was simply numb. Vivian Reid – a woman she'd never met before taking a job at the university – had a connection to her childhood. But if the fragments of the professor's speech were to be believed, Reid had not known Alice was the child she and the older woman had handed – reluctantly – over for adoption. Not until she'd seen Alice wearing the signet ring her mum had given to her before she'd left Ireland.

She tried to think back to that conversation, to how she'd wrongly inferred that the ring had been a *Wyndham* heirloom, but she couldn't quite recall it now. Patricia Wyndham had never worn it. Why would she? The much younger Vivian Reid had left this ring for Alice. And yet, she was nothing like the Vivian Reid that Alice knew: arrogant, volatile, sharp-tempered, with little regard for anyone else. She had gone by a different name in the memory, too: Catherine Rose.

'Are you ready to talk?'

Her eyes darted up to see Crowley looking down at her with concern.

She nodded. 'Yes. I'm ready.' She took a deep breath and told him everything. Everything that had happened since she'd returned to the university, even her trip to The Necropolis with August, the attacks, everything – right up to the moment she'd arrived on his doorstep.

'The earthquake,' he said at last. 'Vivian Reid—'

'Crushed by a dislodged ceiling joist,' she said, looking around at the kitchen, just now noticing it was untouched by the tremors that had so disturbed her university apartment.

'And it was this afternoon?' Crowley clarified. 'Not yesterday, at the same time as the midsummer disaster?'

'No,' she said slowly, confused. Of all the things she'd revealed to him, why had he focused on this one? It was the third quake to hit the Rookery – he must have felt it too. She frowned again at the kitchen. And yet—

'Alice,' he said, his voice feather-light with patience. 'There has been *no* earthquake today.'

19

'What?' said Alice, incredulous. 'Of course there . . .' She trailed away.

She hadn't seen any new damage to the university grounds when she'd fled the building to come here. If what he was saying was true . . .

'Oh my God,' she murmured. 'There was no earthquake. Reid tried to tell me.' She rubbed her face wearily with the flat of her hand. 'Reid said, "He did this; he's here." But I didn't . . .' Alice tipped her head back to the ceiling in thought.

'Someone wished to silence her?' Crowley asked. 'To stop her speaking with you?'

'I don't . . . Maybe,' said Alice. 'She wanted me to go with her – to her apartment, I think, to see what was left of her research. She mentioned . . . Crowley, she mentioned Crane Park Island. I mean, she was distressed and not making much sense, but . . . it sounded like her research project had something to do with it. Or at least she *felt* it did.' She pored over the moment a panicked Reid had thrown out those words. Was it just Reid being arrogant? To assume that whatever she'd been working on was capable of such a thing?

'She's safe now,' Alice murmured. 'I think. The university nurse went with her in the ambulance. She was sure Reid would be okay, but . . . she won't be out of hospital for a while.'

'Do you know where Reid lives?' Crowley asked tentatively.

'Islington,' said Alice. She'd travelled to the Rookery's version of Islington to drop some papers off to Reid months ago. 'Why? You think we should break in and look for whatever it was she wanted to show me?'

He raised a musing eyebrow. 'Is it breaking in if nothing gets broken?'

She gave this some thought. Whoever had tried to silence Reid hadn't yet discovered her address – that's what she'd said. How much time did she have before they found it? And should she try to get there first? Prioritize the test or Reid's apartment?

'My next membership trial is so close,' she said, her voice strained. 'I have to pass that test tomorrow. I can't risk a failure. Maybe . . . afterwards, we could go?'

They lapsed into silence again. Her thoughts were a fog of uncertainty. Frowning, she reached into her pocket and pulled out a photograph. 'I grabbed this before I left,' she said, passing it to him. 'I found it with another photograph in Reid's drawers when the lab was trashed.'

Crowley's stare turned blank as his eyes ghosted over the picture. It was the old group photo of the picnic. Half a dozen smiling girls and young women sat between two middle-aged ladies. A magnificent townhouse towered over them.

'There's Reid,' she said, pointing to the girl named on the back as Catherine, who sat with her arm around a wet Labrador.

The Reid in the picture was glancing at something out of the frame, a half-smile on her face. She couldn't have been more than thirteen. Next to her, a scrawny girl a few years younger stared up at her, eyes gleaming. Marianne: Crowley's maternal aunt. His face stiffened when he caught sight of her.

Alice pointed at one of the older women – in her forties, tall, with a stately bearing. Her hair was pulled back into a bun and her dress patchy with wetness – from the dog, Alice assumed.

'Do you know her?' she asked.

He shook his head, his eyes drawn instead to a face at the other end of the row: Helena, his mother and Marianne's sister.

Alice returned to the older woman and the words on the back of the photograph: *Look at Tilda's wet dress! She told me she's banning either dogs or pond-dipping next year! I almost told her I'd rather she banned herself but I bit my tongue to keep Mother happy!*

Tilda. *This* woman had appeared in Reid's memory. Tilda had pretended to be a social worker signing off Alice's adoption. Tilda knew the truth about where Alice came from – because she was the one who had left her in Henley-on-Thames. This woman had had a hand in her adoption. She'd been there, right at the very start.

'Do you recognize the others?' Alice asked quietly, mindful of Crowley's drawn expression.

'Other than my mother and Marianne, only this one,' he said after a moment, tapping the young woman on the end. Brown hair in long braids and smiling warmly at the camera, she could only have been in her late teens. 'Leda Westergard. Future Rookery chancellor. This must have been taken years before she took office.'

Alice nodded. Her skin prickled as she saw a signet ring on her little finger. The same ring from the other photo.

'The Annual Jarvis Fundraiser,' she said, referring to the words on the back. 'Do you think they were all friends? Family friends, maybe – that would account for the range of ages.'

'I think,' Crowley said quietly, 'that back then lots of the established families understood the values of quid pro quo better than the value of friendship. The Northams, Westergards and Roses had much more clout than they could ever hope to have today. Now, they're no better than anyone.'

He glanced up. 'May I keep the picture?'

She hesitated. The fire sparked in the grate, the only sound. The picture was her only real clue. But then she wondered when he'd last seen his mother's face, and nodded.

'This . . . Vivian Reid,' he said, glancing at the pencilled writing to double-check. But of course, the name listed next to Marianne's was Catherine, not Vivian. He frowned and laid the photograph flat on the table. 'The Roses were a big House Pellervoinen family. Her father – Catherine Rose's father – was the founder of the Fellowship,' Crowley said, his voice brittle. 'She disappeared over two decades ago.'

Alice sat back. *Catherine Rose. The Fellowship.* No wonder Reid had had that leaflet. Had she been an active member all this time, or had she left the Fellowship when she'd abandoned her name?

'Why did she disappear?' Alice murmured.

'It was . . .' Crowley cleared his throat. 'Not long before the . . . Cranleigh Grange dinner party massacre.'

Alice noted the tension in his jaw. The Cranleigh Grange massacre was the night that Marianne had descended on his family home and slaughtered his mother and grandparents. Crowley had been very young, and his sister a newborn. Marianne had led the slaughter in revenge for her sister polluting their bloodline by marrying a non-Väki – non-magical, human 'filth'. Crowley had harboured a hatred for Marianne all his life.

'The news from the time,' said Crowley in a tight voice, 'suggested that when her father died, Catherine had been seen as a voice of reason, a modernizing force within the Fellowship. It set her at odds with Marianne Northam, whose preferred methods are brutally old-fashioned: wholesale slaughter. The Fellowship almost disintegrated in the wake of the Cranleigh attack. It survived, unfortunately, but its mania was . . . diminished. It stopped attracting new members so easily and Marianne – the new leader – had to resort to other methods to . . . coerce membership.'

Other methods. She'd used hemomancy, blood magic, to trick new members and swell the ranks with compulsion.

'Catherine Rose vanished – and many suggested Marianne had killed her.'

'She went to the mainland,' said Alice – the world on the other side of Marble Arch. 'Reid travelled Europe, taking short posts at different universities to further her research. She left the Sorbonne under a cloud.'

'But . . . why did she reappear twenty years later as Vivian Reid?' Crowley mused.

'Because of her research project on souls,' said Alice.

'Which she herself destroyed?'

'Yes. The bulk of it.'

'Strange,' said Crowley, 'to have found something important enough to resurface – after a decades-long absence – only to obliterate that very thing within a year.'

Alice nodded. It certainly was strange – but it wasn't the only thing. Something nagged at her, something that didn't seem to fit.

'Crowley?' she said slowly. 'You're talking about Vivian Reid as though you've never heard her name before today. But . . . you were the one who told me about the job working with her in the first place.'

He glanced at her. 'It wasn't me – it was Sasha who found the advert in the newspaper. It didn't mention your employer's name, only Magellan's. For an aviarist, it seemed perfect.'

She nodded, lapsing into silence. It *had* been perfect for her. Until Reid had destroyed everything.

'I think Catherine – Reid, whoever she is – knew my biological mother. But if Reid was in House Pellervoinen, and a member of the Fellowship . . . is it possible my mother was too? Have I got this wrong, assuming she was in House Mielikki?' She shuddered a breath. 'The legacies aren't always that clear, are they? You can have a bit of any of them – be a jack of all trades,' she said, remembering Cecil's words.

'That's true,' said Crowley. 'But to pass for a House you must have a dominant legacy. The jacks of all trades don't usually pass.' His eyes narrowed, searching hers. 'You have a House Mielikki parent; I'm certain of that.'

She hoped he was right, because if not, the second test might kill her. Alice shifted in her seat, one nagging argument against his theory refusing to slide. 'But you passed for House Ilmarinen,' she pointed out, 'and you're . . .' She searched for the right word.

'Prodigiously talented with the doorways?' he offered, his mouth tugging into a faint smile.

'Yes.' She hesitated. Then, 'I should have thanked you earlier. For what you did for my parents. The safety door.'

His eyes held hers. 'It was my pleasure.'

Alice felt something in her chest begin to thaw. She nodded and looked away. Crowley and his doorways. He could open almost any door for travelling. There was virtually nowhere closed to him, and nowhere he couldn't go. And yet, it wasn't Ilmarinen who had created the doorways – it had been Pellervoinen.

'Your dominant Ilmarinen legacy wasn't diluted by your Pellervoinen one,' she said.

He smiled to himself. 'That's . . . not quite correct.'

'Well I'm glad anyway,' she said after a moment. 'I'd rather you were in Ilmarinen. Mielikki and Pellervoinen were at odds with each other. I think you and I have enough problems without our opposing Houses getting in the way.'

He laughed. 'Pellervoinen and Mielikki weren't in opposition.'

She cocked an eyebrow. 'No? She created the most incredible tree in the world and he went and slapped a big bloody abbey round it. He literally imprisoned her greatest creation.'

'Non-factual rubbish,' said Crowley.

She glared at him, aghast. 'Why on earth are you defending him?'

Crowley gave a long-suffering sigh – designed purely to irritate, she had no doubt. 'They built the foundations of the Rookery *together*, tree and stone.'

'Well, given that the foundations seem to be disintegrating under our feet,' said Alice, 'their teamwork skills weren't up to much.'

'You can thank Mielikki's unmanageable contribution for that,' he said.

She shot him a dark look.

'Look, Pellervoinen didn't place the abbey around the tree to imprison it,' said Crowley. 'He placed a monumental stone abbey around her tree . . . to protect it. To keep it safe for her.'

Alice shook her head sceptically.

'They didn't despise each other; they loved each other,' he pressed. 'Why else do you think they built the foundations of their Houses so close together?'

She hesitated, unwilling to cede the point to him – though she didn't really know why. Habit, she supposed.

'Alice,' Crowley said in a low voice, his gaze locked on hers. 'Look at my nightjar.'

Four small words that sucked out the air in the room. She stared at him. She had only ever seen his nightjar once. He'd always gone to great lengths to hide it from her – one of the few people who could. And now he was offering it up for inspection – the guardian mirror of his soul?

Her eyes began to drift, searching, but she shook her head. 'No. I don't need that from you.'

Once, the curiosity had almost driven her mad. But she'd learned since then that her gift came with responsibilities, and that no one owed her their deepest self. Though it meant something to her that he'd offered.

Crowley leaned closer, his shirtsleeves pushed up and his elbows resting on his knees. 'Please,' he said, his eyes glittering with something like mischief. 'Just look.'

She hesitated – before nodding.

Her gaze left his face, tracing a path from the glowing cord around his wrist to the dark-feathered bird resting on the table, watching her. Sharp-beaked and strong, it had a series of short intersecting lines on the breast feathers – as expected from a member of House Ilmarinen – but the overwhelming pattern was of speckles, barely visible against the dark mahogany vanes, like those from Pellervoinen.

Confusion lined her brow and she shuffled closer to be sure, before backing away again.

'The pattern . . .' she said. 'It's mostly Pellervoinen. But then why aren't you a member of that House?'

He sat back and tugged down his shirtsleeves, and she had the sense that having exposed himself, he was buttoning himself up again – literally and metaphorically.

'I could never belong to the House in which Marianne Northam, murderess, is a member. They didn't expel her, you know. They know what she's capable of, but she was never officially charged. Apparently, murder only counts if it's committed on this side of Marble Arch.' He shook his head bitterly. 'Allowing her to retain her membership – it legitimized her; it legitimized what she did. I could never be part of that. So I trained harder than you can possibly imagine, under Josef Skala, honing a weaker legacy to pass their tests and hoping that my weaknesses wouldn't kill me off during my membership bid. But I passed, and the rest, as they say, is history.'

They fell into a silence. Alice wasn't quite sure what to say. She'd known he had the mental strength of iron, but to sharpen a weaker legacy to such an extent was remarkable. And to throw off a legacy he didn't want was just as incredible.

'Do you ever regret it?' she asked.

'No.' He shook his head. 'I've made my peace with it. Though I have no doubt my mother would turn in her grave to see me in another House.'

'The Northams were another big Pellervoinen family, like the Roses?' said Alice.

He paused, considering his answer.

'The Northams *were* the Pellervoinen family,' he said with a quick, tight smile. 'Or . . . the tapered end of it.'

Alice frowned, not quite processing his meaning. 'Do you mean—'

'My grandmother was a Wren. Rumours that the Wrens were really Pellervoinens had circulated for years,' he drawled. 'My grandmother neither confirmed nor denied them. She was, apparently, far too sharp for that; she knew that there would have been expectations and demands made of her if it was confirmed.'

'Crowley,' Alice repeated. 'Are you *actually* saying that the Northams – as in, you and Marianne – are descended directly from Pellervoinen?'

He shrugged offhandedly. 'Everyone is descended from someone.'

Alice's eyes widened and she laughed into the silence, a shocked sound. She stared at him, incredulous.

'You're serious?'

He raised a coy eyebrow.

'You're . . . the heir of the man who helped build the Rookery's *foundations*? The foundations that are starting to—'

He shook his head to forestall her. 'My lineage gives me a talent for opening doors, that's all,' he said, 'not for rebuilding the shoddy foundations of an entire city.'

'But Crowley—'

The front door creaked and she glanced over her shoulder as the rumble of chatter and laughter came from the hallway. Footsteps approached, and then the kitchen door was batted wide. August, chewing on a hunk of sourdough bread tucked under his arm without a cover on it, grinned down at them.

'Not interrupting anything, are we?' he said.

Crowley's eyes narrowed. 'You are always interrupting *something*,' he said. 'Unwanted appearances are your way of life.' He sighed. 'Alice was just . . . preparing for her test, that's all.'

'Oh. Let's see then,' said August, dumping his bread on the counter while Jude wheeled into the room, with Sasha following close behind. They stared down at her expectantly, and she turned to Crowley with a faint glare. This was his fault. He raised an eyebrow, clearly amused.

Alice sighed and reached up to the fireplace mantle for one of the pot plants in a ceramic container. She placed it on the table and dug her fingertips into the soil, allowing warmth to massage through them. She pressed harder, and the drooping spider plant was taken over by a growth spurt, shooting up, the stem thickening, bursting with a flurry of new leaves. She removed her hands and sat back down with a satisfied smile.

'In the last test,' she said, 'they pitted us against objects tainted from the other Houses, to see if we could withstand—'

Crowley waved a lazy hand and her plant burst into flames. Fire ate holes through the smouldering leaves.

'*Crowley*,' Sasha shouted in laughing admonishment.

He gave her an innocent look. 'What? I was just checking if it could withstand—'

Behind him, August snapped his fingers. A hovering balloon of water appeared to grow out from the soil and exploded, dousing the flames.

'Thank you, August,' said Alice, shooting a glance at Crowley.

But August had overdone it with the water. It sloshed like a wave over the kitchen table.

Jude pulled a coin from his pocket and flipped it in the air. It reshaped itself, widening into a broader disc, the edges rising. When it landed in his hand, it had transformed into a bronze cup. He held it under the table's edge and caught the water pouring across the surface.

He winked at Alice, and there was a moment of stunned silence in the kitchen as he raised the metal cup – and drank the lot.

'Did I ever tell you that I was the three-time Cream of the Crops champion – rock, paper, scissors round?' he said.

The room erupted with laughter, and Alice felt a weight on her chest lift as she looked around at them all.

'I have a present for you,' said Jude, leaning closer while the others fell to bickering. He reached into the side bag on his wheelchair and pulled out a small box.

'The signet ring?' she said. 'Did you have any luck?'

He flipped the lid open in answer and she picked it out with careful fingers.

He'd worked a miracle. The ring gleamed in the light, the engraving on the burnished gold clear as day. If it was a crest, it was an unusual shape: an oval, made of intertwining branches and leaves, with a handful of simple shapes around the edges. What she'd taken to be scratches now looked like birds.

'You mentioned Chancellor Westergard's ring,' he said quietly so the others couldn't hear. 'So I checked for you. It's not the Westergard crest, Alice.'

She let this sink in for a moment, and then nodded. She knew it had been a long shot anyway. 'Thanks for this – if nothing else, it was special to someone once, and now it looks good as new. How did you restore the detail so well?'

Jude laughed. 'Magic.'

20

There was a chill in the air, and Alice burrowed her hands into her pockets as she crossed the road. Overhead, the falling sun hid itself behind thick grey clouds, and a lone star twinkled in the darkening sky. They were in for rain. Not the warm summer rain welcomed with relief – the cold, lashing rain that drilled into your clothes and left you sopping and miserable. The woven branches and leaves that formed two of House Mielikki's walls might be glad of it, however.

'This test is different to the first,' said Bea as they crossed the road towards the House. 'Tonight *is* a competition. You won't speak to the others beforehand, and that's for the best. And if you see them at all during the test, don't speak to them, don't look at them, don't make yourself small out of politeness.'

Alice nodded. She had no intention of losing out of misguided civility. This was too important. But she felt ready – even despite the emotional upset of the past few days. The return of Sasha and the others to Coram House had ended her conversation with Crowley. She'd been left with multitudes of unanswered questions, but their presence had lifted her spirits in a way she hadn't realized she'd needed. She'd slept in her old room, and she'd slept well. A solid eight hours. She hadn't had time to speak privately with Crowley before she'd had to leave for some final hours of practice with Bea, but he'd wished her luck and offered to wait outside the House for her. She'd declined – she hadn't wanted to risk any distractions – and he'd respected her decision.

Alice paused outside the entrance, absentmindedly rubbing her signet ring.

'Should we warn someone?' she asked suddenly. 'About what Reid said? About Crane Park Island being her fault? It might give them something more solid to investigate.'

On their walk to the doorway for travelling, Alice had given Bea a shortened account of Reid's panicked claims. She trusted Bea implicitly. But there were some things she had left out about her encounter with Reid – private things she wanted to probe mentally before she shared them with anyone other than Crowley.

'I can't see how one university professor could be responsible,' said Bea. 'You don't think it smacks of delusions of grandeur? Our tree – the Summer Tree – is the most powerful force in the Rookery.' Bea snorted dismissively. 'She isn't even a member of Mielikki's House. Which does she belong to?'

'Pellervoinen,' Alice replied, her brow furrowing as she considered this in light of her conversation with Crowley. If both Mielikki and Pellervoinen had built the foundations and Mielikki's offering had somehow begun to fail, could House Pellervoinen be responsible? But why would they want to destroy the Rookery? They would gain nothing. It made no sense.

Bea's nose wrinkled. 'As a precaution, I suppose we should report it to the Runners,' she said, although it had been House Mielikki's authority figures Alice had been thinking of.

'If you're heading to Islington to retrieve Reid's research, I'll come with you,' said Bea. 'I used to live in Islington myself.'

Alice shook her head. 'Thanks, but it's okay – I've made

arrangements already, and I'll be keeping it short and sweet.' It wasn't quite the truth – if she had the opportunity, Alice planned to see what else Reid was hiding. The remainder of her research was one thing, but Reid had had an intimate connection with Alice's past, and she wanted to know what it was.

Alice glanced up at the arched bough that shaped the House's doorway. Warm light flickered invitingly in the shadows beyond it. She took a deep breath and stepped inside. Behind her, slithering vines and branches crept across the gap, knitting together to close off the entrance.

'Ready?' whispered Bea.

'Yes.' Time to stop thinking about Reid and focus on herself.

Bea squeezed her arm and swept off down the corridor, leading Alice into Cecil's office.

The room was unchanged from her last visit. All luxurious walnut furniture, leather chairs and crowded walls. Ornamental wooden and terracotta animals jostled for space with the framed portraits of House Mielikki's most prestigious members – chancellors, governors, rectors and treasurers – and in pole position was the current governor, Gabriel Whitmore, his unreadable face staring out from a particularly elegant frame.

Cecil was seated behind his desk, suited in a dark grey three-piece, his glasses hanging on a chain around his neck.

'Is the governor here today?' she asked lightly.

'No,' said Cecil. 'He was here first thing this morning, but he was called away. A shame. He'd expressed an interest in staying for the tests, but circumstances being as volatile as they currently are . . .' He trailed away and gave her a knowing look over his glasses.

Alice considered this while he busied himself with paperwork. Hadn't Cecil said last time that the governor only dealt with the test-takers if they reached the final stage and he had to confer membership on them? Why would he be interested in watching them at this early stage?

Alice took a seat and tried to ignore the portrait of Governor Whitmore, which her imagination now had her half convinced was watching her.

Cecil scooped up the dangling pocket watch and checked the time.

'Would you like to stay?' he asked Bea. 'Or did you have other business in the House?'

Bea nodded. 'I might just catch up on some news in the club-house bar. Is Tom already here?'

Cecil winced. 'He is. There's been some discussion among the others. Some of the other candidates have requested that he doesn't administer their binding draught, after the incident with Holly Mowbray. He's putting a brave face on it, but an arm around the shoulder wouldn't go amiss if you have time.'

Bea sighed. 'Just what he needed,' she said.

'He can administer mine,' Alice told Cecil. 'He made up the draught I took last time – I know there was nothing wrong with it.'

Cecil peered at her over his glasses. 'That's very . . . confident.'

Her cheeks warmed. Of course – she'd jumped to the assumption she was going to pass the test well enough to be *offered* the binding draught. Well, she thought, sitting up straighter, she wasn't going to apologize for her optimism.

Bea winked at her and mouthed, 'Good luck, darling,' before hurrying out.

'So,' said Cecil. 'You feel prepared?'

'Yes.'

'Good.' He poured her a drink from a teapot, pressing a cup of piping-hot amber liquid into her hands.

'Thank you,' she said, 'but I don't really—'

'Drink it,' he said simply.

She hesitated and then nodded. She sipped at it, careful not to burn her lips. She recognized it as valerian root tea and quickly set it down on the table. Valerian was a known herb to treat insomnia; it made you drowsy and dulled the mind. Why had he given her this? She'd sabotage herself if she drank it all.

'Thank you for the book,' she said.

He blinked as though surprised, and smiled with pleasure. 'I hope it proves useful to you.'

'Can I ask about the front cover? About the portrait of Leda Westergard?'

'It was from the day she took her oath of office,' he said, gesturing at the wall behind Alice.

She turned in her seat. Her eyes quickly picked out the same image, but this time framed and lined among the pictures of other luminaries from the House's history.

'And am I right in thinking it's an official portrait, released by the Council?' she asked.

'Yes,' he said. 'They commemorate every new chancellor in the same way.'

'So there's nothing especially significant about the picture itself,' she said, more to herself. Reid only had it because they'd known each other in their childhood, then, and she'd kept a photo of an old friend who'd gone on to achieve success.

Cecil smiled fondly. 'Oh, I'd say the picture is very significant – to us, certainly. Chancellor Westergard may have ruffled a few feathers in her time, but no one was more loved by the public. Which is why Governor Whitmore insisted she be given pride of place on our alumni wall. They made quite the pair, in their heyday.'

'A pair?' said Alice, frowning.

'Oh,' said Cecil with a smile, 'nothing like that. They were the youngest chancellor and the youngest governor the city's ever had,' he said. 'A formidable duo. We could have asked for none better.'

Alice stared at the picture a moment longer. It was a little more prominent than the others, the frame a little bigger. 'The ring she's wearing – is that ceremonial, along with the chain of office?'

'Not that I'm aware of,' he said, and she knew it must have seemed a strange question. His eyes flickered to the portrait, his expression ponderous. 'It looks like a signet ring to me. Usually they're adorned with family crests, but I couldn't say for sure.'

Alice curled her fingers to hide her own ring. She'd studied the portrait on Cecil's book cover and the one she'd taken from Reid's office. Whatever Jude had said about the Westergard crest, she was becoming convinced it was the same ring. The scratches were clearly now birds, thanks to Jude's handiwork, but their placement was identical.

'And she was never married?' asked Alice.

Cecil gave her a considering look. 'No, never.'

She had thought that perhaps the ring Leda wore actually belonged to someone else. If it didn't bear the Westergard crest, it was reasonable to think it might have belonged to her husband's family, except she didn't have one. Leda could have been in a serious relationship without a marriage, however.

Alice ran a thumb over the engraved surface. Reid had left this with her as an infant. Leda Westergard was wearing an identical ring in her official portrait and in the picnic photo. How had Reid ended up with it, and why had she passed it on to Alice? Had Reid stolen it? Or – was the truth quite different?

'You are aware of the unfolding political situation?' asked Cecil, and she was jerked from her thoughts.

She nodded, wondering briefly if this was part of the test.

'The issue with the Summer Tree has lost us some support. The harm caused at Crane Park Island and the subsequent problems . . .' His voice faded away. 'But we lost some of our own that night, too,' he added.

He sighed gently, and in the silence Alice felt an old, nagging fear rise to the surface. 'You told me once,' she said, her voice tentative, 'that when we bind ourselves to the Summer Tree, it can . . . damage us through that connection, but that we can't damage it in return.'

He looked at her, blinking in mild confusion. 'That's correct. Are you concerned you might be harmed by the changes in the Summer Tree?'

She shook her head. 'What if, somehow, I – we're damaging the tree? Sending something *bad* through the link, and that's causing—'

'The tree isn't damaged, Alice,' he said kindly. 'If anything, it's the very opposite. The tree has never been stronger.' He paused, noting her unconvinced expression. 'Think of the connection like a river pouring from a towering mountain. The water flows downwards. A stream at the foot of the mountain can't force the water back up it, to its source at the top. And if the source of the river is polluted, that will spread down the mountain. But if a stream at the bottom is polluted, it can't spread upwards to the river's source.'

'So it's . . . one-way,' she murmured.

He nodded, and she lapsed into thought. Reid was convinced

she was to blame. Even if she was to be believed, *how* had her work caused the tree to grow?

Cecil shuffled his papers pointedly, and she sat straighter in the chair, giving him her attention.

'The political situation,' he said. 'We have always counted House Ahti as an ally. The link between our legacies is clear, since nature is sustained by water. House Ilmarinen, on the other hand, has always maintained a neutral position towards us; nature, trees and plants give oxygen to the world, and fire feeds on oxygen. But House Pellervoinen and House Mielikki have always been at odds,' said Cecil, clasping his hands on the tabletop.

'Because the legacies are . . . opposing?'

'Because the whole world was once a garden,' he said. 'And then men carved houses from rock, cut back the trees and grew brick and stone cities where forests once stood.' He paused. 'But nature . . . fights back. Fungus and mosses layer themselves over damp stone, tree roots damage building foundations, and weeds grow through the cracks of abandoned buildings. The battle between urbanization and nature has lasted thousands of years. And so, House Mielikki has been forced to adapt, to coexist despite the battle for dominance. House Mielikki itself is made of brick and branch – a display of power our neighbour calls arrogant.'

How could their Houses dislike each other so much if they'd built the Rookery together?

Cecil paused and gestured at the cup of valerian tea. 'Please,' he said. 'Drink.'

She reluctantly took a sip and set it down again.

'Our Houses are side by side,' he continued. 'Geographically, we are the closest of the Houses, but in every other way, the furthest apart.'

'We balance each other out,' she said, 'with our differences.'

'Yes,' he said, with a grunt of laughter. 'Well put.'

There was a moment's pause while he examined her curiously.

'You should remember these things when you take your test. There are four candidates, but only two will go forward. The strongest. Once they have succeeded in the test, they must make their way to the grove to imbibe the binding draught.'

She nodded. Two spots. Two chances.

'Alice?' Cecil was watching her calmly. 'You must now finish your drink. I insist.'

She exhaled softly and looked down at it, her lip curled. It tasted vile, and would leave her too drugged to compete. But maybe this was part of the test – drink the herbal tea and resist its effects. She took a large mouthful while he watched patiently.

As the valerian began to cloud her mind, she tried to sharpen her focus on the room in a bid to stay awake.

'Where are the other candidates?' she asked, turning to look about for them. But there was no sign anyone else was coming. She squinted at the sea of framed faces on the wall, tilting her head sideways to better study them through the descending haze.

'Cecil,' she mouthed. 'Are you trying to make me . . . fail?'

A dense fog began to settle on her brain, coaxing her to close her eyes, and she swallowed hard, trying to resist. Her breathing slowed and the room seemed to be fading away as the valerian swamped her senses.

'No,' she moaned softly as her eyelids slammed shut. 'Mustn't . . . mustn't sleep . . .'

21

Alice woke with a jolt. She was on her hands and knees in a dark room. The floor beneath her was cold, rough and gritty beneath her fingertips. She licked her lips and gave herself a mental prod. Her head was clear and her senses alert. The valerian seemed to have passed out of her system.

She pushed herself into a sitting position, and something in the darkness skittered and clanked along the ground. She fumbled for the source of the noise – a heavy metal chain screwed into the floor – and followed it to her ankle, where it was clamped in place. An iron band pinched her skin tightly. She tried to claw it off but it was immovable, and panic began to march a beat in her chest. *Stuck fast.*

A bead of dancing light bloomed in the shadows above her and she flinched. It was a firefly. *Lampyridae.* Then another flared to life, and another, until so many glowing specks of light hovered and buzzed overhead that if she squinted, she could work out where she was.

It wasn't a room. It was a concrete box. If she attempted to stand, she would bang her head on the ceiling, and with both arms stretched wide, her hands would scrape the sides. The concrete was in poor condition. It had been invaded by some sort of plant growth. Clusters of purple bamboo-like stalks had burst through the stone, sprouting heart-shaped leaves. The concrete had warped under the intrusion and angular cracks criss-crossed every wall. Knotweed, she realized.

Alice sat very still while she considered her position. She was chained to the floor of a concrete box infested with knotweed. A brief examination of the box suggested she was inside a real-life Jenga game. The walls were fragile and unsteady. If she attempted to yank her chain out of the ground, the ceiling and dislodged slab walls would collapse on top of her. If she used Mielikki's legacy to force the knotweed to recede, it would destabilize the concrete block and falling slabs would crush her. At the moment, as much as the plants were responsible for the instability, they were also the only things stopping the concrete from collapsing – the walls were balanced against the cane-like stems, each supporting the other.

She adjusted herself to see better, leaning back on her hands. So . . . she couldn't will the knotweed to leave the box – but maybe if she drew it further in and used it to choke the concrete – to destroy the slabs before they fell? She frowned. No. She might avoid being crushed, but the falling chunks of concrete would be like bricks raining down on her head.

Cecil's pre-drink conversation about a political crisis now gained new meaning. *Pellervoinen*, she thought, her eyes wandering over the concrete, *and Mielikki*, entwined. Stone and plant, the eternal battle for control. Alice exhaled slowly. She knew what to do. This wasn't about gently extricating the weed from the concrete. This was about dominance.

Alice spread out her arms and walked her scrabbling fingers along the walls so that she could lay her palms flat. The coarse stone scraped her skin and she leaned into the sensation. There was more knotweed, right there, just beyond the walls. And *those* were the plants she needed, pressed against the outer walls. Her hands grew warm. Her fingertips tingled. Alice closed her eyes, focusing every thought on the pulsing electricity in her hands. She sucked in a sharp breath, reached into her mind and *pulled*.

An explosion of knotweed smashed through the concrete like a bomb. The slabs disintegrated on impact, the sheer force of the invasion blasting them to dust. A cloud of powdered grit mushroomed upwards and Alice gasped a lungful of clean air before the dusty flecks dropped back to settle on her hair and clothes and what remained of the box.

Coughing and spluttering, she shuffled sideways. There was no resistance from the chain around her ankle; it was no longer anchored to the wall. She grabbed handfuls of the knotweed surrounding her and used it to wrench herself upright. She was in a forest. Another one. How many doors in House Mielikki opened into forests? Turning, she found that there were other concrete boxes nearby, and her pulse quickened. The other candidates? Was she the first to finish?

She listed sideways to peer into the distance, shifting her weight to see between the trees. Their concrete blocks . . . She squinted. The others' boxes seemed intact, their knotweed twisted and woven through the cracks in the concrete, combining stone and plant more tightly together, knitting them like the walls of House Mielikki. But how, then, had the inhabitants of the boxes escaped – or had they even attempted it? With a sinking feeling, it occurred to her that the point might not have been to evacuate the box. Maybe she was supposed to stay inside it and render the precarious walls more stable. Stabilize, not destroy. A case of keeping your friends close and your enemies closer.

Shit.

There was a faint rumble, like the crashing of distant waves, and Alice's skin prickled. She clambered from the undergrowth, her feet sinking into the mossy forest floor. Where was the grove with the binding draught – perhaps she had to find it? She spun in the other direction, peering through the trees and listening for signs of movement.

It began as a shudder in the belly of the earth. Soil vibrated and brushwood began to bounce in the undergrowth. With a thunderous clap, stems of knotweed burst out of the soil, one after the other – two dozen, three dozen . . . They erupted from under tree roots, tilting their trunks until they fell. Echoes of crashing trees, whining as their roots pulled taut and snapped, ricocheted through the air.

A crooked oak swung towards Alice, its branches snagging and leaves raining from its shattered crown. She dived to clear the area, watching in horror as it landed squarely on her disintegrated concrete box with a terrific *whump*. She scrambled over the collapsed trunk, scraping her arms on the rough bark and sharp branches. *The grove. Get to the grove.*

'Help!' a panicked voice, muffled and hoarse, called out.

Alice spun round, her eyes widening.

'Get me out!'

There was someone in the nearest box! Her stomach churned as she glanced in the opposite direction, grinding her teeth. *Stay or go? The grove or—*

'Please!'

Alice exhaled sharply and powered off through the grass. She held her breath as she skirted a teetering pine. The shaking had stopped, but she had no doubt the respite was only temporary. *This* was part of the test. It wouldn't stop until there were two winners.

Alice skidded to a halt at the first concrete box. A hand poked out through one of the holes.

'I'm here!'

The hand drew back inside and a man's face pressed against the gap.

'Part of the ceiling's collapsed on the metal chain. I can't move it. I'm still bolted to the floor.' He was panting in distress. 'If another quake hits, I can't escape!'

Overhead, the leaves rippled on the trees, fluttering far more than was natural, and Alice watched them warily.

'Tell me what you did with the knotweed,' she said.

'Wove it through the concrete,' he replied. He reached out a hand again and rapped the outside with his knuckles to show her. 'It was stable, but I can't get out. It's not going to be stable *enough* if it happens again.'

'Okay,' she said. 'Just . . . hang on.'

She moved around the box, trying to find a weakness, her mind discarding dozens of possible solutions as too dangerous. Something cracked – something above. Alice's head darted up. The trees had begun to sway again. No time.

'Shit!'

'Get me out!' he shouted hoarsely.

Alice hurtled over to the fallen oak, scrabbling through the splayed branches, searching. There! An acorn! Snatching it up, she raced back to the trapped candidate and slammed down onto her knees.

'Use your legacy to hold up the roof in the corner!' she barked.

She thrust the acorn into a tiny crack in the concrete, a small gap where the knotweed had been laced through.

'This is going to be fast,' she said. 'I'm going to smash the concrete where the chain's bolted. Pull your leg clear as soon as the chain breaks.'

'Just do it,' he rasped.

Alice pressed the flat of her hand against the acorn, focusing her thoughts on the pressure point against her skin and the feel of its smooth base. With her mind, she *pushed*. The acorn's skin split open. Tiny roots poured out, unravelling to the forest floor, thickening, and then with a ferocious whip-crack a sapling burst from it – with such force it shattered the concrete piled inside. Grey dust bloomed out through the gaps.

'Are you okay?' Alice shouted, coughing on grit.

'It worked!' he yelled. 'And it broke through the other side. Can you move the cracked piece?'

She sprinted around the box and found a broken chunk of concrete leaning against the roof. Alice hastily shouldered it aside; it thunked into the grass. The man trapped inside released the knotweed he'd been using to shore up the roof and bolted clear. Collapsing in a heap in the grass, he grinned up at her; his short blond hair and even his eyelashes were caked in dust.

'Fucking knotweed,' he said, leaning over to hack and cough into the grass. 'Thanks.'

'Do you know if the others got out?' asked Alice, peering at the two other boxes. A tree had landed on one, and the other had almost completely collapsed.

'Didn't see anything,' he said, wiping his mouth on his sleeve and sitting up groggily. He couldn't have been much younger than Alice, but he was far stronger. Broad-shouldered and thick-necked, his trouser leg had torn, revealing tanned, muscular calves.

A muffled groan stiffened Alice's spine, and she glanced at the man she'd just rescued.

'What's your name?' she asked.

'Phillip.'

'I'm Alice,' she said, then spun round and darted towards the noise.

The first box had been destroyed by knotweed – a failure in the test, then, rather than the quake. She ducked the low-hanging chunks of concrete and eased closer, to search for the candidate inside. She was already too late.

Her stomach lurched and Alice recoiled from the box, bile rising in her throat. The candidate inside – a thin man with curled hair – had been strung up by the knotweed like a scarecrow. It had invaded his body like a thousand daggers, impaling his shoulders and piercing his chest, blades of the plant stabbing upwards through his ribs. The box was a mess of blood and carnage.

Stumbling away, she blinked hard against the clinging images and swerved towards the moans of pain seeping from the remaining box.

'Hello?' she called, her voice faint.

'Can't breathe,' came the mumbled response.

It was the tree. A thick rowan, bursting with beautiful red berries, had crashed down on the roof, compressing the space inside. If they could just lift it off . . .

She rose up on her toes, eyes scanning the forest. 'Phillip?' she called. 'Help me lift the tree!'

There were distant signs of movement, and then Phillip staggered upright. He cricked his neck to loosen his muscles and Alice rounded the box, hunting for the best place to grab the branches.

Beneath her feet, the floor juddered. Her head snapped up, and she and Phillip locked eyes. The creak of listing trees grew louder – and Phillip shook his head.

'There are only two winners,' he said, gesturing at himself, Alice and whoever was in the box. 'Leave them and we'll share it.'

A pulse of anger throbbed under Alice's skin, and she looked from Phillip to the collapsed rowan tree, clenching her jaw. He shrugged and sprinted off through the forest, and Alice floundered, her mind battling her instincts. *Go now – get the final place!* She shuddered, pressing the ball of her palm into her eyes. *Think!* She couldn't fail this test – she needed that spot. But she also couldn't leave someone to die like the other poor soul in the box. Yet if she saved this one and helped them to the grove, which of them would take the pass?

The rumbling began again. Gently at first, like falling pebbles, but growing louder every moment. The compacted soil shook her off balance and she thumped into the grass, sitting upright. The forest see-sawed around her, trees oscillating. Leaves rustled and branches cracked. Alice tried to stand, but the tremors increased and gravity pinned her down.

The rowan tree began to shimmy with every quake, and with a yawning creak, its trunk slipped from the concrete. Alice rolled to the side just before it smashed down in the space she'd occupied. The momentum helped her dive upwards and she staggered to her feet, careening back towards the box. The pieces of broken concrete vibrated and clinked together, and Alice lunged at them, shoving them aside, clawing through to uncover the candidate inside.

A slender young woman, her dark skin coated with grey dust and a trickle of blood dribbling from her temple, lay curled on the floor. The chain bolting her to the box had snapped. Liberated from the weight crushing her chest, she gasped, and Alice sank down next to her while the remaining walls trembled.

'Can you stand?' Alice demanded.

The woman nodded, and Alice quickly slid a hand under her back and pulled her upright. Stumbling together, they hurried from the battered concrete shell. Alice tensed at the sound of something whistling through the air nearby. A teetering pine tree swooped to the ground, landing with a clatter.

'Let's go,' Alice breathed, the woman's arm over her shoulder.

Weaving through the long grasses, tripping on fallen logs and clawing branches, they navigated a path through the forest while trees crashed down around them.

'Look!' hissed the woman in Alice's ear. 'Should we check him?'

Phillip was splayed out in the undergrowth, the snapped trunk of a fallen rowan tree smashed right through his chest. His eyes were open, his face frozen in a mask of shock. His nightjar was gone and no sign of the gleaming cord remained.

'No,' said Alice, walking on with a shudder. 'He's dead.' Relief and dismay raged through her mind, but one thought won out in the end: there were only two candidates now.

There was a gasp beside her, and Alice's head darted up. An elm tree sliced through the air towards them at speed. Alice instinctively flinched as the branches struck her shoulder. The other woman's arm shot upwards and she screamed as her palm hit the falling trunk . . . and obliterated the entire tree. An explosion of sawdust flittered around them, dusting their hair and sinking into the cotton of their clothes. A bubble of exhaustion and nerves rose in Alice's throat, and she began to laugh – she didn't quite know why. Together, the two women creased over, eyes streaming. Engulfed by grains of shattered elm, they slumped down in the dust together, their nervous laughter echoing through the trees.

'Congratulations on a successful test.' A man's voice, gentle and proper: Cecil.

He appeared from between two trees on a ridge, smiling down at them, and Alice's laughter died out.

'Follow me,' he said. 'The door to the grove is just through here.'

There was a moment's pause, and then Alice rose from the grass. She held out her hand to the other woman.

'I'm Shobhna, by the way,' said the woman, her dark eyes shining.

'I'm Alice. Thanks for saving my life.'

Alice pulled her to her feet.

'Thanks for saving mine,' said Shobhna, shaking dust from her sleeve with a smile.

'Are you injured?' asked Alice, looking her over.

'I think my ankle's sprained, and my chest hurts,' said Shobhna, 'but the binding draught will fix it. Shall we go?'

Alice nodded, a grin creeping over her face. The binding draught *would* fix it. It fixed everything.

Alice stepped out onto King Edward Street sometime later with her heart still pounding and the elated feeling in her chest almost lifting her off her feet. The binding draught had healed the scratches that the branches had drawn over her skin, and Alice felt invincible. She wasn't at all anxious about going straight to Reid's apartment – so what if someone else wanted to get hold of the research? Alice grinned; she and Crowley would simply get there first.

It took several seconds before she realized there was something odd about the street. It was unusually crowded. Drifts of people were pouring out of buildings and looking around at each other – some confused, others irritable.

'What's wrong?' she asked a nearby young woman.

'Power outage,' she said. 'All the electricity systems have gone down. It's got to be the earthquakes' fault again, hasn't it?'

Alice nodded blankly, the niggling signs of more Summer Tree havoc puncturing her good mood.

22

Crowley was leaning against a street lamp outside Coram House, his hands in his pockets. When he saw her, holding open the door to the void, he instantly straightened, drawing himself up to his full height to study her.

'You passed,' he said, a satisfied look in his eye.

'How did you know?' she asked.

'You're alive,' he said with a smirk. 'And why wouldn't you have passed? You're *Alice Wyndham*.' He strode up the stairs of the derelict building they always used for travel and stepped in beside her with a raised eyebrow. 'You see? I can be charming when I want to be.'

She rolled her eyes, but a blush had formed on her cheeks. 'Have you been practising in the mirror?'

'Yes.'

She barked a laugh at his unexpected response and closed the door behind him, pitching them into instant shadow. Frigid blasts of air chilled her to the bone and she shivered. Crowley inched closer as though to lend her some warmth, but paused when his hand inadvertently brushed hers. He glanced down at her, swallowed and looked away. She was very aware of his breathing, of the rise and fall of his chest.

'Congratulations,' he said, a husk to the edge of his voice that raised the hairs on the back of her neck. 'There wasn't a doubt in my mind.'

Alice smiled invisibly into the gloom, and then gave herself a mental shake. No distractions. Time to get down to business. Crowley had no idea where they were going: Alice was in the driving seat for this trip.

Reid's apartment was in Islington. Alice had once dropped off some photocopying to her, pushing it through her letterbox on a Saturday morning. She tried to visualize it in her mind's eye, staring into the darkness surrounding her. Her nose began to stream and she bowed her head into her chest. One hand thrust out in front of her, groping the darkness, searching . . . *Reid's apartment . . . Reid's apartment . . .* She pictured the glass-fronted lobby, the steel beams and stone walls.

A rounded shape slotted neatly into her curved palm with a dull thwack. The door. She twisted. The lock clicked and she pushed against the blustering wind. Light blazed into the void as the door gave way, and she leaned into it, stepping forward, into the entrance to Reid's apartment block.

Reid's front door was locked to travel; she was far too mistrustful to allow anyone access to her flat. Fortunately, however, Alice had brought with her the one man capable of opening any door he pleased. Pellervoinen's heir, no less.

'Third floor,' she whispered. 'We'd better not take the lift. Too loud.'

She hurried purposefully towards the stairs, Crowley keeping pace with her. At the top, she nodded and he gently pushed open the fire door. She put a finger to her lips and moved past him in silence. The corridor was empty. Reid's apartment was at the end – she occupied one of the small corner plots.

Creeping towards it, Alice froze. There had been no need to bring Crowley – because the door was already open. She felt him stiffen behind her. He placed one hand on her arm, in warning, and she nodded. Then, using just the tip of her index finger, she pushed the door. It swung open with a muffled creak.

A flurry of motion followed the sound. *There was someone inside.* Alice shoved the door wider and stepped into Reid's tiled inner hallway. Her pulse was thrumming. She clenched and unclenched her fists, readying herself to call her legacy to her palms. Her back suddenly warmed and she glanced over her shoulder. A haze of warm air shimmered around Crowley, like the calm before a storm, as he drew his power to him: Ilmarinen's, the House of fire.

She stepped forward, the floorboard creaking beneath her foot.

'Hello?' a cautious voice called out to her from another room. 'Is someone there?'

Alice frowned, some of the tension lifting off her shoulders. She knew that voice.

With a quick glance at Crowley, who was stony-faced, she moved through the apartment, into Reid's cramped living room. It was a comfortable enough room, but the only real luxury was the tiny balcony overlooking the main road. Through the glass, Alice caught sight of a vintage double-decker bus, a winding staircase on the back and an advert for Bovril splashed on the side. And in the living room window's reflection, Alice spied movement over her shoulder.

'Alice?' said Tom as he emerged from the kitchen, his nose wrinkling in confusion. 'Did they send you too?'

She stared at him for a moment, running through a dozen possible reasons for his presence.

He gave her a quizzical smile, his eyes drifting to Crowley. 'Have we met?'

'Who's *they*, Tom?' she asked, her voice measured.

He adjusted his glasses. 'The university welfare team,' he said. 'They asked for a volunteer to collect some of her things to take to the hospital. Apparently she'll be there for weeks.'

She wasn't watching his face. Her eyes were on his nightjar. A long, lithe bird with a complicated patchwork of browns, its neck was unusually thin. Every time he spoke, it tucked its wings closer around its body as though using them as a barricade.

'I didn't realize they'd asked you too,' he said, his blue eyes looking thoughtful.

Alice's mouth tightened briefly. 'They didn't ask me, Tom.' She paused. 'And I don't think they asked you either.'

Warring emotions crossed his face, and she tensed, expecting him to continue the lie. But instead, his shoulders sagged with something like relief.

'Okay,' he said with a pronounced sigh. 'Let me show you – but you absolutely can't tell anyone outside of the House.' He beckoned her towards the kitchen, but paused, casting Crowley an awkward glance. 'I'm sorry,' he said. 'If the governor found out I'd spoken about this with . . .' He trailed away and looked to Alice for support. 'What House is your friend in?' he murmured to Alice.

'Ilmarinen,' said Crowley, answering for himself with a raised eyebrow.

Tom threw him an apologetic smile and swallowed.

'Okay,' he said. 'I . . . All right. *Both* of you then. Look—'

He disappeared into the kitchen and reappeared clutching a biscuit-coloured folder: what remained of Reid's notes.

'While you were busy with your test, Bea spoke with the committee. She said one of her sources had confirmed that Vivian Reid had been doing research into something that might have harmed the Summer Tree. Something that might have caused the damage our House is being blamed for. If it's true,' he said a little breathlessly, 'this could exonerate us. Reid's a member of House Pellervoinen – who's to say they're not behind all this and the tragedy at Crane Park Island?'

Crowley shifted, leaning back against the living room wall, his arms folded.

It was, of course, something she'd considered herself. But as Alice searched Tom's earnest face, the pleading look in his eyes felt like a blow to her chest.

She exhaled deeply, trying to push away the doubts. This was Tom – who'd been bullied by Lester and was distraught over Holly; who had lain on the university's lawn with her, drunk cloudberry wine and laughed at the stars; who had helped her train for her tests and had administered her binding draught. Tom, who had snuck into Vivian Reid's apartment to steal her research.

'Tom,' she said quietly, her voice strained, 'I wish you weren't lying.'

It was his nightjar. It laid him utterly bare. He looked taken aback, and for the slightest moment, she saw the sincerity in his eyes harden and vanish.

'You were the one Reid tried to warn me about, weren't you?' said Alice. 'She kept saying "he's here". She meant at the university. You set off the quake in my apartment to stop her talking—'

Tom's lips curled back into a bitter sneer. He clenched the folder under one arm and hissed, 'Get out of my way, Alice.'

She held her ground, and from the corner of her eye she saw Crowley silently stride up behind her. 'Give me the folder, Tom,' she said, trying to inject her voice with a calm she didn't feel. Her heart thumped violently against her ribs and her fingers twitched.

Tom dropped to his knees and slammed his palm against the oak floor. The moment his skin touched the wood, the boards beneath Crowley disintegrated. With a shocked yell, he fell through them, but they reformed rapidly, trapping him waist-deep in the floor.

Tom raised a mocking eyebrow at Alice. 'Move out of my way.'

She reached for the wooden dado rail running around the room, intending on forcing her legacy into it, and he smiled.

'I don't think so,' he said, pressing harder against the floor.

Alice's feet vibrated with warmth as Tom's legacy seeped closer.

'Alice, look out!' hissed Crowley, battling to free himself without falling into the apartment below.

She dived just in time as Tom obliterated the floorboard beneath her. Panting, she hit the wall when she landed and reached upwards. Alice slammed her hand over the dado rail and mentally *pulled*. *Crack-crack-crack*. It snapped off the wall and she snatched it closer. Pinching it between her fingers in a carving motion, she sharpened the tip and threw it – slicing the air – at him.

Tom ducked and gritted his teeth, whipping his arm out in front of him. Reid's wooden coffee table lifted into the air and catapulted towards Alice.

She gasped and braced for impact, but it exploded in a burst of flames before it reached her. She glanced at Crowley – still trapped – and shouted, 'Thanks!'

Thwarted, Tom slammed his palms to the floor again, but this time he made no attempt to eat through the wooden boards; instead, branches unspooled from the knots, but unlike those from her first test, these were like waxy saplings.

Kuu suddenly swooped into view and called out in a shrill voice, as though directing Alice's attention. The bird circled Tom, wings striking urgently above his head, and she understood. Tom's nightjar hovered behind him, its eyes wider than she'd ever seen them and its claws tucked up as though to attack. She tried to focus, to exhale slowly, but her breath came in short pants. If she could just cloak herself long enough to gain the upper hand.

'Look away,' she hissed to his soul-bird. 'Look away.'

The nightjar blinked. It appeared to lose interest in her and began to turn. But her concentration slipped and its head spun back round. It flapped its wings aggressively, its glare now locked on her face. Kuu expressed her disappointment at the failure with a flurry of ruffled feathers, and then vanished again.

Tom grunted and the saplings pouring from the floor snapped towards Alice. They grabbed her ankles, their grasping reach curling higher around her calves. She was reminded, forcefully, of the attack from her window frame. Just as *that* night she'd been reminded of another.

'It was *you*,' she breathed. 'You were the one attacking me. The window, the corridor, the flowers . . . You wanted me to think . . . but it was *never* Lester.' Her eyes darted over his face, frantic. 'You were the one who left the messages calling me a murderer. You were there, in the grove that night. Not just Bea and Cecil, and *Lester – you*.' She bent and grabbed handfuls of the vines, tearing at them, but they were thickening and pulling taut.

'Move your hands,' shouted Crowley. He clicked a flame onto

his fingers, inhaled sharply and breathed fire across the room. Tom's saplings burned to cinders and Alice lunged at him.

Tom shot to his feet and backed up towards the kitchen as she advanced, fists clenched. 'I didn't murder Holly,' she said, her voice dangerously low. 'You were the one who gave Holly that draught, not me. Did you tamper with it?'

'There was nothing wrong with the draught,' he snapped, his shoulders hunched. 'It was the Summer Tree – it was already growing and she was just too weak to control it.'

'Why Reid?' she flung out. 'Why are you taking her research? You should be making it public, not stealing it away.'

Tom leaned into the kitchen and snatched a glass, hurling it at her. It smashed at her feet. Then another, and another, until glittering fragments carpeted the ground. Distracted, he glanced around for something else he could use, or for an escape route, and Alice took the opportunity to beat him at his own game. He'd sent tremors through her living quarters, and Reid had taken the brunt of it. Now it was his turn. She sank to her feet and struck the wooden floorboards with her palms, gritting her teeth and willing them to move. The interlocking boards vibrated, their corners lifting and beginning to overlap each other. Cursing, Crowley yelled a muffled protest, but Alice's attention was fixed on Tom.

The boards below Tom parted like a broken jigsaw and his foot slipped through the gap, throwing him off balance. He clattered onto his back with a winded breath. Reid's papers were thrown into the air and scattered across the room as they drifted down.

Alice swallowed and held her nerve, pushing a new energy into the boards. The convulsions stopped, and waxen twigs slithered out from the floor. They wound around Tom, holding him still, trussing him up tightly.

Alice leapt up and stood over him, breathless. Her forehead was dusted with sweat. The vines around his wrist tightened, splaying him immobile on the floorboards.

'If Reid's project,' she managed after a moment, '*was* responsible for Crane Park Island, then stealing the evidence only means no one can reverse it. You're enabling it. And meanwhile, the tree . . .' She trailed away. 'The tree grows,' she intoned blankly. 'And the power of House Mielikki rises. Is this about power? You don't *want* to stop the tree because it's boosting your legacy?'

She toed the twigs lashing him to the floor. 'Well guess what – it's boosting my legacy too.'

A sharp blast of fire heated Alice's back, and she turned to find a furious Crowley extricating himself from the boards, some of them singed like charcoal. Somehow, he managed to make it look elegant when he pushed his weight onto his arms and climbed free of the hole.

He paused only to dust himself down before striding towards her.

'A little late,' she said, raising an eyebrow.

'You seemed to have it in hand,' he drawled, walking around their captive to examine him more closely. He went very still, and Alice glanced at him, concerned.

'You have her mark,' Crowley said softly, his eyes flashing with menace.

He shot a spray of fire at the vine holding Tom's wrist in place. It burned rapidly, the embers smouldering on the floor. Crowley seized his freed wrist and yanked it closer. With a bony click, it slipped its socket and Tom gasped in pain as Crowley shoved back his sleeve.

There was a ragged scar on Tom's forearm. Crowley dug his finger into it, his face twisted in disgust. 'This is Marianne's handiwork,' he said, turning to Alice, twisting the arm towards her. 'She cuts them with the lancet and takes pride in leaving a nice bold scar behind.'

Crowley glared at Tom. 'How long have you been a member of the Fellowship?' he barked.

Tom shook his head, his eyes screwed up.

'Do you know who she *is*?' Crowley demanded, gesturing at Alice.

'Can't . . . breathe . . .' Tom managed. 'Please . . .'

The vines had curled around his chest, crushing his ribs. Crowley glanced up at Alice, and she nodded.

With his mouth drawn into a line, Crowley pressed his hand against the vines, and fire raced along them like a candlewick. Lines of dark ash criss-crossed Tom as he was liberated.

'You're going to tell us everything you know,' said Crowley, his voice like thunder.

He grabbed Tom's shirt and yanked him to his feet. He took three steps and slammed the technician against the balcony doors.

'Just . . . let me . . . catch a breath,' said Tom.

Crowley's hands must have relaxed for a fraction of a second, because Tom scrambled for the door handle, and before they had time to react, he'd managed to shove open the door.

Crowley hissed in cold rage and lunged for him, but Tom dived out onto the balcony. Alice raced to stop him escaping but he slammed the door against the hinges and it swung towards her, giving him a second's advantage, alone on the balcony.

He threw her a quick smile through the glass. Overhead, his nightjar flapped frantically, tugging away and circling him in distress.

But Tom's face was calm. 'Alice . . . I'm sorry.'

And then he hauled himself onto the stone safety wall and – without pause – stepped off, into the cool night air.

The thud as he hit the pavement seemed to reverberate up her legs and sent her teetering. Down on the street, someone screamed, and Alice's stomach lurched. Crowley grabbed her and she latched on to his lapels, squeezing them while he pulled her closer.

'We have to go, Alice,' he said urgently. 'The Runners will be coming.'

23

The next morning, Alice moved through the university corridors in a trance. Bea had insisted on dragging her downstairs to breakfast, to toast her success in her test, and Alice had been forced to play along.

'I can't stomach cold tea and bread,' muttered Bea, glaring at her plate. 'This is bloody prison food, darling.'

There was no electricity. Not in the whole of Westminster. The power grid was sound but some of the distribution lines had been so weakened during the Summer Tree's last growth spurt that they'd finally given out.

'There's talk of an enforced blackout at dusk so they can fix it,' said Bea. 'The lights and Ditto machines are down, and the rector is refusing to allow matches and uncontrolled fires to be used indoors – which means that tea, coffee and food are now served at the mercy of the faculty from House Ilmarinen, with their so-called "controlled fire", and at the moment the bastards are refusing. Apparently, they're here to develop the minds of the next great thinkers, not to boil pans and barbeque food for the entire staff.'

Bea shot a glare at the Dean of Philosophy, who was busy

blowtorching a piece of toast with his bare hands, and who appeared to have a piping-hot cup of tea with steam curling off it.

'On the plus side,' said Bea with a heaving sigh, 'the Council are coming under terrific pressure to restore normality. Geraint's been having kittens, apparently.' She smiled brightly. 'And what's fantastic about it is, it's deflected some of the attention from our House for a change. Ilmarinen sort out the electrical systems, and they're being blamed for poor maintenance due to the Council's budget cuts. Serves them right,' she said, with another icy glare at the Dean of Philosophy, who raised his cup to her as though in greeting.

She took a sip of her own – cold – tea and baulked at it. 'I wonder where Tom is,' she said, peering around the dining hall. 'Wait until he finds out we can't even power a kettle and the entire faculty is about to descend into civil war.'

Alice said nothing. She couldn't bring herself to tell Bea that Tom would never be sitting down to breakfast with them ever again – that he had been a liar and a traitor. So instead, she ate in virtual silence.

A scream from the other side of the dining room jolted Alice upright and her eyes raced to search out the source. It was the young student couple she'd once watched over breakfast.

'Help him!' the girl screamed. She lunged frantically across the table, scattering cups and plates. She brushed back the long hair from her boyfriend's face, pleading with him to be okay.

'What happened?' bellowed the Dean of Philosophy, jumping to his feet with such force his tea spilled over the table.

'He – he was carving me an orchid from the wooden coaster,' she breathed. 'It was just a splinter, in his thumb. Just a tiny splinter . . . and look what it's . . .' She trailed away in panic.

By now, Bea had flung her napkin onto the bench and was

marching over to help, but Alice was frozen in stunned dread. It was Holly all over again. The splinter had corrupted the young student, somehow – dug its way into his bloodstream, perhaps. Because as they watched, it grew through his body, branching into his veins, forking through blood vessels like an invasion until every space inside his body was filled with wood and twig. With terrible realization, his skin began to tear, pinpricks of blood appearing on his shirt, and the dining hall echoed with his pained screams.

Alice trembled with guilt and horror – frightened to ask Kuu to end his agony and risk releasing her soul again, but unable to bear the remorse of doing nothing. She took a lurching step towards him, but with a ragged gasp, he fell silent. His head flopped back, and Alice blinked in shock as his nightjar soared away from his lifeless body, a luminous glow pulsing at the end of its broken cord. It ended just as quickly as it had begun, and an awful silence fell over the dining hall, broken only by the soft weeping of the student's girlfriend.

The rise of House Mielikki? Was this really what Tom had wanted? A legacy so strong and uncontrollable that it could tear you apart just as much as its talisman, the Summer Tree, had torn apart Crane Park Island? Alice shuddered. Was the price of wielding such power too high?

Alice sat on her bed, Reid's folder opened flat and its contents spread out over the blankets. In a bid to block the morning's scenes from her mind, she had chosen to spend the afternoon numbing her thoughts with paperwork and a detached search for answers about Crane Park Island. She had separated Reid's research into two camps. The first: everything relating to her work for the Magellan Institute; the second: a miscellaneous pile of newspaper clippings. But it had soon become clear that there was not even the slightest reference to anything related to Crane Park Island. Had Reid been delusional with panic? Why had Tom – and therefore Marianne – wanted these notes?

Alice's fingers sifted through the pile again. Reid's research for the Magellan Institute centred around proving the soul consisted of three different parts: the itse, henki and luonto. Each had a different function: henki gave life to the body; itse gave one a sense of self and conscience; and luonto brought good fortune and, according to Magellan, bound the three parts together.

Alice's eyes darted over the notes again. Reid had scribbled frantic details across several pages, explaining that the henki was the life-giving spirit delivered by the nightjar at birth – an injection of life, like a blast from a defibrillator, bringing a pulsing heartbeat, rushing flow of blood, heaving lungs and the crackling spark of neurons. And at the moment of death, the henki finally escaped to be collected by the Lintuvahti – the reigning Lord of Death. Alice swallowed thickly. The long-haired student's nightjar – the pulsing glow trailing at the end of the cord – had that been parts of his soul?

The other two parts of the soul were quite different. Magellan called the luonto the gatekeeper. Reid's notes claimed that in the moments before death, the luonto was the first part to escape the body, to encourage the nightjar to cut the cord and free its other parts. However, the gatekeeper was not infallible. It could be weakened by trauma, leaving the other parts to slip free before their time. Only once the henki left was the body actually dead.

It was the itse that seemed to have claimed most of Reid's attention. Itse was your sense of self – your thoughts, beliefs, your personality. After death, it was the part of your soul that travelled to the Land of Death to find its peace. If the luonto was weakened, the itse could depart the body temporarily, following grief, trauma or illness – leaving the person emotionally detached, often in the wake of a loved one's death; the loss of the itse was often mistaken for depression.

Reid's notes included a citation from a text:

> *(Kosonen, 1911) Following the loss of his wife, Petri Jääskeläinen descended into a state of vacant melancholy. The desperate Jääskeläinen family contacted a local shaman, who diagnosed him as itsetön, 'without spirit'. To cure him, the shaman agreed to retrieve Petri's lost itse: a common practice, in which the shaman would fall into a meditative state and send out his own itse to find and bring back that which was lost . . .*

In the margins next to the citation, Reid had scribbled something largely illegible. Alice turned it sideways, trying to decipher the comment . . . *Pellervoinen safeguard holds?* Her lips pressed together. That link to Pellervoinen again, this time in black and white. She squinted at Reid's handwriting. Pellervoinen *safeguard?* She would have to show Crowley.

Alice stared numbly at the pages. This was all there was. Nothing else. Why had Reid not destroyed these notes along with the others – and had the others contained something more illuminating? Reid had already spoken of the three-part soul, and Alice herself had read Magellan's book, *Sielun*. But other than her odd scribble, there was nothing particularly new or shocking here, Alice thought, staring hard at the pages. Why had Tom been so desperate to get his hands on it? Had he assumed it would reveal more than this? Had he not realized exactly which notes had survived Reid's destruction?

Alice sat back. For years the Fellowship's aim had been the same as the Beaks': to purge the Rookery of life. Marianne had imagined herself offering the dead as sacrifices to Tuoni. And now, here she was again, connected to something that might succeed. But Marianne had Pellervoinen's legacy, not Mielikki's. Like Crowley, she was his heir too. Alice bit her lip, glancing at Reid's notes. It made her uneasy – this spider web connecting Reid's work, Marianne and herself.

'Kuu?'

With a snap of white wings, Kuu burst into the room. Alice held out her hand, and the nightjar's pin-sharp claws latched on to her fingers. She pecked affectionately at her ears. Alice pulled the bird closer to examine the cord joining them. It draped from Kuu's leg to Alice's wrist – luminous, pulsing with energy . . . and completely intact. She studied it with growing relief. Sir John Boleyn had sliced it at Marble Arch, but the reigning Lord of Death had fused it back together, the cord binding her tightly to the bird.

'You'd never let me down?' she whispered.

Kuu's head spun round, and Alice saw herself reflected in her dark, shining eyes. The bird looked affronted and turned her back. Alice let out a short laugh.

'I *do* trust you to do your job, Kuu,' she said.

With a prideful flutter, the nightjar vanished, and Alice's eyes drifted over to the other pile she'd found in the biscuit-coloured folder: the newspaper clippings. They were old and fragile, some of them yellowed, the print tiny. But they all focused on the same thing: Leda Westergard's many achievements. There were several articles about her election win, others about her swearing-in ceremony when she'd taken her oath of office and some that spoke of her success in changing the House membership system for the better.

Alice read them several times, but to her uninitiated eye there wasn't quite enough information to glean exactly what she'd done with the membership arrangements. She wondered if Cecil's book might provide more insight, and scrambled from the bed to reach it.

Flipping through the pages, she tossed the book onto the floor in frustration. The chancellor's section was nothing more than a brief chapter skating over the same details. Westergard had somehow made the membership system fairer and introduced the mentorship scheme that had resulted in Alice being paired with Bea. But the exact details of what she'd done were missing – probably, he'd assumed his readership were already familiar with them. Maybe she could ask him.

Alice sighed shakily and moved to trail her fingers through the clippings. The other one that had stood out was the smallest, tucked away at the back: the chancellor's obituary.

She had died the same year Alice was born. Alice allowed that to sink in for a moment, her eyes drifting from the signet ring on her finger to the one the chancellor wore. She moved to the window to examine the faded picture better in the light. There was something about the slant of Leda's mouth, and the shape of her eyes . . .

'She looks . . . a bit like me,' Alice said out loud. 'And I'm *sure* this is her ring.' She whipped her hand down and threw the article on the table.

If Leda was her mother, then she had known Crowley's mother, Helena. The old photograph swam into her memory. Their parents had known each other, and she and Crowley had found each other without them.

Leda, Helena, Reid and Marianne. All four of them linked in a way she didn't yet fully understand. But so much seemed to come back to Marianne – the woman who worshipped Alice's father, who had sent Tom to attack her and whose youthful face smiled out of a photograph next to Alice's possible mother.

But there had been another woman in that photograph. Tilda – the older lady, who'd been involved in her adoption alongside Reid. Alice exhaled shakily. There was so much she wanted to understand.

'I need to see Marianne,' she said out loud.

She would find August. The necromancer was the only one who might know how to find the Fellowship's current headquarters. And she would do it now, before the evening's blackout meant she had to operate in the dark.

'Who says crime doesn't pay?' said August, his cheeks hollowed out as he smoked furiously on the corner of Warren Street and Grafton Mews in the Rookery's Bloomsbury. 'Always lands on her feet. Always somewhere nice for her to move on to.'

'Which one is it?' asked Alice.

He gestured at a tall, brown-brick Georgian townhouse. 'Red door,' he said. 'I'm coming in with you.'

'No, you're not.'

He threw the cigarette on the pavement and stamped on it. 'Like fuck I'm not.'

She laid her palm on his chest, pretending not to notice the necromancer's slight tremble of nerves. Marianne had left him badly scarred – mentally and physically. The scars Tom had had on his forearm were nothing to the ones on August's.

'August, I don't want you to. This is between me and Marianne.'

'When Crowley realizes—'

'I can take care of this one myself,' Alice said firmly. 'I'm ready for Marianne and whatever she wants to throw at me.'

He opened his mouth to speak but she cut him off.

'Listen, don't even think about telling Crowley.'

'But—'

'If you tell Crowley I'm at the Fellowship, I'll tell him you dumped me here and left.'

His mouth fell slack and he stared at her, wide-eyed. 'Fuck,' he breathed. 'If that wasn't so evil I'd be impressed.'

She smiled and patted his arm. 'Don't wait for me,' she said as she crossed the road and jogged up the steps. There was a knocker on the door; she'd seen one like it before. It had oscillating spikes to cut the hands of Marianne's visitors. Anyone requiring entry to the hemomancer's house was expected to make a blood payment. Of course, the blood then gave her a measure of control over them, and Alice knew that game too well to play it today. Marianne's control led people to step off third-floor balconies without a parachute.

Instead, juggling a biscuit-coloured folder in one hand, Alice reached into her pocket for a stone and hurled it through the nearest ground-floor window. The glass shattered and she heard the stone bounce across a hard floor, crunching through tinkling shards.

The door flew open and a tall woman with a face shrouded in fury bore down on her.

'Hello, Marianne,' Alice said calmly. 'I think it's time we talked.'

Incense curled through the sitting room, infusing the patterned rug and the mounds of cushions on the plump sofa with odours of sandalwood and jasmine. Alice's eyes followed a bloom of smoke as it wafted up to the ceiling and thinned out against the plasterwork. There was no door. Thanks to Marianne's Pellervoinen handiwork, it had disappeared the minute Alice had entered. Four plain brick walls and no escape route. But it was all part of the game, and so Alice suppressed the fleeting urge to stiffen before it had time to take hold, crossed her legs and gazed steadily at Marianne.

Marianne held court on her favoured Queen Anne chair against the back wall, her gaunt wrists curved around the armrests and her many bracelets and rings catching the light in bright slashes of colour. It had only been a year, but she looked much older than Alice remembered. She had always assumed Marianne was in her mid-forties, but now she'd be surprised if she was a day under fifty. Marianne was still brunette – her hair piled high and pinned to the back of her head – but the greying streak at her temples had now begun to take root all over; the heavy make-up powder was no longer too pale for her skin tone, and the thick mascara seemed only to emphasize the smallness of her shark-like eyes. She reminded Alice of an old beauty queen gone to seed.

They sat across from one another, sizing each other up like prizefighters before a bout. Marianne smiled. Always a bad sign.

'Bridget?' she called out, her voice deep and velvety. 'A moment, please.'

She smiled again, and Alice sat back to better track Marianne's nightjar. It was a muscular bird with glossy, unblinking eyes and wide feathers flattened against its broad head. It was perched on the back of Marianne's chair, in a proud and domineering pose. If it made any sudden moves . . .

Marianne glanced at Alice, as though to check she was watching, and then held up her hand, spread her fingers wide and clenched her jaw in concentration. *What is she doing?* Alice's muscles tensed and her eyes flitted between Marianne and her nightjar. The wall juddered and a cloud of dust and plaster rained down. A sound like a puckered kiss reverberated through the room and the brick wall disintegrated. Alice's instinct was to scramble to safety at the other end of the room, but she forced herself to sit still; she could afford to allow Marianne her little power moves. Proctor had once berated her lack of poker knowledge. Well, Alice had had some time to perfect her poker face in the year since, and now she sighed and affected a bored expression as the brickwork exploded into grains of red dust.

Marianne's other hand joined the first and she turned them in a cupping motion. The chunks of fragmented bricks, the red dust and grit . . . were suspended in the air. Inert, floating above the floorboards, utterly still. A shadow appeared behind the wall of floating grit – and then stepped through it, a young woman emerging like a figure from a sandstorm. Marianne's fingers twitched, she pushed her hands forward, and the red dust quivered. Dust stuck to dust, stuck to chunks, stuck to blocks . . . until the bricks reformed. With a rasping thunk, they slotted back into their original stacks – and the wall was once again whole and rebuilt.

'You remember Bridget,' said Marianne, her rapid breathing the only sign of her exertion.

Alice did remember her. Bridget Hogan, a small blonde with freckles and a nightjar about as lively as a stuffed toy. Alice had once used her identity to sneak into the Bow Street Runners' HQ. She was completely under Marianne's spell, and Alice had no idea why Marianne had called for her. Perhaps it had just been a display of power, or a taunt.

'Hello, Bridget,' said Alice with a nod.

The other woman sat by Marianne's feet like a docile puppy and gave no indication she'd even heard Alice's greeting.

'A little security,' explained Marianne. 'You attacked me once . . .'

Alice had once grabbed Marianne's cord – not a method she was keen to try again. Touching a person's cord caused them unendurable pain; unfortunately, when their defence mechanisms kicked in, the pain rebounded along the cord.

'. . . and I doubt you'd hesitate to attack me again,' Marianne continued. 'But I think you might hesitate to attack an innocent.'

She laid a hand on Bridget's head and softly stroked her hair. Alice frowned. Of course she wouldn't hurt Bridget. But why—

'If you make a move on me, I'll have her cut her own throat.' Marianne smiled again and gestured to Bridget. The blonde pulled out a knife and laid it flat on her lap. Marianne patted her head indulgently. 'You're familiar with that, I think?' she mused.

Alice's poker face slipped and a flash of pained rage darkened her expression. How *dare* she mention Jen? Jen was off-limits.

'What do you *want*?' said Marianne, her tone sharp with impatience, and Alice knew the preliminaries were now over.

She stared at her for a long moment before answering. 'Tell me about Tom Bannister.'

Marianne leaned back in her chair, an exaggerated pose of relaxation. 'I can't say the name's familiar.'

'That's a shame,' Alice replied coolly, 'because last night he died trying to retrieve this.'

She pulled out the folder wedged under her arm: Reid's research folder. Marianne became very still, her face a frozen mask, but her nightjar shifted uneasily.

'And I assumed he wanted it for you, because he was a member of the Fellowship.' Alice shrugged. 'But perhaps not.' She made as though to put it away, and Marianne's nostrils flared, though she said nothing.

'Tom was a friend of mine at the university,' said Alice. 'Except, not really in the end.' She looked Marianne in the eye. 'You sent an attacker to my door – and I think that's an interesting conflict of interests, given who I am.' A faint, goading smile curved her mouth – she preferred to see Marianne on the back foot, all spitting rage and poorly considered impulse. 'Shouldn't you be on your knees, worshipping me?'

Marianne sat more stiffly in the chair, her hands now clenching the armrests with such force her fingers were bone-white.

'I devoted myself to Tuoni,' said Marianne with a clear bite of anger, 'not his unworthy leech of a daughter. You aren't fit to walk in the Lord of Death's shadow.' The cords in her neck were rigid. Alice wondered if Marianne realized that Tuoni's reign had ended. That someone else, who wasn't her father, had taken his place. Alice cleared her throat. It might disadvantage her if Marianne knew.

'There is no conflict of interest between us,' Marianne said derisively. 'You've done nothing in Tuoni's name, whereas I've proven myself loyal every day for almost thirty years.'

Alice stared at her. *I've done nothing in his name?* She sat taller in her chair. *Good.* She smiled coldly. 'And who's been loyal to you, Marianne?' Alice asked. 'Thirty years of loneliness would be enough to send anyone mad. And you are alone, aren't you?'

Marianne's eyes cast about, looking towards Bridget.

'I don't think she counts,' Alice said. 'I don't think any of your followers count. Not when they're tricked and forced to stay with you.'

'They're here because they want to be,' she snapped. 'Because it's an honour to be devoted to something greater than yourself.'

Alice nodded thoughtfully. 'But there were others who didn't want that honour,' she said, probing for a response that would take her in the direction of Tilda without arousing Marianne's suspicions. 'Catherine Rose. Your sister, Helena. Both older than you, weren't they? Both ahead of you in the line to lead the Fellowship, and yet here you are instead.'

Marianne froze. Very slowly, she sat back in the chair, her mouth pressed into a firm line. 'Catherine . . .?'

'Rose,' said Alice, looking for a reaction. 'Catherine Rose. Her father was once the lea—'

'I know who her father was,' she said softly, and glanced away. 'How do you know about Catherine?'

'I've been doing my homework.'

Marianne turned back to look at Alice with a contemplative eye. 'Strange.'

'What is?' asked Alice.

'You, coming in here, talking about a name I haven't heard spoken in over twenty years.'

Her gaze tracked over Alice's face. It was clear her curiosity had been piqued.

'You were friends,' said Alice.

Marianne shook her head bitterly. 'We outgrew each other.'

'I saw a photograph,' Alice ventured, stoking the fire a little further. 'A group of you at a picnic. You were in it – only a child. With—'

'At the old Jarvis house?' said Marianne, eyes narrowing in confusion. 'One of the annual charity fundraisers?'

Alice shrugged. 'Maybe.'

Marianne rose from the chair and Alice tensed – she was ready. If Marianne wanted to try—

'Stay here,' murmured Marianne. 'Bridget? Entertain our guest.'

301

Alice inhaled sharply, staring at Bridget in horror. The blonde had calmly sliced the knife across her forearm. She held it still on her knee, rich rivers of blood pouring into the cotton folds of her skirt.

'Please don't stain the rug,' said Marianne with a sigh. She touched Bridget's shoulder lightly, and the blonde put the knife down on the floor and squeezed her arm to stem the blood. She gave no indication at all that she was in pain; she was like a sleep-walker. And yet, the already pale woman was growing paler as the blood spilled out.

Marianne rolled her shoulders to loosen them, her bones cricking. 'Wait here,' she said, striding to the wall.

The bricks pivoted outwards with a snap, opening a hole to the hallway beyond. They spun back into place as she disappeared, and Alice turned to examine the room. But she couldn't concentrate. Not with Bridget silently bleeding out on the floor. Her breathing was laboured and she was so pale she was almost transparent, save for the tinge of blue cyanosis in her fingertips. Bridget's head swayed as though she struggled with its weight. When her eyelids began to flicker, Alice dived for her. She whipped off her jumper and wrapped it around the blonde's arm, one eye on her nightjar's cord while she searched for the slow pulse. *Fucking Marianne.*

Almost as though conjured by thought, Marianne swept back through the wall, the brickwork clicking into place behind her.

'Bridget,' Marianne said sharply. '*Stop that.*' She flicked a finger, and the blood pumping from Bridget's arm instantly clotted, hardening into a tapering, ridged scab.

On her knees, Alice peered up at the repulsive woman, her lip curled with distaste.

'A photograph like this one?' Marianne asked, flourishing a small, glossy photo.

Taken by surprise, Alice reached for it just as Marianne thrust it at her . . . and Alice nicked her finger on the edge.

'Paper cut?' said Marianne, grabbing her wrist to examine it with false sympathy. 'Poor thing. Sometimes the smallest cuts hurt the most. Shall I fix it for you?'

Alice yanked her hand back, her adrenaline racing and her fingers trembling as she checked the cut. Had the hemomancer done that on purpose? There was a tiny speck of blood. Was it enough?

Marianne grinned. 'You're almost as pale as she is,' she said, nodding at Bridget. 'Oh, don't worry, Alice. Daughter of my Lord. Blood of Tuoni. You can trust in *me*.'

The tone was mocking, and Alice's skin crawled with agitation. But she clamped down on it, parcelled it away for later so that she could focus on the here and now – and on the photograph clenched in her other hand.

It was almost identical to the one she'd found in Reid's drawers. Except that in this one they were even younger. Marianne, clearly the youngest, couldn't have been more than eleven. The group of women and girls were stretched out on a huge checked picnic blanket, smiling up at the camera and shielding their eyes from the sun. Leda Westergard was laughing at something in the distance. Alice studied her closely, eyes roving across the image for clues, desperate to know what had so amused her.

'There's Catherine,' said Marianne, interrupting her thoughts. 'We were a unit, a pair. The others were older, but we had each other.'

'You had Helena,' Alice pointed out. Her sister.

Marianne tutted irritably. 'I didn't have Helena. *Leda and Emmi* had Helena.'

Alice had to bite her tongue. She couldn't probe Marianne for information about Leda. It would be reckless and would give her far too much ammunition she could use against her.

'After our mother died, Helena preferred her friends to her family,' said Marianne, 'because she didn't care about what was important. About tradition and reputation.' She paused, her gaze distant. '*I* cared. I should have been the firstborn. I should have had the birthright she didn't want, but Mother gave all her secrets to Helena and not to me. Still. I had secrets of my own, anyway.'

Alice frowned, uncertain of her meaning. She moved to the chair far from Marianne and sat down.

Marianne's face was sour with remembrance. 'I was glad when Helena moved away to study. We barely saw her for years. But then . . . she twisted the knife by ruining us.'

'And so you got revenge by burying the knife in her back?' Alice shot back, a flicker of anger crossing her face. Marianne was utterly deluded. She really did believe she was the victim.

'It was her own fault,' snapped Marianne. 'She took every opportunity that should have been mine. You have no idea. And your little friend – that filth that shares my blood—'

'Crowley?' Alice asked sharply. Marianne's nephew?

'I think it's clear that she didn't pass my mother's secrets to him, isn't it?' She tipped her head on one side, lips pouted, feigning sympathy. 'Perhaps she knew he was unworthy of the duty she'd been given.'

'What are you talking about?' asked Alice. The thread of the conversation had unravelled in a direction Alice hadn't anticipated and didn't understand. What duty had Crowley's mother had? Did he know more than he'd told her?

Marianne smiled viciously. 'Never mind,' she said, sweeping her verbal detour away with a hand.

Alice's fingers twitched with the urge to lunge forward and grab Marianne's nightjar, to peel all of its secrets away. And yet . . . she sensed something in the hemomancer's soul-bird. It radiated ignorance and jealousy. Whatever secrets Crowley's mother had had, the nightjar suggested Marianne didn't know them.

'You've heard the old adage that blood is thicker than water: family over friendships,' said Marianne. 'Well, the Northams learned the hard way that blood and water are *both* weak. Father was demoted because of Helena's marriage choice – and it was Catherine's father, Edgar Rose, who ordered the demotion. Couldn't be helped, apparently. It hurt him just as much as it hurt us.' She shook her head bitterly. 'The humiliation ruined us. Edgar made sure we weren't welcome at any more charity fund-raisers afterwards,' she said, nodding at the photograph. 'Even though it was the Northams whose pockets were far deeper than the Roses'.'

She withdrew from Alice, standing with a manic gleam in her eye. 'The Northams descended directly from Pellervoinen blood. What could the Roses claim? What right had the Roses to lead the Fellowship, when they were such minor players in House Pellervoinen?' She clicked her fingers – and an entire wall disintegrated in a curtain of falling dust.

Alice stared at Marianne, stony-faced, her thoughts circling. *Pellervoinen blood. Helena's secret duty.*

'The Roses might have been able to dictate the goings-on in the Fellowship, but it was the Northams who could press home their advantage in the House. And now, the Northams are the ones who remain, who outlasted the rest.'

'Catherine—' Alice started.

'She changed,' Marianne said dismissively. 'Like Helena, she went away to university, and came back with a head full of ridiculous ideas. I was the one who stayed. The most loyal, always.'

Marianne laughed, and Alice glanced back at the photograph as the older woman flopped lazily into her Queen Anne chair.

'But credit where it's due,' said Marianne with a tight smile. 'Catherine bested me in the end.'

'How so?'

'She died,' said Marianne. 'So she had the honour of meeting Tuoni first. But then again, I always think first place is overrated – better to save the best for last.'

Alice clamped her lips. Marianne was wrong, but it wasn't Alice's place to put her right. Reid had clearly gone to great lengths to change her identity, and Alice wouldn't give it up without good reason.

'Now. I think,' said Marianne, 'that it's time to give me the folder under your arm. You wouldn't have brought it if you weren't planning to give it to me.'

Alice glanced down at it and smiled. 'This old thing?'

Marianne straightened and gripped the armrests tighter. Alice's hand slid into her pocket, gently pulling out a small mass of plant growths: creeping rootstalks from a knotweed. She'd kept hold of them from her last test at House Mielikki.

Alice's eye was on Marianne's nightjar. When the bird began to flutter in agitation, she squeezed the rootstalks until her palm tingled with sensitivity. Her muscles tensed.

Marianne clicked her fingers, and the wall behind Alice crumpled. A waterfall of bricks slammed through the air towards her. But the nightjar's advance notice had sharpened Alice's reactions. She didn't flinch; her hand snapped open and the knotweed roots exploded into the air around her, thrusting their stalks in all directions and smashing the bricks to dust.

With a frustrated hiss, Marianne made to leap from the chair, intent on reaching Reid's folder. Alice's jaw clenched and she slammed her hands on the wooden armrests of her own chair. Her fingers pressed into the grains of wood. Alice's eyes were fixed on the polished sheen of the Queen Anne, catching the light through the hole in Marianne's wall.

'You should never have—' Marianne began, stalking towards Alice. But with a shocked yelp, she was whipped off her feet and snatched backwards into the Queen Anne. The grains shifted, pouring like sand through the armrests. The wood curled around Marianne's wrists, holding her in place, while knots in the chair legs had sprouted twisting branches that wound around her ankles, pinning her down.

Marianne's face was puce with rage. Her eyes bulged and her teeth were bared as Alice approached. The folder was held carelessly in one hand.

'Well that wasn't very nice,' said Alice. 'No wonder all of your friends left you behind.'

'You can't hold me like this forever,' hissed Marianne. 'And when I free myself . . . What Tom did to you is nothing to what I can bring down on your head.'

Alice's face grew blank and her eyes cold. She could leave Marianne here, like this. Let her starve to death in this chair. Soil herself. Show her the same mercy she'd shown Crowley's mum, Helena – none. She watched her struggle for a moment, considering.

'You won't be freed from this chair unless I allow it,' said Alice. 'Haven't you read the newspapers? House Mielikki is on the rise.' Her tone was mocking. 'Our legacies will beat yours every time.'

She paused. 'It's strange, isn't it? Because I heard a whisper that this research' – she twitched the folder – 'might be connected to the Summer Tree's growth, and therefore what's causing the House Mielikki power surges. But if that's true, why are you so keen to get your hands on it? Do you *want* our legacies to grow stronger than yours?' Marianne didn't respond – Alice didn't really expect her to. 'Are you doing something to the Summer Tree?' she demanded.

She raised an eyebrow, but Marianne's lips were clamped shut. There was nothing in her nightjar's demeanour that indicated whether this was true or false. Alice's fingers twitched. She wanted to probe her about the comment she'd found in Reid's notes – *Pellervoinen safeguard*. Marianne might know more than Crowley. But Marianne wanted the notes, and so Alice couldn't simply dish out the highlights without knowing if it might be more dangerous to do so.

Alice studied the older woman and sighed irritably. She almost – almost – had the impression Marianne didn't know quite as much about the contents of the folder as she'd thought. It was odd, certainly, that Marianne had no idea this was the work of her old childhood friend.

'Look, I don't want to humiliate you, Marianne. In fact, I want to be reasonable. So how about a bargain?'

'What the fuck do you want?' Marianne rasped. 'Spit it out!'

'There was an older woman in the photograph,' she said. 'A woman named Tilda. I want to know where she is.'

Marianne stared at her as if she was deranged, and then she began to laugh – a hoarse, throaty sound.

'You want to know where that judgemental old bitch is?' she said. 'What's it worth?'

Alice took a deep breath and held up the folder. 'This.'

Marianne's mouth fell open. Then suspicion clouded her face. 'I don't believe you.'

'Here,' said Alice, tossing the folder to Bridget. 'Catch.'

Bridget made no attempt to reach for it. It thwacked the floor and lay by her knees. Alice moved backwards and retook her seat, allowing Marianne to note the distance between her and the folder.

'Tell me about Tilda,' she said.

Marianne blinked and scrutinized Alice more closely. Alice knew she'd thrown all her chips into the pile – Marianne's curiosity had been sparked and she would certainly follow up on it later – but the gamble was worth the prize. Alice was sure now that she'd made the right decision not to ask after Leda Westergard too.

'Tilda Jarvis,' said Marianne at last, glancing down at the folder and back over at Alice, 'squandered the family fortune on charitable ventures. She disappeared for a few years, working in one of the Council's least glamorous departments, before reappearing as a librarian in the Abbey Library.'

Alice stared hard at Marianne, her eyes wandering to check her nightjar.

'And where is she now?' she asked, her heart beginning to race in anticipation.

Marianne sneered. 'The last I heard, she was still there. Withered and dried up as her books.'

Alice glanced back at the photograph, her eyes darting from the young Catherine, Leda and Helena to the older Tilda Jarvis. If she still worked at the Abbey Library, Alice would stake it out until she found her.

'Are we done here?' snapped Marianne.

Alice nodded distractedly as she rose. 'Yes. I think we're done for good.'

Marianne smiled and her voice dropped. 'Mind you don't give yourself any more paper cuts.'

Alice ignored her, striding through the hole Marianne had caused in the wall, towards the front door. She paused on the step as she tried to commit her visit and all that Marianne had said to memory. She had to go to the library. She had to find Tilda Jarvis – she needed to know what the old woman knew about her past. The question was, when? Now? Or should she take some time to prepare without charging in? Maybe she should take some proof with her, something to convince the old woman of her identity: Reid's photograph, maybe.

Before she stepped out into the garden, she cast one last look behind her. Her bent fingers flexed, and she heard Marianne gasp as the bindings pinning her to the chair suddenly disintegrated. The sounds of Marianne scrambling for Reid's research folder accompanied Alice out onto the street. She paused – waiting – her fingers tingling.

There was a scream of rage from within the house, and Alice nodded in satisfaction. The folder of blank paper had rotted and blackened, disintegrating in Marianne's hands, while Reid's notes sat safely in Coram House.

As Marianne's frustration echoed down the street, Alice smiled. That one was for Crowley.

24

Alice flinched. There were two uniformed Runners leaning against the door to her apartment. She'd grown exhausted on her trek through the campus – it had been a long few days – but her mind raced at the sight of her visitors. She backed down the corridor, towards the end where the stairs lay. Her spine hit the door to the fire escape and she fumbled behind her for the handle.

'Miss Wyndham? Is that you?'

She froze and squeezed her eyes shut. 'No' hovered on the tip of her tongue, but she sighed and pushed away from the door.

'Yes,' she said flatly.

'Mind if we have a quick word?'

Yes, she did mind. She wanted to be left alone to think. She didn't want to wonder what, exactly, they might be here for – a word about Reid's lab? An account of what she'd witnessed at Crane Park? Or Tom? She snorted bitterly. Pick one.

Head down, she trudged towards them and made to open her door. It was only when a shaft of dying sunlight illuminated not just one but both Runners that her hand paused on the lock and she froze, her temper sparking instantly.

Reuben Risdon, commander of the Bow Street Runners. *Again.* He nodded solemnly at her. Silver-haired, with sharply slanted eyebrows and eyes that appeared grey in the right light, he looked like a man dipped in liquid mercury.

'Good evening,' he said.

She clenched her jaw and cut him a dark look.

'What do you want?'

'We have some enquiries to make about one of your colleagues, Tom Bannister.'

She tensed and moved to stand in front of her apartment door, barring it from them.

'Oh? What about him?'

Risdon looked up from his notebook. 'He's dead.'

Alice's face paled. 'I'm . . . sorry to hear that.'

'Are you?' he asked mildly.

A bloom of pink rushed to her cheeks. What was that supposed to mean? 'Yes,' she said. 'Why wouldn't I be?'

He held her gaze for a moment and then nodded.

'How did he die?' she asked.

'A broken neck,' said Risdon. 'He fell from a third-floor balcony. We're trying to establish whether he stepped off or whether he was pushed.'

Alice licked her lips, trying to figure out how to buy some time. Why had they come to her, and how much did they know?

'We weren't colleagues,' she said carefully. Risdon appeared to scribble this down. 'We worked in different departments.'

'But you knew him?'

She shrugged. 'I'd seen him around.'

'That's interesting,' said Risdon, his gaze flickering over her, coolly assessing.

There was a pointed pause. Risdon nodded at the other Runner, a young, freckled man with a side-parting and exceptionally shiny shoes. Inexperienced and eager to please the higher-ups, thought Alice.

'Mr Bannister seemed to know *you* quite well,' said the young Runner. 'He had your work schedule pinned up in his kitchen. It seems he'd been making an observation log to keep track of your movements.'

Alice's mouth slackened. What the fuck? He'd been logging her whereabouts? It was one thing to imagine him carrying out a few opportunistic attacks, but to find that he'd been following her too? Stalking her all that time he'd been feigning friendship? Her stomach churned in revulsion. She felt violated in a way she hadn't before.

'We understand this must be quite distressing to hear,' said the young Runner. The badge on his pocket said *Gibson*.

'No, it's not,' she shot back. 'Not if he's dead.'

Two silent faces stared back at her. Risdon had a shrewdly probing look in his eye.

'I'm sorry,' she said, too tired to hide behind lies, 'but if he's been spying on me, then to be honest with you it's a relief that I don't need to worry about what he might do next.'

'Oh, I – we completely understand,' said Gibson, shooting an anxious glance at Risdon. 'Personal safety is always at the forefront of – of Runner operations and—'

'Mr Bannister's body was found outside the apartment of your employer, Professor Reid,' Risdon said smoothly. 'To your knowledge, were they in a relationship?'

Alice's eyes widened in surprise. 'No. Why?'

'It might have explained why he was there,' said Risdon. 'Particularly as Professor Reid is still in a serious condition in hospital.'

'Oh.' She nodded.

'Do you know of any other connection between Mr Bannister and Professor Reid?' asked the young Runner.

She shook her head. 'Other than the fact they both worked here and had seen each other around, no.'

Risdon closed his notebook. 'We're investigating whether, given our findings in his apartment, Mr Bannister was, in fact, the individual targeting you. At the moment, the only connection we can find between him and your employer . . . is you.'

She tilted her chin.

'Could I ask where you were last night?' he said, his tone light but a faint frown creasing his forehead.

'Sleeping,' she said tightly. 'Now if you will excuse me, I have to—'

'We have an officer looking into his last movements, so that we can form a clearer picture about exactly what happened,' said Risdon conversationally. 'Eris Mawkin – I think you know of her?'

Alice's breathing slowed. The Runners used the necromancer to pick up on signs of a struggle, imprints of distress left by the dead. What would she find?

'Good,' she said, pushing open her front door. 'I'm sure you'll find her very illuminating.'

'If you think of anything that might be useful later,' said Gibson, 'please feel free to—'

'Thanks,' she said, closing the door on them.

Alice waited until their footsteps took them away before shrugging off her jacket and slumping onto the edge of her bed. She leaned over, head in her hands, utterly spent. What was Eris Mawkin going to find? Her stomach churned with the injustice of it; she was the one who Tom had attacked, tricked and made a fool of. He'd killed himself and it was only good fortune he hadn't killed her too. She was the victim, and yet now she might be the one forced to defend herself from the Runners.

Flopping back onto the mattress, she threw her hand over her eyes. They were hot and gritty with exhaustion. She crawled up the bed and sank into the pillows. Tomorrow. She'd find Tilda tomorrow, but first she needed to rest.

Red hair. Always. Jen darted between the black trees, her red hair flying out behind her like a living thing. The crooked trees striped the frosted landscape like iron bars. Alice glanced down at her bare feet as she crunched through the glittering carpet of snow.

'Jen!'

Alice sped up, her feet burning with cold as she chased shadows through the forest.

'Jen, wait!'

On and on. Her feet numb. Pounding the snow. Clambering over tree roots, ducking low-hanging branches, weaving between the trees standing sentry.

And then Jen stopped – so abruptly that Alice skidded to a halt a short distance away, panting and dizzy. Jen turned, and the hair whipped across her face like a spray of blood.

'Alice,' she said, and her voice was strange – a husky rasp of a voice.

Jen darted behind the trees, calling out her name, and it seemed to come from every direction. A thousand sing-song voices, taunting her.

Alice spun around, searching for the lash of red hair. The moors tilted with her, the monochrome frost and black trees morphing into a grey blur strobing around her. Her vision flickered, and then she saw it: the Summer Tree. Here, in this place it didn't belong, its roots submerged in the glittering snow, its crown a canopy over the whole forest. It towered over the frosted landscape, the tree's twisted branches blackened just like those of the Arbor Talvi – the winter trees, the trees of death. Alice shuddered at the sight of it: so monstrous, so magnificent. Her eyes tracked up the crooked trunk, utterly entranced.

'Alice!'

Her head turned sharply to the noise, but as she looked away from the shadowy Summer Tree she almost missed the flurry of movement from its branches. Her eyes snapped back to the tree as hundreds of nightjars burst out from the leaves, spiralling into the dark skies of the Sulka Moors. She laughed delightedly.

'Alice?'

The smile froze on her lips.

'Alice!' Tom's voice, not Jen's.

She tensed and backed away, her heels crunching through the thick frost. Somewhere nearby, Alice's nightjar shrieked a warning as a root from the Summer Tree untethered itself. The ground rumbled as it shifted and bunched. The contraction sent a wave of compacted soil and snow ploughing towards her, and she stumbled sideways to avoid it.

Her hair fell across her face and she roughly dashed it away. A shadow loomed over her. Not Jen's. This one taller, broader, steadier. Tom stood over her. He wore the same shirt he'd died in, his glasses askew and his beard matted with blood. He peered down at her with a cold look in his eye.

'Tom—' she said.

He clicked his fingers and another root burst free from the ground. Swaying like a python, it swiped her onto her back and she landed winded, the back of her head smarting. She scrambled onto her elbows but the root slid over her chest, crushing her beneath it, while Tom looked on grimly.

Alice gasped. The weight on her ribs clamped and tightened, bending her inwards. And the pressure in her head . . . Bright sparks popped across her vision. She was going to pass out. She . . . The weight on her lungs . . .

'Tom, stop,' she rasped. *Stopstopstopstop* . . . The echo rolled across the moors, demanding and pleading.

Alice didn't have the energy to raise her head. Her cheek was pressed against the snow, raw with cold. Her breaths were shallow. She fought to push the weight off her chest, and failed. She slumped back, her arms splayed out and her head ricocheting off the ground. Her skull rang with the crack. She tried to focus her blurred gaze on the shadow stepping closer with a heavy, deliberate tread. It paused, Tom's shadow slanting across her body, and she flinched. *Fightbackfightback* . . .

'Kuu?' she mouthed.

The nightjar appeared with a snap of air. Hovering behind Alice, its body arched in a fighting stance that swelled her heart, the bird screeched angrily.

She glanced up at it, urging it with her eyes. 'Go.'

Kuu instantly glided to the left and swooped away like a lightning bolt. The glowing cord that stretched between them was pulled taut, and thinned under the pressure of Kuu's distance.

Alice tipped her head back, the landscape swimming around her, and closed her eyes. With one final puff of breath, she exhaled sharply, pushing herself out from her body, expelling herself into the air like a formless gas. Her deadly soul shattered into a million glittering particles, suspended above her body. And then – a throb of movement from Tom was like a beacon in a frozen sea. The dark cloud made of Alice, the invisible, shapeless thing she was, vibrated. She spread herself wide, seeping through the air, and reached for him—

Her eyes flew open. Heart hammering against her ribs, she dragged air into her lungs and bolted upright, trying to get a grip on her surroundings. It was dark. Her room was black and she was hopelessly tangled in the sheets. She wriggled sideways and fell out of bed, clattering onto the wooden floor. The sheets slipped and she struggled out of them, bursting up onto her feet. The back of her neck tingled, and her fists were clenched as she stood hunched in the space next to her bed. She waited for a movement or a sound in the darkness, but there was nothing at all. Flicking the light switch, she remembered the blackouts. No electricity. She moved to the window, where a small glimpse of moonlight lit a corner of the room. She squinted into the gloom with a wary eye. Nothing. She waited a while longer. Still nothing.

'My God,' she breathed, climbing back into bed. 'Forget that bastard Tom, these bloody dreams are going to kill me.'

As she closed her eyes, Jen's voice – not Tom's – rang through her mind, harsh and rasping in a way the living Jen's voice never had been. The nightmarish echo was disconcerting, and Alice's eyes flicked open. *Not Jen's voice at all*, she realized suddenly. She recognized it. It had been Marianne's voice issuing from Jen's mouth. Alice shuddered under the bedcovers. Was it a nightmare because she'd been to see Marianne? Or had Marianne induced this nightmare with her paper cut – for fun or a threat, to show that she could wheedle her way into Alice's dreams if she wanted to? Or in anger, because Alice had tricked her out of Reid's research notes.

'Kuu?'

Her nightjar fluttered down to join her on the mattress and Alice reached out to stroke her. Her feathers were chilled, and Alice's fingers tensed at the memory of the icy landscape and the sensation of expelling herself from her own body.

'Will you stay close tonight?' she asked the bird.

Kuu churred in response. The nightjar shuffled closer and tucked herself into the crook of Alice's arm, rubbing her soft head comfortingly against her cheek.

Alice sighed and tried to sleep. Until she was sure Marianne's paper cut wasn't a threat, she'd start taking valerian or lavender before bed, to shut out any nightmares.

It was half past six in the morning and Alice had been huddled in the Abbey Library's entrance for thirty minutes. Its opening hours were seven till midnight and not twenty-four hours, as she'd believed when she'd dragged herself out of bed that morning. Bea was expecting her to roll into the library for an update at nine, so she only hoped that Tilda was one of the librarian's early birds.

Cramp buckled Alice's legs, and she moved out from the arched entrance to pace the cobbled square and release the tension in her calves. The shadow of the ancient abbey, with its spire and bell tower, loomed over her. Ivy crawled up the face of the crumbling building, smothering it. *Like knotweed*, she thought, turning away.

At dead on the hour, the door clanked open and Alice, along with a handful of rather more studious-looking people who had also been waiting, tramped inside. The abbey was empty, the space simply an enormous dusty room with a hole in the floor leading to a winding subterranean staircase. Alice trudged after the others, through the hole and down the stairwell. Flickering oil lamps cast shadows over the rough walls; their faint lights illuminated the many darkened corridors that sloped off from the stairs. Alice plunged further into the bowels of the building, finally emerging into the upper floor of an immense atrium.

In the centre stood the vast Summer Tree, its tangled roots embedded in the ground-floor courtyard, five storeys below. The leafy crown stretched far overhead, its tapered leaves and crooked branches crushed against the glass ceiling.

The tree always took Alice's breath away. Its towering magnitude made her feel she was in the presence of an otherworldly creature. It emanated power. Like a frozen warrior trapped in an endless battle with the walls caging it beneath the abbey, its thick boughs lashed out at its confinement, pressing their weight against the stone. An army of branches and twigs, like foot soldiers ordered by their general, invaded every empty space, coiling around pillars and curling into arches. The Summer Tree was wonderful and terrible in its immensity.

A granite staircase spiralled around the twisted trunk, leading from the top floor to the bottom – from crown to roots. Landings ran off it, leading to floors of bookshelves, tight passageways and discreet alcoves: everywhere crowded with books. Despite the early morning sky, clusters of fireflies drifted through the atrium, glowing like fairy lights.

Alice hurried down the staircase to the courtyard on the ground floor, and inhaled sharply at the scene of devastation. One crooked tree root bulged outwards, rising from the soil like a sea monster and dislodging the tiled floor. Down one narrow corridor, the walls listed and the ground tilted at an impossible angle. A rope cordoned it off, preventing access, but Alice could see heaps of damaged books scattered all over the floor. This was what had happened to Crane Park Island. The tree roots had grown and fractured the land. And this was where it had started, with a tumescent root burrowing deeper at one end and rising up to cause chaos at the other. She stood back to study it.

Footsteps over her shoulder caused her to step aside without thinking, but when she saw who they belonged to, she tensed in shock and hurried into an alcove. The shelves were still upright here, but they leaned heavily to one side, and all of the books had fallen into a haphazard clutter or had slipped off entirely. She flattened herself against the shelf, flinching when it began to sway against her. The whole thing might come down on top of her, and then they'd certainly hear her.

Gabriel Whitmore was talking to someone she couldn't see. *Talking* was perhaps generous – he was whispering animatedly in the shadows of a corridor. Alice inched closer, curiosity spiking her adrenaline.

'. . . death and destruction . . . the entire city . . . and there's nothing that can be done about it!'

A calmer voice murmured something that Alice didn't quite catch.

'No one else can get down there,' Whitmore hissed. 'Do you understand? *No one.*'

Alice's eyebrows slanted in suspicion. Who was he threatening? She leaned out further, but a rustle of paper nearby startled her and she darted back into the corridor. She watched as Whitmore strode out from the corridor, glanced around as though to check for observers and then swept up the stairs. Alice waited before slipping out and glancing down the corridor he'd exited. She just caught sight of a grey-haired woman vanishing down it and squinted after her thoughtfully.

'Are you lost?'

Alice jerked in surprise. One of the librarians – a young woman in a long, sweeping dark dress with a pocketed apron filled with books – was stacking manuscripts and sheaves of paper in a neat pile by the alcove.

'Can you tell me where to find Tilda Jarvis? Does she still—'

'Third floor,' said the woman, with barely a glance away from her manuscripts.

'Okay, thanks.'

Alice eyed the staircase and set off to climb it again. On the third floor, she was sent to the fifth. Then the second, the ground, and back to the third again. By the time a small, wiry-haired man with red hair had sent her up to the empty fourth, she was beginning to seethe. Alice planted her hands on the spiral banister and looked out over the tree. Somewhere in this building, the woman she needed was avoiding her.

She considered calling for a bird's-eye view from Kuu, but it always unsettled her, and made her vulnerable – she couldn't protect her human body while she was squatting in a bird's mind – and even when it alerted her to danger, valuable seconds were lost readjusting to her heavy human frame. No. A bird's-eye view here might send her accidentally swaying and tripping down the granite stairs. Instead, she slowed her breathing and tried to block out all noise, all sensation, and just listen. Maybe she or Kuu would somehow sense this woman's nightjar. After all, Alice had met her once, when she was too young to remember. But sometimes, she'd found, memories masqueraded as instincts. She closed her mind, shut down her thoughts and focused.

Somewhere, on the other side of the trunk, was a gentle churring . . . the flap of feathers . . . the rustle of wings in flight, gliding out of sight. In a trance, Alice reached out towards the sound . . .

'*Don't*,' a sharp voice hissed in her ear, and Alice jerked to her senses and dropped her arm.

She turned to find a tall, angular woman with steely-grey hair pulled back into a bun staring at her. She wore a glove on one hand, and when Alice glanced at it without thinking, the woman snatched it off to reveal she was missing a finger.

'The Lampyridae bite,' she said sternly. 'Don't put your hands on the tree. Read the signs.'

Alice nodded vacantly. She'd met this woman before. Here, on these very steps, with this very same warning ringing in her ears.

'I wasn't trying to touch the tree or the fireflies,' Alice murmured. 'I was just . . . I heard a . . .'

She trailed away, her eyes fixed on the woman's face. It hadn't changed much. More lines, certainly, given she must now be around eighty years old, but it was undoubtedly the same woman from Reid's memory. And – if she wasn't mistaken – the same woman Whitmore had been remonstrating with.

'You're Tilda Jarvis,' said Alice. 'I've been looking for you.'

25

Alice stared at her. Now the moment had come, she seemed to have lost the ability to speak. Tilda, perhaps sensing this, took her by the arm and walked her to a quiet alcove, pushing her down onto a cushioned bench by the shelves.

'Are you quite well?' said the old woman, eyes bright as she studied Alice closely. 'Your library fines must be appalling, judging by your—'

'I think you helped arrange my adoption,' Alice murmured.

The old woman's smile instantly faded. Her face a mask of shock, Tilda lowered herself onto the bench next to Alice.

'And why, exactly, do you think that?' Tilda asked quietly.

Alice's fingers crept to her pocket and she pulled out Reid's photograph. 'Because I think that this is you with Catherine Rose, who was also involved. And I think that the young woman on the end . . . might be my biological mother.'

Tilda swallowed thickly, the aged muscles in her neck strained. 'You think that Leda Westergard is your mother?' she asked. 'Everyone knows Leda Westergard was childless when she died.'

Alice nodded. She slipped the signet ring from her finger and held it out to Tilda. The old woman glanced down at it and released a shaky breath.

'What . . . name did they give you?' she asked.

'Alice Wyndham.'

Tilda's skeletal fingers tightened reflexively around the pocket of her apron. 'Wyndham,' she said. 'Yes, that was their . . .' She trailed away and shifted in her seat, turning to fully examine Alice.

Alice took the opportunity to do the same. Tilda was a tall, sinewy woman, handsome, with a strong face and high cheekbones. Her hands told a story of their own; all wiry tendons and tiny scars, they spoke of strength and battles won and lost.

'I saw you . . . in a memory,' said Alice.

Tilda seemed unfazed by this strange admission. She nodded, her expression stern and yet softening.

'You will have some questions. Ask me what you want to ask,' said Tilda, without any preamble at all.

'Was Leda Westergard my mother?' Alice asked baldly. It was what she most wanted to know. No use building up to it.

'Yes.'

A great breath rushed out of Alice. She shoved the signet ring back on her finger, her thoughts swamped. Leda Westergard. It was true. Chancellor Westergard.

'I always hoped . . .' Tilda shook her head and squeezed the apron again. 'I must tell you – there's a book. Here, in the library. I wasn't sure . . .' She trailed away.

'There's – a what? A book?' asked Alice. 'Which book?' A sudden thought came to her – she remembered Reid, in the memory, saying that Tilda had planned to burn a book. This one?

'Disguised as your mother's biography. *Chancellor Westergard: A Life in Service.* I made it so that only Leda's daughter could open it. No other borrower.'

'But what's—'

'I wanted to destroy it, but . . . those were Leda's own words to you. It would have been wrong to rob her of a voice in death.'

Alice couldn't speak. Her throat closed up and there was a tremble in her fingers. She wanted that book. Badly.

'Catherine pushed for me to leave it for you, and she was right in more ways than we could ever have realized at the time.' Tilda made as though to rise from the bench. 'I suggest you read it. You may find more of the answers you're looking for in there, if—'

Alice grabbed her elbow and Tilda paused, glancing down. She searched Alice's eyes, her expression pained, and then sat back down.

'I only want a few minutes of your time,' said Alice. 'Whatever happened – I don't begrudge you for what you did. I have the best parents, thanks to you.'

Tilda blinked hard and glanced away.

'Catherine Rose and Leda – they were good friends?' said Alice after a moment. 'That's why she was with you for the adoption?'

Tilda nodded. 'Yes. Leda was closest to Helena, but she died around the time you were born. And . . .' She cleared her throat. 'Dear Catherine wanted so much to help Leda. She took her failure very badly. For a time, she blamed herself for Leda's death.'

'She . . . Why would she blame herself?' asked Alice, with a cramped feeling in her stomach.

'Because she was a medical student and she thought her training would allow her to save Leda's life, but she was wrong. No one could have saved her. Leda knew that herself. It was why she chose your parents, while she still carried you inside her.'

Alice jerked back at this. Reid had said something similar, but she hadn't realized *Leda* had been the one to find her a new family.

Alice blinked away the sudden threat of tears and Tilda leaned closer, her eyes serious. 'She chose well?'

Alice turned away to steady herself. 'Yes,' she replied shakily. 'She did.' There was a short pause, and then, 'Did she die in childbirth?'

'Yes.'

Alice stared hard at the wall. Growing up, she'd assumed her parents had died when she was very young, in an accident maybe. But this . . . Leda had never even seen her face, never held her baby. It felt so much more tragic, and fresh sympathy for this poor woman she'd never met swept over her.

'Why was it – why was I – kept secret?' asked Alice.

'Oh,' said Tilda with a brittle smile. 'Your mother hid her pregnancy – first because she feared her political rivals might try to step in, and then . . .' Tilda shook her head. 'Only Catherine and I knew. Me, because I'd known her since she was a child, and her parents had died when she was barely in her twenties. And Catherine – well, Catherine latched on to Helena and Leda to try to separate herself from Marianne. We supported Leda as best we could. We tried, between us, to follow through with her wishes, but Catherine found it all very difficult.'

The old woman paused. 'And when both Leda and Helena had passed away, Catherine left the Rookery herself – couldn't bear the sight of it any more. I lost track of her over the years. I know that she turned away from practising medicine. I think she considered it a waste. She'd failed to save a life even before her career in saving lives had begun. She grew . . . hardened by her experiences. So she took herself off to one of the London universities to further her career – in research, I believe. Changed her name so she couldn't be found, changed everything.' She paused again, noticing that Alice's eyes had dropped to her lap in thought.

Alice tried to sift through the bombardment of information to make sense of it. Her mother, the chancellor, had told hardly anyone she was pregnant. But she'd known she was going to die, and had picked out a pair of adoptive parents for Alice. And Tilda and Catherine had been the ones to deliver the baby to her new family. It felt . . . so odd, like someone else's story.

'Your mother had warned me not to return to watch you once she was gone, and I'm ashamed to say I ignored her. I watched you for a few months, just from a distance, but then your adoptive parents moved and I finally followed her wishes. I didn't hunt you down to your new address. I . . . let you go.'

She was right. They'd lived in a different house in Henley when Alice was small. They'd moved when Alice was still in nursery, to the house next door to Jen's. It would have been better for Jen if they'd never moved at all.

'So I lost track of you,' said Tilda, 'and I lost track of Catherine, and instead, I stayed here to monitor your mother's tree as best I—'

A puff of dust ballooned from the ceiling, sprinkling them with debris. They stared at each other in shock as white powder pattered into their hair and the walls of the alcove shook. The legs of the bench bounced and vibrated, and Tilda shot to her feet as a terrible groan reverberated through the library; it was the sound of a dying giant, or a—

'The Summer Tree,' said Tilda, her voice tight. 'It's happening again. We lost a whole corridor last time.'

'What do you mean, my mother's tree?' asked Alice.

The books on the alcove shelves juddered and slid off. The bindings thudded onto the stone floor and the books fanned open, their pages splayed out like fallen birds' wings. The floor rumbled beneath them and the force threw the books out of the alcove, onto the landing.

'You haven't asked me about your father,' Tilda said quickly.

Alice's head snapped up.

'Listen to me,' said the librarian, growing urgent. 'He did love her – but his love killed her.'

Alice's eyes widened. Tuoni had *loved* Leda?

'But darkness can't love the light, Alice. The two can't coexist – they cancel each other out,' said Tilda. 'The moment your father reached for your mother, he destroyed her. She spent her last few weeks hiding from him. And *you* . . . you must not let him do the same. Understand?'

'No,' she said, more confused than ever. 'I *don't* understand. What do you—?'

Glass shattered. Tinkling shards fell, a jangling waterfall of music as they collided with the stone floor. Tilda dashed from the alcove and across the landing, skidding to a halt at the banister. The glass atrium ceiling . . . was gone. Half the steel girders designed to support the ceiling now held nothing at all; the other half had fallen to the floor, smashing holes in the stone flags. Glass debris littered the courtyard floor, and glittering crystals lay in chunks on the Summer Tree's lower leaves . . . and the upper leaves and much of the tree's crown now fountained through the ceiling.

'Alice!' said Tilda. 'Can you feel it?'

'Feel *what*?'

'Its power. Your power.'

Alice gestured helplessly. 'What do—?'

'You haven't taken the binding draught?' shouted Tilda above the echoing rumble.

'I'm still—'

'Leda Westergard's daughter should belong to her mother's House,' said Tilda in a reproving tone. 'You must apply to House Mielikki – everything depends on it!'

'I'm trying to!' Alice responded. 'But why?'

'The anchors are broken,' she started, breaking off at another creaking groan from the tree. A rumble in the underbelly of the building echoed ominously from the walls, and the pages of the scattered books began to flutter.

'Come and find me when it settles again,' said Tilda, with an impatient shake of her head. 'I'll explain everything to you then. The roots . . . You heard about Crane Park Island? You know the danger?'

'Death and destruction . . . the entire city,' said Alice. 'I heard you – I think it was you – with Gabriel Whitmore.'

Tilda's eyes widened at his name, and she nodded at the stairs. 'You need to find somewhere safe and stay there!'

'But I . . . Where would I find Leda's book?'

'The ground floor. Biographies, under *920 WES*. But not now,' Tilda shouted, stepping aside as a surge of people hurried up the stairs. 'When it's safer.'

'I don't—'

Tilda shouted something that Alice only just managed to catch. 'Mile End?' Alice checked.

'Yes!' said the old woman. 'My address. I'll meet you there tonight and we can talk!'

Tilda hurried down the stairs, pushing against the tide as the other librarians and visitors rushed up them, desperate to escape the atrium.

Alice raced after her and the old woman stopped, chest heaving, and looked back. She put up her gloved hand to stop Alice following.

'Go! Find somewhere safe!' Alice hesitated, and Tilda threw her a quick smile. 'I'm glad you've come home,' she said. 'We need you.'

The fragments of glass on the stairs began to vibrate, and they watched it for a split second, the vibrations gaining momentum, before staring at each other. And then Alice nodded, and in perfect synchronization they whirled away from each other. Tilda hurtled down the stairs and Alice dashed up them. Behind her, the tree strained against its roots, and the echoing crash of falling bookshelves chased her out into the square.

Alice had made it all the way to the derelict doorway opposite Coram House before the voice in her head won its argument. She wanted Leda's book, and she wouldn't settle if she didn't at least try to find it. So she'd slammed the door shut and dived back into the void, fixing her destination in mind.

When she arrived, the Summer Tree had stopped trembling the earth all around it and the square was deathly quiet. Everyone inside had fled. Which meant that there was no one to pay her any attention at all as she slipped into the abbey and made her way down to the atrium.

Even in the dim light from the oil lamps on the walls, she could see that the ground floor was an absolute disaster. Stone flags were upended and scattered at random, a mass of engorged tree roots were tangled over the floor, and books littered everything, tucked into nooks and crannies formed by curved roots and propped-up stones.

No Tilda Jarvis, she suddenly realized. No librarians here now at all. She cast about her, realizing quite suddenly how futile this would be. How could she expect to find a specific book in this utter chaos?

She searched the corridors, her stomach leaping at her good fortune when she found the corridor Tilda had indicated. Many of the signs had fallen off the walls, but the biography section's merely hung slanted.

The corridor was uneven. Where a bookshelf had tipped its load, the books were piled against one wall like rubble, but then the bookshelf itself had collapsed and landed on top. She was forced to clamber over the unsteady unit to reach the far end of the corridor, which darkened the further she moved away from the natural light at the entrance.

When Alice finally reached the shelf she was looking for, number 920 – cracked and hanging by a nail – she almost laughed out of sheer hopelessness. Her good fortune had lasted long enough only to jeer at her. She would never find this book. No one would ever find anything among this clutter. She couldn't even see down here; it was so dark she had no idea where she was standing, and would probably trip and break her neck at any moment.

'Kuu?' she whispered.

There was a pale flutter in the air above her head and she reached up to stroke her nightjar, who came to rest on her hand. She bestowed a few gentle brushes with a curled finger and then held the bird up to her shadowed eye.

'Can you find it, Kuu?' she asked. 'The way you once found Reid's philosophy book?'

Her nightjar lifted into the air, its claws briefly pinching her skin as it shot upwards. Alice bent to her haunches and began her own search while Kuu helped from the air. She pulled out books, scanned the titles and stacked them to one side. Book after book after book. It was slow-going in the shadows. She squinted at a title and held it up, angling it to see if the light might glance off it so she could identify it.

She bit back a frustrated sigh and put it down again. It was no use. She couldn't see a bloody—

A tiny light bloomed to life overhead and she froze. There was a whirring hum near her ear and she forced herself not to recoil from it. Another light joined the first. Then a third. A small congregation of fireflies drifted closer, shining their soft glow on the books by her feet. She held her breath, bit her lip and lifted another book, holding it up to their generous light. The fireflies . . . the lethal, carnivorous fireflies . . . were helping her.

Kuu tugged at the luminous cord wrapped around Alice's wrist, and she dropped the book she was holding. The nightjar let out a shriek and swooped down to stab at another book with her beak. The force of it sent the book rolling end over end towards Alice. She snatched it up, her heart pummelling her ribs, and ran a hand over the front cover. In the soft yellow glimmer from above, the words stood proud. *Chancellor Westergard: A Life in Service.*

This was it! Leda's book. The one Tilda wanted her to have. The temptation to flip it open and scour it was overwhelming, but she forced her desire aside. It would have to wait. She needed to get out of here. Struggling to her feet, slipping and sliding on fallen books and shelves, she scrambled out of the corridor and back to the ground floor of the atrium. The fireflies followed obediently, lighting her path. *Strange.*

Alice paused for a moment to appreciate the magnificence and awe of the Summer Tree. It was so vast it seemed on the verge of exploding through the walls of the abbey. A sobering thought. She looked about her, suddenly feeling overcome with the need to leave. Now. What she'd once thought beautiful was now unearthly and eerie. It was too dark, too broken down here – too silent. The only sound was the creaking wood, straining from the roots, pressing against the stone walls. It was almost—

She stilled. Every muscle and every sinew in her body tightened. Her own breathing was too loud, and she hushed even that as she turned her face up to the tree, her eyes searching. She could hear . . . something. She darted a glance at Kuu, but there was no one else here. No doubt the Runners were outside securing the area with safety barriers this very moment. But . . .

She shuffled closer to the trunk and peered up through the knotted branches. The hairs rose on the back of her neck as she stood up on her tiptoes to see better. The overlapping branches were too thick, the leaves too impenetrable. She could see nothing, but she could sense . . . She swallowed her confusion.

There was a nightjar in here. Somewhere in the atrium, there was a nightjar that didn't belong. A nightjar flying freely, attached to no one. Alice was sure of it.

26

The door to Coram House swung open and Alice stumbled over the threshold. Crowley caught her by the shoulders. He held her at arm's length, his eyes searching hers with growing alarm.

'Alice?'

She shook her head. 'I'm okay, I . . . Can I just sit for a while?' she murmured. 'With you?'

Relief washed over his face, and without a word he took her by the elbow and guided her to the stairs. He hesitated, just momentarily, before leading her onwards – not to the kitchen but towards his private quarters in the basement.

Crowley's rooms had been built for comfort rather than elegance. The wooden furniture was plain, with chunky legs on the wing-back chairs and worn velvet on the seat cushions. But the cushions were thickly padded, the rug soft, curtains draped in a pile to the floor, and a dying fire crackled in the grate. He waved a hand at it and the fire burst to life, heat pouring off it like the sun.

She cast an eye over the rest of the space. A desk, set diagonally under the basement window, gleamed in the cold early morning light, and was stacked with books, a tray of spirits and crystal glasses. One entire wall was given over to bookshelves, and through a crack in the door, Alice caught a glimpse of a handsome bed dressed with a plump quilted blanket and soft pillows. It looked the sort of bed you could dive into and sink to the bottom of. Everything was wood and sage-green furnishings. It looked more like the home of a House Mielikki member than an Ilmarinen's.

Alice opened her mouth to speak. She ought to tell him what Marianne had said about his mother, about her jealousy over some secret birthright. But she couldn't seem to focus on anything but what she'd learned from Tilda.

'Leda Westergard is my biological mother,' she said as they moved to sit by the fire.

He jerked in shock, but he didn't question what she'd said. Alice stared absently at the flames in the grate, casting distorted shadows over the wall. She felt there was a tight band around her ribcage, compressing her breathing along with every emotion other than dreadful anticipation.

'This is hers,' she said, holding out the book to him.

Frowning, he took it and lowered his eyes to the cover. He made to flip it open, but failed. Confused, he tried to slide his thumb between the cover and first page, but there was no give. Tilda had said she'd made it so that only Leda's daughter could open it. Alice had wanted to make sure.

She held out her hand, and he returned the book to her. She ran her palm over the faded letters, *Chancellor Westergard: A Life in Service*. There was a picture of Leda on the cover, sitting in an oval frame with an air of stateliness, her brown hair plaited and pinned up, a calm but steely expression on her face. She looked like the sort of woman who was used to having all the answers.

Alice took a sharp breath and opened the cover. The pages

turned easily, and she felt faintly like King Arthur pulling Excalibur from the stone. Alice's eyes dropped to the opened page, her heart fluttering and a strange, muffled sensation settling over her, crowding out the room, Crowley's voice and everything else but the book. The book, which was filled with blank pages – except for the first few. Blue ink looped and scratched across them. Leda's handwriting. Leda's hands had touched these pages . . .

My darling kulta, the message began. The sight of it stirred something inside Alice's chest; Leda had never known the name Alice would be given. To Leda, the very concept of Alice must have been a barely formed thing.

'Crowley . . .' said Alice. 'Is Kulta a girl's name? Was that the name she'd picked out for me?'

'No,' he murmured. 'It's a term of endearment. It means "gold".'

Alice nodded, her focus drifting back to the book.

My darling kulta,
I am so sorry, and so ashamed. And I am so very, very tired. I pray for sleep every night. But every time I close my eyes, I hear his whispers taking root in my mind, his pleas and promises. I worry you can sense it – my exhaustion, my guilt – and that somehow it might harm you. I remember Helena's pregnancy; she bloomed with good health, yet I've robbed myself of that – and you, too. If there had been any other way, I'd have taken it. I've broken him, and I regret it more than he'll ever know, but he isn't blameless. We are, in the end, both ruined. But you, little one, are not.

Alice shuddered. Was this a message to her or a maudlin diary entry, towards the end of Leda's pregnancy? Her eyes dropped back to the page.

I've protected you as best as I can, and found anonymity for you in the hope that this will protect you when I'm gone. They're good people. I've watched them. They'll love you in the way that love should be expressed: healthy, and not the poison ours has become.

And though I have so many regrets, I know I'd make the same choices again. I've always done the things that needed to be done. I've never turned my face from the hard decisions. You are all that matters, in the end.

So I'll bear my pain here, in private, while Tilda fusses over my health and Catherine takes to her books for a solution she won't find. Helena has gone. I'm not sure where. Perhaps to nurse her guilt, as I do. Shame binds people like nothing else; she won't ever tell what we've done, and soon I won't be on this earth to tell another soul either. My only hope is that the cost of what we've done won't be borne by others. We're certain nothing has been endangered – that we've not damned all to hell – but it's poor comfort when we three have already paid an unimaginable price.

Each night, when sleep refuses to come, I remind myself that I didn't lie when I took my oath of office – though I have broken it since. It brings me no relief to know that I intended to hold fast to the values of my chancellorship, even if I've fallen short. The Houses are blind to what we've done, and Gabriel, if he ever loved me, will let me have this one, final secret. Not that it matters now – my legacy is no longer going to be the achievements of my office. My legacy is you. You'll never know the burden of the Westergard name, or the duties expected of the last of the Gardiner line, and for that I'm glad. I hope that I've relinquished those on your behalf. You'll be a Wyndham, and it will be a name that brings you a freedom I've never had. I hope, also, though every cell in my body craves to know you, that you'll never read these words and that you'll never know me. What I wish most for you – and what I've fought for, and betrayed for – is that you will have the freedom to be no one other than yourself.

    Leda

Alice trembled, her thoughts in chaos. She squeezed the book compulsively, and then reread the words again several times over. Was Leda saying . . .?

'I think . . . I think I might be a Gardiner,' Alice breathed.

Crowley stared at her, his face ashen with surprise.

She looked up at him. 'I think I'm a Gardiner. The last Gardiner. Which would make me—'

'Mielikki's heir,' he whispered in stunned disbelief.

'Look,' said Alice, thrusting the book at him.

He glanced down at it. 'It's blank.'

Alice frowned. Crowley couldn't see Leda's writing?

'Read it to me,' he said quietly.

He listened in silence, only emitting a shaky breath when Alice mentioned his mother's name.

'What were they so ashamed of? What did they do?' said Alice. 'And who was she protecting me from?'

Crowley shook his head, his mouth pressed into a tight line, and Alice's eyes fell to her signet ring. It wasn't the Westergard crest Leda had worn on her finger. Could it be something much older – the Gardiner crest instead?

Crowley exhaled steadily, apparently mastering whatever emotions were roiling through him.

Finally, he spoke. 'Gabriel?'

Alice stilled. She didn't dare breathe.

'If *Gabriel* ever loved me?' said Crowley, his voice hoarse. 'Alice . . . could Gabriel Whitmore be your father?'

No. She squeezed her eyes shut tight. No. It couldn't be. Tuoni . . .? Why would Tuoni have come to the Rookery and masqueraded as an actual man, with a job and a life? She flung her eyes open. The Lintuvahti had once said that her father, Tuoni, had grown weary of his duties and had found that his place was elsewhere. Was his place in the Rookery – as the governor of House Mielikki?

'Gabriel Whitmore and Leda Westergard?' Crowley murmured.

Alice's mind jumped back to Cecil's office, where Leda's portrait hung in pride of place. *They made quite the pair . . .*

Alice pressed her fists into her eyes. 'It can't be true,' she said. 'I'd have . . . I'd have sensed it. I know I would.'

'Can Tuoni age?' said Crowley. 'Whitmore was a young man when he became governor.'

Alice shook her head. 'He isn't Tuoni,' she said, shoving aside the sickening feeling in her stomach. 'He just isn't, Crowley.' Alice's chest was too tight. 'Tuoni isn't just a man living an ordinary life.' She shuddered. 'I don't trust Whitmore – he lied about being in the grove when the siren went off; he lied about the tree growing at the abbey; he threatened Tilda, telling her there was nothing to be done about the destruction of the city moments before another quake; and he – oh God, what if it's true about the book?'

'What book?' Crowley asked sharply.

'Tom and Bea . . . There was a rumour that Whitmore had a copy of a book. Some sort of Latin book about how the Rookery's foundations were built over the Summer Tree. Bea once said it was nonsense – but what if it wasn't? What if he's doing all this, Crowley? Wouldn't the head of House Mielikki have access to hidden knowledge the other members don't? The House's legacies are growing stronger. Maybe it *is* a power grab.'

'But Alice,' said Crowley, 'who wants to rule over a broken kingdom? If the Rookery is destroyed, his power is meaningless.'

They fell silent, and Crowley began to pace the tiny room. 'The Westergards were descended from the Gardiners? That's what Leda suggests in her diary?' He stopped, turning to her abruptly. 'Alice,' he said, staring at her like he'd never seen her before, 'regardless of Whitmore – if you're a Gardiner, this changes *everything*.'

She was thrown back to the memory of Tilda's words.

Your mother's tree . . . You haven't taken the binding draught? . . . Can you feel it . . .?

Alice couldn't sleep. Hunkered down in her old Coram House bed, Leda's words and Tilda's questions played through her mind on repeat. She was a Gardiner. And if ever in history a Gardiner was needed, it was now. But Leda was only half of Alice's make-up. How much would her Tuoni ties prevent her from assuming any of the duties a true Gardiner might have been able to perform?

And yet . . . buried so far down that she didn't dare give it room to grow was the tantalizing prospect: could she become something other than what she was? Leda had wanted her to have the freedom to be herself, but Alice's concept of self was so warped by her dread of Tuoni's influence that she had begun to fear herself. Was this a chance for reinvention? Was this her absolution for what had happened to Jen?

Bea had said all control over the tree had ended with the last of Mielikki's line. If she took the final binding draught, linking herself fully and irreversibly to Mielikki's Summer Tree, might she somehow be able to control it? To regress its growth? To safely prune it the way a gardener might – and stop it from damaging the city? To save the Rookery from any more destruction?

'If Gabriel ever loved me . . .' Alice stared up at her shadowy ceiling. Gabriel Whitmore. Tuoni? She tried out the idea in her mind, but Alice had never felt more numb in her life. What was wrong with her? She gave herself a mental prod, seeking some sort of reaction, but her mind was anaesthetized. Leda wasn't with him when she'd died. Why? What had he done? Leda claimed she'd broken him – by leaving him?

Tuoni . . . She took a deep, shuddering breath. If Tuoni was alive and well, living in the Rookery . . . then he was no longer an abstract concept, or a bogeyman: he was a man with shrewd blue eyes and thinning hair. It was so normal it was laughable. But he simply couldn't be Tuoni. Surely she'd have felt it in her bones when they'd first met. Whatever the case – whether he was Tuoni or not – Whitmore had known Leda. He'd loved her, even. So did he know that Alice was really her daughter? And if he was blind to her real identity, might that give her an advantage while she investigated further? Alice exhaled heavily and pulled the blanket up over her head. Downstairs, Crowley would be tossing and turning too, no doubt. He'd grown so deathly quiet after the mention of his mother in Leda's book that she hadn't been able to face telling him she'd visited Marianne. Not tonight. They'd fallen into a silence, both consumed by their own thoughts.

Tomorrow, they were going to follow up with Tilda Jarvis. She'd written down the address so as not to forget it. Tilda might be able to tell them more about the odd link between their families. She might also be able to tell them how Alice could save the Rookery from Mielikki's tree.

27

'Are you sure this is it?' asked Alice, her teeth chattering in the frozen void.

'I know this area well,' said Crowley, pushing open the door to a narrow street of Victorian houses. 'I once took a case near here. A husband who was accusing his wife of running off with most of their savings. He wanted me to track the money down – but of course he really wanted the wife.'

As a thief-taker by trade, Crowley tracked down stolen goods and returned them for a reward. The Runners tolerated him for his usefulness and he despised them for their incompetence.

'Did you find her?' asked Alice, shivering. It was summer, and yet the build-up of exhaustion made it difficult to withstand the icy cold every time she travelled.

Crowley glanced down at her. 'Of course. She was living over in Bermondsey. But it turned out she'd run off with their savings because she'd taken one too many black eyes from him.' He squinted out into the street. 'I gave her the money he'd given me to find her and locked all of her doors to travel. I doubt the idiot was bright enough to find her himself, but even if he did, he'd never be able to get in.'

They stepped out from the void, the wind chasing their hair and rippling Crowley's long coat around his legs.

A creaking open-topped bus rolled past them, a winding staircase spiralling to the upper deck and an advert for *Oxo's Motoring Chocolate, only twenty shillings!* stretched across the side. It threw up a draught as it passed and Alice shivered again. Crowley frowned down at her, concern in his eyes.

'Take this,' he murmured, pulling off his coat.

He wrapped it around her shoulders, his fingers accidentally brushing her throat, and his eyes caught hers. Crowley stilled, his fingers on her collar and his expression inscrutable, and then cleared his throat.

'We should go,' he said, faint reluctance in his tone. 'I think it's just up here.'

Alice sank gratefully into the fabric of his coat. Her stomach fluttered with awareness: it was still warm from his body.

The Jarvis family had allowed their fortune to dwindle in the intervening years. Their original family seat in Kensington hadn't survived their lavish spending and had been sold almost thirty years ago. Tilda Jarvis now lived in a cramped terraced house in the Rookery's Mile End. Inside, it was filled with the most elaborate interior design Alice had ever seen, as though Tilda had taken lessons on home decoration from the royals. It was such a contrast from the ordinary exterior that it stopped them both in their tracks.

'They must have managed to retain the furniture when they lost the house,' said Crowley, his eyes tracing the silk upholstery, gilt-edged ornamental clocks and candlesticks, lush velvet curtains and an eclectic mix of darkly imposing Regency cabinets with theatrical baroque chairs and lamps.

Alice's shoulders hunched and she buried her face in the collar of Crowley's coat, squeezing the unbuttoned sides together.

'Crowley,' she said quietly. 'That smell . . .'

A nerve twitched in his temple. 'I know.' She glanced over at him. His eyes met hers and he nodded grimly. 'Can I convince you to stay here?'

'No.'

Tilda had told Alice to find her again when the chaos settled. The answered knock at the door and the rank, coppery stench of blood told her they were too late.

Crowley moved slowly through the ground-floor rooms, his nose twitching and his face tight with disgust. When it became clear that there was nothing out of place downstairs, he made for the stairs.

'You're sure?' he whispered.

Her fingers clenched the coat's collar. 'Yes,' she replied, a rasp in her voice.

He swept up the stairs ahead of her. She lifted up the ends of the long coat, so as not to trip, and hurried after him. The dreadful odour of death was strongest on the landing.

Crowley was very pale, the most terrible indecision gripping his features, pulling down his brows and thinning his lips.

'*Alice—*' he tried.

'Crowley,' she said, 'I don't need you to protect me from death. I *am* Death.'

She stepped past him and into the bedroom, shuddering as she crossed the threshold.

Tilda Jarvis sat at her dressing table. Slumped ever so slightly backwards, her head resting on one shoulder and both hands extended, palms upwards, on the arms of her chair. Her skin was mottled, her face pale, but her limbs were purple where gravity had pulled the un-pumped blood down to settle. A clotted gash had opened up her left forearm, and dried blood had gushed across the dressing table and chair, soaking into her dark skirt. A spray of congealed blood splattered the mirror, and Alice could see her own distorted reflection in it as she entered. Tilda, it was clear, had died of blood loss. But she had not given in without a fight.

I'm glad you've come home . . . Tilda's last words slid into Alice's memory, spoken just as Tilda ran towards the danger. She'd been courageous and strong. And for her life to end like *this . . .*

Desperately trying to regain control of her stomach, which was on the verge of expelling its contents through her gullet, Alice had to turn away from the old woman. While Crowley inspected the body, Alice was drawn to the splintered window frame and the four-poster bed, which was missing three of its posts. She surveyed the remains of an oak wardrobe in the corner and the warped wooden floor. The floorboards had been torn up, the planks twisted and the ends sharpened; it almost looked like a mouthful of teeth, biting upwards. The old woman must have thrown every Mielikki defence she could think of at her attacker.

'She fought for her life,' Alice said numbly.

'Yes,' said Crowley, the toe of his boot sifting through a mound of brick dust strewn by the bottom of the bed. 'But she was bested by someone younger. Stronger.'

Alice's gaze drifted back to Tilda and fixed first on the ravaged arm of congealing blood and then the grit and brick dust – where a single white dove's feather lay, stained a deep red. The one-time calling card of the Fellowship of the Pale Feather.

'Marianne,' said Alice, her voice clipped with anger. 'She did

347

this because of me. Because she knew I wanted to speak to Tilda, and because I tricked her with the rotting *fucking*' – she kicked out at a wooden board, smashing it to pieces – 'research folder.'

Alice clamped a hand on her mouth, her jaw clenched and sudden angry tears in her eyes. *That hateful, evil bitch.*

'You . . . went to see Marianne?' he asked.

She nodded, and his expression darkened.

'There are things I need to tell you,' she said, averting her eyes from Tilda with a shudder. 'Marianne said your mother—'

'*Don't*,' he said, flinching. 'I don't want to know. That woman is poison. You should never have risked it.'

He swallowed thickly, a muscle in his jaw twitching as he tried to master his emotions, forcing down his anger. He hated Marianne even more than she did.

She hesitated before pushing on, more tentatively. 'In Reid's file, she mentioned something about a – a Pellervoinen safeguard. And Marianne hinted that your mother—'

'My mother, the woman she *murdered*,' he said, his voice tight. 'I don't want to hear more of Marianne's twisted lies.' He stepped away from her, hiding his face, and moved to the window to peer out over the street. 'We should go before someone sees us. We can notify the Runners when we return to Coram House.'

Alice nodded. Maybe now – here – was not the time or place for this. She spun round and strode to the door, wanting to bleach the hideous images from her mind. Marianne had murdered an innocent old woman in petty revenge. Alice hated death. She was so sick of the violence and the pain, and the loneliness of it.

Out on the landing, she held up a hand and inhaled sharply as Kuu appeared with a flutter. Needle-thin claws pinched the sleeve of her coat and the little white bird sidestepped higher, from forearm to shoulder, where she nuzzled Alice's neck and churred rhythmically.

'At least I'll never die alone,' she whispered fiercely. 'Not when I have you.'

She stared at Crowley's back as he stood framed by the window, the sun backlighting strands of too-long dark hair. He had mastered the ability to hide his nightjar – quite a feat, considering he wasn't even able to see what it was he was masking. His grip had begun to loosen, however, and she had caught one or two fleeting glimpses of it lately. It hovered in the air to his left, like him, peering down at the street. The sun caught its glossy black eyes and the tips of its feathers, and though it was a dark shade of rich browns it seemed almost to glisten in the light. It was a strong bird, imposing and stiff-postured. If a bird could be haughty, then that one word would describe Crowley's nightjar perfectly.

'Are you okay?' he asked, turning to watch her, his eyes concerned.

Alice nodded. 'Yes. But I think I might like some fresh air now.' She avoided glancing in Tilda's direction as she powered down the stairs on shaky legs before bursting out the front door, onto the pavement. She sat on the kerb, stroking Kuu's feathers.

When Crowley emerged ten minutes or so later, she was finally able to greet him without a quiver of rage in her voice.

'You've . . . stolen her books?' she asked, staring at the two battered books he carried in one hand.

'I hardly think she'll notice,' he said.

Alice's eyes flashed, and she opened her mouth to issue a suitable response, but he cut her off.

'I thought I'd have a quick look before the Runners arrive and confiscate the lot,' he said. 'She's a librarian, who left you a book, and who apparently had further information she could provide us about our guilt-ridden mothers.' He gestured at the books. 'A quick check of her personal library – not as extensive as you'd probably have imagined – was worth a moment of my time.'

'And . . . so what did you find?' asked Alice, frowning.

He held them out to her. 'I found two books . . . that I couldn't open.'

One of the books was nearly empty – all of its pages had been torn out except one on which a slash of ink read, *Natura valde simplex est et sibi consona*. In contrast, the other book was crammed with writing and drawings in every available space. Blotches of ink made some passages illegible, and sunlight had faded others. There were at least three or four different styles of penmanship, making it impossible – without further investigation – to tell whether any of the commentary belonged to Leda Westergard.

The first few pages contained an image drawn in thinly inked lines of a small, enclosed room, the stone walls curved and something indecipherable in the centre. The drawing had been annotated in Latin. In fact – she turned the yellowed pages with great care – the vast majority of the book was in Latin, a dead language that she had very definitely not studied in her comprehensive school.

She had raised an eyebrow at finding two books in Latin so soon after their conversation about Whitmore's rumoured book. Until Crowley had pointed out that there were shelves of Latin texts at the university, and that while it was a dead language now, it hadn't been hundreds of years ago when many were written.

'I can't read them,' she said, frustration flickering in her chest as she turned to Crowley, who was making them a cup of tea in the Coram House kitchen. 'What the hell is "natura valde simplex est et sibi consona" supposed to mean?'

'Nature is exceedingly simple and harmonious,' Crowley responded automatically.

Alice blinked up at him. 'You can—?' She shook her head. 'Never mind, of course you can.'

'It's a quote,' he said with a sharp laugh. 'One of Isaac Newton's. The rest of my Latin is admittedly rusty.'

'Well mine is non-existent,' she said, sitting back and rubbing her face wearily. 'This is just great. I can't read the words, and you can't even see them.'

Crowley couldn't see a single word on these pages either; they appeared utterly blank, like Leda's biography. They had clearly been locked to unapproved eyes as part of some Mielikki legacy trickery.

'I could copy it out for you,' she said, casting a doubtful look over the thick wedge of pages filled with incomprehensible handwriting. She could spend hours copying useless pages before she ever reached anything important.

'Read it to me,' he said, pulling aside the chair and feigning a most un-Crowley-like patience. 'I might be able to translate.'

It was a frustrating process. Alice was pronouncing as phonetically as she could, but Crowley could understand only two words in every twenty. The fire in the grate had dwindled to nothing before they had a breakthrough.

'Say that part again,' said Crowley, suddenly stiffening.

'I can't read it properly, there's a big blotch and then it's faded.' She squinted at the page again. '*Tutela est lapis*, that one?'

'And before that?' he said.

'I . . . It's impossible to see it properly. *Est . . . Es*? Or *aestas*? I'm not sure how to say it . . .'

Alice trailed off, watching as – with sharp efficiency – Crowley snatched his coat from the back of his chair.

She put down her teacup. 'What does it mean?'

He hesitated. '*Lapis* . . . is "stone". And *aestas* is "summer".'

Alice's senses sharpened. Stone and *summer*?

'You mentioned . . . a Pellervoinen safeguard?' he said, clearing his throat.

She nodded, and Crowley swung the coat over his shoulders.

'My mother used to tell me bedtime stories about Mielikki and Pellervoinen laying the foundations of a magical world together. She gave me fairy tales,' said Crowley, 'so that in my dreams I could escape the hell we lived in with my father.'

He reached for Alice's coat and held it out to her. 'I think I know what the safeguard is. Let me show you something – in London.'

28

Of all the things Alice had thought he might be whisking her away to, huddling on a London street corner and staring at a piece of limestone was not what she'd expected. The ugly rock was a fairly uninspiring sight. It sat on a plinth, in a glass display case set into a stone wall on Cannon Street, opposite the train station. A pockmarked, misshapen lump. Of course, as a history graduate, she did appreciate its historical value, but she was uncertain of its relevance to the Rookery.

'As interesting as the London Stone is, could you explain what—' she started.

'What I find fascinating is the fact people walk past it every single day and yet hardly anyone seems to be aware of its history.'

'Its *disputed* history,' said Alice.

'You don't think this stone is the magical heart of London?' asked Crowley. 'The Stone of Brutus, Britain's first king. A palladium, safeguarding the city like the statue of Pallas Athene that protected the city of Troy. The stone that held Excalibur? Or a—'

'Are you showing off?' she asked.

He raised an eyebrow. 'Is it showing off simply to declare your expert knowledge and educate those around you on their deficiencies?'

'Unless you're on an episode of *Mastermind*, yes, it is.'

'Then absolutely.'

She shot him an amused look, and he gestured at the display case. 'So how much of your famed history degree covered the London Stone?' asked Crowley.

'None of it,' said Alice. She moved closer to the glass screen and squinted at the lump of limestone. 'I mean, what is it – a thousand years old?' She shook her head. 'It's a historical artefact, but it's been smothered by so many myths . . . no one knows anything factual about it. It would be better suited to a folklore degree.'

'Or English,' said Crowley. 'Shakespeare wrote it into a scene in *Henry VI*. He had Jack Cade, the revolutionary, strike his staff on the London Stone and declare himself lord of the city. Blake and Dickens also wrote about the stone.'

'Look, Crowley—' she said slowly.

'In the seventeenth century, the Worshipful Company of Spectacle Makers – the most impressive name for an optician's you'll ever hear – had a batch of spectacles that were declared unfit for sale by the courts, so they were ordered to be hammered to pieces on the London Stone.'

She stared at him, wondering exactly where he was going with his bizarre factoids.

'It was recorded in the court papers,' he went on, 'that "the judgement was executed accordingly in Cannon Street – on the remaining part of the London Stone".' He paused, his eyes bright, urging her to understand. 'The *remaining* part of the London Stone. The inference being that it had originally been bigger and reduced in size or fragmented, with a piece broken off.' He shook his head. 'They were absolutely correct.'

She peered in at the stone again. 'That a piece of it was broken?'

'Yes,' he said, tapping the window. 'This is what remains of it here in London. And the fragment that was broken off . . . is in the *Rookery*.'

'There's a Rookery Stone? Then . . . why not take me to see that one instead of this?'

He shook his head. 'It's not . . . quite as simple as that.'

She gave him a speculative look. 'You think this is Pellervoinen's safeguard, don't you?' She paused. 'But what does that even mean?'

'*This* isn't the safeguard,' he said, with a nod at the display case.

'The Rookery Stone, then?' she asked, trying to piece it together. 'The fragment is the safeguard?'

'Did you know the London Stone has a guardian?' he asked, neatly sidestepping her question. 'The stone has been moved several times, but whoever is responsible for the building that *houses* the stone . . . is also its guardian. Once, it was the manager of a sports shop. I always thought that must have been an interesting job interview.' His mouth quirked. 'Tell me, Mr Smith, do you agree to manage our sales and customer service, work on Sundays until noon, and while you're at it do you agree to become a protector of the realm and custodian of the legendary London Stone, defending it from all evils, lest London should fall?'

She smiled distractedly and glanced up at the sleek, modern building that held the display case – an office block?

'Well, I suppose this is probably more dignified than a sports shop,' she offered.

'I expect so.' He moved back to the pavement's edge, his eyes travelling up the pale, many-windowed building. 'So long as the Stone of Brutus is safe, so long shall London flourish,' he said.

'Shakespeare?'

355

'No.' His gaze drifted down to her face. 'As a matter of fact, no one knows who said it. Perhaps that adds to its mystique.'

There was a moment's silence. It was clear the link he was making. If the London Stone was damaged, London would fall. If the Rookery Stone was supposed to be a safeguard and was damaged, was it reasonable to assume that the Rookery would fall too? But it was the Summer Tree causing destruction in the Rookery, not a stone. Unless there was a connection between them.

Alice's energy levels were beginning to sink. Around her, London was coming alive, people threading through the streets clutching briefcases and handbags as they hurried to meetings or brunches. Alice felt like a ghost. Unseen. Standing in the middle of the street, discussing stones and stories while *real life* flowed around her. She didn't belong to this world and this city any more.

'If this one isn't the safeguard, why have you brought me here, Crowley?' she asked, suddenly tired. He could, after all, have told her all this in his kitchen.

'To . . . examine the stone for any defects.'

She frowned. 'Defects? How would you ever be able to tell? It's covered in them. It's a weathered lump of—'

'The Rookery is a parasite,' he said. 'Did you know?'

'A . . .?' She stared at him. 'What are you talking about now?'

'You've heard it mentioned that the Summer Tree gives life to the Rookery. Its roots stretch through the entire foundations; the city is built *on* the tree. Without the tree, there would be nothing.'

She nodded cautiously. 'Yes, Bea told me.'

'And my mother told *me* fairy tales about the Rookery Stone,' he said, striding past her to examine a glass door that led to the ground floor of the building – there was some sort of financial investor's centre inside.

'Or maybe not,' said Crowley. He raised an eyebrow and opened the door, holding it out for her. She'd assumed he was opening the door to the void – which was why her mouth pinched as she stared suspiciously into a brightly lit room with a cosy waiting area and desks decorated with trailing pot plants. This was very much *not* an icy corridor between worlds.

'What are you doing?' she murmured to him. 'Checking your pension investments?'

He grinned and stepped inside. An older man in a pinstriped suit emerged from nowhere and greeted them with a smile. 'Did you have an appointment?'

'We're from the British Museum,' said Crowley. 'I believe you were expecting us?'

The man's smile faltered and he cast about, uncertain. 'Not . . . that I'm aware.'

Crowley turned to Alice. 'You did confirm our appointment?' Before she could answer, he turned back to the man with an apologetic grin. 'It seems my assistant neglected to confirm the arrangements. You really can't get the staff these days.'

Alice gritted her teeth and smiled blithely. 'You'll pay for that later,' she murmured under her breath.

'Is that a promise?' he whispered, whipping around before she could respond.

He turned back to the suited man and gestured at the street. 'It's in the tenancy agreement,' said Crowley, striding around the room, peering into corners and through windows. Then he stopped, turned on his heel and treated the man to a brief smile. 'The lease allows for the British Museum to send a representative every year to check on the safety of the London Stone embedded in your outer wall.'

'Oh,' said the suited man, frowning. 'Well . . . feel free to see what you can, but it's walled off – it's inaccessible.' He paused. 'You'd think the British Museum would know that.'

'Yes, you would, wouldn't you?' said Alice, nodding in agreement and throwing a glance at Crowley.

Crowley gestured at Alice. 'Could you note that down, so that we can pass that on to the legal department?' He sighed and stamped a foot on the wooden floor as though testing its strength. 'Do you have a basement?'

'Yes,' said the man.

Crowley's eyes brightened. 'Excellent.' He turned to Alice and nodded at the door. 'We're very sorry to have disturbed you,' he said. 'We'll come back when you're closed.'

'*Closed?*' the man called after them as Crowley smirked and swept from the building.

'Well that wasn't very enlightening,' he said. 'But the basement sounds promising for a closer look.' He glanced around the busy street and ran a hand through his hair.

'What else did your mother tell you about the two stones?' asked Alice, wandering back to peer through the glass. It really was a very ordinary-looking lump of stone.

'That Pellervoinen opened a door from one world into another,' he said. 'Two worlds layered on top of each other, or perhaps side by side. But the Rookery was barren and fragile when it was first made. It needed a strong foundation. Every house Pellervoinen built collapsed. Every river Ahti created dried up. Mielikki's tree was the only thing that strengthened the land. They built on it and around it, and what they built lasted – all because of the tree and its roots.'

'The roots that ripped open Crane Park Island,' she said, stepping back from the display case, deep in thought. 'There's something interesting about the word "safeguard", isn't there? Safeguards are . . . back-up plans. Plan Bs, used if plan A fails. Do you think that Pellervoinen's safeguard was supposed to prevent the tree growing so recklessly? An opposing legacy acting on it like a block?'

Crowley frowned. 'I don't know. My mother never mentioned anything of that nature, but . . .' He shrugged wearily. 'Why would she? I was just a child. She gave me a head full of stories, not nitty-gritty explanations.'

'But it's logical, isn't it?' she said. 'Just as a possibility? In my first membership test, there was a room full of objects from the other Houses, designed to work against the Mielikki legacy. Pellervoinen's safeguard – the stone – could have been designed the same way.'

'I wouldn't rule anything out at this stage,' said Crowley.

Alice nodded with grim satisfaction. 'Whatever the case, if we assume the Rookery Stone *is* involved in what's gone wrong with the tree, then the tree must somehow be *linked* to the stone. If it wasn't, it would make no difference if the stone was damaged. There has to be some sort of physical connection between them if one is affecting the other.'

Crowley nodded, and his expression grew serious. 'I think that's . . . an entirely plausible theory.'

There was a short pause while they each considered this.

'Have you eaten breakfast?' Crowley asked abruptly, scattering her thoughts.

Alice shook her head.

'There's a cafe up there,' he said, nodding at a distant building.

They set off along the street, side by side. It felt strange. It felt normal. Maybe that was the reason for the strangeness; they'd never had the chance to do the normal things like going for a stroll and a coffee. They'd never had the chance to see how it – how they – might work.

'A full English breakfast, please,' Alice told the waitress, 'with extra hash browns.'

The waitress smiled and turned to Crowley. 'And can I get you anything, sir?'

'Just a coffee, please. Black, no sugar.'

Alice gaped at him as the waitress hurried away. 'You can't do that!' she hissed.

'Do what?'

'Just order a coffee after I've ordered a huge breakfast!'

His brows knitted in confusion. 'Why not?'

She spluttered helplessly. 'I can't sit and gorge myself in front of a – a spectator. It's not decent. You tricked me.'

He chuffed out a laugh. 'Eating is a basic need. But if my non-eating offends you, I'll be sure to avoid watching you "gorge yourself". In fact . . .' He twitched the menu into his hands, opened it up and hid his face behind it. 'There. Problem solved.'

'I'm just saying,' she said snippily, 'it's undignified to eat while someone is staring.' She thought she saw his shoulders begin to shake, and her eyes narrowed with suspicion. She swiped the menu away from him. His face was a blank mask, but his eyes glittered darkly.

'I will do everything I can to preserve your dignity,' he said. 'Satisfied?'

A corner of his mouth lifted and she scowled at the tablecloth.

'Let me show you something,' he said, grabbing the salt and pepper shakers and planting them in the middle of the table. 'Your theory about a link between the stone and tree?' He tapped the pepper pot. 'Imagine this is the London Stone.' Leaning back, he snatched another from the empty table behind him. 'And this one is the Rookery Stone.' He sprinkled a line of pepper grains across the table, placing the pots at either end of the line.

'The two stones,' he said, 'are anchors. Pellervoinen connected them.'

She frowned, something niggling at her memory, though she couldn't think what.

'To hear my mother's stories,' said Crowley, 'you might have believed he single-handedly roped the two cities together.' He smiled at the table. 'Pellervoinen tied the Rookery to an older city with stronger foundations. All it took was one parasitic stone to use as an anchor, the threads of our tie stretching right through the void, from one stone to the other.'

'Like the two trees,' said Alice. 'The Summer Tree in the Rookery and the small replica here in London.'

'Anchors,' said Crowley. 'Joining one world to another. Laying foundations that could be built on.'

'Two trees and two stones in two cities,' Alice said slowly, as her thoughts cleared and a memory struck her like an arrow. 'Tilda mentioned anchors,' she said, her blood beginning to pound. 'In the library, when the tree was growing again. She said the anchors were broken. *Crowley . . .?*'

They stared at each other across the table in uncomfortable silence. She suddenly swiped up the salt pot and moved it to the edge of the table. 'Let's call this the Summer Tree,' she said. 'And . . .?'

Crowley leaned over and grabbed the salt from the empty table.

'Let's call this one the miniature tree,' he said, holding up the purloined salt shaker. He then shook a line of salt over the table's surface, crossing the line of pepper, and placed the salt pot down.

'Two anchors in each city, connected to two anchors in the other,' he said. 'Created by Pellervoinen and Mielikki – laying the foundations together. And then . . . Mielikki's Summer Tree . . .' He pressed his fingers into the salt near the shaker and flicked it out so that it spread across the table. 'The roots spread through the city, through the void, increasing the strength of the anchor. Then they built a city over the roots to prevent the Rookery from collapsing into the void.'

'But that's actually not my theory,' said Alice after a moment. 'In this model,' she said, looking at the individual lines of salt and pepper, 'all the anchors are separate – two connected stones, two connected trees – in pairs, instead of all four connected. If they're separate to each other, why would the trees be affected by a problem with the stones?' She frowned. 'Maybe I'm wrong, but Mielikki's anchors seem stronger. How can a stone – magical or not – be stronger than the Tree of Life? Why can't the tree survive a problem with the stones?'

'Well the tree isn't exactly having any difficulties surviving,' said Crowley. 'If anything, it's the opposite.'

'I think they're *all* connected,' said Alice. She snatched up the salt and pepper pots and shook them together, creating a mixed line from the remaining salt pot to the other pepper pot. 'If Mielikki and Pellervoinen laid the foundations together . . . why wouldn't they have joined stone to tree? Making them stronger.

And if they *are* joined . . . then a problem with the stones would definitely impact on the tree too.'

She plonked the pots onto the table. 'Stone and tree, *connected*,' she murmured. 'Yin and yang. And here we are . . . Pellervoinen's and Mielikki's heirs . . . stone and tree.'

He nodded, and the words unsaid fell into the silence. *If Pellervoinen and Mielikki built the foundations, can we fix them?*

'Crowley, are you . . . crying?' said Alice, staring at him in confusion. One eye was beginning to well up and he rubbed at it roughly.

'No,' he said. 'You wafted the damned pepper into my eye.'

Alice's eyes widened and she tried to appear solemn and regretful. But it was difficult when the waitress appeared seconds later and surveyed the mess of salt and pepper grains all over the table.

'We . . . had a bit of an accident,' said Alice. 'Could I borrow a cloth?'

'What else do you remember about your mother?' asked Alice, blowing on the steam curling from her second mug of tea. The plate in front of her was empty save for a few errant baked beans.

Crowley frowned and rubbed his chin. 'Presumably, I'm supposed to say 'her perfume' or 'her kind smile' or something along those lines. But I can remember neither of those.' He gazed out of the cafe window, into the distance. 'I remember her stories, and I remember feeling safe.' He paused. 'Or maybe it was only that I felt unsafe with my father, and so I associated her presence with safety.' His eyes darted to Alice's, and there was a bitter smile on his face. 'Whatever she was to me is shaped by a comparison with him. She doesn't get to be a memory in her own right.'

He shook off the bite of anger in his tone and glanced out of the window again, returning to face her with a blank expression. Always shoving his emotion behind a mask, thought Alice. She instinctively moved to search out his nightjar but caught herself just in time.

'According to photographs – which you have of course seen,' he said, 'she had brown hair, bright green eyes and a very noble, one might say *patrician* proboscis.'

Alice's face screwed up. 'Proboscis?'

He gave her a withering look. 'The nose, Alice. She gave me the nose.'

She bit her lip to keep from laughing. 'And a very splendid nose it is.'

Crowley nodded in acknowledgement.

'Many of my memories are sketchy. Sylvie tried to bring them to life, but . . .' He shook his head.

Sylvie was the aviarist who had awakened Alice's gift. It seemed like a lifetime ago that she'd sent Alice a feather from her nightjar – every dying aviarist's nightjar shed a feather to pass on and catalyse another's sight. Sylvie had also taken Crowley in when he'd needed a refuge from his father. She'd stepped into his life when he was a teenager, lost in grief for his sister, and taken him under her wing.

'I used to think it was coincidence that we met,' said Alice. 'But it wasn't, was it?'

He set down his cup to listen to her more carefully.

'Sylvie's nightjar made me an aviarist—'

'You were always an—'

'All right, well, she opened my eyes to it, then. And you found me because you'd been waiting to find her successor. But she knew your mother, and yours knew mine. And even our oldest ancestors were linked . . .' She shook her head. 'It's just . . . strange.'

'I think it's likely that's the very reason our parents knew each other. Shared histories *are* binding. What's more strange is that they died in the same year.'

'How do you know when—?'

'Everyone knows when Chancellor Westergard died.'

'What did Leda do that made her so well loved?' she asked quietly. 'All I hear is that she was the greatest chancellor the city had ever had, but . . . why?'

'Your mother—'

She laid a hand on his arm. 'I'm not sure I want to call her that any more. I know she is, or was, but . . . I have a mum. I'd rather . . . Can we just call her Leda?'

His eyes softened in understanding. 'Leda abolished all of our old social and class boundaries in one fell swoop,' he said. 'That's why she was loved. She pushed through a law abolishing the old House membership system. Originally, membership was only for the upper classes, and Houses were joined at birth. There was no testing system.'

She nodded, but it occurred to her that there was one glaring issue with that. 'How did that work if your parents were from different Houses?' said Alice.

'Whichever side of the family had the strongest position would usually be the decider – unless the alternative house was more politically favourable at the time. If you married a Gardiner, for instance, your children were going into House Mielikki, whether you liked it or not.'

'But . . . that still doesn't resolve the issue. What if it was the wrong House for you? What if you were useless with that legacy but better suited to the one from your other parent's House?'

'Then you kept it to yourself and practised in private.' He shrugged. 'No one questioned the system because, as legacies are inherited, it was seen as the deepest insult to question someone's right to membership – an insult to the whole family. The inference being, you are questioning whether my child has weak blood, and therefore whether my own blood is weak – or worse, you are questioning whether my child is really my child.' He paused.

'That must have actually happened, at some point,' said Alice. 'People finding themselves in the wrong House, feeling like they just . . . didn't fit. Affairs and concealed parentage – that sort of thing has been going on for years.'

He smiled. 'Ironically, although the upper classes were determined to keep membership within families, the old political system actually diluted the legacies. Marriage became nothing more than a horse fair.' He ran a hand through his dark hair and gave her an amused look. 'The families were very vocal about which Houses they belonged to, but showy displays of legacy prowess were treated with contempt on the grounds of crassness. Of course, the real reason was absolute terror that you might publicly fail – because you were in the wrong House – and shame your family name forever.'

There was a long pause. 'What if you weren't from one of the richer families and didn't automatically join a House at birth?' asked Alice.

'Then you were not allowed to join, or even attempt it. Membership was divvied out among less than a hundred families. But Chancellor Westergard abolished all that. She made deals with anyone prepared to help her agenda and she was able to gain a majority in the Council without even needing the support of the four governors. It was unprecedented. Automatic membership was prohibited, and membership was awarded on merit alone. The tests democratized the entire House system. And as a result, the Houses actually grew stronger in terms of their magic, pulling in the most skilled instead of the best connected. But it wasn't just a matter of the legacies. It broke the hold of the upper classes – of contracts awarded under the table, of agreements that denied workers' rights decided over a malt whisky in the House Ilmarinen bar. Opportunities were opened up to the masses, not just a tiny fraction of the population. It changed everything, Alice. And she did it. It could only ever have been her that pushed it through.'

'Why?'

'Because it had to be one of their own. She was a Westergard. The last of them, and they had been one of the most respected House Mielikki families for years. It meant that she was able to turn the few voters to her cause who might otherwise have rejected her proposals before she'd got them off the ground. She turned the Jarvis, Florilynn and Derbyshire families to her cause – families who had watched her grow up, who were sympathetic and running out of heirs so had nothing to lose.'

'But the tests are brutal,' she said. 'Is it really *better* to have a system that kills and maims people who just want to belong?'

'The tests weren't always so deadly,' replied Crowley. 'They were made so by the Pellervoinen chancellors that followed her. Don't let it eclipse what she did for democracy.'

They grew silent, each lost in their own thoughts before Crowley spoke again. 'Leda Westergard and Helena Northam,' he said quietly, running his finger around the lip of his cup. 'Friends who grew up together and had all the opportunities they could wish for. One went on to change the face of the Rookery for good, and one abandoned it forever.' He glanced up at Alice. 'What might have been, I wonder? If my mother had stayed – as Leda did.'

Both ruined by love, Alice realized. Leda had broken her oath of office for Tuoni, and Crowley's mum had married the one man who grew to despise everything the Rookery stood for.

'Your mother never had any designs on Council or House leadership when she was younger?' Alice asked.

He shook his head. 'Apparently not. According to Sylvie, she had a grander purpose.'

Alice stared at him in gradual understanding, remembering Marianne's words about Helena's duty.

Crowley smiled humourlessly. 'My mother was the custodian of the *Rookery's* London Stone.'

29

Watching Crowley stride through crowds of London tourists and city workers was a thing of wonder. He sliced through them like a blade, groups parting around him and flowing back together as he passed. Maybe it was the fact that he dressed like a scruffy undertaker, or some sort of decadent land pirate with a sweeping coat. Or perhaps it was the permanent frown that promised dire consequences if you got in his way. In any case, in a city as busy as London, this Moses-like ability was something of a superpower.

She trudged after him, her pace slowing to watch the crowds of people hurrying past, unaware that the world was so much bigger than they realized. While London's tourists and general population used the tube to travel the city, she and Crowley used the doorways. And it occurred to Alice, as they went from door to door, that she didn't know quite what her relationship with London was any more. Her flat and job were gone, and her visits here infrequent.

'*I'm* a tourist now,' she murmured to herself.

By the time they made their final crossing, striding through Marble Arch in London and exiting through Marble Arch in the Rookery, only yards from Goring University, Alice knew immediately that something was wrong.

The campus was deathly silent. No students crossed the lawns, the main doors in the Arlington Building were firmly shut, and the blinds and curtains were drawn. All were signs of a lockdown drill.

'Crowley . . .'

'Can you hear sirens?' he asked, turning on the spot.

The streets were too empty – only a handful of cars were rolling past, and the few people they could see were dashing inside.

'That's an old air-raid siren,' Crowley murmured, gazing off into the distance, his face tight.

'Where?'

He turned on the spot, listening carefully. 'Towards Millbank and Vauxhall Bridge Road, on the edge of the Thames. The Council used them in the fifties, when they wanted to clear the streets for maintenance work.' He tipped his head on one side. 'I think . . . there's still one by John Islip and Atterbury Street.'

'Okay,' said Alice, striding off towards the janitor's outhouse by the side of the Arlington Building, the gravel crunching beneath her boots. 'Then let's go.'

'Alice, wait,' he shouted. 'It could be dangerous. If the Summer Tree—'

'Exactly,' she called over her shoulder. If she was a Gardiner – a Mielikki – then she needed to see what was happening.

Crowley was wrong. The siren was wailing from half a mile away – because there was no Atterbury Street. Alice stood on Vauxhall Bridge, pressed against the red-and-yellow railings and clutching the barrier so tightly her knuckles hurt. Just over on the other side, near the water's edge, half a dozen streets were missing. No Atterbury Street and no Herrick, Erasmus or Causton

Streets either. And while Regency Street had been spared, Ponsonby Terrace was also gone. The roads had fallen – literally fallen – into a vast crack in the land.

Ponsonby Terrace was rubble and dust, swallowed by the river. Where the street of Georgian houses had once been, now there was only debris, floating in the water and carried under the bridge by the tide. Five streets – gone. Houses, offices, shops . . . people. All gone. Cavernous fractures had opened up in the earth like sinkholes, widening into canyons. They branched off, eating up buildings, foundations, pavements and roads like the open maw of a hungering beast. The river had burst its banks and swept into the cracks, sudden whirlpools appearing as the water collided with the remnants of crumbled buildings, spraying frothy foam into the air.

Alice scanned the landscape, nausea twisting her gut. The air was alive with shouts for help – to move blockages, for first aid, for extra blankets. On the other side of the bridge, people worked quickly to sift through the disaster, searching for signs of life. Bricks were rolled aside at the wave of a hand, walls were torn in half with a finger click, and on the remains of Millbank, the governor of House Ahti stood at the front of a large gathering, sweating and grunting as they worked together to redirect the flow of the river before it drained entirely into a fracture.

Alice peered through the gaps in the railings, at the roiling water splattering the legs of the bridge. Risen from the Thames, like the curved spine of the Loch Ness Monster, was a partially submerged tree root. And whether it was her imagination or not, she could *feel* it drawing her gaze towards it, and something in her fingers began to tingle. She clenched her fists to shake it off.

'The Summer Tree,' she said. 'It's causing *subsidence*. That's how it's damaging the city. Subsidence. It's so simple.'

All tree roots were capable of it – shrinking or expanding, dislodging the soil bed and destabilizing the foundations of a house so badly it could collapse into a dip in the land. The Summer Tree's shifting roots were collapsing the entire Rookery.

Alice shook her head and turned to Crowley. 'But we can stop it. Can't we?' she urged.

Before he had time to respond, she had set off along the bridge. 'There might still be people,' she called out, her jog soon becoming an all-out sprint. She was vaguely aware of Crowley hurtling after her as she drew closer to the devastation, leaping over mangled parts of the bridge's railings and chunks of disjointed masonry.

Alice was so focused on reaching the fallen buildings, where there might yet be people still alive, that she missed the subtle change in consistency of the ground. She didn't see the way the small potholes increased, and she didn't realize that one end of the bridge had twisted, weakening the whole structure.

Her foot landed at an awkward angle and the floor dropped suddenly. With a shocked gasp, Alice threw out a hand to steady herself, but the shifting weight caused the masonry to roll beneath her – and break away. A fragment of the bridge fell to the river below, and Alice slipped with it, through the gap. She flung out her other hand and latched on to a chunk of broken steel poking through the edge of the hole. Crowley's alarmed face appeared overhead as he dived for her. But Alice's scrabbling fingers slid from the metal. She plummeted from the bridge, her mouth forming a small 'O' of surprise.

She hit the icy water like a bullet. The cold was paralysing, and she sank deep into the murky depths. The silence of the dark water pressed in around her, muffling every sensation, the pressure shrinking her lungs. *Swim!* But her limbs felt like iron. She cracked open an eyelid and peered into the gloom. Beads of air bubbled up around her nose and her brown hair floated up like a halo.

And then something flickered: a buzzing sensation underneath her skin, a vibration in the water, as though something recognized her presence. *The Summer Tree.*

Swim! She forced herself to kick. Slowly at first, a half-hearted upwards punt, then harder, faster.

Alice broke the water with a ragged gasp, her hair slicked down her face – but her buoyancy was short-lived. The momentum of the water dragged her back under. She lashed out with her feet and propelled her arms to the top. *Harder! And again!* Bursting up to the surface, she spun onto her back and heaved in a great lungful of oxygen. Eyes screwed shut, the water splattered her face.

'Alice!'

Her eyes flew open. A figure was standing on the bridge, frantically tearing off his coat. Crowley.

Alice shivered. It felt colder now. The breeze scraped her skin, leeching more heat from her bones. She raised her chin higher above the water, spitting out a mouthful and kicking her legs to stay near the churning surface. The Thames was a pattern of ripples and whirls as the water flowed around the littering debris and pushed it further downstream. Alice tried to swim with it, hoping it would push her towards the riverbank, but it soon became clear it was pushing her towards danger. The Thames was pouring into the fractures caused by the Summer Tree. She was drifting towards the sinkholes – and picking up speed. Heart slamming against her ribs, the numbness fell away and she thrashed against the water pressure.

But as the river pooled into a convergence, it collected a watery mass of destruction. Shards of splintered wood butted against chunks of plaster and broken furniture, all rushing through the water together: a chaotic soup of city life. Alice arched sideways to avoid a smashed bottle, but a spray of water sent it rushing faster than she could move. The sharp glass sliced her cheek and she hissed in pain, spinning into the path of a block of wood. The wood punched the back of her skull and the blow arrested her movements. She dipped below the surface, water sweeping into her mouth and eyes, pulling her down and down.

Battered by wreckage and detritus, she struck out for the surface but the back of her head was warm and her energy had evaporated. Blood seeped into the water, blossoming out like roses made of ink. Her skin prickled as she dropped deeper; she sensed a wave of tremendous power below the surface.

And then a hand clamped around her arm. Another around her waist. And she was dragged upwards. Sunlight fell across her frozen face and Crowley's wet hair was crushed against her neck as he swam, pulling her with him, tight against his chest.

'Alice?' he shouted above the roar of the water. 'Don't kick, just breathe!'

Alice screwed up her face and nodded. The cold and the knock to her head had dulled her senses. But she was in Crowley's arms, and she was safe, she thought absently. Only, not really, because he couldn't seem to clear them from the slipstream. Now, instead of only one of them drowning, they were going to drown together. She tried to concentrate, to focus on this thought. But every time she tried to grapple with it, it slid further away.

Focus!

With her free hand, she pinched her arm, trying to inject herself with some urgency. But she was so cold and so tired. Behind her, Crowley was breathing harder as he tried, and failed, to tow her through the water, away from the pouring rush.

'Are we dying, Crowley?' she managed.

'Let's just say,' he managed through gritted teeth as he sent a bolt of fire at a chair hurtling towards them, 'it's not going as I'd planned.' The chair exploded into ash, but others raced through the river alongside it, and it was no use. He couldn't fight off the overwhelming onslaught of debris and keep them both above water while trying to kick them away from the nearest fracture, into which, like a waterfall, they were headed.

'Let me go,' she said in his ear.

His arm tightened around her in response. 'No.'

A wave of water slammed into them, leaving them gasping, but his grip held.

'I'm not being *noble*, Crowley,' she said, wedging an elbow between them to crowbar herself free.

Crowley shook his head, grimly determined. 'I'm not letting you go.'

She managed to turn sideways in his arms. He was deathly pale and strained. He thought she was trying to sacrifice herself to give him a better chance – she could see it in his eyes. Exhaustion was written all over his face. Droplets of water glistened on his cheekbones and on his mouth. And as they were buffeted by rubble from every direction, swaying with the movement of the icy river, she leaned up and without any warning at all pressed her icy lips to his. It lasted only a second. Caught off guard, his eyebrows flew up, and he lost his grip. Satisfied, she slipped free from his arms and kicked away. He lunged to grab her with a shocked cry, but she shook her head.

'I'm *not* being noble!' she shouted.

And then she raised her arms above her head, streamlining her body as best she could, stopped kicking and sank. This time it was much faster. They were closer to the fracture now, and it sucked the river towards it like a black hole. Below the surface, she offered no resistance as the water swept her deeper, praying her lungs would hold out.

The tingling in her fingers grew more insistent. A throb of magic spasmed through her arms, legs and chest as she plunged towards the fracture and the exposed root of the Summer Tree. Its power was magnetic. Ripples of warmth pulsed through the icy water like a welcome.

The water pressure shifted suddenly, pushing backwards, and Alice's movement stalled. Something drew closer, slithering along the riverbed. The whining groan of a heavy mass straining against its bindings echoed out above the surface. And Alice's blood was on fire as a bunched-up curve of the Summer Tree's root surged up beneath her like a life raft . . . and pushed her to the surface.

Water sprayed out around her as she emerged from the river, standing on the crooked root. Raw energy crackled beneath her feet and her muscles thrummed with a strange vitality. She thrust out a hand to snatch Crowley's sleeve as she passed and clenched it tight as he scrambled up beside her, gasping on all fours.

Panting, and shoving wet hair from her face, Alice peered over at the mass evacuation effort underway on the other side of the river, a small crowd searching for survivors.

'Do you think,' she breathed, 'anyone saw us?'

30

'I felt it,' said Alice, 'beneath the water. Its power. I don't know how, but I did.'

They were sitting in Alice's university quarters. Visitors were not allowed, but Alice no longer cared about breaking the rules. It was unlikely anyone would ever find out, anyway – there was no one around to see. The entire campus had been silent when they'd arrived. The university buildings and all the surrounding streets were pitch black. It had been eerie to step out of the janitor's outhouse and find the street lamps extinguished and a blanket of darkness as far as the eye could see.

The rector had maintained the campus-wide ban on matches, candles and uncontrollable fires, so they sat at Alice's table with one of Crowley's flames dancing on a saucer between them. He had dried them off with a flick of his wrist the moment they'd reached land. Still, she couldn't seem to get warm. She was wrapped in the blankets from her bed, her legs crossed on the wooden chair.

'Look,' said Alice, stabbing a finger at Reid's biscuit-coloured folder. In the margins, Reid had scribbled *Pellervoinen safeguards hold?* 'Even she knew about the stone.'

Crowley gave an imperceptible shrug. He looked exhausted, and she wondered when he'd last slept a full eight hours.

She sighed heavily. 'Reid – God knows why – thought that her soul research caused the tree to grow. She once claimed *plants* have souls, so maybe she was researching whether the Summer Tree had a soul and thought she'd damaged it, I don't know. But she clearly thought that the Pellervoinen safeguard would be strong enough to resist any backlash to the city's foundations.' She pointed again at Reid's scribbled handwriting. 'Is it common knowledge about the anchors and the Rookery Stone?'

He shook his head. 'No.'

'Then maybe your mother told her. They knew each other, Crowley. They grew up together. The fact that Reid knew how important they were . . . We need to examine the Rookery Stone.'

He stared at the flames on the saucer. 'I've never known where it is,' he said. 'It's why I've spared it little thought over the years.' There were shadows under his eyes that were less to do with the flicker of firelight and everything to do with weariness.

She stared at him, unable to comprehend. 'But . . . we need to check it,' she said. 'If Tilda's right about broken anchors . . . The London Stone seemed intact, but the Rookery Stone might be damaged.'

He sighed heavily and turned to her, his expression pained. 'My mother never told me its location, Alice. If I've inherited the guardianship from her, then I am the custodian of a needle in a haystack.'

Alice sat back in her seat, all of her ideas cut off at the root. How could they find a single stone in a city so sprawling? She opened her mouth to speak but found there was nothing much she could say.

Crowley stared blankly into the flames, his expression morose.

'It isn't your fault that you don't know how to save the world, Crowley,' she said at last.

He shot her a dark look, and she knew she'd hit the target. Another thought began to creep around the edges of her brain, and she wasn't sure this was the moment to bring it up, but she sensed they were running out of time.

'Crowley – the Beaks . . .'

He grew very still. His father, Sir John Boleyn, led a government faction dedicated to wiping out the Rookery and its people. The Judicium, they called themselves, though they were known in this city as the far less impressive-sounding 'Beaks'.

'Do you think they know that the London Stone is an anchor?' asked Alice. 'If they knew they could use it to damage the Rookery—'

'They don't know,' Crowley said quietly. 'Whatever my mother's naivety in marrying him, she never told him that.'

Alice nodded, but the look in Crowley's eyes was stricken. She swallowed and reached for a change of subject.

'Those books of Tilda's,' she said. 'They mentioned a stone and the Summer Tree. We should check them again. Maybe Bea can open them, too – they might be linked to House Mielikki members rather than just her heir. Bea can probably read Latin – it's the sort of thing lords and ladies can do, isn't it?'

Crowley nodded, and then neither spoke for a long time. His dark eyes, shining in the dancing light, drifted up to steal glances of her when he thought she wasn't looking. Her hands tightened on the blanket as she listened to the gentle hum of his breathing and remembered the shock on his face when their lips had met.

'No, darling, I can't read Latin,' said Bea later that night. She'd been busy at the House since the siren had sounded, returning before midnight. Crowley had stayed to meet her, and Bea had looked him over with an appraising eye before giving Alice a subtle nod. The librarian looked weary – the dark circles under her eyes, Alice suspected, were caused by the news of Tom's death. She was glad it had been announced in her absence.

'We had the option of Latin or Ancient Greek at school. I went with Ancient Greek because the teacher was rumoured never to give homework, which incidentally turned out to be a lie.' Bea swept out from one of the library's dark aisles with an exhausted sigh.

Crowley's contraband light – now in a jar on the check-out desk – was just enough to see by. The shelves cast shadows along every narrow corridor, but the huge window provided some low moonlight to the centre of the library. A stripe of dim light illuminated Bea, her mass of thick, glossy hair pinned back and her patterned dress clashing gloriously with the beads around her neck.

'Tell me the quote again,' she said.

Crowley cleared his throat. 'Natura valde simplex est et sibi consona.'

'Nature is exceedingly simple and harmonious with itself,' said Bea.

'You know it too?' said Alice, incredulous.

'It's Newton,' said Bea. 'Everybody knows Newton.'

Alice shook her head. 'Not everybody.'

'That's not just a quote, it's also a book,' said Bea. 'The one we spoke about. Very famous for a book no one's ever seen.'

Alice stared at her. 'The one we spoke about? You mean . . . the one Whitmore's rumoured to have a copy of?'

Bea snorted. 'That rumour only started because he refuses to let anyone access his personal library at the House; people started to suspect he had all sorts of illicit materials in it. But frankly, by the number of dog-eared books the students return to me here, I don't blame him for keeping his collection private.' She stopped and sighed. 'I wish he did have it, of course I do, but just because the book was written by his ancestor, doesn't mean he inherited a copy.'

Alice darted an alarmed glance at Crowley but said nothing. How could Gabriel Whitmore be Tuoni if he had ancestors? But whether he was Tuoni or not, he'd been behaving suspiciously every time he'd been involved with the Summer Tree, and now another link had come to the fore. This warranted her attention. Who was he really, and what was his connection to the tree's destruction?

'Just so we're clear,' Alice said slowly, 'the book is a study of the Rookery's geography and foundations?'

'Apparently so.'

'And by foundations . . .' Alice trailed off as she glanced again at Crowley, whose expression was serious.

Foundations – surely that meant the anchors? The two stones and the two trees. Was there a book out there that could tell the heirs of Mielikki and Pellervoinen how to fix the city?

'Look, I told you, darling,' said Bea. 'The book burned in this library.' She looked around the shelves. 'It's partly why the rector's already threatened to sack anyone found with candles indoors. The original Goring House and its successor, Arlington House, both burned down in London on this very site. The place has practically been cursed by fire. No wonder he's not taking any chances. Anyway,' said Bea, turning back to Alice with a calming breath. 'Your book? *Natura Valde Simplex est et Sibi Consona*. Real mouthful. Terrible idea to title a book with a complete quote.'

'The book was once here, in *this* library?' asked Crowley.

'Yes. A few hundred years ago, but the library burned down here too, and all the books with it. It was one of them. I still have a copy of the old stocktake, believe it or not.'

'Why would you remember the name of this one specific book anyway?' asked Alice.

'Because of the public outcry about its loss at the time. And I *am* a librarian, darling; there's such a thing as professional interest.'

Alice met Crowley's eye. They had an empty book cover with that Latin name. All the pages were torn out, but they weren't singed from a fire. If Whitmore's ancestor wrote the book, maybe the rumours were true. Maybe he had a spare copy. Or perhaps Whitmore had the missing pages. Either way, they needed to make sure. Because if a copy of that book did exist, and had the information they needed – it could save the city.

It was long after midnight, but the door to House Mielikki was still open. Muffled, haunting music swayed out from the arched bough that formed the entrance, a sign that the clubhouse bar was still open for business. People needed to find solace somewhere, she supposed. Alice's eyes traced the slants of moonlight striping the pavement like a ladder, highlighting a path to the magnificent botanical and stone facade. The leaves rustled in the breeze as the seasons transformed the outer walls.

'How do you propose we do this?' asked Crowley, his voice such a close rumble in her ear that it lifted the hair on the back of her neck.

They were standing on the corner of Angel Street, aiming for an air of inconspicuousness while they pored over their options.

'I'm not allowed access to the bar until I get my membership,' she said, 'so that rules out having a drink and sneaking through the building to find Whitmore's office.'

'I could attempt to travel inside using a doorway,' said Crowley. 'But I can't imagine the doors won't be locked and alarmed against members of other Houses, which would amount to a smash and grab.'

She shook her head. 'If we broke in with force and I got caught, that would be my membership bid up in smoke.' She turned to him and found he'd moved closer, so she had to tip her head back to see him clearly. 'We've been here before,' she said, offering a wry smile. 'Trespassing?'

'Indeed,' he said, tracing his lips with a finger.

But it was different this time; she couldn't jeopardize her membership. There was too much riding on it. Tilda had told her she needed to bind herself to the Summer Tree. As Mielikki's heir, the Rookery's survival might depend on it.

'A more subtle approach then?' he said.

She nodded. 'How much leeway do you think ignorance might get us? If, say, we were refused a drink at the bar and acciden-tally . . . took a wrong turning on our way out?'

If they came across anyone, Alice could always cloak them both. It'd failed with Tom, but she knew she could do it if she was given time to focus.

'Let's go,' she murmured, hurrying across the road before she changed her mind. As she charged towards the House, she tested a few possible excuses in case they were discovered. About the most plausible was that she'd come to ask Cecil to autograph his book, which meant they really couldn't afford to get caught.

She stepped into the entrance, warm light flickering overhead, and then turned to gesture for Crowley to follow her. With a swift glance around him, he entered the corridor, peering at the willow walls with curiosity.

'I've always wondered what it was like in here,' he said, just as a clawing knot of vines and branches snaked out from either side of the corridor, blocking their path forward and sealing off the entrance behind, entrapping them.

'Shit,' Alice murmured.

She flexed her fingers and grabbed the thicket barring their way. Then she poured all of her frustration and anger into her hands, down through her fingertips and into the wall of branches. The branches rotted and hollowed out under her grasp. She twitched her hands, strengthening her hold, and they disintegrated into ash and sawdust. She stepped over the heaped dust and wiped her hands on her thighs.

'Not quite the welcome we were hoping for,' said Crowley.

He moved in step behind her, but the willow wall rippled again. The branches unravelled and wound across their path, blocking them from continuing. Crowley caught Alice's arm and tugged her backwards, but another wall of branches wove itself around them from behind, capturing them in the middle. This trap was tighter, the weight of the branches pushing them together. They were wrapped in the walls like a blanket, Alice's arms pinned to her sides.

She tried to elbow herself some room. 'We must've triggered an alert,' she hissed.

She gave up struggling. It was no use. They were hamstrung. But the House could hardly dismiss her from the membership tests for this – she'd only stepped through the bloody entrance.

It would put paid, however, to their attempts to access Whitmore's private library tonight.

'Cat burglary really isn't your forte, is it?' drawled Crowley. 'Might I suggest you look for another career? To my knowledge, you've been caught trespassing every time you've attempted it.' His breath ghosted the back of her neck when he spoke, and she suddenly became very aware of his presence.

Her back was pressed against his chest. Crowley's arm was down by his side, next to hers, the backs of their hands lightly touching. And though she should have been focused on what she was doing at House Mielikki and the fact that they were trapped in the corridor, every sense had instead honed in on the feel of his hand pressed gently against hers. They stood deathly still for several agonizing minutes, neither quite sure how to break the strange deadlock.

But then a knuckle brushed her skin, just barely. A touch so light she might have imagined it if not for the electric sensation it left behind. Crowley stared straight ahead, as though his movements were utterly detached. And then she felt a finger, gently questing, reaching out – and then another. Alice swallowed hard as his wrist turned in the cramped space and his hand reached for hers. Their fingers slid together, locking like jigsaw pieces, and they stood for a moment in the flickering light of the corridor, holding hands in silence.

'What happened in the river . . .' he murmured.

She swallowed hard. The kiss. But it had only been an attempt to distract him.

'Did you . . .?' he began, but the willow wall surrounding them suddenly disintegrated and she staggered forward, breaking their hands apart.

Crowley caught her by the shoulders, holding her steady, as a door swung open at the end of the corridor. A door she'd never seen before. And Gabriel Whitmore stood before her, with a piercing look in his eye. He held her gaze for a long, drawn-out moment, and then nodded his acknowledgement.

'Your friend doesn't belong here,' said Whitmore. 'Ask him to leave, and then we may talk.'

31

'I see you've inherited your mother's gift for theatrics.'

Alice's breathing stilled. 'How long have you known?'

He leaned back in the sumptuous leather chair. Across the impressive polished desk, his gaze was penetrating. 'Only a matter of days. Tilda came to me with the news. I should have seen it earlier. You look . . . very alike.'

She had never scrutinized the governor up close. Now she took the opportunity to explore his features, searching for her own face in his, some small image of herself mirrored there, but she found nothing. He was sandy-haired, his eyes a deep ocean blue where hers were brown; his skin was a milky alabaster next to her rosy-cheeked complexion. And the way he held himself, sturdy but long-limbed, precise and elegant; there was nothing at all she had inherited from him – he couldn't possibly be her father.

'Why did you . . .?' Questions swarmed her mind, but she couldn't seem to latch on to any one of them.

He leaned forward, planting his elbows on the table and resting his chin on his fists. For some reason, she couldn't stop staring at his extravagant cufflinks. Maybe it was better than staring into his eyes, which were scrutinizing her carefully.

'Where's your nightjar?' she asked, suddenly noting its absence.

He tilted his head to watch her with greater interest. 'You're an aviarist like your mother? She taught me to hide my nightjar when we were children,' he said.

Silence fell and Alice's thoughts raced. Leda was an aviarist too?

'You were *children* together?'

'We were. The Whitmores and Westergards were neighbours.'

Alice blinked rapidly. 'So you're not . . .' She stared at him. 'You're definitely *not* my father, are you?'

The tightness in his face relaxed and his bright eyes regarded her with something like sympathy.

'No. I'm not your father.'

She nodded, but her thoughts slammed into a brick wall. Leda's message. The book. *I remind myself that I didn't lie when I took my oath of office – though I have broken it since . . . The Houses are blind to what we've done, and Gabriel, if he ever loved me, will let me have this one, final secret.*

'Leda said . . . She thought . . .' Alice stopped and shuddered a breath. *Not my father. Whitmore isn't Tuoni.* Her wits were in danger of deserting her. She shoved aside the uncertainties and renewed her focus on the things she did know.

'You were in love with her,' said Alice. 'You knew her secret. You knew it, and you didn't tell anyone because you loved her.'

His face paled and he sat more stiffly in the chair, his hands falling from beneath his chin to clasp over his desk.

'I was young. What's the point of youth if not to fall in love a dozen times a day, with every pretty girl that crosses your path?' He winked at her, as though inviting her to join him in laughing at his charming caddishness. She didn't laugh.

'I saw you coming out of the forest after my first test,' she said, squeezing the arms of her chair until her fingers whitened. 'I saw you leave that door, just before the siren went off. And I saw you with Tilda at the Summer Tree before it erupted.'

Whitmore's eyes flicked over to her face. 'Your point?'

What did she have to lose now? He could hardly refuse her the final test because of poor manners. 'Have you done something to the tree?' she asked baldly.

He slammed his palm on the desk, his expression bitter. 'Your *mother* is the cause of all this,' he snapped. Whitmore seemed to rediscover his restraint, leaning back in the chair, his arms casually draped over the armrests.

Alice tried again to seek out his nightjar. 'Leda is the cause of the Summer Tree's problems? But she's been dead for over twenty years. How could she possibly—'

'First, do no harm: the Hippocratic oath,' he said in a soft, unsettling voice. 'It forms part of the chancellor's oath of office. And quite the hypocrite she became in the end.'

Alice swallowed thickly. 'What did she do?'

His eyes narrowed. 'You're sure you want me to taint her memory for you?'

'Tell me,' she croaked. 'Please.'

'Very well,' he said. 'Your mother was a Gardiner. Did you know?' He paused to study her reaction before continuing. 'The Summer Tree was linked to a stone laid by Pellervoinen.'

'Both of them?' she interrupted. 'The London and the Rookery Stone?'

He paused. 'Well. You have done your research, haven't you?'

'Yes,' she said, her eyes never leaving his face. 'I've been trying to find a book to complete my research. The title is a Latin quote from Sir Isaac Newton. It vanished over a century ago.'

He frowned at her, his expression wary. 'As to your question,' he said stiffly, refusing to be drawn on the book, 'the stones were linked together, that's true – but only the Rookery Stone was directly linked to the Summer Tree. The aim was to use it as a counterweight. An opposing force to prevent the Summer Tree from uncontrollable, damaging growth.'

All the breath rushed out of her, but he didn't seem to notice. So she'd been right, there was a link between them. The stone's task, as an opposing legacy, was to keep the tree in check. It *must* have been damaged.

Whitmore paused and ran his index finger over his bottom lip, deep in thought.

'Your mother, as a Gardiner, was entrusted with maintaining the link between the stone and tree, as every Gardiner and Westergard had done before her. But instead . . . she severed it.'

Alice's head snapped up and her eyes searched his face, but he stared calmly back at her. He was serious. Her blood chilled. *Leda* broke the link between the Rookery and London? She removed Pellervoinen's safeguard?

'Not alone,' he said. 'She had help from Helena Northam. And then, Helena was never heard from again, and your mother went not long afterwards.'

Alice's muscles turned to stone. Oh God. This was what Leda had meant in her diary. This was their shameful secret.

'And so I was left to monitor their mistakes,' said Whitmore. 'Just as they expected me to clean up their messes when we were children. I've been watching the miniature for years, and I've been trying to access the Rookery Stone, waiting for the pigeons to come home to roost. And now they have.'

Alice's mind was racing, trying to keep up. Whitmore had been trying to keep an eye on the tree?

'You . . . you know where the Rookery Stone is?' she murmured.

'Yes. But no one can get to it. It's in a lower chamber of the Abbey Library, behind a concealed door in one of the corridors. It won't open.'

She caught herself just in time. Didn't he know Crowley was Helena's son and Marianne's nephew, and that he might be able to open it? She took a breath. If he didn't, she decided it wasn't her place to reveal it. Not yet. Without being able to pry on his nightjar, she wasn't willing to trust Whitmore. She'd been burned before.

'I can help,' she said. 'I'm a Gardiner too. I have a link to the tree – I've felt it.'

'You won't even be allowed within two feet of the Summer Tree,' he said, with a bite to his voice. 'The Council has seen fit to remove our privileges. The House no longer has any jurisdiction over the tree.'

'What do you—'

'They've banned us from it,' he said. 'They no longer trust us to discharge our duty. Fools. No one is allowed inside – not our representatives, no one. The Runners are in charge now.'

'But . . .' Alice frowned, trying to hurry her thoughts. 'I might be able to help. A Council ban is irrelevant if I can just—'

'You're not yet even a member of this House,' he said silkily.

'Then bring the final test forward and let me take the binding draught,' she said. 'If I'm a Gardiner, it's a formality anyway, isn't it? Seal my membership. Strengthen my link to the Summer Tree and let me fix this.' She paused to gather herself, continuing more calmly. 'Tilda thought I could help. So let me.'

He stared at her for a moment, his eyes narrowed in deliberation. Then he stood abruptly and moved to the door. 'Wait here.'

She couldn't sit still. Her pent-up energy made her knees bounce and her fingers tap involuntarily.

He returned sometime later with a small folder of paper. He nodded for her to open it and she pulled it out. It appeared to be the torn-out pages of a handwritten book. Blue ink scratched across the pages.

'This book was what caused the damage,' he said softly. 'Leda was always so curious about it, and I . . .' He swallowed. 'I gave it to her because I always gave her what she asked for.' He paused and sat up straighter, the look in his eyes hardening. 'She found a ritual in it about how to sever the link. Not specific instructions,' he said, 'but that it was possible. It was my great-uncle's book. He wrote about—'

'I know it,' she managed. 'I know the book. I have the covering the pages were ripped from.'

Whitmore's words echoed through her mind as she left the House in a daze. He was not her father, and Leda had caused the tree's destructiveness. Leda and Helena, custodians of the Summer Tree and the Rookery Stone, had severed the link between the two, reneging on their duties together. Leda had been filled with shame and guilt even at the end of her life. How could she have been naive enough to think that the other anchors would be strong enough to keep the city safe? All those changes she'd made to improve the Rookery for the better were gone, wiped out in the face of her selfish and reckless act. How could she have taken such a risk?

Alice had a sudden and desperate need to see the tree in person. The tree and the stone. She knew where the stone *was* now. She glanced down at the pages in her arms – and soon she would know how to fix them.

Crowley stared into the fire. The twisting flames licked the sides of the grille, spitting and hissing sparks, casting shadows across his face. His legs were stretched out in front of him and his arms rested on the sides of the worn green armchair in the corner of the kitchen. His shirtsleeves were rolled to his elbows, his top button loose, and a glass of whisky dangled from his right hand.

'Why did they do it?' he murmured.

The flames crackled in the grate. Alice watched them as she skirted past the hearth and drew out a wooden dining chair from the table.

'I don't know,' she answered, though she sensed he was talking only to himself.

Alice turned slightly to watch him. She'd never seen Crowley so dejected; he prided himself on being able to think two steps ahead, and now he looked like someone whose footing had been utterly lost. Alice was worried about him.

'Crowley . . .?'

The leaping fire was reflected in his pupils. He swirled the amber whisky dregs around the bottom of his glass.

'Our mothers took it upon themselves to destroy our city – our home. It makes no sense. So much . . . for her fairy tales.'

Draining the whisky, he wiped his mouth on his wrist. He stood abruptly and walked to the sink. Planting his glass on the counter, he slid it away and rested his elbows briefly on the edge of the metal basin. His head dropped into his hands, and he waited there a moment, before releasing a deep sigh and straightening up. 'Maybe,' he said slowly, 'we're not supposed to save it. Maybe we're supposed to let the city burn.' He gave her one last anguished look before striding from the room. As the door swung shut behind him, the fire exploded in the grate and she shoved her chair back in shock.

'I need your help, Crowley,' she called after him. 'We have to put this right.'

She lapsed into silence, her gaze fixed on the flames. How did you sever a link from one object to another? Had something similar to a nightjar cord linked the tree and stone? Something tangible that had been physically cut in half?

She looked down at the papers on her lap. Whitmore was right: they didn't provide specific instructions. All they did was reiterate the importance of the link and the location of the Rookery Stone. As far as she understood, there was a chamber beneath the abbey that led beneath the Summer Tree. It was there that the Rookery Stone sat, in a tangle of the tree's roots.

Whatever the case, Alice needed Crowley to be on his best game. This wasn't something she could do alone, even if somehow she was able to get close to the tree. Two legacies had caused this. Two would have to fix it.

32

'The steel girders were still attached?' Jude asked for the third time.

'Yes,' Alice confirmed. When the Summer Tree had smashed through the atrium ceiling, most of the girders supporting the glass roof had still been in place. 'They *were* attached a while ago. But I can't guarantee that's still the case.'

'It's all right,' said Jude, stowing a container of ball bearings in his wheelchair's travel bag. 'Our back-up plan is the water pipes.'

'The water pipes are not our back-up plan,' said Sasha, affronted. 'They're our plan A.'

'You're right,' he said, dissipating the nervous tension. 'They're *our* plan A, but *my* plan B if the girders have already fallen.'

Sasha nodded and turned away to pull on her long burgundy coat. But Alice had spotted the strain in her jaw. 'Are you sure you want to do this?' she asked.

Sasha flicked a glance at her and pulled a tight, dismissive smile. 'Please. I was born for this. Uncontrollable destruction is my middle name.'

'Sasha Marie-Antoinette Uncontrollable Destruction Hamilton?' drawled Crowley from the doorway. 'It rolls so beautifully off the tongue. The traditional names really are the best, aren't they?'

Before Sasha could fire off a retort, he turned to Jude. 'You have everything you need?'

'I think so,' said Jude.

Alice watched Crowley carefully. He had needed this call to arms. The sense of purpose spurring him on had lifted him from his despondency.

'The ball bearings are magnetized steel,' Jude continued. 'I can get them to the girders, but I might need some help with the heat.'

Crowley nodded, glancing at Alice and offering her a brief reassuring smile. 'I'll make sure to find a suitable position around the square.'

It was a relatively simple plan: destruction and distraction. Alice wanted to access the Abbey Library, and with every possible doorway guarded by Runners, the only way to reach it was through the main entrance – which was, incidentally, also cordoned off by Runners. Far too many of them to cloak herself from sight – at most, she'd only ever managed to blind three nightjars to her presence.

The only people allowed through the entrance were the team of Runners guarding the tree inside, and they had been camping around it in shifts. The only circumstance in which the Runners would leave en masse was if the tree grew and damaged the building. If this happened, Risdon had ordered every Runner to evacuate immediately and find safety. If the Runners fled the building, Alice could slip inside unhindered.

However, she couldn't chance waiting for the tree to burst into spontaneous growth; the pattern of its growth was unpredictable – she might be waiting weeks and still miss it. It was Sasha who had scoffed at their cautious wait-and-see plans and thrown the wild-card into the mix: the tree didn't have to grow; the Runners just had to *believe* it had. They were going to convince Risdon's men that the tree was disturbing the abbey's foundations and threatening to crash it down around their ears.

They staggered their arrivals to prevent suspicion. Crowley and Sasha went first, striding across the road together and vanishing through the door of the derelict building opposite. August went through alone, and Alice and Jude hurried over soon after.

As they approached, the steps that led from the pavement up to the doorway shuddered. The mortar thinned out and there was a clanking thud, followed by the rasp of stone scraping stone as the steps repositioned themselves. The steep angle of the steps decreased, pavement cobbles rising and the first few steps sinking lower. It was the only thing Crowley ever gave the Council any credit for: half a century ago, they'd ordered House Pellervoinen to adjust every set of steps in the Rookery so that they'd be more accessible to those who might otherwise find navigating stairs difficult. The steps responded to a small piece of white Bath stone bracketed to Jude's wheelchair, morphing into a ramp whenever the stone was sensed nearby. The gradient now shallow, Jude's wheels rolled up the flattened steps and through the open doorway. Alice pulled the door closed behind them and shivered at the biting winds knifing through her jumper in the darkness.

'I think we left the ball bearings on the—' she started in a sudden panic.

'I have the ball bearings,' he said with a calming smile. He patted his side bag and she nodded. They were using them as pressure points to rip the girders from the library ceiling.

'Do you think I should've brought my—'

'Alice,' he said. 'Open the door.'

She flexed her fingers and took a deep breath. 'Okay. Okay, yes, the door.' She thrust her arm into the shadows, the sharp wind needling her fingers, and fixed the image of their destination in mind. Three swipes of her hand and her palm glanced off a solid metal ring. The door handle. She latched on to the ring, turned it and pushed the door open an inch. Crooked light folded into the gap, and she scanned left and right before she shouldered the door aside and exited. There were no steps this time, and Jude followed her out, directly onto a quiet side street. The others were nowhere to be seen.

'You know where you're going?' she asked. This suddenly felt like a bad idea – it was one thing for her to take the risk, but to put this on her friends too? The whole square would be swarming with Runners.

'Yes,' he said. 'And Sasha and August too. Sasha is focusing on the mains water pipes, and August on the sewers.'

She glanced anxiously at the top of the road. Something popped, and she looked down to see Jude prising open a vial of amber liquid.

'Rosemary and willow bark,' he said.

'For pain relief?' she asked, concerned.

He nodded and swallowed the liquid. 'It's been one of my bad weeks.' He stowed the empty vial in the side bag on his wheel-chair.

'Jude, are you sure—'

'It's fine.'

'But—'

'I've got some of Mowbray's lavender waiting for me when

398

we're done,' he said. She hesitated, before nodding and glancing back up the street.

'Did you know that August thinks he's related to Bazalgette?' Jude said mildly.

Alice frowned into the distance, distracted. 'Bazal . . .' She trailed away, and her attention drifted back to Jude. 'What were you saying?'

'August thinks he's related to the architect that designed the London sewers.'

'I can well believe it,' she said. 'His mind is a cesspit.'

Jude grinned up at her, and some of the nerves churning up her stomach eased.

'Thanks,' she said.

'Are you ready?' he asked.

'Nope.'

'Good. I've come to realize that being ready is overrated. What you need is adrenaline and the ability to think fast and react *faster.*'

Jude spun one wheel and his chair turned sharply in the opposite direction. He shot down the street, wheels blurred as they turned circles, and the shock of his sudden disappearance almost caused her to call after him. She bit down on her lip to silence herself, put her head down and moved off in the same direction. However, where Jude crossed the road and went straight on, she took a right turn, putting the Abbey Library on the left of her field of vision.

She'd been right about Runners swarming the area. Behind the abbey was the enclosed, cobbled yard that had once surrounded an immense piece of thick glass. The top third of the Summer Tree's crown had burst through it, smashing the ceiling into glittering fragments. A metal safety barrier now circled the rising tree, manned by Runners wearing weary expressions. Small groups of bystanders gathered nearby, peering over at the branches reaching upwards while the Runners regarded them cautiously.

Somewhere nearby, Jude and the others would be settling into their positions; they might even be watching her now. It was tempting to scour the crowd, seeking out their faces for some silent reassurance, but that might only draw unwanted attention. So instead, Alice slid her gaze away from the busy square. Face set determinedly forward, she trudged along the street just across from their cordon. Just as Crowley had told her to, she found a suitable unused porch twenty metres or so from the corner. It was the entrance to a boarded-up shop: *Horrocks's Horticulturals*. She stepped neatly off the pavement and into the shadows. And there she waited.

Alice ran a finger over her bottom molars, testing them for cracks. She'd been grinding her teeth solidly for at least an hour, and either her jawbone or her enamel was going to pay the price. The constant tension had driven harmless flutters from her stomach and replaced them with a tight cramping; it felt like her intestines were being wrung out like a dishcloth. She wasn't sure she could wait much longer. If she hadn't been alone, it might have been easier. But this constant waiting in the dark was taking its toll. She wanted to leave the doorway; it was musty and the sharp tang of urine scented the air. Still. She supposed that August had the worst of it. By now, he would be somewhere below her, huddled alone in the sewers. Assuming they'd avoided the Runners, Sasha and Crowley were around the other side of the square, as close to the cordon as they could get without being visible. And Jude wouldn't be far – he was aiming to get to the opposite side of the square, though with his magnetized ball bearings he could operate blindly in a way Sasha couldn't.

Alice tugged the neck of her jumper over her nose and breathed in the warm – but cleaner – air. She slouched back against the wall and stared out at the bright pavement, watching footsteps march past. Though her eyes were open, she slipped into a dull trance and was almost dozing when the first bang rocked the square.

Jude! Alice's spine snapped upright and she bolted out to the pavement. People walking on the streets had paused mid-step; the Runners had turned slowly to stare at each other. But it hadn't hit home yet. There was a syrupy confusion in the air, but no desperate panic. *And again, Jude!* Alice braced herself and set off at speed. *Don't run*, she reprimanded herself; running would draw attention. She slowed her hurtling canter to a business-like pace, swiftly navigating the road and the bystanders until she was on the outskirts of the square.

She had one foot on the kerb when the second thunderous explosion burst. Alice slammed her hands over her ears, wincing as the sound reverberated around the streets. Then a metallic vibration rang out, followed by a series of thudding booms. The last remnants of the shattered atrium glass broke loose from the ceiling and rained down into the hollow abbey. The leaves of the Summer Tree trembled, the branches creaked . . . and pandemonium struck.

'Code zero, code zero!' a Runner screamed in her face.

Alice backed away and circled round again when he raced off, yelling to his colleagues. Navy uniforms shot in all directions. Bystanders rushed towards doorways, shoving each other aside to dash into the safety of the void. And amidst the ruckus, the water pipes that ran under the street ruptured, sending fountains of gushing water rocketing across the cobbles. *Well done, August and Sasha 'Uncontrollable Destruction' Hamilton.*

Come on, Alice urged. *Evacuate the building.* She caught her breath when a troop of Runners poured around the side of the abbey itself, scurrying across the square. *Yes!*

'Code zero!' a uniformed woman shouted over the slow whine of an air-raid siren. 'Clear the area!' The cobbled ground rumbled again and panic widened the Runner's eyes. She dashed across the road, corralling the few Rookery citizens standing around, too slack-jawed for self-preservation.

Alice scrambled to the side wall of the Abbey Library and threw one last glance over her shoulder. No one had noticed Jude's tiny steel ball bearings rolling across the square towards the Summer Tree's crown. Alice bit back a grin and darted around the corner.

She hesitated briefly at the entrance to the building. Runners had surged out of this door only moments ago, following Risdon's instructions to evacuate in the event of the Summer Tree's growth. But what if some had ignored his orders? Her lips pressed tightly together, she squared her shoulders and hurried through the entrance. It didn't matter if there were Runners inside; she had one chance to get in and she was going to take it.

When she reached the first set of narrow, winding stairs, she sat on the bottom step and whispered into the gloom.

'Kuu?'

Her nightjar appeared with a nervous flutter.

'Bird's-eye view,' she murmured.

Her vision jumped and her body staggered. No longer viewing the world from the safety of her own cranium, she observed her physical self from Kuu's higher vantage point. With one flick of the head in the direction of Alice's body, the bird arced sideways.

Kuu's tight, controlled flight blurred the roughly hewn walls as she swooped around the corner. Dark corridors led off from the stairwell. Off-limits: they would take her nightjar too far from her body. The shadows receded and the stairs opened into the vast, bright atrium. Kuu held back. Wings flapping, suspended in the air like a spider on a silken string, she darted her head around the stone wall and back again. There were four Runners on the upper floor. The staircase that spiralled around the tree was clear, but they would spot Alice as soon as she approached. She could cloak herself against three, maybe, but four at once would be a struggle – and there could be others on lower floors.

Kuu leaned out into the atrium again, imprinting the scene in Alice's mind. The Runners were jumpy. A spat had broken out, and one appeared to be threatening to leave while the others demanded he stay.

Shit. If he leaves now, he'll find me on the stairs.

One of the Runners was absolutely still, holding a boulder in one hand, his jaw clenched. Another was pacing and clicking his fingers anxiously, producing a bloom of fire on his thumb while he snapped at the others. A third was clutching a granite spear and fighting to keep hold of the fourth Runner, who was ready to run. At random intervals, all four swatted at the air with the panic of someone striking out at an attack of wasps.

The nightjar's head darted upwards. The steel girders holding up the glass ceiling had begun to come apart. A third of them had slipped loose and fallen, smashing onto the courtyard flags below, causing the deafening banging. The Runners had assumed it was because the growing tree had dislodged them, when in fact it was Jude.

He had sent hundreds of ball bearings rolling towards the shattered glass, and they had attached themselves in magnetized clumps to the girders. Placed just right, with Jude's will and Crowley's combustion, the ball bearings had put pressure on the weakest points, ripping them from their bindings. Not all – just a few. Just enough to suggest the tree had damaged them. Just enough to send the Runners scrambling from the abbey. The other girders had been left in position in case some of the Runners disobeyed Risdon's instructions and stayed behind to protect the tree – like the fractious four who remained.

With a last swoop, Kuu saw the girders now glowing like metal heated in a forge. *Stage two. Nearly ready.* Crowley and Jude had willed a blazing heat into the ball bearings – and the heat had spread. Alice needed to be in position.

Kuu glided silently back up the stairwell, the cord linking her to Alice glowing brighter as she closed the distance between them. Alice was sitting on the steps, her head leaning against the wall, when Kuu landed on her knee. The bird nudged Alice's hand with her beak and Alice snapped upright, inhaling sharply as her vision leapt back into her own head. She glanced down at Kuu and gave her a shaky pat before shoving herself up from the steps and hurrying to the stairwell's exit.

Alice aligned herself with the edge of the wall, carefully peering out for reassurance that the four upper-floor Runners had remained in place. She glanced up at the scorching steel girders.

The air sizzled. A plume of steam spewed downwards into the atrium. Alice's pulse raced and her hands shook with anticipation. This was it. The Runners leapt back from the stone banister in shock and confusion as the steam billowed. But it wasn't enough, Alice realized. Had August and Sasha run out of water?

There was a wet roar and then a gushing waterfall poured through the shattered glass ceiling. Spilling from the square outside, it cascaded over the tree, over the steel girders . . . and as it hit the hot metal, it erupted into a blast of warm vapour. A pillow of steam rolled into the atrium, turning the air grey and impenetrable. The entire space filled with it, fogged and indistinct – perfect for someone who didn't want to be seen.

Alice leapt to action, dashing out across the floor. She flattened herself against the banister, trying to pierce the haze for some sign of the Runners, now shouting in panic, and the possibility of others below.

Her steps sure and swift, she hurried to the top of the spiral staircase. After a pause to catch her breath, with one hand gripping the banister tightly she ploughed down the stairs.

At the bottom, she stepped carefully over the uneven, root-damaged flagstones. Her feet slid into cracks and sloping pockets between the stones. Now would be a bad time to twist her ankle. She needed to keep open the possibility of a quick escape, because it was likely the Runners had set traps around the tree.

Her thoughts drifted away like steam. She smiled and tipped her head back as the glow from a thousand fireflies danced closer and warmed her face. The swarm hung in the air above, floating like a luminous cloud. Were they one of the Runners' traps? Alice reached up her hand and they drew closer. She turned her palm over and their sparks left trails of lightning against her skin. These were no threat to her. They had never once hurt her, and they never would. Mielikki's blood ran through her veins. This tree was hers, and they had no need to defend it against her. She wondered if she had the power to command them – perhaps to chase off any remaining Runners – but dismissed the thought quickly. The fireflies were too savage. She flicked her fingers and they drifted off, a dim glow growing fuzzy in the steam.

Alice moved forward, examining the base of the massive trunk and its roots. She was searching for some sign of a cord, a broken link to the Rookery Stone trailing in the roots. Something ethereal, or ghostly, or—

Her heart leapt against her ribs. Her breath came in dizzying fits and starts. She saw it draping down the back of the Summer Tree, tangled in the leafy branches, so thin it was almost translucent. Alice stumbled towards it, barely believing her eyes. She reached out a trembling finger. Transfixed by the gently pulsing twine, she ignored the flutter of pale wings overhead and the shriek of a bird. *Not now, Kuu.*

But it wasn't Kuu.

A white bird, its leg looped to a glowing, incandescent cord, swooped out from the cloud of grey steam. Alice's arms fell away from the cord, and she stared at it in shock. A nightjar was tied to the tree. The cord didn't belong to the Summer Tree. It belonged to this *bird*, lashed to the trunk. A white nightjar. So like her own.

In a daze, she reached out to stroke the bird. Its eyes darted to hers, shining darkly like polished black marbles. The throbbing cord cinched its leg, backlighting its feathers with pulses of dazzling light. Alice stared, entranced. Amidst the brightness, the bird's dark gaze drew her attention and locked on hers. Around her, the atrium flickered and vanished. Her vision tunnelled and she mentally pitched forward, falling towards the nightjar's black stare. She sank into its mind, the weight of her presence dispersing memories. Visions shot past her, the echoes of sobs and laughter and screams fading into the darkness. She screwed her eyes shut and inhaled slowly. And when her eyes snapped open, Alice found herself somewhere else entirely: in a memory.

Whose mind was this?

33

Alice shivered. She was someone else – not Alice – and the room was unbearably hot.

The chapel had been dressed with silks and roses. He watched her. The chancellor. She was smiling and complimenting the beautiful decor, but her lips were stretched just a little too wide and her eyes just a little too glassy. She clearly hated it. He allowed himself an inward smirk. Aviarists were usually good liars; she was clearly the exception to the rule. Still, she was correct. The richly elegant silks were gaudy against the chapel's simple arches and pillars. The vaulted nave might have been an extravagant focal point, as it was in other chapels, but this one was plain and lacking in grandeur. He greatly admired it. The White Tower chapel's simple, solid Romanesque architecture was infinitely preferable to the ostentatious baroque of St Paul's Cathedral. He raised his eyes to examine the triforium gallery, the arches like something gouged from stone. It was beautiful in its simplicity. The silks were a poor attempt to make the space opulent, to change its very character.

He reached out to stroke one of the roses twined around the pillars. The petals dulled and crisped in his hands before falling away, scattering over the stone floor and leaving the flower head bare. *Better. Strip everything back to its essence and you are left with the truth.*

She stepped out from behind the pillar, her boots crunching the petals, and his back straightened in surprise at being caught off guard.

'Good evening,' she said, amusement dancing in her eyes. 'I'm Chancellor Westergard, and I must inform you that we don't usually divest the chapel of its decoration until the *end* of the Council's annual banquet.' She glanced over her shoulder in pantomime and leaned in close to whisper loudly, 'If you vandalize the chapel, you might well be sent to the tower dungeons. Apparently, the chancellor is a real stickler for law and order.'

She winked at him, and he took in her plain dress and cloak. A gleaming, ceremonial chain of office was draped around her shoulders. Amidst the garish costumes of the aristocratic peacocks here, who couldn't hope to reach her status, she was beautiful in her simplicity. He smiled down at her.

Leda. Alice latched on to the thought. Was this a memory of the night her biological parents had met? Like Reid's memories of the adoption, Alice was viewing the scene as an actor onstage, not as a member of the audience. *The main actor.* And then the chapel dissolved like sand in the tide, and a new memory rose up under Alice's feet.

Pregnant. No. It couldn't be. It was simply not possible.

He stared at her in horror. He had dreamed of *living*, but this . . . this was how dying must feel.

'Listen to me,' Leda begged, pulling at his limp hands, placing them on her abdomen. 'This is a miracle. *You've* created life. *We've* created life, *together.*'

He snatched his trembling hands back. She didn't understand.

This baby, this monster, would destroy her. And he had done this. He had ruined her.

'I'm keeping this baby,' she whispered. Then, stronger, 'I'm keeping her. All my life, I've weighed up risks and taken chances others haven't. I've given every ounce of my energy to my public office, to fighting for others. And now I'm *taking* this risk. She's a miracle and she'll do miraculous things.'

He was a block of stone and her words chipped away at his edges, fragmenting his body and carving away at the pieces of him. They hadn't created a life; they had created death. This child would kill her. It would be a hungry, grasping thing. When it was pushed into the world, it would seek out the only source of warmth it could find: Leda's life. The child would slice her cord the moment it was born. Its first breath would be her last. The shame and grief hollowed him out. He had given Leda a piece of himself that would consume her.

His love had killed her.

She could not keep this child.

The room disintegrated and Alice watched as the determined face of Leda Westergard blurred and washed away. Colours spiralled around Alice, a bright smear, disorienting her. Lightheaded, she fought to focus as the space settled. This time it was dark. Leda's voice was a harsh rasp in the shadows of a doorway.

'Stay away! I know what you mean to do. You will *not* kill this child – not to save me!'

He surged closer. 'Leda, please,' he whispered. Desperation was burrowing beneath his skin.

She swiped her hand through the air and a clutch of fast-growing weeds burst from the cobblestones and lunged for him, whipping him off his feet. He clattered onto the street, his knees smashing against the stone.

He wouldn't stop. She must know it. He wouldn't stop until he'd removed the threat hanging over her life like the sword of Damocles. The child would have to die. Even if Leda hated him for it. He didn't need her forgiveness. He only needed her to live.

She stared down at him, her face softening. 'Don't make me do this,' she pleaded. 'Don't make me choose.'

He glanced up at her, and his face was a study in perfect misery. He *had* no choice. Didn't she understand? He'd given up who he was. Everything he had been, he'd abandoned. He couldn't lose her now, not when he'd spent so many lifetimes waiting to find her. And she deserved to live. She was everything good in the world; she'd *earned* a place here. What use was his stolen life if she wasn't in it?

Leda stiffened, and then nodded with steely resolve. 'So be it,' she said. 'It's all I can do.'

And then she closed the door on him, her voice carried away by the wind blustering through the void.

Alice lost her grip on the street. It was swept out from under her, and a new memory formed. A ticking clock in the gloom.

He sat in the darkness of his living room, staring blankly at the wall. The moon's light curved through his window, illuminating the clock face on the wall. Time was irrelevant now. Everything . . . was irrelevant now. She was dead. He had failed, and she was dead. The child? Somewhere. Perhaps. Perhaps it too was dead. Perhaps they were together, and he was the only one alone. Left behind. Trapped.

What she had done was monstrous. And yet, he was equal to it. He would never see her again. She had robbed him of that. They would never reunite. Not even on the moors: a consequence of her decision. He was trapped here until the end. Leda must have known it, but she'd deemed it an acceptable consequence to keep the child safe. She had sacrificed her own life. But she had also sacrificed his chance of a true death.

He prodded his chest but the skin was numb. He glanced over his shoulder, his eyes tracking for the familiar sight of his nightjar, but it too was gone. No Leda. No nightjar. No itse. Leda had taken it and imprisoned it in the Summer Tree. Balance. Pellervoinen had once provided the counterweight, with the London Stone's twin here in the Rookery, but Leda had severed it. To maintain the balance the tree required, she had parcelled up part of his soul and offered it to the Summer Tree as a bond: his raw, deadly soul neutralizing the all-consuming life bursting from Mielikki's tree.

It was the itse-soul that travelled to the moors after death. Without his, he would never return to his homeland and he would never reunite with Leda. He would be trapped, and they would always be apart. His only hope of restitution was to reverse what she had done, to liberate his soul and go to her. Let this puppet body go, and seek her out in the moors.

He stood abruptly, his eyes falling on a book lit by the moonlight on his shelf. He snatched it up, scanning the title with desperation. This was her book. She had carried it with her like a bible. How many of her secrets might he uncover? Perhaps it could reveal to him how she had done it – and how it could be undone.

Magellan's Metaphysical Treatise: Sielun.

He stroked the cover her fingers had once held. Leda had considered herself an expert on Magellan. She'd had access to his private papers and manuscripts – not because of her Council position but because she'd been a Westergard and the name carried weight. He needed that same access; he would scour the Rookery for information about Magellan. And once he had it, he would

411

make plans to release his soul from the tree. To be reunited with Leda in the moors. To forgive her, and to beg her forgiveness in turn.

Alice's hand slipped from the nightjar's soft feathers and the atrium blinked into existence around her. The walls tilted and the tree see-sawed across her vision. She threw out a hand for stability, but there was nothing to grab. She swung sideways and clattered to the floor, the sharp edges of the flagstones pressing into the side of her ribcage. *Deep breath. Deep breath.* Alice drew her knees up to her chest and pressed her fists into her eyes. *Deep breath.*

When she finally looked up, wincing, the light was still too bright, too stark. She lurched to her feet and peered up at the tree. Where had the nightjar gone? There was no sign of it. Maybe it was crouching on a branch, camouflaged by the dense thicket of leaves, watching her. She hadn't summoned the bird; it had come to her of its own accord.

Tuoni's nightjar.

Tuoni's nightjar was tied to this tree because part of his soul was caged inside it. Her face paled and she reeled backwards at the thought. Leda had used her link to Mielikki to push a soul into her tree. A *soul*.

Alice clapped a hand to her mouth, muffling a moan of horror and realization. Leda had done this for *her*. Tuoni had been so determined to save Leda he'd set out to kill his unborn child. So she'd trapped the most dangerous part of him to keep Alice safe.

A chill swept through Alice's body. If the Rookery Stone had been the original counterweight and Leda had swapped it for Tuoni's soul . . . she must have assumed that his powers of death would keep the Summer Tree's powers of life in check. But something had gone wrong, because the tree's growth was now unrestricted; it was damaging the Rookery, obliterating buildings and streets and tearing the land in two.

Tuoni had wanted to free his soul. With the original link severed, the price would be the Summer Tree's growth. Had Tuoni been successful – in part, at least? Where was he now, and what had he found in Magellan's writings? What had . . .?

Her hand fell away from her mouth. Magellan . . . the Magellan Institute. Tuoni had been determined to retrace Leda's steps, and they had taken him to Magellan's manuscripts.

Alice shuddered, a sickness deep in her belly. Who, exactly, had Reid been working for? Was the Magellan Estate simply Tuoni masquerading as a wealthy financial backer? Reid had blamed herself for Crane Park Island. Had Reid destroyed her research to stop this – because Tuoni was using her findings to free his soul?

34

The campus was deathly quiet when Alice made her way across the gardens many hours later, with Tilda's two books clutched in one hand. The mulberry trees swayed drunkenly in the breeze, the only sign of movement. Some of the students and staff living on-site had left, driven out by fear of the university falling into a sinkhole like the streets by the Thames. She had Coram House, if she'd wanted to leave, but it was no safer there than here. Her friends had been busy trying to reinforce the building when she'd slipped out; she'd told them she needed some time to think.

Alice skirted the side of the Sydenham Building and made her way to her favourite bench in the quadrangle. It was almost midnight, and thick grey clouds hid the moon; it was dark, cold and calm. There were no lights on in the windows of the Arlington Building. Word had probably spread that there had been another incident with the Summer Tree; no doubt it would be morning before they realized it was a false alarm.

She swung her knees up and lay on the bench, hugging the folder to her chest and looking up at the marbled sky. There were more stars in the Rookery than in London – not because they had a greater number but because with the poor electricity systems here, there was less light pollution to camouflage them. She searched for the North Star, but wherever it was, she couldn't find it.

She remembered her dad, when she was a teenager, trying to teach her about the constellations. He'd focused on Aquila and Cygnus, patiently drawing them when she'd been unable to see them, embellishing them with feathers and wings and beaks to show her there were birds made of stars, and weren't they beautiful? But she'd never been able to follow the join-the-dots path he'd tried to make with his finger, no matter how many times he'd traced them across the skies for her.

'It doesn't matter that you can't see my birds,' he'd told her. 'I know they're there, just over my shoulder every night. I can appreciate them for what they are, because they really are beautiful, but I can ignore them too. When it's daytime, I can't see them at all. And at night, I can choose to step into the garden and admire them if I want to. *I* decide.'

She'd boxed away her own birds soon after, the ones *she'd* decided not to see – the nightjars that haunted her every waking moment. Of course, she'd thought they were hallucinations at the time, but her dad had tried to give her some control over them, some agency. He had always put the reins in her hands, always encouraged her to make her own decisions. She'd made some bad ones, undoubtedly, but they'd been *hers* and no one else's. He'd always been proud of her independence and her wilfulness, even when he'd hoped she might temper it with caution. Well here she was, learning at last.

Alice sat up and wrapped her arms around herself. The mulberry tree in the centre of the quad had grown. Its berries were brighter and heavy with juices, its canopy a little wider. Maybe all the trees in the Rookery would benefit from the Summer Tree's domination. Unchecked, it might churn up the land, but new life might blossom in the cracks. Perhaps nature would flourish as it once had, before the world had been concreted over. House Mielikki would certainly rise above the other Houses then. If there were any left.

She smoothed a hand over the book cover. Whitmore's torn papers had been useful, from a theoretical standpoint. But the book crammed with drawings and annotations had, in the end, proven more useful still. They'd added a practical element to Whitmore's book of theory.

The handwritten notes in different inks and styles – some in Latin, others in English – were laid out erratically. Sentences scattered here and there across the pages, expanding on a paragraph or a phrase written by someone else, like a collective body of research. The newer additions, Alice had finally realized, were in Leda's handwriting. She'd lined the diary and the book side by side, scrutinizing their form – the way Leda looped some of her letters, the sharp angles on the others – until she was in no doubt. Without meaning to, Leda had left her a breadcrumb trail through the pages.

Alice had tried to show the annotations to Crowley, but he hadn't been able to see, neither the newer nor the older text. She was glad, in the end, that he hadn't been able to read Leda's words. If he had known what was expected of her, he would try to stop her. He would try to save her.

A memory rose sharply in her mind. Wet through and shivering, Crowley at her back, his arm wrapped tightly around her. *I'm not letting you go.* She swallowed hard and leaned back to look up at the stars.

'Kuu?' she murmured.

Her nightjar appeared, fluttering down to rest on her lap. She stroked its pale feathers, ignoring the tightness in her throat as it leaned into her touch. The glowing cord on her wrist pulsed vividly, highlighting the sheen on Kuu's wings.

Tree becomes stone, and stone becomes tree. Leda had annotated the words in the margins. Alice glanced over at the lawns, where the Cream of the Crops competition had once taken place. The students from Houses Mielikki and Pellervoinen had fought a contest there, the Pellervoinens attempting to petrify a piece of wood, to fossilize it by replacing its elements with minerals. To be successful, the wood couldn't be allowed to rot, or there would be nothing for the stone to replace. Petrification needed water and heat, but no oxygen. Those were the ingredients in petrification by normal means. A process that took millions of years in a world without magic.

Tree and stone must be bound together to fix the broken link between the anchors. Joined completely – fused together – in a way that hardly seemed possible. Leda's annotations had been useful, but Alice couldn't quite *picture* what she was expected to do, or how. It was . . . too big. She could see the smaller parts, but not the whole.

Water. Heat. No oxygen. It couldn't be allowed to rot.

Alice's eyes traced Kuu's cord – so bright, so vivid. So warm, when she touched it. Raw power and energy. Enough, perhaps, to generate the heat required. The nightjar churred softly and nuzzled at her fingers, and Alice had to look away.

Mielikki had used her cord's energy to fuse her tree to Pellervoinen's stone. And Alice would follow in her footsteps. She would sever her nightjar cord to complete the ritual. Kuu would leave her for good. And to prevent her deadly soul from escaping and striking down an innocent – as it almost had at Marble Arch – Alice would step into the Sulka Moors, the Land of Death, where she belonged – where she could do no harm. Forever.

417

'Alice? Is that you?'

She sat up again, peering over the back of the wooden bench.

'Bea?' she murmured, her nightjar vanishing at the sound of the librarian's approaching footsteps.

'I've been searching for you for hours,' said Bea, breathless. 'Governor Whitmore wants you to take your final test tomorrow. I think the timing is awful, and the whole thing should be postponed, but he was adamant.'

Alice nodded. Of course he was. He wasn't just adamant, he was desperate. He thought she stood a chance of fixing this mess. And so she would. And maybe, along the way, she would seek out Tuoni at last and make sure he could never threaten the city's safety again. She closed her eyes. What a curse her parents had been on the Rookery. Yet now it was time to dig deep into her soul and learn which part of her was strong enough to save it: Tuoni or Mielikki.

'Dandelions?' said Alice as they hurried along King Edward Street. The atmosphere in the Rookery had changed; people seemed to scurry everywhere, heads down and with little time to waste.

'Watch out!'

A bearded man with a thick waist swung a suitcase apparently filled with all his worldly goods directly into Alice's path. She veered around him, the corner of his suitcase clipping her ankle.

'Singular,' amended Bea as they both paused to watch the man lug his heavy suitcase away. Was this a sign that people were abandoning the city? But where would they find safety? In the mainland with the Beaks?

'*One* dandelion,' said Bea, refocusing on the matter at hand.

'It's nicknamed The Dandelion Test.' She tugged absentmindedly on her necklace. 'It's an unexpected choice,' she said, glancing at Alice. 'I shouldn't really be telling you this, but . . . Cecil told me that Whitmore wanted to push through the last batch of membership applications quickly. Only you and one other made it to the final test.'

'Shobhna? The woman from the knotweed forest?'

She nodded. 'But Cecil got the impression Whitmore was treating it as a formality – hurrying them through because, frankly, the House has enough to deal with right now. Honestly, darling, we both assumed it would mean you'd be given one of the easier final tests.'

Alice tried to keep her face blank. The timing was right. The test was only a means to an end now. She just needed the final portion of binding draught to tie her to the tree so that she could sacrifice herself in its honour.

Bea tutted loudly and Alice mentally scrambled to catch up. 'For Whitmore to turn around and select The Dandelion Test, he's not gone for the easy option at all, and yet—'

'Dandelions sound pretty innocuous,' said Alice. 'What exactly does this process . . . entail?' she finished cautiously. Alice held her breath, fearing she'd made a misstep that would lead them to the subject of Tom's absence. Today, a stranger would have to administer her binding draught, if she passed, instead of Tom. He'd become an elephant in the room. Bea choked up every time his name was mentioned and Alice couldn't bring herself to tell her the truth about his betrayal.

Bea reached into the voluminous pocket of her housecoat. After a rummage, she pulled out half a dozen yellow dandelions. 'Here. Practise while we walk,' she said, and Alice breathed a sigh of relief. 'There are variations but the general idea is the same.

You'll be given one of these and instructed to speed its growth into a white, fluffy head. Then you'll have to take it from the starting point to the finish line without losing a single seed. It has to be intact at the end of the journey or you'll fail.'

There was a brief pause. 'That . . . doesn't *sound* too difficult.'

Bea pulled a face. 'The obstacles are deadly and combative. You have to meet them head-on without a single fluffy bristle floating free. The year I took my final test, two girls died in this test: one drowned in a bog and the other was crushed by rocks. The year after, three died. The last candidate got caught in brambles and was cut in half by the thorns. His family reported the House to the Runners.' She shook her head. 'The House wasn't liable, since most families willingly accepted the risks, but it caused a stir at the time. After that, the House broadened our range of tests.'

Alice's pace quickened. The sooner they reached the House, the sooner she could get this over with. 'So is there a trick?' she asked. 'To keep the dandelion from disintegrating?'

Bea's eyes sparkled briefly. 'Of course there's a trick. It's all about timing its life cycle perfectly.' She selected one of the dandelions and stroked its head. The yellow petals contracted, closing up into a green bud. The petals dried out and fell away, and when the bud opened, what was left were the white tufts of a dandelion clock.

'Pause its growth so that the bud opens to reveal the fluffy head, but not all the way. Keep the bud from turning inside out; keep it semi-visible so that the tufts are kept in place,' she said, handing the dandelion to Alice. 'The more tightly packed together the tufts are, the less likely they'll be blown away by an accidental flick of the wrist or a puff of air.'

She gave Alice a grim smile. 'If you can master the dandelion, all you'll have to do during the test is avoid being drowned, burned, garrotted, stabbed or crushed.'

Alice gingerly reached for a flower. 'Oh,' she mumbled. 'Is that all?'

As she observed House Mielikki from the pavement opposite, Alice allowed the flutter of nervous tension buried under her skin to grow. Her heart pounding like a piston engine, she inhaled deeply, imagining the crackle of electricity in her veins. Jude was right. Nerves were good. Adrenaline was good: an evolutionary superpower.

'Bea?' she said suddenly. 'Do you trust him? Whitmore?'

There was a pause. 'Years ago, long before I was a member of the House . . . In something like the early nineties, there was a scandal around House Ilmarinen's links with the mainland steel industry – a deal the governor had done with Thatcher. They were sanctioned for interfering and the Council banned them from taking part in the House-weighted voting system. Politically, they lost their voice in parliament. It went on for well over a year.' She frowned. 'It was Whitmore who lobbied for them to have the sanctions removed and their votes restored.'

Alice stared at her, waiting to see where she was leading.

'Without House Ilmarinen, every vote went in favour of Mielikki and Ahti. Long-time allies, they always voted together. But Whitmore lobbied for Ilmarinen's rights to be restored, knowing it would mean the end of his House's hold on the votes. That it would bolster House Pellervoinen and give the deciding vote back to the chancellor. And yet he did it anyway, because he felt it was the right thing to do. So . . . yes. I think he's proved himself honourable in the past. I don't find him very *warm*, but I trust him to do the right thing.'

Alice nodded thoughtfully. Leda had trusted him once, when he'd loved her and kept her secret for over twenty years.

She stepped off the pavement and hastened towards the House. With a quick glance up at the boughs draped over the archway, she entered the building and pressed ahead. The glimmering ceiling lights lit her way.

A figure stepped out into the corridor, his shadow falling across her path. Cecil Pryor.

'Hello, Alice,' he said, offering her a reassuring smile. 'Are you ready?'

'As I'll ever be,' she said.

This time, he didn't walk her to his office. With a solemn nod, he gestured for her to follow and turned on his heel. She squared her shoulders and strode after him.

'This is for you,' said Cecil, startling her from her thoughts.

She reached out for the yellow dandelion he was offering. A shot of warmth blossomed in her stomach. Alice waited for his instructions, which were as predicted. In her hands, the dandelion aged into a fluffy white seed head, the green bud gripping the ends of the bristles tightly.

'Deliver the intact dandelion to the door, and there your test will end,' said Cecil. 'If you have succeeded, Governor Whitmore will be waiting by the door to award you with the final portion of binding draught.'

Alice gave him a searching look. 'Has Shobhna taken her test?'

He looked surprised. 'She passed this morning.'

'That's good,' she said, nodding. 'I'm glad.'

Cecil raised his hand, and for a moment she thought he wanted her to pass the flower back. He smiled and took her hand, shaking it with an encouraging squeeze.

'Take care, Alice,' he said, his eyes bright behind his glasses.

He swung open a door in the corridor, and she stepped through.

35

Her boots crunched onto loose topsoil and brushwood. Not the grove that housed the miniature Summer Tree but another forest – shadowy, the air fresh with the earthy scents of nature. Maple trees stretched above her head. Cedar, beech, horse chestnut, oak, even a rowan tree bursting with red berries – trees of every variety and shape crowded around her. Their dense canopies hid the sky, their trunks – crooked, slender, thick, smooth, ridged – carrying the weight of their leafy crowns with ease. She turned towards the door, but it, and Cecil, had gone.

Clutching the dandelion, she carefully moved off. Her eyes swept back and forth, hunting for danger: a sudden rock face, a watery marsh – anything. Alice ducked under a gnarled hornbeam, its leaves fountaining from the centre like a weeping willow. There was no path and no tracks to follow, but the way was obvious; the trees seemed to herd her onwards, ushering with their outstretched arms and whispering leaves.

Alice's every sense was primed. She peered into the dappled shadows cast across the forest floor, gripping the flower tightly, taking care not to walk too fast and dislodge a seed from the head. She glanced up, in case the threat might approach from overhead, but other than the creak and sway of branches, there was no sign of movement at all. And eventually, as she plunged onwards through the grass, it became clear – there was no threat. There were no obstacles in her path. No falling trees, or boulders, or watery graves. There was just Alice and the quiet sounds of the forest as it breathed into the night.

When she emerged into a small clearing, she saw the door. The branch of a gnarled oak tree curved to the ground, and tucked between the branch and the trunk was a door made of a blackened wood, crooked and fitted to the shape of the tree's embrace. She stepped carefully around it, but it led nowhere. Beside it was a carved stump, and resting in the centre was a wooden chalice filled to the brim with the binding draught. The last portion.

She stepped back from it and peered around. Was it a trick? She would lift the cup and an assailant might rain down from the trees?

'Hello?' Her voice was muffled by the wall of shrubbery around her. 'Governor Whitmore?'

She paused, ears pricked. But there was nothing. Maybe he hadn't set her any traps because he'd simply wanted to rush her through the final test without being seen to show bias. House reputation rested on the fairness of their membership bids. But there had been no one here to see Alice walk through the forest untested – and no one to see as she laid the dandelion on the stump and lifted the chalice.

She tilted the wooden cup and examined the wheat-coloured liquid, ribbons of gold skating over its surface. She hesitated for just a moment. Holly's terrified face chased through her memory – imbibing the draught was as much a test as anything. But she had Gardiner blood. Mielikki blood. And the Summer Tree was already a part of her. She looked around once more, checking for signs of Whitmore or Cecil – someone from the House who ought to have been present. But the only other life in the forest belonged to the trees and the grasses.

She didn't want to waste this chance. The draught was here – all she had to do was drink it. This was her opportunity to save the Rookery. Bind herself to the Summer Tree and use her Mielikki legacy to control it. *Go on*, she urged herself, *just do it*.

Alice took a sharp breath, raised the chalice to her lips and drank deeply. The liquid warmed her throat and chest as it slid into her body. For a heartbeat, nothing happened. And then she began to tremble all over as sparks of electricity crackled through her arms, drove into her legs and surged through her veins. Her blood was effervescent, every particle vibrating, firing her senses. Her nerve endings tingled and buzzed, and a feeling of completeness and utter bliss swept through her – like the lights flicking on one by one in a dark house, the draught lit her up inside until she felt she was glowing with euphoria.

Alice stared at her hands, flexing her fingers. They throbbed with energy and she laughed in delight. Dropping to her knees, she placed her palms in the grass and *pushed*. Flowers burst to life all around her, buttercups growing in the gaps between her fingers, a ring of daisies, gypsophila and chrysanthemums blooming outwards across the forest floor.

She got to her feet and staggered at the sudden deep rhythmic beat marching against her ribs. When had her heartbeat grown so loud? It filled her ears, a sonorous echo in her chest. She leaned over, hands on her knees and eyes closed, trying to focus as it ricocheted through her mind like the clanging of a church bell. *It's not my heartbeat*, she realized. She knew it – she felt it. The rhythm of her pumping lifeblood was aligning itself with another. *It's the Summer Tree's heartbeat, in sync with mine.*

Alice took a breath as she straightened, finding a measure of control over this strange new connection. She peered into the gaps between the trees, and where before she'd only seen shadows, now she saw the ripple of every blade of grass and the grains of crusted bark on every tree; she saw it all. She was nature itself, and it was free and exhilarating and—

Her smile froze. There was something odd about the fall of light and shadow in the shrubs opposite the black door. A shadow where there ought not to be. Forehead lined in confusion, Alice picked her way closer. There was something partially hidden by loose brushwood. She flicked her fingers and the camouflaging branches and twigs rolled away.

Gabriel Whitmore lay dead in the grass.

One arm was outstretched and his tie was strewn over the ground. His mouth was slack, his face pale, and his dark blue eyes stared up at Alice, unseeing. Her stomach lurched in horror. *How?*

A shiver of cold dread ran down her spine and she backed away. Whoever had done this – were they still in here with her? Her mind raced, trying to piece together who else might have had access to this testing place, but she found herself unable to turn away from the sight of Whitmore's glassy eyes.

Behind her, there was a shuffling noise in the undergrowth and she froze. Were there animals in here? She spun around, straining to listen to the sounds of the forest, but there were so few. The gentle swaying of leaves, the occasional groan of wood, maybe, but nothing more significant.

And yet. There it was again. A crack.

She waited, eyes searching, her legs ready to spring away. Nothing. She straightened up and rolled her shoulders to ease some of the tension in her back. Taking a quiet, steadying breath, she turned to the black door, wrapped in the arms of the tree branch. Time to go.

Crack.

Alice spun around.

Reuben Risdon was standing beneath an elm tree, one hand resting against the trunk. She stared at him in shocked silence. He made no move to approach; he studied her face from a distance.

'What are you . . .?' she began, trailing away when he pushed himself off from the elm.

Her spine straightened and her hands bunched into wary fists at her side. Risdon moved past her, his shabby blue greatcoat sweeping out behind him. Alice watched as he bent to his haunches and examined Gabriel's body, eyes narrowed in concentration. Still crouching, he shifted round, the brushwood crunching beneath his feet, and peered up at Alice.

'He was a good man,' he said, gesturing at the body. His fingers reached out for Whitmore's skewed tie and placed it neatly in its proper position. He smoothed the silk down with a sigh.

'Isn't that . . . tampering with the scene of a crime?' said Alice, a harsh rasp to her voice.

'Yes,' he said, turning towards her, his expression curious, 'but I have always believed in dignity for the dead. Do you begrudge him that?'

Alice said nothing. What was Risdon doing here? What did he want, and where had he come from?

'What do you think happened to him?' she asked, trying desperately to bring herself up to speed.

'Oh, I think he met his death here in the forest,' said Risdon, his grey eyes shining.

She frowned at the obviousness of this statement as he laid his palm on Gabriel's forehead . . . and within seconds, the body disintegrated to ash and dust. Alice's throat tightened, and she moved an inch backwards to the door.

'Ashes to ashes,' said Risdon, rising and brushing his hands on his coat. 'Isn't that what they say?'

'What are you doing here?' she whispered over the buzzing noise in her skull.

His slanted eyebrows lifted just a fraction. 'I came to congratulate you.' He glanced at the chalice lying sideways on the stump. 'You passed. Allow me a moment's pride.'

Pride? Why should he be proud?

Alice stared at him, afraid to blink in case he moved any closer. 'Tell me . . . what happened to Gabriel Whitmore,' she said, her voice faint.

He tilted his head, observing her. 'I told you, Alice. He met his Death in the forest.'

A great shuddering breath rushed from her lungs as he stood there, drinking in the sight of her. Her throat was too tight. Her brain functions had dimmed. She was only aware of the pulse of her own heartbeat roaring in her ears.

'Are you . . . *his Death*?' she whispered.

He nodded, the look in his eyes solemn. A long silence fell between them, and when he spoke again, something in the atmosphere had changed.

'Hello, Alice,' he murmured gently. 'We were never introduced properly when we first met – but I know who you are now.'

She shook her head and took another step backwards. Her hand, behind her, hunted desperately for the door. It was locked.

'Do you know who I am?' he asked.

'Reuben Risdon,' she hissed.

'Yes,' he said. 'And no.'

It couldn't be true. It couldn't be true.

Her brown eyes searched his face. The face of the monster who had killed her best friend, who had warned her about Crowley's lies, who had once asked her to work alongside him, who had offered to protect her – who had made her a figure of death.

'*Tuoni*,' she breathed. '*You're Tuoni?*'

36

'It's been a long time since anyone has called me by that name,' he said, his eyes raking her face with interest.

'How can you be . . .?' Alice whispered, the tension in her head growing so tight her skull felt cramped. She swallowed and shook her head. 'Why are you here?'

'I wanted you to know me,' he said, regarding her with curiosity. 'Before the end.'

'Before you free your soul and destroy the Rookery?' she managed.

How? How can he be Tuoni? This man who she despised. She wanted to run, to get away from him, but her legs were leaden with disgust and horror. Her chest was too tight, a heavy weight pressing against her ribs, squeezing her senseless.

'No.' A small, regretful sigh escaped Risdon – Tuoni – as he turned his attention to a crooked elm tree. 'Before *you* free my soul and destroy the Rookery.'

She stared at him as he peered at the tree's trunk. Panic clawed its way up her throat and she fought to tamp it down.

'I'm Mielikki's heir,' she said. 'I'm not going to destroy the city. I'm going to save it.'

He turned back to her, a faint smile on his face. 'You're *my* heir.

You're Death. You take life,' he said simply. 'It's just what you are. People worry over whether their souls are good or bad, how stained they are with sin. But your soul . . . is Death. Good or bad doesn't matter. Death takes everyone. And *like* Death, your soul can cut through nightjar cords; your mother knew that before you were born.

'I begged her,' he said, his voice soft. 'I warned her you wouldn't be able to help yourself. Infants have no self-control.' He paused and turned away, shaking his head. 'You are still that infant, Alice. I knew it the moment I saw your soul escape in Marble Arch. You lost control.'

He moved back to the elm and stroked one hand down the bark. Alice watched in mounting dread as flames sparked from his fingertips and he trailed fire across the rough wood. What was he doing?

'House Ilmarinen?' she whispered. The House of fire. Crowley's house.

'House Tuoni, I think,' he said with a wan smile. He snapped a blackened branch from the tree and crumbled it between his fingers. 'All four Houses have destructive gifts at their heart. Fire is death.' He tilted his head to observe her from an angle. 'If you had spent your time embracing who you are rather than resisting it, you might have discovered gifts untold.'

'Death isn't a gift,' she snapped, her eyes flashing with sudden fury.

He pushed away from the tree. 'Not so,' he said, and there was an earnest tone in his voice. 'It can be the kindest gift of all, in the right circumstances. Death can be merciful.'

'And vengeful,' she said, her words hitting the air between them like bullets. 'And harrowing. And unfair. And—'

'Yes.' He nodded his agreement. 'Those things too.'

'You killed my best friend,' she said, a knot of rage unfurling behind her ribs, filling her up and making her tremble.

'You killed the only woman I'd ever loved,' he responded, his voice like a whip-crack through the forest.

Alice flinched as though he'd slapped her. 'I was a *baby*,' she spat. 'It wasn't my fault.'

He sighed. 'Nor was your friend's mine. It was simply necessary.'

Necessary. Because if he hadn't found a way to send Alice's soul back to her body, it would have gone on to destroy the Rookery. Jen had died for Alice's sins.

'I became a killer so that you wouldn't have to,' he said.

'But I am anyway,' she replied roughly. 'You said it yourself. I killed Leda. This is what I am.' She knelt and snatched up the dandelion on the log. Holding it out, she watched as it crumpled and rotted to a fine powder. Staring at him, she reached out for the lowest branches of an oak tree, wrapping her hand around them. The bark curled and flaked away, and the branches rotted to dust. 'Death,' she said, wiping the decayed remains on her jeans.

Tension thickened the air between them and they fell silent – assessing each other, waiting to see who made the next move. Fire had raced up the length of the elm tree, jumping from leaf to leaf. Orange flickers danced in her eyes.

'My job,' she said, 'at the Magellan Institute—'

'I wanted you there,' he said. 'I left the advert on Sasha Hamilton's desk. I knew she'd pass it on.'

Alice's stomach clenched and her mouth ran dry. 'When did Reid realize she was working for you?' she asked hoarsely.

He smiled. 'It took her longer than I'd expected. When I pushed for her to shift her focus, she grew suspicious.'

'You wanted to know whether the three-part soul existed,' said Alice.

'No, of course not,' he said with a wry look in his eye. 'I'm Tuoni. I know the make-up of souls. Catherine was asked to begin researching how to *split* a soul without the subject knowing.'

She searched his face. The gentle flicker of orange flames from the burning elm cast eerie shadows across his jaw.

'And why would you want to know that?' she asked, her voice faint.

'I think you know,' he murmured.

She blinked rapidly, the hammering of her heart drowning out the crackle of fire consuming the branches above his head.

'Spell it out for me,' she said.

He glanced up at the flames racing up the length of the elm and back to Alice. 'My nightjar is keeping my soul in the tree – and you are capable of severing nightjar cords.' He gave her a thoughtful look, as though they were discussing something inane and small. 'Souls are surprisingly fragile things,' he said. 'Trauma can weaken them. And every time yours was freed, it chipped away just a little more at the cord tying my nightjar to the Summer Tree.'

Alice held her breath, trying to compute what he was saying. Every time she'd told Kuu to 'go' and sent out her itse-soul to defend her from an attacker, she'd released her soul – that was true. But it had never gone far. He had to be lying.

'Tom was working for you,' she rasped.

He nodded. 'In a way. He was working for Marianne, and everything Marianne does is for Tuoni.'

'Those attacks . . . my soul escaping . . . It never happened anywhere near the Summer Tree. I didn't even see the nightjar until a few days ago. I couldn't have—'

434

'You couldn't have helped yourself,' said Risdon. 'As soon as you bound yourself to the tree, you created a pathway. A direct line from your nightjar, and your soul, to my prison.'

Alice remembered, suddenly, the first time she'd met Cecil and discussed the binding draught with him. He'd framed it as an honour to link your life force to the life force of a tree, but she'd considered it servitude; members were forced to take the greatest care with it because if the tree was damaged, the binding passed on that damage to you. Its benefits were given with conditions attached to guarantee your service. But Cecil had said it was a one-way street. Members of the House couldn't damage the tree in return – otherwise every time someone linked to the tree died of old age, their death would damage it. But they didn't. The tree was too powerful to accept such insignificant damage.

'No,' she said. 'The binding draught doesn't work like that. The link between the tree and the members of—'

'You are not a member of House Mielikki,' Risdon said softly. 'You *are* House Mielikki, just like your mother. Your connection to the Summer Tree runs deep. It's in your blood.'

Alice stared at him, her mouth dry. All this time, she'd been blessed with the benefits she'd received from the Summer Tree, unaware that – with her Mielikki blood – she was passing back something of herself, her own damage, to the tree.

'Every time you strengthened the link' – he nodded at the empty binding draught chalice – 'you chipped away at my bonds.'

'But Holly,' she said desperately. 'She died because the tree was *already* growing; the draught was too powerful for her. But that was before I'd linked myself to it at all, so I couldn't have—'

'Your first test almost killed you,' he said. 'Your soul suffered a trauma while you were standing in Mielikki's House, a corridor

435

away from the replica of her tree – its anchor. You were so close to it, and you were so weak.'

Alice's eyes searched his face. 'But I—'

'Infants have no self-control,' he repeated with a grim smile. '*You* are the one who has been liberating my soul from Leda's trap. You're the reason the Summer Tree has grown. And now – the bonds are so fragile, Alice – you've had the final binding draught. It's time. I want my soul returned to me.'

Alice pressed her hands against her ears to muffle his words. No. She was Mielikki's heir. She was going to save the Rookery. People had died because of this. People had . . . people . . .

She sucked in a ragged breath, the truth striking her so suddenly that she swayed on her feet as though she'd taken a blow to the temple. He was right. She was Death. She had tried to run from it, but there was no escaping who and what she was. People had died because she'd tried.

'Leda won't forgive you,' Alice murmured after a long moment. 'If you go to her, in the moors, she won't forgive you for using what she did to destroy the Rookery.'

'I'll take that chance,' he said. 'I'm tired of this existence. Please. Let me rest, Alice.'

He flicked his fingers and the burning elm flamed more brightly. Smoke peeled away from the canopy, billowing through the air and leaving an acrid taste in the back of Alice's throat. Powerful heat pressed against her face, stinging her cheeks, but still Alice stood in silence, watching.

The fire jumped the distance between the trees, snagging the leaves of the neighbouring poplar . . . then the oak . . . and the hornbeam at her back.

'Alice,' said Risdon, his weary voice carrying through the trees. '*Run.*'

37

Her boots kicked up soil as she plunged through the under-growth. Fire swept through the trees behind her, consuming the dense canopies. Twisting columns of flame stretched into the glowing skies. Leaves turned to ash. Scorched branches were tossed from the sizzling inferno. Expanding pillars of smoke pumped out above the trees, a churning grey smudge against the gold-streaked sky.

Alice threw an arm across her face to protect it from the searing heat at her back. The smoke drifted down to blanket the forest floor, obscuring the safe passageways between trees. She stumbled through a copse. *Wrong turn. Shit. Stay ahead of the fire.* She swung back round, searching for a gap. The air rippled with heat haze, and Alice's eyes stung, but she ploughed onwards, darting past a smouldering cedar. Spiked brambles whipped her skin and pulled at her hair, but she quickened her pace. The fire had caught her up. It bloomed out between the trees, latching on, spreading . . . *Wildfire.*

Embers rained down from above, a shower of glinting cinders hitting the brushwood. Alice leapt aside with a gasp. A spark flared to life at her feet, snagging her bootlace. She stamped it out with her other foot and swayed back and forth, light-headed with smoke. The forest tilted around her, a smear of orange and gold on a dark canvas. *Head for the shadows*, she imagined Crowley shouting at her. *There's safety in the shadows.* Her footsteps slow, she lurched onwards. Shadows. Find the shadows.

'There's nowhere left for you,' shouted Risdon, raising his voice above the crackle and hiss of flames.

A scorched maple branch thudded onto the ground at his feet. He kicked it aside and stepped closer.

The fire had torched the trees and left blackened skeletons behind. The flames had amputated their crooked limbs, and their kindled remains lay in tumbling piles over the forest floor. The fire consumed them from within, like a parasite. Everywhere was dancing flame and thick, funnelling smoke. Sweat beaded Alice's face and stuck her jumper to her damp skin. The air was too hot to breathe. She maintained her wary stance, staring at him as he approached.

'Look at you,' he said. 'Refusing to be bowed by fire.'

Her muscles tensed. She swiped away the sweat dripping from her brow.

'Fighting to save a city that doesn't know you. You have Leda's bite.' A burning rowan tree shed its branches and smoking wood thumped to the ground between them. 'I think . . . in a different life . . .'

He shook his head and waved his hand. The fire flared brighter. The flames exploded outwards from the trees, their rippling peaks just inches from her skin. Risdon's face, painted by shadow and fire, stared through the flames with an eerie calm. He was untouched. The fire glanced off him. He flicked a finger, and the spitting flames roared and tightened around her. The air swelled with blistering heat, walling her in from all sides. She couldn't breathe; the boiling air flayed her throat and ignited her lungs.

What did he want? To burn her alive? Cauterize his wounds by destroying the child who should never have existed? But that wouldn't bring Leda back. This attack was senseless; he'd never be . . .

Her thoughts skidded to a halt. An attack. Just like the others. Tom's attacks hadn't been senseless; their purpose had been to threaten her so that she'd unleash a piece of her soul to cut down her attacker. Risdon wanted her to fight back. He wanted her to unleash her soul on him like a bomb . . . but her soul would sever his nightjar's cord. Finally and completely. Alice shuddered. She could *not* send Kuu away. Her soul couldn't save her this time.

She dropped to her knees, one arm raised to shield her watering eyes. She scrabbled through the hot brushwood, searching for something she could use – a weapon, anything – and found a thick branch, one end blackened like charcoal. She launched it at Risdon. As it struck the fire it disintegrated to ash. He smiled grimly at her and she shook it off. Her brain scrambled for possibilities. *What can I do? What can I do?* She groped for something else to hurl through the flames. But her hand caught the edge of the fire and she yanked it back with a yelp. It was getting closer. *Think.*

Roots. The roots were underground. Hidden from the fire. She plunged her hands into the warm earth. Scraping mud aside, she burrowed deeper with her fingers. Her chest tightened with apprehension. She dropped her head onto her chest, ignoring the sizzle and pop of the flames only inches away, and sent every ounce of concentration into her arms. She pushed her will through her wrists; it spread across her palms and seeped into her tingling fingers. Damp grains of mud coated her hands, caked into the lines of her skin. Thick wads of soil were embedded under her nails. She rolled clumps of moist earth between her fingers. Mielikki's soil. Mielikki's trees. The soil began to vibrate. Particles ricocheting off particles, a wave of movement rippled underground. Sweat – from the heat, from concentration – dripped into Alice's eyes, but she maintained her focus. *Move.*

Outside the ring of fire, tree roots erupted from the soil. They smashed through the surface, raining clumps of muck as they wound upwards. A tangle of creeping roots slid through the undergrowth and through the fire. Flames snagged the bark but the roots poured ceaselessly across the forest, with just one destination: Risdon.

A flexible vine whipped around his knees, pinning his legs together. A root curled around his chest. *Squeeze.* The root pinched around his ribs. He puffed out his chest to fight against the pressure. Like a moving spider's web, the snarl of roots wrapped their burning arms around him and hugged him tight. The fire around Alice stuttered and she raised her head, a spark of hope lighting in her eyes.

But Risdon wrenched his arms out to his sides and the roots disintegrated. *No!* Charcoal and ash flittered to the ground like snow. Ash streaked his face and hair, tinting his skin statue-grey. He snapped his fingers and the fire rushed closer, caging Alice. Fury and fear descended and she yanked her hands from the soil. The ends of her hair curled as the heat drew in.

'You have two options,' he shouted over the flames. 'Fight me – the only way you can win. Or die.'

Save her life by sending out her soul to attack him . . . or die and her soul would be released straight to the moors – harmlessly stepping into its natural home, where he couldn't use it? He was wrong. There was only one option. She would not release her soul to attack him and his bonds – she would not destroy the Rookery; she would not risk the lives of those who would die when it crumbled beneath them; she would not fight him. She would die. And with her death, his chances of releasing his soul would die too, and his chances of reuniting with Leda. Without Leda, he had nothing to live for. But Alice had something worth dying for.

This was it.

She put aside all thoughts of fighting and crouched on her knees. Sweat slid down the back of her neck. *Don't think of the fire. Ignore the heat.* She groped for something else to focus on, to distract her. She thought of the pictures she'd seen in history books, of the victims of the Pompeii eruption, ashen and huddled in their death poses. Would House Mielikki block off this forest entirely, or would they one day open the door to find the fire doused and Alice here, in just this position? She thought of Joan of Arc and Thomas Becket, and the World War One poet Wilfred Owen. Martyrs to a cause. Could she claim martyrdom? What was Owen's famous poem? *Dulce . . .*

The fire licked at the sole of her boots and she pulled her legs in closer. Her head nodded dizzily. *No oxygen.*

Dulce et decorum est pro patria mori. That was it. *It is sweet and fitting to die for one's country.* Sarcasm on Owen's part. But now she was going to follow him down that rabbit hole. Only, no one would ever know what she had done, or what she had sacrificed. There would be no blue plaque outside Coram House for her, no Rookery-issued medal to console her loved ones with tales of her bravery.

She thought of her parents, who would never hear her voice again, who would wonder why she had never returned home. Maybe they would assume she had found a more exciting life than the one they had offered – that she had finally set them aside to pursue her glamorous new life in the Rookery.

She thought of Crowley. Crowley – who would be furious with her for dying, for allowing this to happen, for being tricked, for leaving. And proud, too, she hoped. Helena and Leda's actions had almost destroyed the Rookery. And now Alice's *in*action would save it. She would right both their wrongs.

The flames crested against her cheek and Alice clenched her jaw to keep from crying out. Something fluttered against her neck and she flinched, expecting pain. A gentle churring in her ear shushed her fears. Kuu. The tension in Alice's chest unspooled and she reached for the bird with a choked sob. Kuu's head nuzzled her face. Her pale wings shone brightly, untouched by fire. Kuu was a nightjar, not a phoenix, and nothing could harm her – not flame, nor anything else.

Falling embers scorched holes in Alice's trousers, singeing her legs. She hissed at the sudden burning and Kuu flapped her wings restlessly.

'Stay,' Alice murmured. 'Stay with me till the end.'

Risdon stood on the other side of the rippling fire, like a demon in the flames. The fire swept nearer and set her sleeve alight. She desperately batted it out and pressed her arm into the soil to soothe the pain. She closed her eyes against the brightness.

'Let go,' he said. 'Dying for the Rookery is not necessary. Tell your little nightjar to save you.'

Alice frowned, her conviction wavering in the throb of pain from her arm. *No.* She gritted her teeth.

'Nightjar,' he called. 'I'm talking to you. I might have been your master, once. You sense me, don't you? You know what I am.' Kuu's head darted up, listening, and Alice groaned. 'Your job is to protect her. And protect the world from her. Tonight, you can do both. You don't need to compromise.'

'Don't – don't listen to him,' Alice managed.

'You can save her if you leave,' said Risdon. 'It won't be her soul that destroys the Rookery, it will be the Summer Tree. She won't be responsible. *You* won't be responsible.'

The white nightjar tipped its head sideways as though considering his words. Could she really hear him?

'Kuu, no,' Alice whispered. 'Don't.'

'Save her,' said Risdon.

And then he brought both hands together, and the fire took her. Alice's trousers ignited, the fire eating through cotton. Hot spikes of pain drove through her skin. Her mouth fell open in a silent scream, and her body began to spasm and buck as waves of boiling agony swept through her. Alice's fingers clenched and a soft moan slipped from her clamped lips. She was too far gone to think, to have awareness of anything beyond her agony.

One eye slid open. Panting, her cheek pressed against the soil, she scanned sideways for her nightjar. For comfort. The glowing cord looped to her wrist was . . . too thin. She scrabbled to reach for it, to pull Kuu closer. But fire engulfed her jumper and the cord slid from her fingers. Trembling, she gave herself up to the pain.

A bolt of lightning slammed into her spine and she snapped backwards with a gasp. *No, Kuu!* Her breath rasped out from burning lungs – and with it, something *else*. Her very essence – potent energy and ravenous darkness – poured out from her body. Like motes of glittering dust, she hovered in the air, lost to all sensation except one: hunger. The steady pulse of warmth nearby drew her closer and she stretched herself wide in yearning. Warmth. Life. Close by. She reached for it . . . but a brightly glowing rope swung across her path, barring her progress. Every gleaming particle of her soul vibrated. A wave of raw power surged forward, slicing through the incandescent barrier . . . A nightjar shrieked . . . not her own. Not Kuu. *Tuoni's nightjar* – its cord had been *severed*.

And then a fluttering of pale wings wafted pockets of air and she spiralled backwards. Kuu cried out and Alice shrank back . . . back . . . shrank *back*.

Alice exhaled sharply and collapsed onto her side. Her eyes flew open and the forest loomed over her, trees blackened with charcoal and soot. The fire . . . was gone. Every flame doused. No fire . . . no Risdon. She was alone. Alone with her burns and her blistered skin. She panted softly through the pain. *Can't stay here. Got to . . . got to go.* Alice pushed herself upright with a scream of agony. The skin on her back stretched and tore open. Her arms trembled but she increased the pressure and forced herself to her feet just as Kuu swooped down to settle on her shoulder.

'What have you done?' she moaned, as the ground began to rumble beneath her.

38

House Mielikki was empty when she staggered along the corridor. Bursting out onto the pavement, she swayed groggily at the sudden city noise and crisp breeze. One hand grappled for support and latched on to the House's botanical wall, her fingers slipping through the gaps. The knitted branches of willow, cherry blossom and horse chestnut, colours shifting, buds and flowers blossoming, were a wall of constant motion.

But in her hands, the branches hardened and the buds withered. Pink and white petals curled and dropped to the ground, discarded. The plants wilted, growth ceased and the branches cracked under the weight. Before her eyes, the wall began to decay. Alice snatched her hand away in alarm and stumbled across the road on leaden legs.

Get to Coram House. Sanctuary. Before the Summer Tree could—

The road's cobbles shuddered and clacked together. She lunged for the safety of the pavement, hissing at the flare of pain in her back. The noise was barely noticeable at first, but the thudding stone grew louder until a cacophony of sound followed her along the street.

Get to the door and travel away. She flung the door open in a panic. The pavement lurched and threw her off balance. She careened sideways, her shoulder slamming into a stone wall and robbing her of breath. She shook her head to sharpen her focus and pushed off from the stone. But before she could hasten through the open doorway, the entire pavement juddered and dropped several feet, sinking deeper into the Rookery's foundations. A yawning gap opened up between the road and pavement and Alice scrambled to avoid it. She grabbed the edge of the doorway and hauled herself inside the void with a wince.

She watched in horror as the pavement shook. A hole opened up in the centre. Bricks, stone, concrete . . . The hole sucked everything inside, widening the edges, growing broader. A sink-hole. The tree . . . Tuoni had taken his soul, and the tree was growing. Subsidence was beginning to disturb the city's foundations. The Rookery . . .

In the distance, a siren began to wail.

Alice shivered and slammed the door shut, taking refuge in the void.

'Cygnus Street,' she shouted. She fixed the destination in her mind's eye. The derelict building opposite Coram House, its black door littered with fly posters belonging to the Fellowship. The door that had been her gateway to so many other doors in the city.

She groped the darkness expectantly, searching for the door handle to take her home. Blackness enveloped her, the chill wind biting at her burns. Too cold. It didn't soothe her wounds; it exacerbated them.

'Cygnus Street,' she pleaded. 'Come on. I can't . . . I need . . .'

Her energy was too depleted to think straight. And so she stood numbly in the darkness, like a lost soul, with no idea what to do next. The door wouldn't open. She cast out again, searching for the door handle. Nothing. Helpless frustration ballooned in her throat. *I just want to get home. Please.*

'Cygnus Street,' she whispered.

Nothing.

She pressed her fingertips to her eyelids while she tried to think what to do. There was another door she could try one street away, an old teashop. Their door was always open for custom. Alice exhaled shakily and pictured the entrance, the solid wooden door engraved with a bronze plaque, *Caddison's Twenty-Four-Hour Tea Rooms*. The metallic doorknob bloomed from the darkness and Alice grabbed it as though it might disappear. She twisted the knob and hurtled through the doorway. The door fell shut behind her and she limped through the streets, skin throbbing, to make her way home.

A stitch jabbed the muscle below her ribs and she pushed a hand into the gap as she reached the end of the road. Not far now. Fifty metres or so once she rounded the . . . She stopped dead. Her hand fell away. Shock heaved her stomach and slackened her mouth.

'No,' she moaned quietly. 'No . . .'

And then she was running, despite the pain. Past the stunned people standing around, and those knee-deep in rubble, shifting bricks with purpose. Past the wreckage of the houses she'd grown so familiar with. Past the yawning gap that had once been the site of the neighbouring buildings. Past the rift in the city's foundations that had swallowed the derelict building whole. Coram House . . . Thank God! It was still standing – though half the street had gone. Collapsed. What if one of her friends had been—

The door to Coram House flew open before she had the chance to knock. Crowley bore down on her, anguish written on his face. Her shoulders sank with relief. He was alive. He snatched her into his arms and slammed the door shut behind them.

'Where have you been?' he shouted into her hair, clutching her tight against him. She flinched in his arms and he released her, regret on his face. 'I thought you were . . .' His apology trailed away as he noted the singed and blackened clothing. He frowned at her, his eyes searching. 'You're hurt.'

She winced. 'My back.'

He moved to inspect her, but she turned to block his view.

'What have you . . .' His face drained of colour. 'Burns? How?'

She shook her head. 'It doesn't matter. Crowley, the street outside.'

'Gone,' he said hoarsely.

It was only then that she noticed the smudges of dust on his face, the grit in his hair, the ripped trousers, the white shirt stained with dirt, the bloody gash on his thigh.

'Help is coming,' he said roughly. 'I've been doing all I can. Four survivors so far, but . . .' His eyes glazed.

'I'll help,' she said.

His attention snapped back to her. 'No. You're injured. It feels like things have settled for now – you should take the opportunity to go up and rest. Are they burns from ordinary fire?'

She nodded. 'I think so.'

'Bad?' He looked at her, concern in his eyes. 'May I see?'

'I've taken the final draught. I think they'll heal quickly.'

He didn't look convinced. '*I* can heal them.'

'You're busy,' she said. 'I can wait.'

'Don't be—'

'The draught,' she croaked. 'I've taken it. It will help.' Her skin shrieked with pain, but she set it aside. What right had she to claim injury when there were people out there who might never . . . 'Are Sasha and—'

'They're helping the coordinated response. Jude has gone to check his forge and to help the efforts there. Sasha and August are four streets away.' His face softened. 'Show me your back.'

Alice shook her head. 'It can wait. You go, and I'll . . .' She trailed away.

He hesitated before nodding sharply. 'Then please – rest. Sleep, if you can.'

'I can't sleep while people are out there—'

'Please, Alice,' he said wearily. 'For once. Please don't fight. None of the rest of us are injured. Rest now and you'll be better placed to help later if . . .'

Crowley trailed away. If there *was* a later.

He turned on his heel and hurried back out to the street. She slumped down on the stairs and put her head in her hands.

'Are you sleeping?'

'No,' she said, her eyes snapping open in the dark. Shit. How long had she been out? She'd showered the soot and sweat off her skin and meant to sit on the edge of the mattress for only a minute. Just to catch her breath before she ignored his instructions and made her way outside to help.

It was eerily silent.

'What time is it?'

'Two o'clock in the morning,' he replied. 'Things have calmed for now, but—'

'How many streets have been lost?' she asked, sitting up with a wince.

'No official figure has been released yet.'

'And unofficially?'

His face tensed. 'Many. Half of Oxford Circus has gone.'

She quailed and sagged back onto the pillows. The cotton rubbed against her burns and she inhaled sharply.

'May I see *now*?' he asked.

She nodded.

He waited expectantly, and she shuffled to the edge of the bed. After a moment's pause, she unbuttoned the shirt she had borrowed from him. She slipped it over her shoulders, exposing her back. Behind her, she heard his breathing pause at the sight. She'd seen the raw blotches, sticky with plasma, in the bathroom mirror; they were red and angry and agonizing. When the cool water had sluiced over them, her sudden tears had mingled with the shower water rinsing dirt from her skin.

'You said you could wait, but Alice, these are—' He stilled. 'How did it happen?' he murmured.

Falteringly, she told him all that had unfolded since she had left them to return to the university. He maintained a stony silence when she told him of Whitmore's death and of Risdon – Tuoni – waiting for her in one of the House's portal forests.

He laid a cool hand on her back and she sucked in a breath at his touch. The sting began to fade under his palm and she relaxed to his ministrations as she recounted her confrontation with Risdon. At the mention of the fire, his hands tensed and he paused for several long moments before he continued. She considered whether to remain silent on her part in the Summer Tree's growth, but it tumbled out with everything else.

He healed her back, and she told him of her nightjar's desperate act to save her, and of what they must now do to re-link the Summer Tree and the Rookery Stone – to stabilize the tree and the city itself in the absence of Tuoni's soul. But she was silent as to the particular role she would have to play, saying nothing of the final step she alone would have to take. He couldn't know what she had planned. If she could just have this short time with him to sustain her through it, it would be enough. Sitting here in the dark, remembering the feel of Crowley's gentle hands on her back. This would be enough.

'Tell me again,' he said quietly, 'what the book – the one Leda annotated – said about the final step. How can we expect to know if it has worked?'

She hesitated, stiffening under his hands. Was she imagining the disquiet in his tone?

'Tree becomes stone, and stone becomes tree,' she said.

'But what does it actually mean?' he murmured. 'Isn't it simply a flowery way of saying they join together?'

'I think its meaning is literal,' she said as his fingers skated along the back of her neck and paused. 'I think . . . the tree roots have to be petrified. Turned to stone, so that the Summer Tree and the Rookery Stone can be fused completely. Each . . .' She searched for the words. 'Becomes the other.'

'In doing this,' he said quietly, 'we're going to see something that only Mielikki and Pellervoinen have ever seen before. Just we two, and them.'

Silence fell between them, and she forced herself not to break it. She would not risk the fragile tension in the room by revealing the truth to him: that she wasn't only going to bear witness to a remarkable event – she was going to sacrifice her nightjar cord to make it happen. And once she was done, her soul was too danger-ous to remain in the city. The Sulka Moors was the only place fit for her.

'I know,' Crowley ventured in a hoarse voice, 'that chaos exists outside this room. Outside this house. But for once – just for one night – I would like to close the door on it.'

'Me too,' she said. 'But Crowley—' Her words fell away at the press of his lips against her bare shoulder.

Her breathing stilled. Every thought in her head dissipated. Her focus sharpened to the feel of his mouth tracing a path across her skin. His fingers slid down her spine, leaving tingles in their wake, and she shivered.

'Alice?' he murmured.

She twisted on the mattress to face him. His eyes caught hers and held her in place. She flushed at the intensity in his heated gaze. The mattress springs creaked as he leaned closer, his dark hair swinging down over his forehead. His warm breath puffed out across her skin and she met him halfway. His lips pressed against hers, once, twice – chaste kisses, checking this was invited. Alice reached up to sweep his hair back and her fingers settled at the nape of his neck, pulling him closer.

He inhaled sharply and opened his mouth to her tongue. The warmth thrumming between them ignited. She pulled him backwards, their mouths unbroken and desperate. His tongue slid inside, exploring, while she reached for his shirt buttons. She arched upwards, her fingers struggling to free him of the shirt. They twisted and pulled but there was no give in the cotton.

'Crowley,' she murmured. 'Your fucking buttons are stuck.'

He rumbled with laughter and pressed a quick kiss to her temple before leaning back and pulling it over his head. He tossed it aside and reclaimed her mouth. She gasped at the feel of his hand sliding up her thigh, reaching for her underwear. One finger hooked around the cotton and he tugged it gently – but the hem tore and he swore quietly.

'I was aiming,' he panted, 'for a little more sophistication.'

She pulled him down and kissed him hard before easing her hips off the bed so that he could tug her underwear down her legs.

He made to move down her body but she grabbed his arms.

'No,' she breathed. 'I don't want to wait.'

Crowley's eyes glittered in the darkness, his pupils liquid ink. He kissed her deeply, his tongue lighting fires in her fluttering chest while she surged beneath him like a wave. She wanted to drown in him. Death by drowning was better than the death she had planned. She squeezed her eyes shut and pushed away every dark thought. No. *Just for tonight, let me have this. Please, let me just have this.*

Alice moved her hands to the buttons of his trousers, and they were dispatched with speed. He rose on his forearms above her.

'You're sure?' he asked, his voice ragged.

She stretched up to kiss him and slid her knees apart, pushing herself against him. This was the only thing she was sure of. This one thing was all she needed in the world.

Crowley's head dropped forward, his breath on her collarbone. He positioned himself between her legs and she urged him on with gentle pushes and pulls. He sank into her body with a gasp and they began to move together.

And without words, she tried to say her goodbyes – with soft sighs and hitched breaths, pressing him into her forever so that she had this one good moment to take with her.

39

There were no Runners. Those manning the barriers outside had vanished, and they had met none on the stairs. Perhaps they'd deserted their posts at the same time as their commanding officer, or perhaps they'd begun to escape the Rookery like many others. The hairs on Alice's arms lifted with suspicion at their absence, but in the end it was irrelevant; if there was a trap waiting for them, they had no choice but to walk into it with their eyes open.

Glass crunched beneath Alice's feet as she stepped into the devastated atrium. Cool, sterile daylight poured through the shattered ceiling, casting harsh shadows against the walls, the dark outlines of rubble, heaps of broken wooden shelves, piles of books and broken flagstones. Everything was under a layer of glittering glass fragments. So much destruction.

Alice peered up at the towering tree, studying the creaking sway of branches and the fountain spray of tapered leaves. She moved closer, clambering over its wooden limbs to stroke the gnarled bark. Her palm smarted, tingles trailing through her arms, and she let go a trembling breath. She closed her eyes, imagining Tuoni's soul inside, trapped like a butterfly under a glass. Long gone now, and his pale nightjar too.

'Alice?' Crowley murmured.

She turned to him as though sleepwalking and withdrew from the tree. Crowley was standing a few feet away, watching her with concern. Their gazes locked for several seconds, and then Alice shivered and hoisted Tilda's book from under her arm. She flipped it open and devoted her attention to it, forcing her emotions behind a wall. They had a job to do.

'The corridor I saw Whitmore coming from,' she said, spinning round, clutching the book, 'was that one.' She jerked her head at a narrow opening that led from the atrium.

Alice glanced down at the book again. There was a hand-drawn image of the chamber, scratched out in thin lines of ink. It showed a small enclosed room, the stone walls curved and something that had once been indecipherable in the centre – but which she now recognized as the Rookery Stone.

The rubble of broken flagstones shifted under Alice's feet as she marched off towards the corridor. Crowley followed close behind, reaching to steady her when her foot slipped into a crack.

Heaped books littered the tight space but trailed away as they ventured further in. The sunlight didn't stretch far enough to light the deepest end of the corridor. The walls either side were roughly hewn and poor at reflecting the little light they did have, and so they were fumbling about in the dark.

'I can try to call the fireflies,' said Alice.

Something flared, and warm flames cut through the shadows to illuminate Crowley's face. 'No need,' he said quietly. He held a ball of fire, cupped in his palm.

He traced the light over both walls, searching for an opening, or a doorway – some secret entrance to the chamber created by his ancestor. He moved back and forth along the corridor, crouching down to the flagstones and up again to the ceiling. It was a painstaking process.

Their breaths filled the small space, adding to the insufferable warmth created by the flames and the lack of air. Crowley's shirt-sleeves were rolled to his elbows, and his top button was open. Crouching down, his hair swung into his face. He swiped it from his eyes, taking care with the cupped flames, but it hung down again seconds later. Alice reached down to tuck his hair behind his ear, and he glanced up at her. She smiled at the echo of Crowley fixing her crown at midsummer – but his eyes narrowed and his expression suddenly grew serious.

'There,' he said, rising to point at the wall behind her.

She turned to examine the stone, but in the flickering glow she could see nothing.

'No bigger than a thumbnail,' he said, 'and so shallow it seems non-existent. It's Pellervoinen's mark – from his tapestry.' He leaned closer. 'Or is it?' He frowned, squinting at the wall. 'It could just be a scratch, from when they carved out this part of the corridor.'

Crowley squeezed his palm, and the flames winked out. In the darkness, she felt him running his hands along the wall, fingers questing. Then he took in a sharp breath that stiffened her spine.

'I can feel it,' he whispered. 'It's here.'

There was a spark of white light in the gloom, a glowing pin-prick on the stone wall. Alice watched, her skin prickling as the tiny grain of light was joined by another, and another, until there were thousands.

'What is it?' she said in awe.

She felt him shake his head in the dark. 'I don't know.'

The shining pinpricks suddenly grew stronger and larger until they formed a clear shape. Light bled from the outline of a door. They heard a grinding rasp of stone against stone, and the rectangular door shuddered open.

Crowley reached for Alice, but she had already taken a step towards the opening. Peering all around her, she crossed the threshold. She found herself in another corridor, this one sloping downwards.

'Are you sure?' asked Crowley, a cautious voice over her shoulder.

'Yes,' she said, and set off into the darkness. It was no brighter here. In fact, the shadows seemed to cling tighter. But she held both hands out, brushing the sides of the walls as she trudged slowly along the path.

'I can't create a flame,' said Crowley, frustrated. 'I think . . . Pellervoinen and Mielikki may have managed to block out the other legacies down here.'

Alice said nothing. The heat and energy she needed to carry out the final step would not be coming from a fire of Ilmarinen's making; it would be coming from her nightjar's cord – far more powerful.

They walked on in silence, following a winding journey below the tree and the courtyard until, finally, their footsteps gained an echo when they stepped into a wider space. This was the chamber – the stone room with curved walls drawn in the book. Except that, unlike in the drawing, the walls were threaded with tapered, winding roots. The Summer Tree had wrapped itself around the chamber walls and ceiling. It looped over the floor, disappearing below the stone and rising up elsewhere like two fabrics knitted together. If Mielikki and Pellervoinen really had loved each other, this room of inseparable legacies was the clearest expression of that love.

'The Lampyridae—' Crowley started in warning.

'They won't hurt you,' said Alice, turning as a drift of incandescent fireflies seeped towards him. Their glow lit the planes of his face, and he held out his hand in awe, watching as they settled like flames on his palm. A moment later, they floated off to hover lazily around the room, illuminating the strange chamber with their eerie light.

'There's the Rookery Stone,' said Alice, sliding carefully past a root to examine the centre of the room. It lay on the ground, cradled by a nest of roots. The ground was damp beneath it. Ground water?

'It looks every bit as ordinary as the London Stone, doesn't it?' she said.

Crowley shook his head, a flash of wonderment in his eyes.

'No,' he said in a ragged voice. 'Can't you see it?'

'See what?'

'The threads of light,' said Crowley, reaching down as though to caress the stone but stopping short. He swallowed hard and then moved off, staring at something Alice couldn't see. He hesitated before stroking the wall on the opposite side of the chamber.

'I think there's a door here,' he said. 'You really can't see the light?'

She shook her head.

'Threads of blue light,' he said quietly, 'surrounding the stone. They're weak, certainly – but they lead to this wall. If there's a door here I think they lead to a path out of the chamber – maybe to the void.'

Alice nodded. She stared at the stone, trying hard to see what Crowley saw – but to her, it was nothing more than a pockmarked monolith, smaller even than the London Stone and less impressive for it.

She moved closer to examine it, noting the way the Summer Tree's roots nestled it, but otherwise there was nothing holding it in place, no connection. It was strange in a room made so completely from their union. But of course, Leda and Helena had severed the connection. It must have looked very different decades ago.

As Alice stepped back, something crunched under her feet. She picked up a chunk of broken stone; it had a grain in the surface like wood. Her breath stilled, and she peered more closely at the roots nestling the stone. They . . . were broken. The tips at the ends were greyed, not like wood at all. Alice glanced at the stone fragment in her hand and dropped it back to the floor.

'They severed the link by snapping it,' she said to Crowley. 'The roots were petrified at the ends, connected to the stone, and they just . . . broke them. I doubt anyone else would have had the power to break Mielikki and Pellervoinen's magic but their heirs, but . . .' She trailed away.

Crowley moved closer, looking into her eyes as though to give her reassurance. 'Are you ready?' he asked.

'Yes,' she said, placing the book gently on the ground. She knew what she had to do, though she wasn't certain of the outcome. The book had made a vague reference to what Mielikki had done, but not why. Alice had had to reason it out herself. To petrify normal wood, it must be dead but not rotted. Mielikki had not sought to kill off her own tree. Instead, she had withered the Summer Tree's roots. An act that might otherwise have filled Alice with dread, but the Rookery was so unstable now that they no longer had anything to lose. It would be destroyed if they did nothing. This way, there was at least hope.

'Try not to lose your grip on the Rookery Stone,' said Alice. 'I think it will recognize you.'

He nodded and scrambled to position himself where he could lay his hand on the stone. There was symmetry to the plan – she would wither Mielikki's tree and he would push Pellervoinen's magic towards it. Together, they would begin to petrify the roots, turning them into stone until a final burst of energy was required to complete the process . . .

Alice took a shaky breath and crouched down on her knees. Shuffling to the nearest root, she hovered a hand above it, glanced at Crowley, nodded and pressed her palm against it.

A surge of raw energy thundered through her arm and she gasped as the sensation almost threw her off. The air crackled, and static lifted the ends of her hair. Pulsing waves of power throbbed through her body, unlike anything she'd ever felt before. Her bones vibrated with it, her neurons sparked and tingled and her blood sang. This was life and growth – wild and pure. Something shifted and creaked. The roots had slithered lower, their wooden arms cradling the stone tightly while Crowley tried to retain his connection with it.

Alice closed her eyes, forcing herself to focus on the rough bark beneath her palms. She imagined the tree's power beneath her dwindling as she forced it back. Pressing her fingers harder, she willed the root to shrivel. *It can't be allowed to rot.*

She opened her eyes and her stomach clenched. The root was as firm and vibrant as ever. Gritting her teeth, she rose up on her knees to gain the leverage needed to push harder. *Come on*, she ordered. *Wither. Shrink back.*

Nothing happened.

Sweat dusted her forehead as she tried again. And again. But nothing worked.

'I don't understand,' she said, helpless. This was Mielikki's tree. Alice was a Wyndham, and a Westergard, and a Mielikki too. She had taken the final binding draught to link herself to the Summer Tree.

'I'm not strong enough,' she said, withdrawing from the root. She sat back on her heels, her shoulders sagging, staring blankly at her hands. 'I'm not Mielikki and . . . I don't have her kind of power.'

A long, painful silence filled the chamber, and then Crowley cleared his throat. 'You have . . . a different kind of power, Alice.'

Her head shot round in alarm. 'I can't risk that,' she said. 'I'm trying to wither it, not kill it.' Her voice was faint as she murmured, 'I've spent all this time trying to box those instincts away. To be someone else, someone worthy of Mielikki's gift, Crowley.'

Crowley smiled, his eyes searching her face. 'Forget about being someone else,' he said gently. 'Be *Alice Wyndham*.'

She stared at him. He didn't know what he was saying – what he was asking her to do.

'It's too dangerous,' she said. '*You* might get hurt. I can't control it. Risdon said so himself.'

'I trust you,' said Crowley.

'Well you shouldn't,' she snapped.

'I trust you.'

Alice turned away, unable to look at him. A flicker of movement at the corner of her eye sent her pulse racing. But it was only Kuu. She reached up to her nightjar, and the little white bird swooped in close, flying inches from Alice's chest as though for safety.

'It's okay,' she said, putting some force into her voice to dispel her own fear. She smiled and gave the bird a last stroke. Kuu ruffled her feathers and pecked at Alice's fingers.

Alice pursed her lips and exhaled steadily, a soft whistle reverberating around the chamber. Her chin dropped onto her chest and she closed her eyes, trying to centre herself. She leaned in to the feel of Kuu's soft feathers wafting against her cheeks and the cold dread creeping down her throat. Could she really control this?

'Kuu,' she murmured, her eyes opening gently. '*Go.*'

With a loud squall, Kuu arced to the left and glided away. The cord tugged at Alice's wrist and the luminous glow dimmed. Her bird was a ghostly blur swooping through the air. The rapidly thinning cord juddered and a sudden pain squeezed her chest. She doubled over with a gasp, breathing into the sensation. Alice had just managed to regain her focus, manoeuvring herself upright, when a bolt of electricity slammed into her spine. She snapped backwards. Her mouth fell open with a gasp and *something* escaped. Churning, glittering particles funnelled out, seeping into the air. Her soul. It stretched out, spreading itself wide. She thrummed with energy. She *was* energy: a collection of vibrating atoms, shimmering and colliding, reaching out for something warm . . . for something to consume . . . *Not Crowley. Not Crowley.* She rose higher, a sense of exhilaration nudging her consciousness. She was so hungry. So cold.

And then . . . a pulse of life. Vivid, and thriving, and so very warm. Unimaginable power and heat, waves of it, calling out to her. She reached for it, and in her grasp it weakened.

It couldn't be allowed to rot.

The warmth called to her. She couldn't resist as she seeped closer, pouring over the roots like a poisonous gas. So hungry . . .

Stop. That's enough!

Alice juddered. The glittering particles of her soul hesitated. And pulled back. Her nightjar cried out. Kuu darted into view and swooped towards her, wings steady and a fierce look in her eye. Alice shrank back, every particle receding, pulling into the centre. *Back. Back.*

Her eyes flew open and she slumped forward. Her palms took her weight, pressed numbly into the gritty stone floor. Alice exhaled shakily and pushed herself upright. She was herself again. Whole. Corporeal. She had sent out her soul and called it back. She had controlled it, and Crowley—

'Are you okay?' she gasped. 'Crowley?'

He fell back from the Rookery Stone with a sharp breath and crawled towards her, pulling her close. 'Alice,' he said. '*Look.* We've done it.'

Together, they watched in astonishment as the roots of the Summer Tree withered before their eyes . . . but far from crumbling to ash and dust, where the knotted tree limbs had draped over the Rookery Stone they hardened and fused to the monolithic block. The roots petrified before their eyes, the sheen of the rough bark turning grey and gritty.

'The roots,' said Crowley, 'they're turning to stone.'

Alice reached out a shaking hand and stroked a finger over the surface of the stone. Tingles of pleasure rippled through her arm and she gasped. She knew that sensation.

'Mielikki's power . . . It's in the Rookery Stone,' she murmured.

'And Pellervoinen's is in the Summer Tree,' said Crowley, his eyes tracing the stony roots.

Tree becomes stone, and stone becomes tree.

They sat in silence for several awestruck minutes while the fireflies fluttered around the chamber, their glowing lights illuminating the spectacle. This was the counterweight. This was why the Summer Tree wasn't supposed to grow – because its roots were inert. A tree that was inanimate, and a stone that had been animated.

Alice glanced upwards. Kuu hovered over her shoulder, her cord pulsing brightly. *I didn't have to sacrifice my bird.* Somehow, the cord's energy hadn't been required.

'I can see the threads now,' said Alice, her eyes glistening. *Kuu is safe.*

Soft fibres of light, like incandescent gossamer, were spun around the Rookery Stone. And Crowley was right – they led to the wall of the chamber and stopped.

'I think,' Crowley began, 'these are the threads that bind the anchors. They must reach through the void, beyond that wall, to the London Stone.'

And no sooner had he spoken than the threads stuttered. The light dimmed, fading to a dull glow. Small cracks began to appear at the point where the petrified roots and stone were joined. It was breaking.

'*No*,' Alice whispered.

Overhead, the Summer Tree's roots – those unpetrified, draped from the ceiling – began to tremble and creak. The stone walls shuddered and grit shook loose, falling around them.

'Open the door!' shouted Alice over the thunderous quaking of the chamber. 'The threads tying the anchors together,' she said, rising unsteadily to her feet, 'they need access to the void! We're only half finished!'

Crowley staggered upright, confused, but followed her orders. He moved quickly to the wall and flattened himself against it, his hands spread wide on the stone, searching for a door he couldn't see.

Alice jerked her head upwards. Her nightjar fluttered over her shoulder, her wings striking powerfully at the air. She swallowed thickly and turned back to Crowley, trying not to meet Kuu's beady gaze.

There was a resounding click, and then a section of the wall rumbled open like a door. Beyond the gap, the dark void yawned open before them and a blustering wind swept into the chamber, scraping their skin raw and tossing their hair about their faces. Crowley shoved the door wider to allow the threads of ebbing light to eke out, but the force of the raging winds sucked him through the open doorway. Clinging to the door by his fingers, he struggled to find enough purchase to power his way back into the chamber.

Alice glanced at him, and back at the Rookery Stone. The threads were no brighter, despite the opened doorway. It wasn't only access to the other anchors – the London Stone, the replica tree in Oxleas Wood – that was needed. The Rookery Stone was failing, its magic dulled by its defective link to the Summer Tree. Like this, it wasn't strong enough to tie itself to the other anchors. Alice took a step towards the cradled stone and roots. The small cracks where they joined were growing. It would snap soon. The petrification wouldn't hold.

'I'm sorry, Kuu,' she whispered, reaching up for her nightjar.

Kuu nuzzled her hand, her feathers illuminated by the glow from the cord wrapped around Alice's wrist.

'Alice!' Crowley yelled from beyond the door. 'What are you doing?'

She screwed her eyes shut. 'There's a final ingredient,' she called to him. 'You couldn't see it, and I couldn't tell you. More energy to complete the binding. To fuse them fully. To strengthen the join.' Her eyes opened, and she turned towards the door. 'It needs something to tie it all together, Crowley. A nightjar cord.'

Just as Death had once fused her cord after Marble Arch and

used it to bind her to Kuu again, so she would do the same for the tree and stone.

For the briefest of moments, Crowley didn't seem to understand. And then his eyes widened with alarm, and grief transformed his face.

'Not *your* cord!' he shouted, his voice ragged with panic as he fought to re-enter the chamber. 'Alice, wait!'

A cheerless smile crept across her face and she gave the slightest shrug. 'You said – at the university – that you wanted only good things for me.' Her throat pinched. 'I want that for you too. I hope you'll remember that.'

Alice turned away from the door. Crowley's roar of wild fury and pain was stolen by the wind.

'Use mine!' he shouted desperately. 'Alice! Use mine!'

Blocking out the sounds of his determined fight against the gales of the void, Alice knelt down by the Rookery Stone with Kuu on her palm.

The bird pecked at the luminous cord around Alice's wrist and she shook her head.

'Not yet,' she murmured. 'Break it when I've wrapped it around.'

Kuu dutifully stopped and peered up. Alice saw herself reflected in the pale bird's glassy eyes, and her breath hitched. They'd grown used to each other, in the end. *The pale nightjar and the Daughter of Death*. Alice stroked the feathered head with a tremulous smile. But it was over now.

She reached for the pulsing cord and lifted it so that she might loop it around the threads' nexus and the meeting point between the granite Summer Tree roots and the Rookery Stone.

And then a voice cut through the chamber.

'Wait.'

Not Crowley's voice.

She turned towards it, her muscles tensing and her pulse racing.

Reuben Risdon – Tuoni – stood at the entrance to the chamber, a knife in his hand.

40

Alice lurched to her feet. Rage stilled her breathing, and she stared at him, jaw clenched as he stepped into the chamber.

'What do you want?' she hissed.

Risdon made as though to lunge in her direction, and she pedalled backwards, her heart slamming against her ribs. He edged around the room, and she watched him, furious with herself for not standing her ground.

He took no care to clamber over the tangle of live roots that still draped from the ceiling or curled out from the stone walls. They disintegrated at his touch, and he moved with ease to the open door.

'Alice, run!' shouted Crowley, inches from landing his foot at the lip of the doorway so that he could force his way back in.

'Silly boy,' said Risdon with a grim smile. He flicked a finger, and Crowley lost his grip with a gasp. Risdon reached into the void and pulled the door shut, stranding Crowley outside. Then he turned to Alice.

'Open the door!' she snapped.

'I'm sure he'll find his way home,' he said, spinning the knife through the fingers of one hand.

'What do you want?' she repeated.

He held the knife up by the blade's tip. 'Do you recognize this?'

She frowned, and then her chest tightened and a wave of pure anger washed over her. It was Jude's knife. The knife Risdon had used to cut Jen's throat at Marble Arch.

'I kept this as a souvenir,' he said, 'of the night I discovered you were mine. The night I discovered what you were capable of.'

Alice trembled with rage, her face twisted with bitterness.

He tossed the knife at her, and it skittered to a stop by her feet.

'I want you to use it to kill me.'

She gaped at him. '*What?*'

He turned away to examine the walls, studying the collection of roots dropping from the ceiling, their ends tapering to stone – and the other, still-organic roots woven through the chamber walls.

'I have my soul,' he said, 'and I intend to go to the Sulka Moors to find Leda.' He spun back to her. 'Send me to the moors, Alice. Send me home.'

She could hardly comprehend what he was saying. The only emotion he had ever invoked in her was hatred, but she had never – not once – intentionally taken a life.

Murderer.

'I'm tired, Alice,' he said. 'You took Leda from me.' He trailed his hands along one of the wooded roots looping through the wall, and it perished beneath his touch, a bloom of sawdust scattering the ground. Above, the ceiling juddered and stony grit rained down, as though the whole chamber might soon collapse.

'You took Leda from me,' he murmured again, 'and it has taken so long to forgive you. But I do.' He glanced at her. 'Monsters beget monsters. I have no one to blame but myself.'

469

He stroked another root and watched it disintegrate. The wall shook with its absence.

'Stop that,' said Alice, her fists clenched.

'Make me,' he said with a smile, reaching for another.

She dropped to her haunches, scrambling to lay her hand against one of the living roots. Mielikki's legacy surged up to meet her, vibrating against her skin. Her palm throbbed as she pushed her will deep into the root, maintaining her composure when a deep rumble echoed around the chamber. A rasping slither hissed into the room as Alice directed the tree roots outside like a choreographer; they curved through the gaps left by Risdon's decay and wound into the room, propping up the walls.

'Your friend with the red hair,' he said, his voice silky, 'perhaps I'll find her in the moors . . .'

Alice flinched, reflexively squeezing the root in her hands. As her fingers clenched, so too did the roots pouring through the walls. They snapped around Risdon, curling to press him against the wall, trapped within their embrace. He made no move to decay them. Instead, his eyes narrowed and he taunted her with another smile, his face still visible through the meshing limbs of the Summer Tree.

'Perhaps Jen and I—'

The roots tightened, crushing him in their grasp, and he gasped in pain. But still the smile. Alice rose on shaky legs and moved closer. She had expected him to be trapped, unable to struggle against the bindings wrapped around him. But there was blood pouring from his chest.

'How did . . .?' She frowned, her stomach churning

The tree root . . . The thin, jagged end of a root had curled around him and embedded itself in his chest. Like a needle, sewn through flesh.

'But I didn't mean . . .' Her words trailed away as realization dawned. *I did this. I did this. Not with my soul. With my own bare hands. With Mielikki's legacy, not Tuoni's.*

'Alice,' he murmured.

She stared at him in shock. He fumbled to reach a hand through the intertwining roots enveloping him – but his attempts were feeble and the blood was pooling rapidly at his feet. Trembling with confusion and guilt, Alice gripped the branches and broke a hole for him, to free him, but he stopped her. He smiled at her – the first genuine smile she'd seen him offer, his grey eyes shining – and managed to reach through the gap.

His hand, shaking as his strength failed him, reached up to gently touch her cheek.

'Good girl,' he said quietly. 'Now take my nightjar and use its cord.'

Her eyes searched his face and her lips pressed into a thin line. It was why he'd come here: to offer his nightjar. To force her to take it. She nodded, her eyes glistening as he released a soft sigh and his white nightjar flapped into the chamber. His body sagged, and the nightjar tugged away from it, the luminous cord rippling loosely from its leg.

Alice snatched the cord from the air. It shimmered in her hands, beads of glittering light oozing through it, like oil through water.

'Kuu?' Alice whispered.

Her bird fluttered down from her shoulder and swooped towards Tuoni's nightjar, its beak open wide. In one graceful arc, it sliced the other end of the cord, and Tuoni's nightjar blinked, held her gaze and soared off along the corridor, vanishing into the shadows with something bright in its claws.

Alice's breath caught and she peered down at the cord in her hands, losing its shine with every second she wasted. But she wasn't sure what to do. The book had told her what needed to be done, but not exactly how to carry it out. Frustration and panic burst across her senses. If she wasted the chance Tuoni had given her, she would be forced to use her own cord anyway.

And then Kuu swooped down, her wings creating small pockets of air that cooled Alice's face, and snatched the spare cord into her beak.

Alice swallowed against the lump in her throat as Kuu leapt into the air. The nightjar circled the chamber, its feathers rippling. It looped and glided between branches, picking up speed. Tuoni's loose cord fluttered behind, leaving sparkling trails of light. And then her nightjar dipped its head and stretched out its tiny body and dived. Right through the roots dripping from the ceiling, it plunged towards the Rookery Stone and the dying threads of light, spiralling around them, swooping left and right, turning circles. Until suddenly, it swooped up to land on the stone, giving it a cautious peck for good measure. Alice scrambled closer, over the uneven floor, to peer down at it, her heart hammering.

Kuu hadn't just knotted Tuoni's nightjar cord around the stone, the roots and the threads of light leading to the void. It was *fused* around them. And the cracks were vanishing . . . Alice hardly dared breathe. What did it mean? Had Kuu—?

The chamber exploded with light and Alice fell backwards. She threw her hands out to break her fall and thumped onto a chunk of hard rock. The threads of light glimmering weakly at the Rookery Stone now shone with a blinding brilliance. White instead of blue raced along the lines, pouring towards the door to the void. The moment they hit it, the closed door glowed just briefly before disintegrating. Dust blossomed outwards, and wind rushed into the chamber.

Alice stared at the dark rectangle in the wall, willing him to appear. *Where are you, Crowley?* And then he was there, filling the door frame, his hands gripping the edges and his hair blown across his face.

'*Alice*,' he said.

Neither moved for a heartbeat. And then he strode across the room and swept his arms around her, crushing her against him.

'There are no good things without you,' he murmured brokenly. 'I won't let you go again.'

On the floor, the petrified roots of the Summer Tree met the Rookery Stone in a glimmering, marble-like sheen. The connection between them was whole – no imperfections, no cracks. Alice watched in silent awe as Kuu glided and swooped about the chamber, her incandescent cord shimmering. Unbroken. Whole.

EPILOGUE

It was not going well. This was the first official meeting between the two women, and Alice was already regretting the idea of introducing them. Sasha and Bea hadn't said a word to each other.

'Would anyone like any more tea?' she asked, staring intently at Jude for support, but he was too busy watching Bea with an appraising eye to notice.

'Can I smoke at the table?' asked August, pulling out a roll-up.

'*No*,' said Sasha and Bea in unison. They narrowed their eyes, staring at each other suspiciously.

'Smoking is prohibited under the terms of your rental agreement,' said Crowley. 'You may not smoke in the kitchen or your bedroom.' He raised an eyebrow. 'As you well know.'

August ran a hand through his straggly blond hair and stretched out his legs under the table. 'Just as well I've never smoked in my bedroom then, isn't it?'

'Yes,' said Crowley. 'Although Sasha I must admit I was very disappointed to see you flouting the rules.'

She shot him a withering look. 'I don't smoke.'

'Strange,' mused Crowley. 'I saw your bedsheets on the drying rack. Pocked with small burn marks from the tobacco sparks of a roll-up cigarette.'

Sasha gasped in horror and Alice stared wide-eyed at the table, clamping her lips and safely avoiding eye contact.

'Oh God, darling,' said Bea in sympathy. 'Don't be ashamed of your terrible choices in men. I once dated Geraint Litmanen, so think on that.'

Alice shook her head, turning away with a laugh. Her eyes met Crowley's. He was staring directly at her, with such intensity that a trickle of nerves fluttered pleasantly in her stomach. He threw a wicked grin in her direction and she swallowed and looked away. Beneath the table, his questing fingers brushed against hers.

'This is going to be the start of a beautiful new friendship,' said Bea, elbowing Sasha. The icy atmosphere between them had melted in the face of their joint stance on terrible men.

'Hey,' objected August. 'Isn't sexism banned under the terms of the rental agreement as well as smoking?'

'I'm not sure that's sexism,' said Jude, reaching for his teacup. 'It's probably closer to misandry.'

'In English?' said August.

Sasha sighed. 'You need to break down the big words for him,' she said, throwing August a smirk.

'Misandry is a hatred of men,' explained Jude.

'Not all men,' said Bea, treating Jude to a coquettish smile.

Crowley's palm slid into Alice's and she held their joined hands in her lap like a secret.

As August dragged Jude into a lively debate about sexist remarks and Bea interrupted to ask him about his reading habits, Alice smiled to herself. This really did feel like *home*. Life wasn't perfect – nor was she – but she still had her research job at the university, with a very contrite Vivian Reid. She still had her health, her soul, her parents safely tucked away in Ireland . . .

The table rattled and Alice frowned.

'Did I just imagine that, or—'

August's tobacco tin vibrated across the wooden surface, and he cursed and snatched it up. The plates and drained teacups bounced and tipped on their sides, and August shot out of his seat.

'What the hell is—'

The grains in the wood rippled, like sand in the breeze, and Crowley's hand tightened in Alice's. The grains poured together in shifting directions, before rising from the surface to form letters.

'It's a message from House Mielikki,' said Bea. 'Read it, darling. What does it say?'

Alice Wyndham – welcome to House Mielikki

'They're a bit late, aren't they, darling,' said Bea with a sigh. 'You took your binding draught days ago. They're supposed to send you a framed certificate.'

'I expect they've been busy,' said Alice. Her eyes glittering, she turned a thoughtful eye on Bea. 'Has anyone ever refused membership after they've passed?'

The table erupted in uproar and she laughed. But the idea picked away at her mind. House Mielikki and House Tuoni; she was a rightful member of both. Crowley was a member of one House and really belonged in another. Why did it have to be black and white?

Maybe there ought to be a House that welcomed the necromancers, like August and Eris Mawkin, who had been forced to hide their legacies for fear of persecution by the Council. A House that welcomed the daughter of Tuoni and embraced her deathly gifts. If the choice were Leda's, wouldn't she do something radical and brave, like setting up her own House? Smashing the four-House system? Maybe even opening a House for those who didn't seem to fit anywhere else – hemomancers along with necromancers, or those whose gifts weren't strong enough to join any of the Houses and who were left to feel inadequate and unwanted? A House of misfits?

She smiled and reached for her teacup. House Mielikki and House Tuoni?

Why couldn't she belong to both?

ACKNOWLEDGEMENTS

Huge thanks to Bella Pagan, editor extraordinaire – a great support with a brilliantly beady eye and an infinite source of plot ideas! Thanks everlasting to the wonderful Jemima Forrester, who has been the catalyst for every good thing that's happened to me in the writing business so far! Many, many thanks to the teams at Pan Macmillan, Tor, Goldmann, Eksmo, Agave, Argo and David Higham who helped to bring the stories of Alice and the Rookery to life and championed them. Thanks to the fabulous Penelope Killick, Becky Lloyd, Georgia Summers, Emma Winter, Charlotte Wright, Natalie Young, Claire Eddy, Diana Gill, Desirae Friesen, Kristin Temple and Toby Selwyn. Thanks to Emma Coode for her brilliantly helpful insights, to Matthew Garrett and Neil Lang for designing the most beautiful covers, and to Jamie-Lee Nardone and Stephen Haskins – PR legends and the best shepherds I could ever have wished for at Comic-Con.

MASSIVE thanks to the readers and bloggers who supported *The Nightjar*. It's hard to put into words what this meant to me. Writing a story is like shouting into a void – you never know if anyone is going to listen or not – but having you there, not just listening but shouting back, was the most wonderful welcome to the book world. You are just fantastic.

Writing and re-writing *The Rookery* in the middle of a pandemic felt, at times, like playing the violin on the deck of the Titanic while it sinks – only you've forgotten the tune and Billy Zane's* just stolen your bow (probably to use it as an oar). Thanks so much to my family for providing the life jackets: to David, for the endless cups of tea and nudges that fuelled me through the journey, and to Pippa and Chris Davies, brilliant parents and my biggest cheerleaders.

To my lovely boys, Seb Hewitt and Archie Hewitt, whose 'encouragement hugs' proved absolutely priceless. You're the only things I've ever created that were perfect in the first draft and I adore you both. Completely and utterly. Massively and infinitely. The best thing about publishing a book is that I get to say this in print so that the message is like an echo – it will always be out there, somewhere. I am so proud of you, always.

The second-best thing about publishing these books has been the chance to immortalize my two elderly Westies, Bo and Ruby. They sat on my knee while I wrote both of these books, but now they're off chasing rainbows together. The best good girls.

Thanks to the Savvies, who have been a fantastic source of information and support. Writing is a strange old business, and it's invaluable to know others who are navigating the same path.

If you've made it this far . . . please seek out the song Alice and Crowley dance to at midsummer. Loituma's *Ievan Polkka* is an absolute marvel – I loved it the minute I heard it, and I hope you will too.

Finally . . . #ThankYouNHS
* To Billy Zane, please don't sue me for defamation, I was only joking.

ABOUT THE AUTHOR

DEBORAH HEWITT lives in the United Kingdom, somewhere south of Glasgow and north of London. She's the proud owner of two brilliant boys and one very elderly dog. When she's not writing, she can be found watching her boys play soccer in a muddy field, or teaching in her classroom. Occasionally she cooks. Her family wishes she wouldn't. *The Rookery* is the sequel to her first novel, *The Nightjar.*

deborahhewitt.com
Twitter: @TheVimes

Made in the USA
Monee, IL
29 August 2023

41799569R00288